The Border Lord

The Border Lord

By

Jan Westcott

CROWN PUBLISHERS

New York

PRINTED IN THE U.S.A.

To Tante

The Border Lord

Part One

Chapter One

It was the night of June twenty-first, 1591. All day long a thick mist had enveloped the walled city of Edinburgh in gray folds, but at sunset the wind had changed, and a pale moon had begun its rise in the ragged sky. The night was fine, the air sharp, but a certain John Fian, lying in the dungeon of the Tolbooth, couldn't know it. In the bowels of the earth the air is dank and noisome, and besides that, a merciful nature had finally lulled him deep into sleep. Still, the weather and the hurt body of the man to be executed the following day were the immediate causes of the events of that particular night in the Scottish capital. Two apparently irrelevant facts combined, and on the stage that they created other figures moved and talked until the very hour when the climax of the drama occurred. Tomorrow, another misty morning would arrive, and John Fian would meet death, but tonight the condemned man slept fitfully, the moon shone on his turreted prison, and the spring night was cold but clear.

It was cold enough for Sir Patrick Galbraith to draw his cloak around him closely as he came down the steps of the tall front stoop of a house on High Street. His coach was waiting, its lanterns burning, and the horses as nervous as the coachman, who did not dare to show his own impatience. The door banged behind the coach's owner, a footman climbed up beside the driver, the whip cracked and the sound of horses' hoofs rang out sharply on the big paving blocks as the journey down the hill toward the royal palace began. It was just ten o'clock.

The coach body swayed gently on the leather straps on which it was hung. On the soft seat inside, Sir Patrick stretched out comfortably, even though his mind was far from his own comfort. Beside him, his secretary Edwin Chalmers sat silent and rather erect, clutching his bag of papers and thinking with some regret that he had still a good deal of work ahead of him tonight. At their next stop, his services would not be required; it would be necessary again for him to wait while Sir Patrick was occupied. But Edwin Chalmers was so accustomed to have his waking hours planned far in advance, and without regard to his own desires, that he accepted his lot with resignation. After all, he was highly paid, and he was a most discreet man; not for extra hours of work would he abandon a position many men envied. He shot a sidelong glance at his silent companion and wondered briefly what had caused the black look on his face. He knew well enough that he would wonder in vain; enlightenment might come many days later—or not at all. He dismissed the thought with a shrug, unaware that his lack of curiosity was one of the traits that endeared his services to Patrick Galbraith.

The coach moved on down the hill; only a mile separated it from its destination of Holyrood Palace, and its coachman hadn't needed orders. He had received them early in the day, as usual. But the coachman knew too that he had yet another stop tonight: after his master had seen His Majesty, James of Scotland, he had a rendezvous for supper at Ainslee's Tavern. The coachman was not so resigned as Edwin Chalmers; the only thing that compensated him for his extra and long hours was the fact that he drove a coach-and-four—a mark of distinction in Edinburgh, for there were few coaches. Only the very wealthy could afford them. From his perch the driver caught the envious eye of many a pretty girl, but there was little use in being envied from such a distance. He wished he had courage enough to use the coach himself when his master didn't require it, but fear of the awful wrath that would follow discovery held him well in leash. At least, he had one visit behind him tonight; two more, and he could claim his hard bed with relief.

Sir Patrick said not a word as the journey downhill continued. The rooms he had just quitted had seen him suffer a defeat, a defeat to plans that had occupied him a great deal during the last month. He was angry, he was chagrined, and a bit incredulous, and if he regretted the bitter words which had followed the realization of his defeat, he would not as yet admit it. He tried to push the thought of the interview aside; he had two other important affairs to attend to tonight, and there was no use worrying over what was past. Even though he had just had his suit for marriage turned down, the present must be looked to first.

It was quite typical of him that he had presented his marriage proposal in the interval between matters of state and business. His days were rigidly allotted; the very hours fell neatly into the pattern that he himself had set sometimes weeks in advance. He was most meticulous and he did nothing from impulse, for he firmly believed that, as making money necessitated orderliness, so must the life of one who used his days in that pursuit be orderly. Certainly his methods had justified themselves to him, for at the age of twenty-eight he was probably the wealthiest man in Scotland. Where other nobles intrigued and flattered their monarch, Patrick Galbraith bought his favors, and the very simplicity of his dealings had never failed to amuse him. Patrick liked to lay his money on the counter; it enabled him to dress as he pleased, act as he pleased, and do as he pleased.

Men said that he affected his humor, and yet no one was really sure, because he himself was so very casual about it. He wore his blond hair cut short, and contrary to fashion he was clean-shaven. He wore no jewelry, rich as he was, except one heavy, carved gold ring, and he never carried a sword, being content with a gold-hilted dagger. He managed to violate most of the customs of his times, even to his preference for raw Scotch whiskey and his abhorrence of French wines, and it was said there wasn't a man in Scotland who liked him, except the King. It was further said, cynically, that this peculiarity the two shared.

The coach rumbled into the outer courts of the palace and

drew to a stop with much shouting and flourishing of the driver's whip. The horses danced for a minute, then stood quiet; the footman jumped down and flung open the door, and the tall figure of the master stepped out indolently. The whole ride had been completed in silence.

Patrick stood for a moment in the dark of the spring night, drinking in the smell of the sea so near. This time he had not come to buy a favor, but to discover what potion the King and the Chancellor, Maitland, were brewing. He had come to weigh the gravity of the charges of treason which hung over the head of a certain peer of the realm. Looking away from the bulk of the palace toward the city he had left, he studied the way it stretched up the hill. More than a mile away, on the summit of Castle Rock, stood the huge pile of Edinburgh Castle, no longer a royal residence, but a prison, a fortress, an armory. In one room of that castle lay a prisoner whose fate Patrick wanted to learn, and with a last backward glance at the city, he turned, his scarlet-lined cloak swinging behind him, and made his familiar way into the palace. His personal servant trailed behind.

It was an odd hour of night to arrive. When he entered the ground floors, he could smell the odors of food cooking, as the kitchens of the resident nobles prepared a late supper for their lords. He made his way up a large staircase, passed by the galleries, the audience chambers. He walked past the chambers of the Queen, past the turret room which was the Queen's bedroom. In this wing lay also the apartments of the King. He entered a small cabinet, a door was opened, and a lackey announced his name. He was admitted to the presence of the King with very little ceremony; in fact, when he removed his brimmed hat, the servants were slightly surprised. They were waiting for the day when both monarch and subject should sit covered and neither notice it.

James Stewart was standing to the right of his heavy oaken table. A hunting hound lay at his slippered feet; behind him an embossed screen protected him from the drafts of the window embrasure. One hand rested on his table, in the other he held a half-finished glass of wine. His furred robe was open, revealing his plump stocky figure, for James was short for a Stewart. He was twenty-five years old.

"Patrick," he said, surprised. He set down his wine and waved Patrick toward him, eying the elegant figure in its rich dress. Patrick dropped to one knee, and James looked down on the shoulders covered with gleaming black satin, and at Patrick's blond head, where the unruly curls at the top had escaped the barber's shears. Affectionately James put one hand on his shoulder.

"Apologize, sir, for your tardiness. Why did you not come sooner?" A tug on Patrick's suit told him to rise.

Patrick stood; he smiled ruefully.

"To be truthful, Sire, a stubborn wench. But you know the old saying, 'The fort that parleys and the woman who listens—surrender.' "

James laughed, and for the first time Patrick seemed to become aware that there was another man in the room. He acknowledged Lord Morton with a brief bow.

"My lord," he said. "A pleasant evening, is it not?"

Lord Morton smiled. His eyes glittered, matching the jewels that enriched his person and his small ears. "A very pleasant evening, sir, after so poor a day."

"Aye," said James thoughtfully. "No hunting today." He finished off his wine and set the cup down. "But tomorrow I expect to be gone at dawn. Don't I?" He touched the hound at his feet with the toe of one thin-soled slipper, and the animal nuzzled the royal foot as if in agreement. "By God, *he* understands me," James added, with a sigh.

Patrick kept the frown off his face. Stewarts were temperamental, and James's mood tonight was evidently not a good one. Patrick had encountered these moods before; so had everyone at court. He wondered whether a good bawdy joke might bring laughter to his monarch's face; he looked around the room, only half-seeing the heavy tapestries, the carved furniture. Then his eye lit on His Majesty's table, which was covered with the evidence of James's industry that day. "You have been writing, Sire?"

James's eyes lighted. "I was so engrossed, I forgot my nap," he admitted. This seemed to remind him that he was tired. "I am a horse with little staying power," he announced, sinking back again into his mood of dissatisfaction. "Yet my subjects—as my good gossips have it—would complain that I am slothful." He frowned heavily.

Patrick kept a wise silence. James's subjects said that if the King wasn't hunting or drinking he was asleep, but it was not altogether true. His interests were many and varied; they ranged from languages, at which he was expert, to witchcraft, on which he considered himself an authority. Today he had delved into that horrid black magic; he, the King, had gone down into the evil-smelling, badly lighted dungeons of the Tolbooth to watch a man questioned. It was easy to remember with vividness the thud of the mallet as it descended into the iron boot, the whimpered pleas for mercy, and James remembered too the name that had been wrung from John Fian's pain-twisted mouth.

The King turned to the other man. "How was Lord Bothwell today, Morton?" he asked.

He had been alternately standing and pacing the room; now he sank into his own chair and waved Patrick to another. For a brief second the three men contemplated each other, and Morton glanced from his monarch to the newcomer whose presence he had neither wanted nor bargained for.

Morton clasped his beringed hands on his stomach, fat hands over a fat stomach; then he realized that James was waiting and hurried into speech. "Lord Bothwell is most insolent, Sire," he began, trying to collect his thoughts and remember exactly where he had been in his narrative to the King when Patrick had entered.

"So you said." James was visibly annoyed, whether at Morton's repetitiveness, or the insolence of the prisoner.

Patrick smiled lazily. "Do tell us, Morton, what behavior you had expected from Bothwell?"

Morton's eyes met Patrick's in a long look which said, "And why are you interested, sir? Is Bothwell the reason for this call?" However, he only murmured, "I had expected, sir, that Lord Bothwell would not be insensible to the gravity of the charges he faces."

"And you infer that because he insults you, he is unaware that he is in danger?" Patrick turned to James. "Bothwell is reported to have said today that Morton's fat belly is the result of his own undigested lies." Patrick smiled. "After all, Morton, insulting you may be his chief pleasure in his last days."

The King laughed. "You must remember, Morton, that he is half Stewart, and in love with sport. You present his only target. You and Maitland."

Patrick heard these words with concealed pleasure. So His Majesty had not forgot, even temporarily (for he had a convenient memory, as most kings did) that the man under charges of treason was a blood relation.

"He's more Hepburn than Stewart," said Morton, "and hunts women more than the stag." He snorted.

"That I would not say." James had a passion for contradicting. "I would say that the wenches chase him like a pack of badly bred bitches, and he beds them at his own pleasure. When I recalled him from Venice, the Venetian harlots sighed so heavily you could hear them in London."

Morton remarked pontifically, "You recalled him, to heap honors on him. Think well, Sire, how he has repaid you!" Morton shook his head and shut his mouth tightly, as if both in anger and pity for his young and easily deluded monarch. "Why do you forget how he has repaid you?"

James's face set, and Patrick watched him carefully, searching for the right rejoinder to Morton. He found it. "Morton, you would be loved more if you presumed less. I can think of no adequate reason that you should assume the royal prerogatives."

"Aye!" James snapped. "D'ye question the punishment already meted out? God's son, Morton, you weary me!"

Patrick nodded understandingly at James. There were no

servants in the room, and he rose to fill James's wineglass. "If you'll allow me, Sire," he said to James, turning his back to Morton.

"Won't you have some?" asked James, absently watching the yellow Rhine wine.

Patrick replied, "It's a physic. No, thank you, Sire."

James smiled; he felt the better for this exchange. He picked up his wine and tasted it. "Now you may tell me, Morton, what Bothwell was doing today."

Morton hesitated for only a second. "Bothwell, Sire, is as always. Maitland and I saw him this afternoon; we endeavored to question him. He lies on the floor playing chess, his right hand against his left. He carved the figures out of tallow; he told us he was raising a beard for lack of a razor; he said did we know the weather would be fine for golf soon, and the next time we came he would like some dice. Aye," said Morton, warming to his theme, "he lies on the floor, taking up most of the room, and talks about golf, beards and strawberries. And he did tell us a jest; I've been trying all evening to remember it."

Patrick burst out laughing.

"At least tell us about the strawberries, if you can't remember the jest."

Morton spoke reluctantly. "He asked us to tell Your Majesty that he is desolated he cannot bring you strawberries from Crichton this year, but his inability is due to circumstances he cannot control."

James sighed; whether for his stomach Patrick did not know. "Sir, he raises the best strawberries in Scotland. I swear they are this big." He held up one hand with the thumb and index finger making a circle.

Patrick regarded the royal fingers with proper respect. "So big?" he inquired wonderingly.

"I like them with uncrudded cream," said Morton, since they must talk about strawberries.

James shook his head in dismissal. "They are far better dipped in sugar. You take them by the stem," he illustrated as if he were the possessor of a fat strawberry with deep green leaves, "and dust it in the sugar. They are the best strawberries in Scotland," he added plaintively.

Morton made his promise suavely. "I shall certainly see that Your Grace receives berries as fine as his."

James looked vastly annoyed; hadn't he just said that there were none in the country to match those from Crichton Castle? He decided to be offended; he picked up the pen lying on the table and pretended to read the last line he had written.

His attitude told Patrick that the interview had come to a close. Patrick rose, but he had one more question he wanted answered: he knew that Fian had implicated Bothwell in a treason plot. "What did you think of Fian, Sire?" he asked.

James frowned; he studied his writing, and his face was inscrutable. "I think the Devil has devious ways, sir." He paused. "I would be pleased to discuss it with you anon."

Patrick bowed. "Your servant, Sire," he said, backing to the door. When it closed behind him, he turned, clapping his plumed hat onto his head. He was fairly well satisfied with what he had learned, but he was still late, and abandoning his indolence, he strode rapidly in the direction from which he had come.

Inside the room, Morton was almost at the door. He was far from satisfied, for tonight he had failed in his intention to arouse the King's anger. Morton gave a last look around the room. The candles were burning low, and the tapestries stirred in the spring drafts. It was cold, and Morton shivered suddenly; the wind sighed outside, rustled softly through the palace, its ancient abbey and its crypts, whispered through the graveyard. In one of the tombs lay the strangled body of Darnley, James's father; in the cemetery lay the body of the murdered Rizzio, secretary to the late Queen—Rizzio, whose blood could not be scrubbed from the oak flooring of a room nearby. And in England, in her grave, were the pitiful remains of Mary, Queen of Scotland and the Isles, the grizzled head completely severed from the trunk. Violence and blood stained the walls of the palace; violence and blood made a trail from the battlefields of Flodden, of Solway Moss, to the murder of James's father at Kirk o' Field and the executioner's platform at Fotheringay, where his mother had died. Now in a room at Edinburgh Castle, another of the clan faced a bloody death, a death by hanging, drawing and quartering, so that the spikes of Tolbooth could display the severed limbs and head. What had the house of Stewart done that heaven should follow it with such mighty wrath?

On the threshold of the room, Morton, remembering the present, bowed deeply. "Your humble servant, Sire," he said. James didn't answer, and as Morton closed the door, he grimaced and thought his King must really enjoy rudeness more than aught else.

Underneath the rooms that Patrick and Morton had just quitted lay Morton's own chambers. The suite was large, boasting bedrooms, dining-room, kitchen and receiving rooms, but at this hour all were dark and silent save his study, which itself opened off the corridor outside his apartments. On this door Morton gave one sharp knock and entered without preamble, for he was expected. He closed the door behind him carefully, and shot the bolt; then he faced his guest.

John Maitland had been writing; the tall candelabra on the table gave out the only light in the room and threw long shadows into the corners. He looked up as Morton entered. His face was very pale, his eyes deeply shadowed, and Morton thought he looked ghostly. Morton's hand left the big bolt, and he said irritably, "Why don't you use more light?"

Maitland laid down his pen and leaned his head on his hand. "I can see perfectly," he said.

Morton tiptoed into the room, and seated himself in a chair by the bare fireplace. He glanced at it wistfully. The leaping flames would be comforting on a night like this; he felt strangely ill at ease.

"Well, there is not enough light," he said petulantly.

Maitland raised one slender eyebrow. "On the contrary, my lord, there is ample light." His voice was louder than Morton's whispered tones. "There is no need to waste candles."

"Nor wood either, I see," said Morton, thinking that Maitland was as penurious as his enemies said.

"No, nor wood," said Maitland equably, and he waited.

"God's wound, John, I shall not contest the point with you!"

Maitland was unperturbed. "Just so, my lord. But there is no need to lock doors, and to run about, casting glances over your shoulder."

Morton threw him a look of disgust. Whether Maitland knew it or not, there were plots and counterplots going on in the palace, and Scottish lords were most addicted to settling their quarrels with bare steel, feeling that it satisfactorily put an end to political uncertainty. Morton said, "Tonight Patrick Galbraith showed extreme interest in your prisoner." Perchance that would remind Maitland that his enemies were not inactive.

Maitland ran his tongue over his lips. "So?" he murmured, considering this information. "So he wishes to meddle, does he? That's strange."

Morton nodded, as if to say it was exceeding strange, and boded no good. Patrick Galbraith wielded tremendous influence, and Morton did not understand why he suddenly entered this intrigue. "I had not thought we must fight him," he said.

Maitland spoke frankly. "Nor did I. But I have been among politicos long enough to know that everything is uncertain. Still, you say he showed interest. It does not necessarily follow that we shall have him for opponent."

Morton shrugged. "I do not like it. Or him."

Maitland understood well enough that Morton liked none of this affair now that he was involved in it. Two months ago it had seemed like a gift from heaven when two wretches accused of witchcraft had implicated the peer whom both Morton and Maitland wished so heartily out of their way. Maitland remembered the joy with which he had drawn up the accusation: "For treasonable conspiracy against His Majesty's own person, Francis, Earl of Bothwell, had consulted with necromancers, witches, and other wicked and ungodly persons, both within and without this country—some already executed for the deed and some others lie ready to be executed for the same crime."

Maitland thought of the charges. "John Fian dies tomorrow. Then his accusers will all be dead."

Morton wasn't listening; he scarcely cared what happened

to Fian. "I never thought it would turn out this way. I never thought there was a chance of acquittal." He fell silent, and glanced nervously around the shadowed room.

"You are afraid, my lord." Maitland smiled. He seemed bored; he picked up his pen and dipped it into the ink.

Morton did not resent the accusation. What he did resent was Maitland's apparent inability to realize that he too should be afraid. Only fools overlooked a coming storm. "I suppose you think you'd be safe if Bothwell is freed?" As Morton said it he recalled only too well the powerful lounging figure of the man he had talked to in prison this afternoon.

Maitland had already begun to write; he looked up absently. "I shan't allow an acquittal, Morton."

Morton studied his face in the gloom. The words and their calm reassured him somewhat; Maitland was very capable. "But," he began, "you certainly wouldn't dare use the boot—" He broke off suddenly, and his eyes darted to the door. Then he sprang up and was across the room as quickly as his slippered feet would permit. For a second he stood motionless; then he slipped the bolt, impatient of the noise it made, and flung the door wide.

In the long black corridor there was the sound of light footsteps, a hurrying in the air, and then there was silence. Morton started after the sounds. "Bring light," he whispered, and his voice echoed in the room and into the hall.

But Maitland hadn't moved. He still sat behind his table and he shook his head at Morton. "If someone were listening, what odds, sir? Close the door. It is eleven o'clock and naught will occur tonight."

Chapter Two

THE prisoner in the tower of Edinburgh Castle was leaning against his one window, his hands idly grasping the stanchions sunk deep into the stone. He could see the edge of the rising moon, and he spoke aloud. "It must be eleven," he said. He took four lazy strides, came to the end of the room, and turned, took two strides more, and peered down at the chessboard with its tiny tallow figures. He leaned over and moved one piece, contemplated the board, and took two more strides to the window. He leaned on the sill again, and grasped at one bar. It came loose in his hand. He regarded it with some pleasure, then he replaced it carefully, and watched the moon. "Just about eleven," he said again.

He resumed his slow pacing; four times he passed the chessboard, and the light from the one candle threw his shadow, elongated, on the wall. He was very tall, his manacled hands swung awkwardly as he walked, and his big boots rang out sharply on the bare stone floor. His face was unshaven; two months' growth of dark beard accentuated the deep brown hair and eyes. If there were lines, bitter lines, in his face, they couldn't be seen. In fact, as he contemplated the tiny barred square of moonlight that almost touched his chessboard, he was smiling. He paused a second in his stride, and listened. He went to the door, listening still, and he shoved back the small square panel. He heard what he was waiting for, and he went slowly back to his bed and lay down comfortably. He had not long to wait.

He heard the far doors in the corridor open, he heard the tread of heavy feet, and finally he heard his own bolts drawn, his door unlocked. He put his head down and closed his eyes.

The Captain of the Night Watch stared at the recumbent figure on the narrow bed, from the stockinged feet to the tousled dark head cradled on the bound wrists. In the silence he could hear the steady rhythmic breathing of his prisoner. "Your Lordship," he said softly.

Bothwell stirred, raising his head slightly; he stirred as though his name alone had roused him, and he turned over; he swung his long legs off the side of the bed and sat up. "Gibson," he said sleepily, frowning at the Captain.

"We brought you food, my lord, and a half cask of ale." Gibson motioned to his companion, who had already set his burden on the table.

"Good," said Bothwell, still sleepy. He ran his hands through his hair, rubbed his eyes, and the irons on his wrists hit him on the ear and he swore softly. He looked from the table to Gibson, to the other guard. Then he said pleasantly, "But I have no more money. You bastardly knaves have been too greedy." He yawned.

Gibson grinned, but the other guard scowled. He took a step toward the lounging figure on the bed. "You have money," he began truculently, and then the eyes of the Earl of Bothwell made him add, respectfully, "your Lordship."

Bothwell looked up at him, and his gaze went past him to Gibson by the door. "I shall have to give you my ring," he said finally, as if he had just thought of a way out of this dilemma. " 'Tis all I have left." Awkwardly he pulled off a heavy ring, engraved with his crest, and as he took it off, he stood up, his eyes on the piece of jewelry. " 'Tis all I have left," he repeated, and took a last look at the ring cupped in his palm. He extended both hands with the ring displayed.

The guard smiled, his eyes intent on Bothwell's open hands, but he couldn't see very well in the dim light. He bent over, pleased with his gain, reaching out for his prize. He never saw the terrible blow from the chained hands under his chin; his head snapped back under the impact, and he slumped slowly to the floor.

In a sudden show of action, Gibson flung himself on the prostrate figure of his erstwhile companion, his dagger in his hand. This shiny weapon he held to the throat of the man on the floor, and looked up at Bothwell. Their eyes met, and Bothwell smiled, shaking his head slowly. This was a comedy they were playing, and both knew it; no Borderer murders in cold blood. So Bothwell said, gravely, "I think he'll not be much hindrance, Gibson." He put his ring back on his finger and held out his hands with the irons dangling. "Take these things off me, Captain. There's a fine Border moon tonight!"

Gibson bent over Bothwell's hands and the scrape of a key freed his wrists. "All is ready, my lord, but—" He stopped, and the manacles fell to the floor.

Bothwell said, "You have done well, Gibson." He rubbed his wrists gratefully; they were sore from the heavy chains.

Gibson knew they hadn't much time, but he had news. "They do say John Fian confessed today, my lord, and the King himself assisted at the torments."

They gazed at each other, showing their distaste. "Jamie assisted?" Bothwell asked. "His stomach is stronger than it was wont to be."

Gibson nodded. "They do say," he whispered, "that they used the boot on him till the marrow in his bones was running with the blood."

"Maitland was preparing that instrument for me. They asked Fian whether I had commissioned his attempts at witchcraft?"

Gibson nodded again. "And he said yes."

Bothwell said genially, "What shall we do first when we are out? Kill Maitland?"

Gibson forgot Fian and his legs; he grinned. "Gregory is waiting at the top of the steps." He waved his hand in the direction of the south. "He has rope."

"Good," said Bothwell. He pointed to the man on the floor. "Hand me his dagger, and gag him well. Give me your keys, Gibson; I'm going to take my friend across the hall."

Gibson had already obeyed the first command, and Bothwell tucked the knife in his belt. "Come after me when you are ready," he ordered, and disappeared from the room, carrying his candle.

The man across the hall was sound asleep, but the sound of his door opening was enough to rouse him instantly. He sat up, his eyes fastened on the door fearfully, and when he saw Bothwell's face in the flickering light, his mouth opened in amazement. "Is it you, my lord?" he asked incredulously.

"We're in heaven," said Bothwell, and with his dark beard, his smile gave him more the appearance of a delighted Satan. "We all died, George," he added. "How do you like it?"

George struggled up, put one leg on the floor, and then the other. He was trembling from head to foot, for he knew this was deliverance—sudden inexplicable deliverance. Without hesitation he began to pull on his shoes. "How?" he asked, in a whisper. "How did you get out, my lord?"

"We're not out yet," Bothwell reminded him, dryly. "Unhappily, George, we have to climb down Castle Rock."

George stood up; not only his door but Bothwell's stood open, and he could see the flicker of the torch in the next room. "The Captain of the Night Watch," he guessed, remembering it had always been the Borderer Gibson who had supplied Bothwell with food and drink.

"The Captain," Bothwell repeated. "He and a guard named Gregory Cranstoun, a member of a Border family whose motto is: 'You shall want, ere I want.' Gregory has rope."

"Rope?" asked George vaguely, trying to gather his wits.

"Certainly, man. Rope. We have to get down to the rocks first. I hope you can manage to slide down a hundred feet or so of rope." Bothwell eyed George in the light of one candle, because if George should slip and fall, he would fall to his death on the jagged rocks that yawned beneath the walls of Edinburgh Castle. Bothwell frowned. Across the hall, Gibson closed the door of Bothwell's room, bolting it. Then he stood ready.

"Lead the way," Bothwell said curtly.

There was no light now; the hall was dark and silent. Gibson led the way. It seemed to George a long long time before he came to a stop at a narrow studded door. Gibson took out his heavy keys. In the stillness the creaking of the little-used entrance to the roof sounded ominously loud. George grew cold with the thought of what would happen to him if he were caught.

The open door revealed a set of curving steps. At the top of the steps the waiting man saw them come with relief; Gregory Cranstoun had taken up his post early in the evening, and in the cramped space he had felt each minute drag endlessly. He rose to his feet hurriedly.

"Your Lordship," he said eagerly, and watched with amazement when Bothwell held out his hand. Gregory took it in his own sweaty hand. "I've plenty of rope, my lord," he said quickly, covering his excitement by opening the door to the roof. It stretched away from them an almost incredible distance, for they were on that part which lay unguarded and empty except for the cannon. Way over to the north was Half-Moon Battery; the moon shone on its guns. To the west the battlements lay dark. The wind blew; noiselessly they crept toward the walls, the three Borderers with a nonchalance born of a life of endless hazards, and George with great fear in his heart. He could think only of the terrible drop on the other side of the breast-high walls. George had never slid down a rope before, and the rope on Gregory's arm looked slender; it might be tough enough, but it was so slender. George forced his feet forward; now that he was out of his prison he remembered it as a haven. In silence he watched Bothwell's nimble fingers tie the rope around the big cannon named Old Meg. George prayed.

"Over you go!" Bothwell spoke to Gibson in a whisper, for the errant wind could carry a voice to other ears.

George edged nearer the walls; he didn't want to look over but he couldn't help it. Only blackness was below. On this side of the walls there was no moonlight; Bothwell had chosen purposely. He didn't want dangling figures outlined in the moonlight—light which was to guide them down the castle rocks on the side away from the city.

George watched Gibson obey Bothwell; he watched Gibson unconcernedly perch himself for a second on the wall, wave his hand, and disappear. George's stomach turned over; he could feel the sweat running down his sides. "Almighty God," he muttered, staring desperately at Bothwell, and wondering whether he would be ordered over next. He shut his eyes, seeing the rocks below, but worse than that was the distance down; worse than the rocks was the terrible height.

"George." Bothwell said only his name, and George became more afraid of Bothwell than the drop. The habit of long years of obedience to the commands of his peers saved him. He asked one question.

"How do you know Gibson is safe, my lord?"

"He tugged the rope," explained Bothwell impatiently. "When you are down, pull hard on this." Bothwell was holding that very slender rope.

George nodded. He couldn't speak; his heart was hammering so that he wasn't actually breathing. He climbed up, and for one moment he hoped he would fall now and have done with it, but the fear of the dizzy hurtling through space came to his rescue.

For a brief moment Bothwell saw his face, his white face in the blackness; it was stamped with terror and it took even the hardened Earl aback. Under his hand the rope hung heavy with George's weight; every second Bothwell expected it to slacken, every second he expected a wild scream, but below him, George slipped farther, farther, and at last suddenly felt the rocks beneath his feet. He remembered to tug on the rope. Then he fell sideways, clutching at the uneven rock.

George thought he had tugged the rope hard, but Bothwell had hardly felt it. He lifted the rope experimentally; it was free, hanging free. Gregory went on over. It took him but thirty seconds to make the descent, and with a last look at his prison, Bothwell swung over the side. Freedom lay below, and when his feet touched the precarious rock at the bottom of the walls, it seemed the firmest ground on which he had stood for months.

But the journey was only begun; the terrible dangerous descent lay just ahead.

"Done," he said curtly. "You lead the way, Gibson."

Gibson had been the first down. He stood against the upgoing walls of the huge castle they had left, his back pressed against the stone. He turned his head; it was impossible for him to move much, for right below him was a sheer drop of at least fifty feet before the big rocks sloped off more gently. He could see Bothwell plainly; the Earl's white shirt—his cloak and doublet had long since gone to pay for his smuggled food and liquor—his shirt was dirty and stained, but it made a spot in the darkness, and Gibson could make out his face.

Gibson started off; it wasn't necessary for him to crawl, but he could hear George clambering along after him. Gibson rounded the last turn on hands and knees; he grasped a big outcropping of rock and pulled himself carefully to his feet.

The moon shone brightly. All four men were clearly defined as they stood against the castle walls. Below them the craggy rocks plunged downwards; way below them the flat moor from which Castle Rock sprang lay ghostly but safe.

"This is the way?" Bothwell asked, leaning over George, and quickly he knotted a piece of the slender rope around George's waist, fastening it to his own belt. There was just one trail which had been used by intrepid climbers before, one trail by which the formidable castle walls had been breached once in their history. "Then we'll follow it."

Gibson was ready for the command; he was starting down. He lowered his foot experimentally, found a familiar cropping of rock, and his head disappeared. He put his hand up and guided George's foot to the stepping place.

"Now, George." Bothwell spoke quietly. "Start down, and remember you're well tied."

George couldn't speak. Horrified by the thought of the two-hundred-foot drop beneath him, with the jagged teeth of stone waiting to crunch his body, he could see himself hurtling down. He remembered to wipe his sweaty hands on either sleeve, and gripping at the stone, he lowered himself. It seemed to him he was swinging in the air, as he almost was, for the rope around Bothwell tightened, and the Earl braced himself against the pull.

"Look where you're going!" He could see George's face puckered with fright and his closed eyes. "You can't feel your way here; the drops are too far!" George opened his eyes; he was afraid to look down but he forced himself. Then he moved over, and Bothwell dropped down beside him. They went on.

Farther below, Gibson was having the easiest time. He had made the descent a few times; he was not the man to stay in at night with the castle garrison. Edinburgh lay too invitingly near: a little matter of a few hundred feet of sheer rock was a small deterrent, especially since Gibson was partial to his ale in the evenings and the maids in the taverns. He lifted his head and shouted upward, "Halfway down!"

George heard him from a great distance. The blood was singing in his ears. He swayed; the rope tightened, and above him Bothwell dug his fingers into the rocky earth against the pull. Both his hands were raw; he could feel the warm blood running down his sleeve, trickling to the elbow. They went on.

Gibson reached up and guided George's foot onto the next rock. George came down, he felt for a foothold, he looked downward at his feet.

"Oh," he cried out, for his shoe slipped and above him Bothwell had already started to move. He swayed backward; he began to slip.

"Look out below," he shouted, his fingers clutching frantically at the rock he had released. He kept sliding slowly; and Gibson, shifting as quickly as possible to one side, threw his arm and then his whole body over the two men who had come to rest beside him.

Upright, and almost on their faces, they lay against the side of the hill. Above, Gregory was breathlessly silent; in the very place Bothwell had slipped from, he clung, afraid to come any further.

Slowly Bothwell felt for the next rock; his arms were numb; he couldn't feel the wet sticky blood that covered them; only the sharp pain in one finger told him he had ripped the nail from it.

The wind was whistling about the base of Castle Rock, and it told him they were almost to the bottom. He stood there for a second. Then George slipped again, and this time Bothwell knew he couldn't save himself. They were going fast, and he had time only to cry out to Gibson, warning him of the danger. He and George reeled back together, and then they fell.

When Bothwell opened his eyes, he was lying across a smooth rock, the wind was in his face, and oddly enough there was no pain. Gibson, bending over him, spoke calmly. "I'll help you up, my lord. You fell about twelve feet."

Bothwell stood unsteadily. He walked two steps and threw himself down on the wet earth, and the smell of the spring soil was suddenly the most lovely of all smells. He put his face on the ground; he stayed prone for a long minute; then he rolled over and sat up. "Hercules is waiting for us." It was a statement, not a question.

"Aye, my lord. The horses are in your stables."

"Good." As he said it Bothwell remembered he had used that word very often during the last hour, but there was really no other word to use. He was free.

Chapter Three

"Aye, sir," said Edwin Chalmers, "you are late. It is almost twelve." He was following his employer into Ainslee's Tavern on High Street, and he followed him through the inn, down a short hall, and into a private dining room. Behind the two men came Patrick's personal man, Geordie, and the door closed after all three of them. Patrick stood for a moment, surveying the room, and the men in it looked up.

It was a small room, about twelve by twelve feet, and most of it was taken up by a heavy table meant for dining. Except for chairs and two serving tables, there was no furniture. Patrick doffed his hat, his cloak was lifted from his shoulders, and he took the chair pulled out for him and sat down.

"My apologies, gentlemen."

Three men were sitting around the table; at his coming, the cards they had been playing with were thrown down carelessly, and the coins lay unnoticed among them.

"It doesn't matter, sir," said the Earl of Murray, politely, and he smiled, the charming smile that had made the "bonnie earl" one of the best-liked men in Scotland.

Patrick smiled back. "I despise lateness in others; I dislike it more in myself."

Murray shook his head deprecatingly. "We are not so impatient, sir. Please have your supper; we can talk when you have dined."

"Aye," said the Earl of Logan belatedly, because he didn't

care if Patrick Galbraith starved. He wanted to get on with the business of the evening; it was important enough to make him forget he had been betting heavily on the hand he had thrown down. He drew his bushy brows together. "Of course you must dine, sir."

Patrick said, "No, thank you. A little whiskey and water, if it's procurable, will suffice me." As he said it, he rubbed his hand over his eyes. He wasn't conscious of being tired, and he wasn't hungry, even though it was late. But he wanted to be finished with tonight's business, so that he could think. Janet. The name went through his head, the two syllables repeating themselves, and her face hovered just out of reach. He tapped his fingers on the table, on the bare wood, and tried to forget her.

Lord Ochiltree, the third man at the table, was watching him with solemn eyes. Ochiltree was a member of the Stewart clan, as was Lord Murray. "Now about Francis, Lord Bothwell," he said, tentatively, for Patrick seemed to be very far away.

Patrick still tapped his fingers on the table. "Ah, yes," he said. He had had to be polite to his King. Now he felt his bad humor returning and he was under no obligation to be good-humored to these men. He let his eyes rove about the table, looking at the cards, the money, the glasses of wine. "The Stewart clan," he said, and he made his voice amused, as at the antics of children.

Logan and Ochiltree frowned, but Murray smiled, showing his even white teeth and looking faintly deprecating himself. "You must not judge us too harshly, sir."

Logan regarded Patrick across the table appraisingly. "Don't you care for gambling, sir?"

"Indeed I do, but I rarely allow myself indulgence in it."

"Holy God," said Logan incredulously; it had never occurred to him to deny himself anything.

"My vices are many, though," said Patrick bitterly, allowing himself the luxury of a swift anger against the woman he wanted. Again he shoved her from his mind. "Now, gentlemen, you've been very patient, and I shan't keep you much longer."

He took a drink of his watered whiskey (the ban on the liquor did not prevent its being served), and the other three men were silent, waiting.

"Two weeks ago," Patrick began, "I undertook an investigation of the charges of treason which now lie over the head of a peer of the realm. I undertook this investigation at the express wish of the Earl of Murray." He inclined his head toward Murray formally, and turned to his secretary. "Hand me the briefs, Chalmers," he ordered. He didn't really need them; he had the facts catalogued in his head. Chalmers complied instantly, but it seemed as though Patrick were forcing his very interested audience to wait again. He leafed through the papers and brought out one which he laid on top.

"My client," he said, "is his Lordship Francis Stewart Hepburn, fifth Earl of Bothwell. He was the only child of a union between Lord John Stewart, natural son of James the Fifth, and Lady Janet Hepburn, sister to James Hepburn, fourth Earl of Bothwell. On the twentieth of April last, he was committed to ward in Edinburgh Castle under the charges of commissioning an attempt at witchcraft against the body and person of the King of Scotland." Patrick lifted that paper, and put another on top of it. He scanned it briefly, and handed it across the table to Murray. "Those are the evidences got under torture from the Wizard Graham and his wife, some time ago, and from John Fian yesterday. Perhaps you would like to see them."

Murray murmured, "Thank you," and took the papers in his hand; he looked down at the closely written sheets with some trepidation. "How good are they, sir?" he asked. "I can't tell the worth of them."

Patrick was making no effort to be pleasant. "As far as regards the truth, they are worthless; as evidence in court, they are extremely dangerous."

"Aye," said Logan, portentously.

"And," Patrick went on, "James himself heard this evidence; James himself gave the orders for the mallets to strike the wedges into the iron boot."

"Aye," growled Logan.

"However, sirs, let us leave the evidences against Bothwell. Now there is hardly anyone in the country who does not believe that Maitland is behind this business. It's a fine way of being rid of his enemy. Maitland has James—Maitland has Jocko—and he thinks he can make the monkey jump his way." Patrick was using the idiom of his day, which compared the King to the ape, Jocko, who, if you had him, would behave the way you wanted. "At this present time, gentlemen, Maitland has Jocko, but I do not think he can make Jocko bite Bothwell; or rather I do not think the bite will be mortal. And these are my reasons. First, the Queen."

Murray nodded. "She and James quarreled today. About Francis."

"And the quarrel was bitter. Bothwell has enchanted her, as he has all the other ladies. Moreover, she feels that he is her champion against Maitland, who did his best to prevent the King's marriage to her. Second, I think you are all aware how dangerous it might be for all of you—if Bothwell were found guilty. Other heads might fall, sirs." He smiled.

Logan was bristling with anger. He banged his hand on the table. "You're right! This is an infamous charge to be brought against the noblest name in the land!"

"It is, as Bothwell said, a 'poor beggar's charge.'" Patrick didn't keep the amusement out of his voice. "You would all have preferred an outright accusation of treason. So," he continued, "I fully believe that the severe penalty will not be asked, but I do also believe he will not go free. Undoubtedly he will be warded again in some prison, for as long as His Majesty sees fit to keep him there."

Logan muttered, "It is an affront to all of us that the Earl of Bothwell should stand behind the dock and hear himself charged with witchcraft!"

Patrick was satisfied with Logan's response; it bore out his findings. "The nobility are one with you, Logan. Therefore I suggest that we allow Bothwell to come to trial, and I am confident that the preponderant weight of disapproval on the part of the peers of the realm will force Maitland into a stalemate.

And thus we protect Bothwell's titles, his lands. When he comes out of gaol—"

At this Logan interrupted. "The devil with the lands! Four years ago Bothwell told Jamie he ought to be hanged. Jamie has not forgiven that; we have no assurance he'll ever pardon Bothwell, and we have no assurance but yours, sir, that Bothwell won't hang for this!"

Patrick ignored Logan; he looked down at his papers.

"There is considerable land, Murray. There are castles at Crichton, Hailes, and Hermitage; dwelling places in almost every Border town. There are lands in Midlothian, Liddesdale, and Teviotdale; the holdings are extensive." He paused briefly, regarding Murray, ignoring Logan, and feeling very glad that Ochiltree was maintaining such a silence. "Of course, they are heavily mortgaged. On two properties alone there is owing thirteen thousand pounds Scot, and I suggest that we raise the mortgages to fifteen thousand, and clear up all outstanding indebtednesses. His tenant rentals will take care of interest while he is in prison; they will pay off—" he stopped and calculated—"In five years they will pay off the entire debt. He would come out of gaol solvent." He folded up the papers, handed them to Chalmers. "Now give me the agreements," he ordered.

Chalmers laid two papers beside Patrick, and pen and ink. Patrick glanced over the few words; he shoved them across to Murray. "If you will sign both, my lord."

Logan couldn't keep silent any longer. "Is this a trap, sir?" He set his glass down sharply. "I don't like your advice. It's too dangerous. Do you know Maitland has about two thousand armed men in the city? As I see this justice you talk about so glibly, I see Bothwell's head on top of the Tolbooth! Perhaps you plan to salute it!"

Murray roused himself from his reading. "Logan, please permit me—" He picked up the pen, but Logan laid his hand over the paper.

"Don't sign it yet," he said. "What is it?" He kept his hand over the paper and turned to face Patrick. "We're playing with the life of a man!"

Murray said slowly, "Take your hand away, Logan. There is nothing in these papers I shouldn't sign. I am selling coal to the amount of five thousand pounds; half now, and the other half when Bothwell is acquitted. That is our payment to the gentleman."

Logan grunted. "So he, with His Majesty's dispensation, can export the coal, and sell it for twice the price."

"Robbie." Murray's tone was weary. "This is the only way I can pay for Sir Patrick's services. Even if I had the money, this would serve our purpose of concealment better."

Logan repeated, "So Sir Patrick may sell for twice his purchase price abroad. And if he is being paid by Maitland, too? I'm too old to trust to words. I say we should be done with this havering, and help Bothwell to escape!"

"No!" Patrick almost rose to his feet. He stared at Logan long and hard. "You help him to escape and you sign his death warrant!"

Logan snorted; he got up. "Will you excuse me, sirs?" He squared his heavy shoulders, and started for the door.

Ochiltree followed him hastily; he wanted to know what Logan was going to do. "Goodnight, Murray." He bowed formally to Patrick. "Goodnight, sir." And he made for the door in Logan's stormy wake.

Patrick didn't wait until the door closed. "I mean it, Murray," he said intently. "Let Bothwell escape and it will be but the beginning of a battle between him and his King, a battle that can have only one bloody end. Now if you have more questions, sir, I'm at your service."

Chapter Four

THE carved hands of the ornate French clock stood at one, and its ticking was the only sound in the quiet room. The green quilts of the gay yellow and green bed were turned down, and its taffeta hangings looped back. A fire burned lazily on the hearth; the little clock chimed the hour; and in a chair by the fire, an elderly maid woke from her doze. She yawned, settled her cap, and straightened up in the brocaded cushion chair. Fully awake now, she rose, smoothing her dress. The fire was very warm; on the overhanging mantle candles were lighted, and she went about the business of lighting the ones which stood on the table, with its complement of a velvet-topped stool and a large Venetian mirror. That done, she looked around the room again, satisfied, but she didn't have time to resume her seat by the fire. The door opened suddenly and her mistress stood on the threshold.

She was carrying her cloak in one hand; it trailed negligently behind her, one end of the lustrous satin sweeping the floor. Her dress was of white velvet; its ruff fanned out behind her head like the frame of a painting, but no painting could be as lush and as warmly beautiful as Anne Galbraith was herself. She was not very tall, boasting only five feet and four inches of height, and she was not quite seventeen years old. Her hair was the color of honey; the curls clustered high on her head. Women said that her claim to beauty was the lovely shape of her head, but men's eyes overlooked that and lingered on the too full mouth and the lashes so heavy that they seemed to pull her eyelids down at the corners.

She kicked the door to with one foot, dropped her cloak on the nearest chair. She dropped off both shoes and stood wiggling her toes. Finally she discarded the white feather fan she was carrying.

"Marie, it was heavenly." She sat down on the stool in front of her table and smiled at her reflection. "Heavenly," she added.

"*Chérie,*" said Marie. She smiled too, and then shook her head. She pointed to the cloak thrown down carelessly, and at the slippers on the floor. "You should never drag your cape, and kick at doors. How many times—" she began, and stopped, for Anne's violet eyes were watching herself in the glass.

"No one but you is here, Marie," she said, absently. She reached up and unfastened one earring, watching the profile she had turned to the glass. She dropped the earring, yawned, and thrust both feet out in front of her, still stretching her toes. "I don't care for shoes yet, Marie." She watched her feet and ankles. "Was it not sweet of him to give these to me?"

Marie understood that she meant the silk stockings which had been one of the many gifts from her cousin. "Sir Patrick is very generous," she said, her black eyes sly.

Anne looked up. "He is very clever too," she said, thoughtfully. She stood up and began to undo her dress.

"I'll do it, *chérie.*" Marie took Anne's hands from the hooks reprovingly. "Don't wriggle so. Ladies stand still." She thought of Patrick's elderly aunt. "You listen to me. You can learn from her Ladyship. Even if she is old-fashioned. You can learn." She nodded her head, and undid Anne's garters, slipping the stockings off her legs with nimble fingers.

Anne said, "Marie, do you know she supervises every bit of food we have on our table? She even apportions what the servants eat. Did you know that?"

Marie nodded. "Your gown, *ma petite*. And you must learn from her. It is the custom of the chatelaine to supervise the food."

"It is the custom to hire a caterer," said Anne firmly. "And to hire musicians, perhaps a magician or dancers for parties."

Marie laughed. "Will you give parties every night? Hold still a minute." She smoothed down Anne's eyebrow with her fingers. "Ah!" She sounded just as though she had spied an errant spider, and she picked up a pair of tweezers. Anne made a face as the wayward hair was plucked. "You have such beautiful eyebrows," said Marie admiringly. She picked up the string of pearls and the pearl earrings Anne had been wearing. She put in front of Anne a green, velvet-covered casket that was protected by a series of intricate locks.

Anne had opened the box many times; the lid flew back and the candlelight gleamed on the extravagant collection of jewelry thus revealed. On top of rings and bracelets, Anne dropped the pearl necklace, and she drew forth one tremendous emerald on a narrow chain. "Tomorrow I'm going to wear this," she announced, watching it spit green fire as it swung back and forth, catching the light.

Marie frowned. "You should be careful to wear no more jewels than you have already worn. Her Ladyship will be suspicious." Marie didn't really care whether the countess was suspicious or not; she was thinking of the sharp eyes of Sir Patrick Galbraith, eyes that never missed a single detail.

"I don't know why you worry, Marie. I don't know why my mother couldn't have got her jewelry from her husbands. She did have two of them."

Marie laid down the brush she had been wielding. "Husbands are not so generous," she said, only. She moved over to the bed, plumped the fat bolster, smoothed out the linen sheets which were already turned down.

Anne stood up, yawned, and sat down on one side of the feather bed, dropping her velvet mules. Marie let the curtains fall back on one side, and came around to fix the others.

"Please, Marie. I don't like to sleep with the curtains down. It's so dark."

Marie sighed. "It's always dark at night."

"Of course it is, but you know what I mean. The night light—I am used to it. In the country—"

"You are not in the country. You haven't quite lost those freckles, either." She spoke as though that were Anne's fault.

Anne turned over in bed, and looked out the window nearest her. She was used to seeing the black bulk of the house next door; its owner was in prison, and every night its windows were dark and vacant. Suddenly she sat up.

"Why, there is light!" She hopped out of bed and went to the window, pressing her nose against the glass. Just opposite her window a single candle was burning; while she watched, it moved; then, just as suddenly, it was extinguished. Marie peered over her shoulder.

"I see nothing," she said.

"But there was a light." Anne stared. "That is Lord Bothwell's town house, Marie, and oh—what I have been told about him!"

"Get back in bed." Marie fussed again, tucking in the disarranged quilts. She looked out the window for a final glance; the gardens between the two houses were dark; the house next door was dark. Marie swung the bed curtains closed. "You must learn to sleep late, *chérie*."

Anne waited only until the door was closed before she was at the window again, looking. But there was nothing but blackness. She peered through it, decided to open her window, and when she raised her eyes from the catch, was sure she had missed seeing something. There had been—there was—a flicker of light in the same window.

The spring wind fanned into the room; it seemed warmer than it had been; it was softer. Suddenly she picked up her robe, slipping her arms into the long sleeves, tying the sash firmly around her waist. Its fur collar tickled her chin comfortingly; she was out the window and standing on the wet grass in the silent gardens.

Once out, she ran. Catching up her skirts she ran between trees and bushes. The moonlight was waning, but there was enough light to make the shrubs throw long shadows. She ran, always making for the one window; she could see plainly now that there was a light behind the shutters.

Ten feet from the house she stopped in the shadow of a gnarled apple tree. She stood against the trunk, feeling the rough bark with her fingers. There was no sound at all from the big house; only the telltale gleam of light behind a wooden shutter. She gathered her courage, and ran the last ten feet to the house, pressing herself against its stone walls.

She was so excited she could hardly breathe. Motionless, she stood for fully a minute before she edged sideways slowly, craning her head to see through the cracks in the shutter. They weren't big enough.

She waited again before she had the audacity to push a finger through the slats. One moved slightly. She bent down, closing one eye. "Oh," she whispered.

She didn't have much of a view of the tiny scullery inside, but she could see the middle part of a rough table. There was a man lying on the table. She couldn't see his face, only his chest and hips. His hands were fumbling at his coat and bending over him was another man. Anne stared at his bent head. His shirt was filthy, its long full sleeves ripped, in one place from the shoulder to the wrist; his hands were bandaged, the clean linen making a sharp contrast to his stained shirt. He raised his head; she was afraid his dark eyes could see right through the shutter, and she was almost frightened enough to let go of the wooden slat when she saw him reach for the dagger in his belt. She was sure she was to see murder done.

Instead, for some reason, he only ripped away the buttoned coat of the man on the table. Anne saw his lips move.

"Is that better, George?" asked Bothwell, frowning down at him. "Why don't you lie back?"

"I can't, my lord." George pushed the words out with great effort. He closed his eyes; through all the pain he could see again the dangling rope, the terrible rocks; he felt again his hands lose their grip, felt the awful moment when he knew he was going to fall. He opened his eyes, looking up at Bothwell's face. "I'm going to die."

"No, you aren't, man." Bothwell picked up a glass of wine. "Can't you drink some of this?"

George paid no attention. "I want to ask a boon," he said. His breath was coming in quick small inhalations that didn't appear to go past his throat.

"Certainly," said Bothwell, unconsciously lowering his voice.

"The old dame I lived with." He stopped; the pain was all over his body now. "My arms," he muttered, "my side."

"Can I do something for her?" Bothwell asked. He tried to think of the right question to save this man the trouble of explanations.

A nod was the answer. "I found the money," he said, cryptically. "She needs it; it's in the kitchen, and it's hers." He paused again for breath. His eyes were wide, then they closed wearily. "I shouldna ha' taken it. But I only took part; there's plenty left." But the thought of his theft seemed to trouble him; he lay silent and the pain came fiercer; he was raked with it. "My clothes," he muttered again.

Bothwell loosened the dirty shirt; he swore under his breath as he pulled the clothes free from the hairy chest where the pain drove unseen knives into the laboring heart. But he didn't know what else to do. He had never seen a man die this way; always before it had been a bloody matter of shattered flesh ripped with flying splinters from a wooden deck, a matter of a bullet or a sword. This was the anguish of a relentless nature inflicting its bloodless wounds; nature trying to force the rich red blood through the collapsed arteries of a struggling heart. He heard George's voice.

"Her name is Campbell."

Bothwell forgot he could hardly promise to see this woman. He was intent only on fulfilling this man's wish. "But her home? Where does she live?"

There was no answer. There was silence only. Bothwell stared at the still face. Then the eyes opened wide. They were deep blue, and they were very far away, so that the rational words came as a shock to their hearer. "Near to your brother Hercules."

The blue eyes closed; the light lashes lay against the cheek.

Bothwell studied the white face, lifted George's hands. He folded them across his chest, and stepped back from the table.

He didn't step out of Anne's line of vision. With her eyes glued to the crack in the wood, she watched unseen hands wrap the man on the table in a dark blanket. It took only a second, Anne could feel their guilty haste, and then just before the light went out, one hand held a heavy canvas jacket for the tall man she had been watching. Bothwell put it on; then there was complete blackness.

Anne stepped away from the window, hugging the wall until she came to a protruding chimney, and she huddled herself against it. In the stillness she heard a door open.

She didn't dare to move; she didn't see Gibson and Gregory carry George's body into the garden; she stood there breathlessly, in the corner the chimney made. Then she heard a voice say, "I found a couple of shovels for them, Francis."

"Poor devil," came Bothwell's voice. "The trip down Castle Rock was too much, I guess."

Hercules didn't waste time asking why Bothwell had brought George from the castle. In prison a man makes strange friends. He was thinking about George's story, and the money in the kitchen. "I do not know a woman named Campbell, if she does live near me."

Bothwell grinned. "She's a mite too ancient for you, I suspect."

Anne could hear so well that she knew both men were very close to her. They must be standing right around the side of the chimney, at the kitchen door.

"Well," Hercules said, "I'll go see to the horses. It will take Gibson a few minutes, too."

"Aye," was the answer. "I'll wait at the front gate."

Fear swept through Anne. If that man were going to the front gate, he would walk right past her. She huddled back into the corner, turning her face toward the stone, her nose pressing its roughness. She could hear no noise, no footsteps of any kind, but she forgot the grass was soft, and when Bothwell rounded the chimney he stopped for just a moment.

In that time he thought of silencing her immediately. He was close to her, only two feet separated them, but her face was turned to the stone and all he could see was her white gown and her unbound blonde hair. He reached out both hands, taking her around the neck, and he swung her around to face him as though she were a doll. His hands tightened on her throat in a brutal grip.

"Be still!" His voice was low, and with one thumb he flipped her chin up so he could see her face. "Be still, wench, or—" He shook her warningly.

Her face was white; she looked up at him, for he towered almost a foot over her, and she put her hands up at his chest imploringly.

"Who are you?" he asked, angrily.

She couldn't answer, and he loosened his grip a little. "Who are you?" he repeated, his scowl menacing on his unshaven face. "What did you see?"

"Nothing," she gasped.

"What did you hear, then?"

"Nothing," she cried; she was trembling with terror.

"You interfering wench, you're lying! Christ's blood, I ought to knock your featherhead against this wall!"

Anne's knees buckled underneath her; her eyes closed, and instinctively she reached out to him for support. "Play me no tricks," she heard him mutter, but he did put one arm around her, keeping the other big hand on her neck.

Anne didn't faint, but Bothwell thought she had. She was limp in his arms, her head was lying against his shoulder. Suddenly he grinned. He bent his head, letting her soft curls rub against his face, and he whispered in her ear, "Well, lassie. I do favor the blondes, but I have so little time tonight."

Anne opened her eyes instantly. It must be he. "I know who you are now," she said breathlessly. She gazed up at him in awe, but she did remember to lift her hand and push the disarranged strands from her forehead. "Don't let go of me, my lord. I'll fall. You did frighten me so, sir."

He shifted his hand from her shoulder. "I'm sorry, lass," he murmured, watching her lean her head against his arm. He thought how he must look, after weeks in Edinburgh Castle. "You smell like flowers," he said truthfully.

"Do I?" She looked up at him, smiling, delighted with her success in finding him. "You did fright me so, my lord." She closed her eyes and tipped her head back against his arm so that he would have the full benefit of the dark lashes, the full mouth.

"Open your eyes, lass," he said, "I'd love to be ravished of my virtue, but I have not the time."

"Why—" she began angrily, raising her hand threateningly, but he caught her fingers and his smile flashed in his dark face. "That's better. Now, how did you know who I was?"

"Because you were so impudent," Anne snapped. Then her tone became distant. "Because Hercules called you Francis. I know you have a brother Hercules—and this is your house."

"Do not pout. I wonder why women are always angry with me? I was telling you the truth, lassie. I'd surrender my virtue, but I don't know you. 'Tis not seemly so."

Anne thrust out her lower lip belligerently; she wasn't going to laugh at him. "I am Anne Galbraith, my lord," she announced haughtily. "I'm not faint any longer, sir; you may release me."

"Your servant, madam." He stepped back, offered her his arm. "Much as it pains me to take leave of you, I'm now going to escort you back to your bed."

"It is hardly necessary, sir." She picked up her skirts. She was searching her mind for a few appropriate words for him, but he interrupted.

"I would not have you frightened again, on your stroll. But what I cannot understand, lass, is why the man you were going to meet didn't keep his assignation."

Anne stopped walking; she turned to face him angrily. "I had no assignation, sir!"

His dark eyes were intent on her. "Could it be the moonlight," he asked, "or is it that I've been in gaol for two months? My eyes are blinded by you, lassie."

Anne thought they looked far from blind. "But I wasn't meeting anyone, my lord. That is my window," she added, reluctantly.

Bothwell picked her up in his arms. The window was wide open, and he set her on her feet inside the room. He stood outside, leaning on the sill, regarding her. "The next time you go out after midnight, do not wear white. Black is less conspicuous, and men like it just as well. In fact many prefer it. I do."

Anne turned her back on him, whirling around so that her skirts swirled. At the same time, Bothwell put one hand on the sill and vaulted into the room. He laid his hand on her shoulder.

Anne didn't turn. "What is it, my lord?" she asked, in a very small voice.

"Lassie," he said slowly, "this is to show you how ungallant a man I am." Gently he turned her around to face him; she looked up at him with eyes that searched his face.

"Why are you ungallant?" she whispered.

"Because necessity dictates it. There are men whose lives depend on your most kissable mouth. You'll not forgive me, so I'll not ask it. Goodnight, Anne."

His left hand was resting on her shoulder; she didn't see him raise his right fist, it was loosely clenched, and when it hit her chin, he put out both arms and caught her as she fell. One of her slippers came off as he lifted her; he put her in bed with the other one on, robe and all, and carefully tucked the quilts around her; he was sure as he looked down at her face on the pillow that she would hate him the more heartily if the bruise on her chin showed for long. Then he was out the window. He made his way across the dark gardens.

Hercules was waiting for him. "Holy God, Francis," he whispered, coming around the corner of the house to join Bothwell. "Where have you been?"

"Wenching," said Bothwell, and Hercules stared. "I put her to sleep, safely. She will not be talking until we've left the city, and I think that she'll sleep till morning. Undisturbed." He swung up into the saddle of the horse Hercules held for him;

Hercules' surprised face was so familiar that Bothwell smiled delightedly.

Hercules smiled back at him; when he did it was quite evident that they were brothers. Although Hercules was as far removed from his titled half-brother as his pretty mother had been from the Lady Janet Hepburn, the two men were as close together as nature and mutual regard could bring them.

"My lord," said Hercules honestly, "I was not worried—as yet." He turned away, waved a hand at Gibson and Gregory, and mounted himself. With one last look at his house, Bothwell and his three companions spurred off down the Canongate.

The Canongate entered High Street a quarter of a mile above Bothwell's house. Very broad, well-paved and drained, it ran up the hill toward the great castle that frowned over the city, the castle that Bothwell had just left. The houses on both sides of High Street were very tall; some reached fifteen stories, for Edinburgh had grown skyward as it expanded with the centuries. The houses were timber fronted, or gray stone, gabled, and they had fat wooden balconies. They leaned close together. High Street was like a river that ran between tall banks.

Hercules and Bothwell, riding abreast, passed the turreted Tolbooth, in whose dungeons the luckless John Fian waited death on the morrow; they clattered through the square, under the very shadow of the towering Town Cross. They passed the entrances to innumerable narrow wynds, which ran off High Street at various angles, twisting streets that in the daytime swarmed with humans as an anthill with its denizens. They had come to the center of the city, and a few lights burned. They reminded Hercules of news he had heard.

"His Lordship, Murray, was meeting at Ainslee's tonight with Sir Patrick Galbraith. Logan and Ochiltree were to be there, too. Murray told me he had employed Sir Patrick to consider your case."

Bothwell was intensely surprised. "I hardly know the man," he said. "Murray should not have done that."

Hercules said, "He is very clever, and Murray thought he could help."

Bothwell looked ahead. There was a coach in front of the tavern; he could see its outlines plainly. "I think he is still there," he said, and began to smile. "If he is there, Murray may be there too." He came up beside the coach; the driver lay across the seat snoring. "There is no mark on the door."

Hercules reined in alongside. "They say Sir Patrick is waiting for his uncle to die, and then he will paint on the arms of his earldom."

Bothwell considered this piece of information. He dismounted, and behind him Gibson jumped down and took the reins tossed to him. Gibson's face was the picture of astonishment. "If there is trouble—" Bothwell said only that, and Gibson nodded. "Aye, my lord," he said capably.

"Come with me, Hercules." Bothwell was already striding toward the doors, and a sleepy man directed him down the hall.

"The first door to the left," he said—and then incredulously, "Your Lordship!"

"How are ye, Tammie?" asked Bothwell imperturbably. He knocked on the door indicated, and it was opened by Patrick's man Geordie; it closed behind both men before anyone inside the room spoke.

Murray had risen to his feet; his hands grasped the edge of the table and his face was frightened. He stared from Bothwell to Hercules and he said, "Francis!" in a very low tense tone.

Bothwell stood with his back to the door. "You're up late, Murray," he began, jokingly, and his smile was very amused. He took a step forward, and at his motion Hercules took his place at the door, like a guard.

Hercules had a pistol stuck through his belt; he carried a dagger and a sword, and his face was puckered with concentration as he shot glances at Patrick, the secretary Chalmers, and the self-effacing Geordie. At any time Hercules, with a height and breadth worthy of his name, had an air of watchful truculence. Now it was more pronounced; he was so obviously on guard. Then Bothwell noticed the tension in the little room and for the second time tonight he remembered he was fugitive.

He forgot Murray then. His eyes fastened on the face of the

man with whom he was acquainted only slightly. "Sir Patrick," he said, almost as though he were commenting on the fact that he knew the name, and a vision of Anne as he had left her flashed through his mind.

"Your Lordship," said Patrick slowly. "A pleasure, sir. Won't you be seated?"

Bothwell was wondering how foolish he had been to enter this tavern. Would Patrick Galbraith turn informer as soon as he could? Bothwell eyed him, his white hands that rested so languidly on the table; then he turned, with a shrug. It made little difference anyway; no one left this room before he ordered it. "How are you, Murray?" he asked, real warmth in his tone.

Murray noticed that Patrick's mouth was set; he doubted the man himself, and then he too forgot him. "Bothwell," he burst out, "faith, man, I'm glad to see you!" He put his hand into the Earl's and his smile was very eager. "Sit down, Francis. What will you have to drink? Are you hungry?" He smiled again, and stood there, looking at Bothwell as if he couldn't believe it was he.

"I'm not hungry." Bothwell smiled. "But I'll have ale." His eyes left Murray again, and went to Patrick; they were sitting side by side.

Patrick stared back, at the unshaven face, the clumsy jacket, the big bandaged hands. This was the man whose fate he had decided tonight, and he thought to himself that his plans had been perfect except that they had overlooked one element which should never be left out—the human equation. Patrick said so. "You remind me of a pirate, my lord. They should look like you."

Bothwell frowned. "Do not let my uncouth appearance deceive you, sir." He reached up and lazily scratched his head.

"I'm looking past the beard, and the lice which undoubtedly infect you." Patrick moved his chair away a little. "No, I understand there are some nations which look unkindly at the letters-of-marque you have granted captains whom the same nations dub piratical."

Bothwell had evidently found a louse, which he crushed in

his fingers with some satisfaction. The undercurrents in the room were so thick that Hercules stood stiffly by the door; he was relieved to hear Bothwell's even voice. "You are mistaken, sir. On the other hand I have it as incontrovertible fact that it is you who have run through a law against the import of golf balls. It is you who force me to deal with a swindling smuggler whom we all know too well. And I further understand it is you who make the domestic balls we are supposed to buy. Are you aware that they split?"

"I do not play golf."

"I see." Bothwell looked as though he could also see that Patrick was not the man he should be, and that his confession of not playing golf fitted in with the Earl's previous opinion. "You're tall," he said, grudgingly. "You might play well."

"I'm sure your opinion on golf," returned Patrick, himself emphasizing the "golf," "is quite valuable."

"He's one of our finest players," said Murray heartily. He had been listening dazedly. It couldn't be true, but it was, and it was dangerous. That thought kept recurring to Murray; every time he looked at Patrick he remembered the danger; he knew he was listening for noises that might materialize at any moment. Somewhere there must be a rope hanging loose over Edinburgh Castle; one room that shouldn't be empty, was empty. He started to ask a question, stopped because of Patrick, and then continued anyway because it was so important, there wasn't any time to lose. "Francis," he asked tensely, "what are you going to do?"

Bothwell, very serious, looked from one to the other of the grave faces. Patrick who had been in the act of raising his glass to his lips, stopped; even Hercules was watching with intentness. Bothwell said one short word, and his eyes crinkled with laughter. "As soon as I get home," he continued, "and in a soft bed."

Murray burst out laughing, and Hercules grinned. "After all, Murray, I've been in prison for two months." Bothwell leaned back in his chair, satisfied with his explanation of his intentions.

Murray said, "Francis, I've missed you." He turned to Patrick. "The man is never serious."

"But I am," said Bothwell. "I have told you the truth. I'm on my way to Hermitage Castle." There was silence; Bothwell finished off his ale, and he realized his audience had been stunned by his words. They had expected him—they had expected him to run away! He frowned, his dark brows met, and he said suddenly, "Am I a criminal?"

Murray looked down at the table but Patrick smiled. "Just how did you arrive here tonight, my lord? So that we could be favored with your company?"

The tension returned to the room. Bothwell turned slightly to face fully the soft-voiced man beside him. "With the aid of two guards," he said curtly. "I left the castle by way of the roof and a strong rope. Does that answer your question?"

"It does. I think your exact words to me were 'am I a criminal?' I believe you are, my lord. In fact the list of crimes against your name reads like a priest's indictment of a heretic." He tapped his foot insistently. "Does that answer your question?"

"You—" Bothwell broke off; he swung around to Murray. "You asked me what I was going to do. Did you expect me to run away, Murray? Did you?"

Murray looked embarrassed. He fidgeted. Bothwell went on finally, "You have answered me. And I you. I'm going to Hermitage," he repeated stubbornly. "What's wrong with all of you?"

The sudden boyish question gave Patrick his first real insight into the Earl of Bothwell. He half smiled; he asked, "You expected us to celebrate your escape, did you not? You expected us to raise our glasses and drink to your health! This is another successful jest, is it not? Well, 'tis one that will earn you the same fate that overtook your uncle!"

Hercules stiffened as he heard the words; he couldn't see Bothwell's face and this time he was not relieved when he heard the Earl's tone. "I had no notion you were interested in my genealogy, sir."

Patrick leaned back lazily. "Oh but I am, my lord. You have a fascinating background, and a rather sinister one. You are the fifth Earl of Bothwell, and you had an uncle by name of James Hepburn, the fourth Earl. He was like you; he thought there were no laws except those he chose either to break or follow. By that method he became the King of Scotland, and for that ambition he spent ten years in prison—ten years that drove him insane, as they might you. Ten years, and part of that time he was chained. The story goes that he was chained to a post, and that he could not move, except in a half-circle which his restless feet wore deep into the stone of his dungeon!"

Bothwell pushed back his chair and got to his feet slowly. "That," he said, "is a lie. And forgetting his hands, he hooked his thumbs in his belt and stood over Patrick's lounging figure.

Patrick looked up at him. "It is quite true," he remarked. "You mislike to credit it. You would rather think that James Hepburn was kindly treated, that imprisonment did not drive him to madness. No, my lord, James Hepburn was chained to a post, to rot in a Danish castle. I predict that you will too—if you are lucky and if you escape the gruesome death sentence performed on traitors!"

Bothwell's hands unhooked themselves from his belt. He took Patrick by his smooth satin collar. A chair crashed over backward, and Patrick was hauled to his feet. All the pent-up anger Bothwell had felt in prison was released; he shook the man in his grasp and he poised himself to throw him back against the wall.

He wasn't conscious of the pain in his hands; he saw only the white face of the man he held and he was rather surprised to see the vicious anger in the hazel eyes that blazed back at him.

"Take your hands away!" Patrick's voice was low but warning.

Bothwell tightened his grip, his mouth curved in a mocking smile, because he was the stronger by far, and he was about to send Patrick in a heap on the floor, and with that fine doublet torn, when he saw the swift movement of Patrick's left hand.

There was no time for Bothwell to move back. He dropped

his own left hand, dragging the dagger from his belt. At the same time that he brought up his arm, he felt the point of his opponent's weapon pressing just below his stomach.

"Don't move!" The warning was in snarled Italian, and Bothwell answered it in kind. "You weren't quick enough!" The two men stood there, so close that there was barely room between them for the twenty-four-inch-long blades.

On the other side of the room Hercules was stricken by the swift action—but for a moment only. Then he put one hand on the table and vaulted it neatly, coming to stand alongside the antagonists. He laid a hand on each of their shoulders, gently. "If you would both take two steps backward, gentlemen." He kicked the chair aside with his foot, and there was room for Patrick to move.

There was no answer; there was silence. Hercules looked down, sending a quick glance at the two daggers that crossed each other, both poised for a fatal thrust. Hercules drew in his breath. "Sirs, if you will each take two steps backward, you could then remove your jackets. His Lordship's heavy canvas is a hindrance."

There was another pregnant silence, in which Murray hardly breathed, and Chalmers grasped a servant for support. "They'll kill each other," he moaned, to Geordie. Then suddenly Patrick stepped back and Bothwell moved too. Their hands dropped to their sides, and they regarded each other across four feet of space.

Hercules felt his fears return when he saw their faces. Duelling with daggers was the most dangerous of duels; at close quarters, in shirtsleeves, it was often fatal to both combatants. How might he stop them?

"It is very unusual," he began, and they both looked at him now, "to duel in so small a space. Especially with those weapons." Hercules tried not to grimace as he looked at the shining daggers. "You should remove your coats. Your Lordship, your sword."

His heart sank as he watched Bothwell unsheath his sword and lay it across the table. Hercules tried to maintain an even composure. "Now if you would help me move this table, sir." He spoke to Patrick.

Patrick said curtly, "Geordie will help you." He motioned to the shivering Geordie.

"Ah, yes," said Hercules, as though he had forgot there were servants in the room. "Why did you speak Italian to Lord Bothwell?"

"I learned the dagger in Padua," Patrick answered, not noticing what he said, watching Hercules move the table over as far as it would go. That wasn't very far.

"You were uncommon quick with it, sir," Hercules went on. "There's very few men except his Lordship would have blocked you in time. Aye, you're well matched. Lord Bothwell learned the weapon in Italy, too."

Murray had got to his feet because the table was being moved. He stared at both men, at Hercules; he shifted his gaze to Bothwell's dark face. "Francis," he said slowly, "Sir Patrick was my guest."

Patrick interrupted. "Chalmers will second me."

Bothwell was taking off his coat, carefully; at Patrick's words he looked across at him, there was respect in his eyes, and he was beginning to feel guilty. He said suddenly, "I'm willing to apologize for laying hands on you, sir. I am also very willing to name a time or place more convenient to you and me, and a time and place which will not embarrass Lord Murray. If that is suitable to you, sir. I leave the choice of weapons to you."

"You may not do that," Patrick contradicted, and Hercules held his breath again. "It is your privilege to choose the weapon." As he said it he remembered only too well that he couldn't use a sword. But he went on. "The choice belongs to you, my lord."

Bothwell grinned; his smile transformed his face. He put his dagger back in his belt. "Do you use the rapier, sir?"

"Aye," said Patrick evenly, and Bothwell smiled again.

"You lie very well, sir. Almost as well as a Borderer. Man, you have a temper as hot as a Borderer!"

Murray came into the conversation with undisguised relief.

"I believe Sir Patrick's mother was the bearer of an old Border name." Murray's smile was very happy.

"Jardine," Patrick said, his tone still snappish. He sat down.

"Oh," said Bothwell. "Are you acquainted with the Border ballads? Do you know the Battle of Otterbourne? The ballad says the Jardines wouldn't fight. I will quote it for you. 'But the Jardines would not with him ride, and they rue it to this day!'" Bothwell was enjoying himself.

Patrick growled, "They were feuding with the Douglasses!"

Hercules nodded to Murray in a way that said he understood all now. He spoke to Murray as though the other two weren't there. "I've seen this many times." As he talked he was helping Bothwell into his jacket. "They're too hot-spurred," he concluded, pulling out Bothwell's chair.

Murray couldn't resist a few jibes himself. "Does it always end like this, Hercules?" he asked, with no trace of a smile.

"No," he said, thoughtfully. "Sometimes they sprawl on the floor in a good tussle; other times they're at each other's throats with swords or daggers, but usually nobody gets killed, Borderers love to fight."

"Hercules, I'll cry quittance." Bothwell was genial.

Murray abandoned the banter. "Francis, we must be serious. I think you should surrender yourself." He looked to Patrick for confirmation, but Patrick shook his head slowly.

"Oh, no, Murray. The damage is done, I fear. There is only one way out now."

This was delivered with such bland assurance that Bothwell listened. His big hand lay around his ale tankard, but he didn't lift it to his lips. Instead he asked quietly, "What is your view of this situation, in which I so unhappily find myself?"

Patrick's face grew quite intent, he leaned forward across the table.

"My own view," he repeated. "Why, my own view is simply this, my lord. You are a Scot; you are living in a land that is a monarchy and is not a monarchy. Our King has no standing army; he relies on his favorites to raise guns and men, when such force is necessary, either to deal with external or internal enemies. For that reason, you are both a threat and a comfort to the crown. You can raise all your Border clans, should you desire it, and although James was quick enough to name you Lieutenant of the armies when the Spanish threatened, now, in this time of peace, your very power becomes a danger. Especially since you abuse it. Do you remember last winter, when you, in force, actually entered the Tolbooth when James was sitting at trial? At that time, last January, you removed from prison a witness against the Laird of Nidrie. Nidrie is one of your clients; you are his patron, and so you dare to kidnap a man who is a witness against him. I understood you took that witness to Crichton and threatened him with the gallows!"

Bothwell looked guilty.

"True," he admitted. "But one sight of the gallows was enough to close his mouth."

Patrick smiled. "It was a fine raid, the 'Raid on the Tolbooth.' But to continue with Nidrie. When James left this country to go to Denmark to marry, he left you as governor of Scotland. I was abroad at the time," he put in thoughtfully. "James chose you, because of your strength, and you governed Scotland, with Lennox and Mr. Bruce representing the preachers. During that time Scotland was never so peaceful, till your same Nidrie considered himself insulted on the street. He promptly killed the man who he thought had impugned his honor. What did you do then?" Bothwell grimaced and Patrick laughed. "I wasn't here, but the story goes that when Nidrie was brought in, and you were informed of the details, you leaped to your feet, knocked Nidrie halfway across the room, and then had him committed to ward. Let us put it this way, then. When you were 'King of Scotland' you tolerated no lawlessness. Well, my lord, you do remember the incident, don't you?"

"Law and damnation!" said Bothwell explosively, then quieted down. "Aye, I remember it."

"That's the first point you will concede me. So we will take last January's defiance, the raid on the Tolbooth. Do you realize your King was in the building? Do you not see how close to treason you came?"

"No," said Bothwell bluntly. "I didn't harm Jamie."

Patrick leaned farther over the table, his blond head very close to Bothwell's dark one, and he spoke earnestly. "But you interfered with the King's justice!"

Bothwell had just had a taste of the King's justice. "What kind of dunghill justice is that?" he asked.

Patrick shook his head slowly. "Nevertheless, it is law. It holds the promise of order. And let me warn you, my lord. James may be young, but he means to rule Scotland. Never forget that, sir. He means to rule! He will use deceit, perhaps. He may use means that you, who are forthright, will despise, but he is a canny Scot, and he is tired of feuds, he is tired of rebellion, he is tired of nobles like you—and you are the worst, when it comes to flaunting your power. James does not want you to have power! I warn you he is going to rule and rule royally!"

"And so you think I should do—what?"

"I think you should go into voluntary exile!"

"And let Maitland hold the reins!"

Patrick shook his head again. "You see, you will not obey your King. Because you would rather feud with Maitland. And I have no doubt but that in prison you planned your revenge. I have no doubt you have no intention of leaving Scotland. You'll rouse the Border; you'll live at Hermitage in defiance of laws!"

Bothwell half smiled, reluctantly, showing Patrick he had spoken the truth. "Aye," he said easily, "I intend to stay in Scotland. I am a man addicted to life in the Borders."

"You're a fool, my lord. I'll warn you again. You will be outlawed, named thief and felon. You'll not be Admiral of Scotland, or Sheriff of Lothian and Berwick. Your lands will be stripped from you. You cannot fight your King; you should not be sitting here now. When Jamie hears you had the impudence to come to the tavern tonight, he will soil himself!" Patrick had been punctuating his words with the glass he held in his hand; at the last he banged it down so hard that it shattered and the fingers that clenched it were bitten deep by the slivers of glass. He held up his hand and surveyed it. The blood was starting to flow freely. "My first wound. I'll have you know I have already suffered in your cause, my lord." He picked up a small linen towel, wrapping it around his hand.

Bothwell pushed back his chair and stood up. "I am sorry, sir. I am sorry I cannot take your advice. 'Tis you who are a canny Scot, and you are right—I should not be sitting here now. I'm not concerned for myself, but there are three men waiting for me and they'd be hanged higher than Haman if they were caught tonight."

Murray stood himself. Tonight had seen the end of his plans: there would be no peace now, no happy ending. The dice were already thrown, the numbers were showing and he would do the only thing he could do—he would give all the help in his power. He held out his hand, he smiled and said lightly, "So be it, Francis," and did not know the decision was to cost him his life.

Patrick said, "It's been a pleasure, my lord." Instead of bowing, he, too, held out his hand, bound up in the linen, and Bothwell took it in turn.

"We will not meet again, probably, but thank you, sir." The three men stood silently, each for a second deep in his own thoughts.

"If you want me," said Bothwell, at the door, "I'll be at the Hermitage."

Chapter Five

SIR PATRICK GALBRAITH's town residence stood on the Canongate, about a quarter of a mile from the Netherbow Port, whose towers separated the court suburb from High Street. It was only two years old, and although it had been built by an Italian architect, its Scot owner had insisted on purely Tudor lines.

Octagonal towers flanked the entrance gateway at each end of the main front, and the side wings projected so that the rooms could have windows on both sides. It was molded in stone, the windows were bowed and semi-circular, letting in the light, and adding to the charm of the rooms inside. The floors were polished oak, and the second floor gallery was a full eighty feet in length, a long lovely room.

In Patrick's own study, the walls were paneled in Spanish leather; leather also covered the chairs. Today the windows were open to the summer air. Coming into his favorite room, the master of the house banged the door behind him and threw himself down in the chair beside his table. His back was to the window.

He leaned his elbows on the table, put his chin in his hands. He stared at the empty fireplace, his face expressionless. He had sat there for a full ten minutes when he realized he had forgotten something important. It annoyed him, for he was scarcely ever forgetful, and this matter of his cousin was confidential. He had just come from Leith, from which port a ship was leaving, and now he had to go back.

He rose lazily and went over to the window, looking out into the garden. He stood at the window quite motionless, for several minutes. The scene before him brought a smile to his lips.

"What is she dressed in?" he asked himself, staring at Anne's figure. She was leaning back against a number of pillows that she had put on the grass, and even from here he could see her bare knees, under the brilliant red plaid of her skirts. "By heaven, kilts!"

He stepped out of the window, crossing the lawn purposefully. "My lord," he said, bowing to Murray. Then he turned to Anne. "Anne, I want to talk to you now—about that." He waved an encompassing hand at her.

Murray had risen to his feet; he did not try to keep the smile from his face. "You must join us, sir," he invited.

Patrick was not to be deflected from his course. "You'll favor me by putting on that cape, Anne." He pointed to her cape. "In the name of God, are you playing a masque out here, in my garden?"

Murray looked up at the sky, and Anne slowly stood up, shaking out her brief skirts. "Marie did make this short," she conceded politely.

Patrick bent over to pick up her cape; he put it over her shoulders unceremoniously. "That's better," he said with relief. "Now you may come with me. I've a deal to say to you."

Anne stood immovable, and he waved her away. "There, in the coach. I'll be with you in a minute."

The two men watched her go slowly away from them. Patrick said irritably, "Murray, you'll not smile at her. Lord knows she needs little enough encouragement." He sighed heavily.

Murray grinned. "You bear a heavy cross."

"Oh, hold your tongue. I'm beginning to think I do, at that. A very heavy cross."

"One that many men would be delighted to bear. I shouldn't worry, if I were you." He paused a moment. "We were talking of Bothwell."

"Bothwell?"

"Aye. I'd like to see Francis marry her. Since I already have a wife. Anne's a treasure, sir."

"One that I'd gladly part with, or bury," said Patrick, feelingly. "Day by day her dowry goes upward. Well, sir, I who never forget anything, forgot an important message to the captain of a ship that's leaving. I'm on my way to Leith. Forgive the interruption, Murray; I'm sorry."

Murray was still smiling. "I should like to hear what ensues, in your coach."

Patrick grimaced. "I'll endeavor to restrain my language."

"I imagine you will. But will Anne?" Murray laughed. He said goodbye and was away before Patrick could swear at him.

Anne was sitting straight on the seat of the coach, waiting. Patrick gave her a comprehensive stare as he got in; nothing but the cape was visible, and he was momentarily satisfied. "Now," he said, as they rolled down the carriage drive, "what explanations have you concocted to excuse this mad behavior?"

Anne said nothing; she folded her hands primly.

"Well?" asked Patrick. "Are you a puppet? Is this a dumb show?"

"No, sir," Anne said haughtily.

"It might be better if it were." There was another silence, and finally Patrick asked, "What did you buy this morning?"

Anne looked amazed. "How did you know?" she murmured, throwing him a sideways look. "Oh, Patrick, I was very good when you sent me away. You sent me away in front of Lord Murray and I—" She stopped, a rebellious look on her face.

"You wanted to protest. What prevented you from so protesting was the purchase you made this morning. It must have been a large purchase," he concluded.

"It was," said Anne honestly. "You know right well that I've been appointed a lady-in-waiting. I wanted a new gown."

"I'll warrant it's more than one."

"Three, then. And four new petticoats. One is to be gold lace."

Patrick laughed. "But no more kilts," he said. He scrutinized her carefully as she leaned back in her seat, her head lying to one side so that her curls touched the edge of his arm. What did he know about her, after all, except that she had been lavishly endowed by a bountiful nature? Yet there was strong kinship between them; he had felt it the first time he had laid eyes on her, not much over two months ago. He did not remember his father; he hardly remembered his mother. He had been raised by the man whose heir he was, Lord Usher; his elderly spinster aunt kept his house for him. Now he had Anne. "But no more kilts," he repeated.

"I know." She sighed; she was looking out her window. The air was sweet with summer; it was a beautiful day. She relaxed comfortably in the seat, sinking into her own thoughts. "Do you know Lord Bothwell?" she asked, making her tone idle.

"You know very well I do. You have been amply informed of our quarrel."

She smiled; she put her hand over his. "Oh, Patrick," she said lovingly, "I do adore you."

He grinned. "Annie, you stay away from Bothwell. He eats wenches like you, and I want no more duels."

"I hate him," she said heatedly, then remembered to add quickly, "I mean I'm sure I would."

He looked surprised at the vehemence of her tone. "Why should you hate him?" he asked, curiously.

"He sounds hateful. And all the women at court—oh!" She waved her hands. "You would think he was the only man on earth. Besides you," she added.

He laughed. "You never forget the man you're with, do you? Even if he is your kin. Every time I have come to see you in the last three days while you were sick, Marie has told me you were asleep. You have completely recovered?"

Involuntarily Anne's hand went to her chin. "Oh, yes," she said hastily. She shot a glance at him, decided it was time to change the subject. "Patrick," she asked seriously, "are you truly in love?"

He sat up very straight. "Who told you that?"

"Murray. He said that you were in love with a Janet Applegate, and that she had refused to marry you. It is not true, is it?"

"Aye," he said bluntly, turning away from her and staring

out the window. " 'Tis true enough, but I did not realize it was common gossip."

Anne said heatedly, "She must be daft! You—you'll not give her up, will you? I wouldn't!" Privately she was determining to see this Janet. This must be a lover's quarrel. Patrick would be an earl. Anne thought of that and of the lovely clink of money that always accompanied him.

"What else did Murray say?" Patrick had turned toward her again and was regarding her intently.

"He said that you quarreled with Lord Bothwell, and that Bothwell's brother had partly stopped you, and then that you two had sat at the table and talked. To think of his sitting there calmly and talking!" Her eyes blazed.

"Why shouldn't we talk?" Patrick frowned.

"Because," she blurted angrily, thinking of her aching chin—"because it was so impudent," she ended weakly.

"Well, the very thing we talked about, that I warned him about, did happen. He was put to the horn this morning."

"What?" She looked frightened.

"Didn't Murray tell you that too? He must have been concerned only with kilts. Bothwell was outlawed this morning, at the Town Cross. We call it being put to the horn because three sharp blasts of the horn accompany the formal denouncement. It means that from this time on, he is a thief among thieves. It is the duty of any man to bring him to justice, dead or alive, wherever and whenever he can lay hands on him." Patrick's voice was grim. "In other words, if I catch him, I could put a bullet through his head, if it pleased me."

Anne stared up at his face. "Would you?" she asked, fearfully. "You wouldn't, would you?"

He shrugged.

"There will be no opportunity, even if I would. Bothwell will not be in Leith, or Edinburgh, Anne. It would mean certain death."

"I warrant he'd not be afraid," she said, so firmly that he gazed at her curiously.

"You have been told that, I surmise. It is nonsense. Although the legends around his name are rather thick—he won't dare enter Leith."

They were driving rapidly down Leith Wynd, the road that ran from the seaport to the capital. Only a few miles separated Edinburgh from its port; the carriage was in Leith, the town was all around them.

"There are many people abroad." Anne frowned a little, peering out curiously.

The coach came to a sudden stop; the man beside the driver leaped down and came to the door. Other men crowded around him and, at the same time, they could hear the common bell in Edinburgh, ringing, ringing.

Patrick flung open the door. "What's the matter?"

He was very impatient, but when he saw the milling crowds in the street, he was puzzled, too. He waited for an answer, but no one was inclined to give it. There were sudden shouts from the corner up ahead; the coachman was yelling at the men who had stopped the horses, and Patrick jumped out of the coach, slamming the door. Anne waited, afraid, because on the other side of the carriage several armed men peered in at her.

She kept her eyes on her hands, in her lap, but her face paled. Time passed, and still Patrick did not return. After five minutes he finally appeared. "What has happened?" she gasped, pulling at his arm as he climbed in.

He said, incredulously, "Bothwell is in Leith! Somewhere! They're tolling the common bell as warning!"

"He is in Leith?" She repeated his words, and her eyes gleamed. "Of course. Murray told me this afternoon—" She broke off, lowering her lashes, and became very thoughtful. Murray had told her that Bothwell had expected to dine tonight with Captain Maisterton. Anne knew the Captain; he had brought her from France; his house was just down the road.

"What did Murray say?" asked Patrick.

"Oh, I forget," she said hurriedly. The coach was going slowly; they could hear plainly the bells of the city tolling their warnings. "Patrick, I'm afraid!"

"Aye," he nodded. "I'm afraid I cannot leave you at the

docks, now. There'll be trouble there, with Bothwell's sailors. They do not believe in outlawry—not when 'tis their Admiral. Yet I cannot believe the rumor for truth!"

"It must be true," wailed Anne. "Look over there! Why, there must be a hundred men in the street. Why don't you leave me here, at Captain Maisterton's? Why don't you, sir? I'll be safe with him."

Patrick leaned forward and rapped sharply on the wood. "Stop here," he shouted.

The coach lurched to a stop before a large stone house. Patrick had the door open, and Anne jumped out, running up the steps ahead of him.

"You will be safe here," he agreed. He was hammering on the door as he spoke. "Curse Bothwell. I wager he's nowhere near the city."

"I warrant he isn't either," breathed Anne, staring up at the big doors. Would he be here, the impudent knave? The door swung open. "Goodbye, Patrick," she said hastily. "I'll be safe!" She banged the door shut and turned to face the amazed man who had opened it for her.

It was very still inside the house. The noises from the street seemed muted and far away. She couldn't even hear the bells. "You may tell Captain Maisterton I wish to speak with him."

The hall was dark and narrow; the man before her, although not tall, was powerfully built, and—she had to look twice to believe it—he carried a pistol in one hand.

"Captain Maisterton is busy, madam," said Gibson, staring with unconcealed interest at her legs. "You will have to wait."

"Dolthead," Anne said distantly, using Patrick's expression for any erring servitor. "Take me to him."

Gibson looked amazed. "Madam," he expostulated vainly, for Anne was already starting down the hall.

He caught up to her in two long strides. "Madam, the Captain does not wish to be disturbed." They had passed two doors and Gibson was hesitating before a third. Anne could hear the murmur of men's voices.

"Knock," she ordered, indicating the door.

Gibson said firmly, "I'll knock, but his Lordship, I mean Captain Maisterton, does not want to be disturbed, I told you." He leaned forward and knocked on the door.

Inside the room, Bothwell stopped talking; he listened, frowning. "It must be Gibson," he murmured. "Is it something important?" he called.

At the sound of his voice Anne brushed by Gibson before he had time to stop her. She flung open the door.

Bothwell jumped to his feet. He glared at her, a frown on his face, for he had been about to swear vehemently at Gibson, who now said quickly, "She pushed past me, my lord!"

Anne moved to one side; she raised her violet eyes to Bothwell's face. He was so different from the last time she had seen him, and she had forgotten how very tall he was, how wide his shoulders. He was clean-shaven now; she could see the slight hollows beneath his cheekbones. But his smile was the same; it was as delighted and guilty as when he had teased her in the garden, and now he said the very thing Patrick had. "Kilts!"

Captain Maisterton had risen too; he was staring at Anne with astounded eyes. Anne smiled at him sweetly. "Good afternoon, Captain."

Bothwell didn't give him time to answer. "Shut the door, Gibson, and for God's sake let no more wenches into this house."

Anne transferred her gaze to Bothwell. "Well, my lord, I hardly did recognize you."

He grinned. "I hardly knew you either, lass. I had not seen those knees before."

Anne ignored him; she looked at the dining table, littered with trenchers of bread and meat and tankards of ale. "Will you sit, madam?" asked the Captain belatedly.

"Thank you, sir." Anne sat in the chair he pulled out, and Bothwell sat down too, beside her.

"Lassie, do you follow me?" he asked, leaning toward her, his elbows on the table.

Anne put her own elbows on the table. She was about to make a withering retort when Bothwell laid one finger on her chin. "Does it still hurt?"

"You brute," she said angrily. "How did you dare to hit me!"

He said seriously, "Madam, I was escaping from prison. I did not want any little tongues wagging that night. Not even your wee red tongue. Would you like to stick it out at me?"

"Aye, that I would! I—"

"You cannot think of any names bad enough for me. I told you I should not ask you to forgive me, either." He reached for his ale and drank it off. "You'll pardon me, madam, if I continue my meal. Would you fill this for me?" He pointed to a jug of ale, and then cut himself a piece of meat, following it with a chunk of cheese that he was evidently enjoying.

Anne glared at him. But she poured his ale. "There you are, my lord."

"Thank you, lass. Now would you serve me the mustard?"

"Certainly," she snapped. "And will you have the vinegar?"

"I do not use vinegar," he answered, smearing mustard on his beef. There was a strained silence, in which Anne's eyes spat fire at Bothwell eating solemnly. Captain Maisterton forgot his food and stared at both of them. Finally Bothwell said, "Why not join me, lassie?"

Anne started to say she wasn't hungry; she changed her mind. "I think I will," she replied, very politely, and he passed her a platter of meat and pushed the bread between the two of them.

"Perhaps you would ask for some wine for me," she went on, in the same nonchalant tone he was using.

He looked at her and smiled, and Anne looked down at her plate, but she let her eyes stray to his big hands. The Captain poured a cup of wine for her; he passed it to Bothwell, who set it in front of her.

"Thank you, my lord," she said, tasting her wine. She tried a piece of cheese, and addressed herself to Maisterton. "Captain, I warrant you wonder why I intruded, sir. Sir Patrick left me here; he was on his way to the docks, and he did not want to leave me in the coach, at the waterfront."

Bothwell smiled. "That is my fault, madam. It is I who should apologize to the Captain. I no longer hear those bells, though." He was silent, listening.

"They have stopped," said Anne. "I cannot hear them now."

Bothwell nodded. "So that when I'm ready to enter Edinburgh, the alarm will be over." He was pleased with the thought and ate the last bit of meat on his plate.

Anne forgot how badly her head had ached. "Edinburgh!" she cried. "Oh, my lord, you can't go to Edinburgh! You'll be killed!"

She didn't think he even heard her; he was chewing his meat in an abstracted manner and wiping the last bit of mustardy gravy off his plate with a piece of bread. Then he said, "Lass, do not worry your bonnie head over me."

Anne studied him covertly, her eyes sliding from the very top of his dark head to the big boots that were so near her own feet.

He had turned toward Maisterton.

"Captain, I've enjoyed your hospitality. When I came, I did not know I was outlawed, but I pledge you my word you won't suffer for this."

Maisterton said earnestly, "My lord, we served under the Hepburn banners at Otterbourne and we'll continue to serve!" Then he cleared his throat, and rose. "Shall I tell Gibson you are ready to ride, my lord?"

Bothwell nodded assent, and Anne whispered, as the door closed, "Was the battle of Otterbourne long ago, my lord?"

"Over two hundred years ago." He had loosened his coat at dinner; now he fastened it. She watched his fingers, watched him pick up his sword and belt and buckle it on.

"Your Lordship, you shouldn't go! Ah, I mean it! You shouldn't go!"

He looked down at her, she had pushed back her chair and got up, and she had put her hands out to him appealingly. "Lassie, I told you not to worry your bonnie head over me. But you can do something for me, if you will. You can remember not to tell anyone you saw me here, today. You see, the Captain may be in a wee bit of trouble over me."

"A wee bit of trouble?"

"Like hanging. For shielding or receiving an outlaw." He smiled, and at her expression of fright, he said, "Now I have worried you again, have I not? But you leave this to me, and tell no one I was here today. I'll vow it to you, lass, no harm will come to the Captain!"

Anne said solemnly—for there was so little time—"I wouldn't have given you away that night, my lord."

"Wouldn't you?" He was rueful. "Nevertheless, there were three other men dependent on me that night."

Anne looked up at him. "I warrant you would have done it even if only you had been escaping!"

He laughed. "I warrant I would." He was at the door; he was going to leave her without another word. Then he stopped, and Anne waited breathlessly for what he was going to say.

"I'm sorry you did not bring your cousin, lass." The door closed, and he left her standing in the middle of the room.

"The hateful beast," she said inadequately. She picked up a piece of meat in her fingers and chewed at it lustily. There were noises outside the window, and she ran over to it, looking out.

Bothwell wasn't very far from her. He was astride a black horse and Anne stared at him, at the big saddle, at the pistols thrust into the saddle holsters. His cap sat impudently on the side of his head, and he was waiting while someone tightened a girth. A number of other riders clattered from the house, drawing up neatly behind the Earl, their mail coats gleaming in the late sunlight.

Bothwell saw her face in the window. He waved to her, glanced around at Gibson, and then, at the head of his riders, turned into Leith Wynd, on the way to Edinburgh.

If he was conscious of the danger, it was only because a thickening excitement filled his body and brain. He thought nothing of the events which had preceded his outlawry; he was not filled with anger any more; that had passed. As for the hate and contempt he felt for Maitland, they had become part of him. He no longer noticed them.

It was a clear evening. He could see the turrets of the Netherbow in the distance; the tall houses and the outlines of the roofs and chimneys made an uneven hemline in the soft bluish sky. Leith Wynd was crowded, the houses clustered thicker, and where the road narrowed in spots, way was made for the twenty riders who came so fast and with such authority. Dogs, boys and men scrambled to the side to let them pass, and they came into the capital through the Netherbow Port.

Bothwell reined in. To his right the city stretched up the hill, and at angles nearby, narrow wynds left the main street; to his left the court suburb, with its lovely houses, straggled down the hill to the royal palace. Bothwell turned to the left and rode about fifty feet, with Gibson right beside him. Then he reined in again, and Gibson jumped to the ground.

A number of people watched the Earl dismount in a leisurely way. Behind him his twenty men drew up in two rows, neatly, and Gibson, after assisting his master to dismount, stood calmly with the reins of both horses in his hands.

Bothwell sauntered forward. He leaned down and picked up a small stone, absentmindedly tossing it in his hand. In back of him the battlements of the Netherbow climbed up into the sky and the clock in the tall tower showed a few minutes after seven. In front of him, the house of the Chancellor Maitland, with its balconies and double doors, waited for its visitor.

"Ahoy, there," Bothwell shouted; he was within fifteen feet of the door.

One of the double doors opened slowly; a servant peered out.

"You," said Bothwell, hooking his thumbs in his belt. "Tell your master an outlaw is here to see him."

The servant gaped. "An outlaw?" he stammered vaguely.

Bothwell nodded. "An outlaw. Lord Bothwell." His voice echoed through the street; his words floated in through the open windows of the houses in the nearest wynds.

The servant had edged away, and Bothwell waited. Presently the door opened again and the Chancellor looked out warily.

"Ah, Maitland," said Bothwell; he came toward the house. "I hear you wished to speak with me."

Maitland clutched the edge of the door for support. "Your Lordship," he stammered; he cast a hasty glance into the hall behind him, but it was mysteriously deserted. "Your Lordship," he said again, fearfully. He waited with disbelief to hear the familiar lowland twang.

Bothwell flipped the stone in his hand to the ground; he reached toward his pocket. "Well, Maitland, I'm here."

"You dared! How did you dare?" The words were wrung from Maitland; he was breathing hard. "Help!" he shouted, to the crowds of men that were gathering around Gibson.

No one paid any attention to Maitland. "I'm calling on you, Maitland," said Bothwell. "I consider I've been put to your horn, and not King Jamie's. I consider you a puddock stool, that craves to rival an ancient cedar!"

The contemptuous words fell into the street, and the increasing crowds behind Bothwell's twenty men were breathlessly silent, their eyes fixed on the tall figure of the Border lord. He was arrogantly alone, unprotected save for his small escort, yet no one moved to oppose him.

"I thought you knew I was coming, Maitland. I hear you would like to lay hands on me!"

Maitland's narrow face peered out at the grinning crowd; he was holding the door as a woman does when she is bothered by a beggar. "My lord—" he tried to keep his dignity—"you wish to surrender yourself?"

"I do. To you, personally." He waggled his finger at Maitland. "Come out here," he invited. "Come here."

Maitland didn't release his hold on the door; he was ready to bang it shut.

"You won't come?" Bothwell held up a coin. "Forty shillings," he said. "Forty shillings I'll pay you for the pleasure of laying your hands on me. Does that not tempt your avarice, you close-fisted bastard?"

The insulting words rang out loudly, and Maitland's face flushed at the jibing laughter. Desperately he looked past his tormentor into the street; it was full of men, some women. He noted vaguely that the time was twenty minutes past seven; it had taken only a few minutes to gather so large a crowd. Even the dogs had arrived by now.

He heard the noise and the laughter, saw the lengthening

shadows in the streets, and then he heard the clink of the large coin. Bothwell had tossed it to the paved causeway; it rolled, coming to a wavering stop at the very doors.

"Come that far then, Maitland."

The crowd could not resist taking up the chant. "Come that far," they shouted. "Forty shillings!" A gun went off, a second shot rang out, and a man's deep voice yelled out the old battle cry. "A Bothwell! A Bothwell!"

Bothwell acknowledged the shouts. He turned, and inclining his head to them, he lifted his hand, and looked up at the windows of the houses, from which more of his supporters were shouting and waving. Regardless of royal edicts, he, in the center of the city, was immune, and in the very back of his head the voice of Patrick Galbraith was saying earnestly, "It's your very power which is a threat—to the crown."

He swung around to Maitland again, holding up his hand for quiet. He won only a comparative silence, for his audience was too excited to be still, but Maitland heard his next words very plainly.

"A warning for you, Maitland. I expect to be in the city again on Monday next—that will be the twenty-sixth of the month. I expect you to convey that information to Lord Morton—" the mention of Morton's name brought loud jeers—"and I further expect you to report to His Majesty that I offered you forty shillings to do your duty, and that you declined."

The authoritative and mocking voice stopped. Maitland slammed the heavy door shut and threw the bolt. Out in the street, Bothwell turned his back on the house and motioned to Gibson.

Gibson had a wide smile on his face; he had never had such good sport before. Proudly he cupped his hands for Bothwell's big shiny black boot, and the Earl was up in the saddle, pulling on a pair of riding gloves while Gibson himself mounted, and the soldiers with Bothwell wheeled around. In the center of the Canongate, the crowds moved aside hastily, shouting and waving, while one urchin ran over and picked up the unwanted coin.

Bothwell waved his hand. "A Bothwell!" The shout was his

farewell; he and his men moved off under the frowning Netherbow, the way they had come. The clock on the spire showed just twenty-five minutes after seven. It had taken the Earl of Bothwell exactly twenty minutes to show King Jamie that the battle had been joined.

Chapter Six

THE waterfront of Leith woke early. Before dawn the fishermen were up and gone, and in the very early morning, the taverns were awake, the fires lighted, the kitchens scrubbed, and the stablers up and busy.

Outside an inn door, at the back beside the kitchen, a horseman dismounted slowly and gave his orders to a sleepy groom. The mist was thick; off the sea rose a typical Edinburgh haar. It almost concealed the tall figure in riding clothes, and it muffled his voice. The groom took the reins, the animal was led away, and the mist covered the strange actions of the horse's owner. He did not go where he should; instead he flung open the kitchen door, to the consternation of the maid who had just risen from her knees. She held onto her bucket of dirty water with both hands, and stared up, affrighted.

Behind her, the fire burned warmly on the hearth; it flickered over the wet tile floor and shone on the neatly arranged spits. With complete disregard for his muddy boots, the stranger strode forward, leaving an unmistakable trail on the clean tiles. The little maid stared after him; he disappeared into the next room, and she leaned over and followed his muddy path with her wet cloth. When she had finished eradicating his footprints, she emptied her bucket in the yard and came back into the kitchen.

At precisely the same minute, a few miles away in Edinburgh, a group of horsemen were receiving last instructions from the

Earl of Morton. The Earl was restless, impatient, and very eager. Today might see the success of his plans, and today might see him made a fool. Today was the twenty-sixth of July.

"He said he would come," murmured Morton, under his breath. He looked up at the captain of the guard and spoke louder. "Every street, every inn, every tavern?" he asked.

The captain nodded. "Aye, my lord."

Morton chewed his lip. He had tried to think of all possibilities. If Bothwell came, as he had so impudently announced, he must be captured. If he didn't come, the preparations must not be so well known that everyone would laugh at Morton's credulity. At least they would laugh at Maitland more. But that was small consolation. He stood looking after the departing horsemen. They must not fail.

As Morton went back into the palace of Holyrood, the early morning visitor was sitting at a table in the tavern at Leith.

"I want oatmeal, Maggie," he ordered. "And eggs."

"Aye, my lord. I'll tell them to hurry." She whisked off to the kitchen and her tongue must have been busy, for in a few seconds the landlord appeared.

"This is an honor, my lord," he said doubtfully. "Maggie is pulling herbs from the garden for your eggs." He crossed to the bar, and drew a flagon of ale.

Bothwell was hungry. He had ridden from his own castle of Crichton that morning. He consumed his oatmeal and the specially-cooked eggs, together with white bread smeared with honey. The landlord kept his glass full; he was very nervous, and the fingers that grasped the coin Bothwell gave him were damp with sweat. Casually, the Earl left the same way he had come; the kitchen door banged, the maids stared, and he disappeared in the yard in the direction of the stables. Maggie came back into the dining room, and began to clear the plates off the table. When four of the Earl of Morton's men came in the front door in their first search of the day, the only evidence of an early meal consumed and enjoyed was a white napkin crumpled and thrown down carelessly on a table in the common room.

The fog was still thick outside.

"Perfect weather," remarked Bothwell, as he swung up into the saddle.

The groom looked surprised, but before he could reply, a coin was tossed him. He dropped it, and while he groveled to find the copper, the horseman was gone. In the mist he rode by a group of Morton's men; he turned into Leith Wynd. He was going to Edinburgh. While they searched for him in Leith, the Earl of Bothwell rode unmolested into the streets of the capital city.

The day was gray, the city was gray. Occasionally the ragged mists would part, and the great castle would loom up and then be gone again. Bothwell rode under the very shadow of the castle, through the commercial Grassmarket, where the freshly-killed cattle hung bloody, and the piles of refuse from slaughtered animals raised a rank odor. He rode into a narrow close with an arched stone entrance, and at eight o'clock he had reached the stables near Hercules' flat.

Its doors were open; Bothwell entered and dismounted. The stabler came forward and recognized his patron and a slow grin welcomed the Earl. "You did come!" Then he added hastily, "Your Lordship."

Bothwell gave him a coin. "I should return soon. Rub him down; he's ridden far this morning."

"Aye, my lord." The man's voice was eager in his desire to please. He wanted to say he would not betray Bothwell, but he did not know how to phrase the words. "I'll rub him down myself," he said. "There is a stall back there." He pointed to the recesses of the stable.

Bothwell understood. "Thank you, man," he said, and walked out.

He was in a narrow twisting street. He picked his way past piles of heather, tar barrels and bundles of broom. One house stood almost in the center of the street; he went around by a curving footpath, and from above his head came the sound of a window being opened.

"Hold your hand!" He leaped for the center of the wynd, and above him there was a giggle.

"*Gardez l'eau,*" called a warning voice. The contents of a slop jar or garbage pail narrowly missed him; he rounded the turn and spoke to a woman on a second floor balcony that jutted out over his head.

"Could you tell me the whereabouts of a Mrs. Campbell?"

The housewife stopped shaking out her cloth and looked down, surprised. "On the first floor of the next house, sir."

Bothwell increased his pace. It was dangerous to stay on the street. He was well satisfied that no one had seen him enter the city, the stabler he could trust, and the search of Leith should be well under way. He expected them to discover he had been there and gone.

He knocked sharply on the door the woman had indicated. Instinctively, he stood with his back against the left hand of the door, so that he was protected from the back. He looked up the street; he couldn't see its entrance to High Street, but he could hear the sounds of the city and its people. A shuffling in the passage inside told him he had not come in vain. The old lady was inside. The door opened gradually, and a withered face peered out suspiciously.

Bothwell said, "I have a message from your former lodger, George."

Her eyes opened wide. She stood there regarding this fine gentleman uncertainly, and Bothwell threw another glance down the street. The stoop on which he stood was high; the pigs squealed underneath it, and he disliked his conspicuous position. He stepped in the door; the old lady retreated hastily.

"Lord Bothwell," he said.

The old dame released her apron, her sparsely lashed eyes blinked, and she curtsied quickly. "Your Lordship," she stammered.

"Where can we talk, dame?" Then he thought of his message. "The kitchen will do," he said, and strode forward. The kitchen would do in more ways than one. If he were caught here, the street would hardly provide a means of egress; the back door would be more practical. He entered the kitchen with the old woman worrying at his heels.

She sat down at a table and chewed on a piece of meat. "That was George's bed," she said, pointing to a straw mattress lumped in one corner of the dirty kitchen.

Bothwell's eyes went over the blackened rafters, the floors and chimney. "Where does this door go?" he asked, going to the door in question. It looked out into a small yard with cabbages growing under a dying fruit tree. At the back was another tree whose thick branches overhung a wooden dyke that fenced in another yard like this one. "Very satisfactory," he said, wondering whether he would have to climb that tree.

The old woman fidgeted. "Aye, my lord. That was George's bed." She was anxious to prove that George had been her lodger and that it was she for whom the message was intended.

Bothwell was looking around the room speculatively. There was money hidden somewhere in these walls, or cupboards.

"George told me there were monies hidden in this kitchen. You told George about it, didn't you?"

"Aye, my lord."

"George confessed to me that he had found it and taken a part of it."

She stopped in the act of finding the elusive bone in her mouth, and a stream of foul words came out instead. Bothwell found himself congratulating her on her knowledge of obscene epithets, but he interrupted her sharply.

"Be quiet," he ordered. "George said you did not know where the money was. Is that true?"

She was trembling with anger. "Aye," she snapped; then, just as suddenly, her mood changed and she began to cry. "I knew I shouldna ha' told him," she whimpered. "I knew I shouldna."

"No one but George knew there were monies hidden?"

She nodded. "I never told nobody else, my lord, and now it's gone. After twenty-five years, it's gone."

"Twenty-five years?" He frowned. "Are you sure it has been that long?"

"Aye, my lord, I'm sure." She lifted her apron and wiped her face, smearing the tears and grease together into the deep wrinkles.

"Where did the monies come from?"

"Was there so much?" she asked, eagerly. "Was it gold?"

"Answer my question," he said. "Where did it come from? Who hid it?"

She glanced down at her plate furtively, rubbed her finger around in the grease and sucked at it. "My husband, Master Campbell. He's the one who hid it." Her voice was full of hatred and resentment. "He hid it, and he never told me where."

Bothwell regarded her in the gloom. He had closed the kitchen door and the only light came in through a round hole made in the boards over the window; the glass had disappeared long since. He regarded her long and tried to shake off his growing dislike of this place, and its atmosphere of evil. Certainly there was nothing here to fear, nothing to cause disquiet except the obviously twisted mind of the woman who faced him.

"Where did your husband get the money?" he asked.

She had gone back to George and his perfidy. "I shouldna ha' told him," she said. "In twenty-five years I never told nobody."

Bothwell tried another tack. "Your husband has been dead that long?"

She nodded. "Aye, my lord."

"You lived alone all those years? Did you have children?"

"I had a son," she said. "He ran away that many years ago, almost. He wouldna stay and help me."

Bothwell stood up, walked to the door and opened it. Leaning with his back at right angles to the jamb, so that he could see her and also the small yard, he drank in the mist with relief.

"What was your husband's work?"

The fog floated in the doorway, and she hugged herself for warmth against the cool damp air. "He was a stonemason," she said. "That's what he was. A stonemason."

"Ah," said the Earl. He scrutinized the walls and then the fireplace. This was the first bit of information he could use. Where would a stonemason hide money but in the walls or the fireplace? "And your son? He didn't know about the monies either?"

"Him," she said vindictively. "He knew too, but he told me I could have it. But I knew he looked. He didn't find it. He went away."

Bothwell was intensely curious. "Did your husband steal the money?"

"Oh, no, my lord, oh no!" She was afraid; a crime once committed could loom large over her even now. "I swear I didna do nothing, my lord," she said fearfully.

"I'm sure you didn't, dame, but do not lie to me or it will be the Tolbooth for you."

Her tongue was loosened a little. "He earned the money," she said. "He earned it with his work."

It was obvious she was telling the truth as far as she knew it. "And how soon after he got the money did he die?"

She seemed to peer back into the past. "Soon, my lord. That very night, after he came home." She stopped and Bothwell waited, because she appeared to have something else to say of her own volition. He was right. She continued, "One night he went out after supper—it was dark—and he told me he was working. He didn't come home till almost morning, and that's when I found him in the kitchen, hiding it. I was watching him; he had waked me up, and he was so angry, he hit me. He hit me so hard I didna know nothing till the sun was up."

Bothwell tried to reconstruct that day long ago. "He had been out all night working. Then I suppose he slept until afternoon. Did anything happen during the day?"

"Nothing." She shook her head. "After supper he went out again."

Bothwell asked, "When did he come home?"

She giggled. "He was murdered," she said. "He came home with a broken head. They carried him from the corner, outside the tavern where he'd been. He was all blood, my lord."

"He never talked to you again? When they brought him home, he never spoke again?"

"I was that frighted," she said. "They laid him on the bed,

and Alan talked to him. My son talked to him, but I didn't, and he couldn't say much."

Bothwell shrugged. There was no more information to be got from the old crone. He closed the door and walked over to the fireplace. He drew his dagger and began to tap at the top stones of the fireplace, and he came down the side to the floor. There was no hollow sound at all. He tried the hearth next, and still there was nothing. He could swear there was no hiding place in the stones he had examined.

The old woman watched in breathless silence; her eyes followed every movement, and Bothwell turned and stared at her. He was sure she would not hesitate to give him away, if she thought she would be reimbursed for her information. He started, with his improvised tool, up the side of the fireplace. He wished that George had absconded with all the monies and not bothered him with this search, this mystery. His dagger tapped on; he had reached the third stone from the floor, about the height of his own hips, when he was rewarded by a hollow sound. His eyes lighted with interest and he tapped around the stone; the hollow sound was repeated everywhere he touched. He turned the dagger in his hand and started to pry carefully with the shining point. The stone was firmly in place and it was a slow job, even with the broad blade of the twenty-four-inch dagger.

He dropped to his knees, and pried around the base of the uneven rock, for that was what it was. The chimney was hewn from rough stones. Gently he worked around the entire stone. It took fifteen minutes, and as he worked the old woman picked her teeth and stared, her eyes never leaving his back and his large brown hands. When the stone finally moved out so that he could grasp it, she rose and came to stand beside him. Like a magnet drawing her, her feet moved in his direction and her eyes never wavered.

The stone must have weighed close to one hundred pounds. Bothwell inched it out slowly, for his grip was necessarily light until he could get both hands under its edges. Now it protruded far enough, and grasping it firmly, he tugged hard. Three more minutes sufficed; it came free, and he set it on the floor. Both of them peered into the aperture.

"There isna nothing," she cried. She came closer, and Bothwell wrinkled his nose at her odor.

"Aye, but there is," he contradicted. He reached in the full length of his arm and drew out a leather bag. It was heavy; for a second he weighed it in his hand. Then he drew the drawstring and looked inside. "Gold," he said.

He walked to the table with her at his heels. Greed, joy, and fright battled with themselves in her face. If his Lordship had found the monies, would he take them away from her? She gripped the edge of the table with her dirty hands and the long ragged nails bit into the wood. Bothwell spilled the contents of the bag onto the table top, and they both stood astonished. There was a great deal of it, and all gold.

Bothwell eyed it narrowly; he remembered that Master Campbell, who had lost his life after a job for which he had been so highly paid, had used some of it. George had taken part, and still there was this much left.

He picked up one piece and made out the date. It was still shiny and it bore the numbers 1566. Twenty-five years ago someone had paid Mr. Campbell newly minted gold, and why?

"It's a fortune," she said. "It's a fortune!"

"So it is," said Bothwell. He put the coin he had in his pocket, drew forth another gold piece and laid it down. "I'm taking one piece and giving you another," he explained. He had no idea why he wanted one of those coins. Certainly it was far too late to solve whatever mystery there was here. He was conscious of only one desire, and that was to leave this kitchen and its stink far behind.

His gesture of replacing the money shocked her into speech. "Thank you, my lord," she gasped. She was trembling from excitement; she feasted her eyes on the pile of coins, and Bothwell started from the room.

He had one last look at her bending over the table. She didn't seem to know he had left, and he strode through the bedroom and out into the hall. Carefully, he opened the door and looked out into the street. He was just in time to see four horsemen clatter into the close, and into the very stable where he had left his horse. With the door barely open, he peered through the crack. What he had feared then happened.

Four soldiers came out of the stable. Two walked rapidly toward the entrance to the close, the other two disappeared into Hercules' house. The way was barred; for some time, at least, there was no means of exit, unless he wanted to leave his horse behind. Footsteps in the bedroom he had just quitted startled him. He banged the door closed and stepped quickly into the other hall with the common stairway that led upstairs. The old dame would assume that he had left the building.

There was no one in the hall and he mounted the steps rapidly. At the first door at the top he knocked. There was no answer, and he knocked again. Still no one answered. He drew his dagger and began to force the old lock. The wood crumpled easily; in a minute the door swung open and he found himself in a large airy room that was as clean as the one he had just left was dirty. He walked on through to a spotless kitchen, with the ashes still smoldering on the hearth. He went to the kitchen window and looked out. It was twenty feet to the ground.

He threw one leg over the sill and hung by his hands. Then he jumped backward, landing on all fours. Quickly he righted himself, making for the tree. Up he went, gaining the high branches and the thick shelter of the leaves. The whole business had taken thirty seconds, and he had been unobserved, as far as he knew.

He climbed up farther, and selected a large limb about forty feet off the ground. From his vantage point he could see nothing beneath him; even to the sides his view was obscured by the foliage and the fog. He settled himself comfortably. Here he could stay—if need be, until darkness. Here he could stay while the search of the house of apartments was under way, for he had no doubt but that the old woman would give him away.

On his leafy perch he sat tense. He could hear men's voices, doors banging, and occasionally he caught the sounds of thuds and noises inside the flats. More than an hour passed, during which he sat opposite the third story windows and waited.

Then there came a spell of silence and now he had a stroke of luck. The third story window was open, and from it came voices.

"They are searching the next house," he heard a woman's voice say. "I hope he gets away."

Another woman answered. "He will; they won't catch his Lordship!" She laughed. "I knew he would come today; he had breakfast in Leith."

Bothwell frowned. The news had traveled fast; he had expected to keep his movements secret for a while longer.

"Have you seen Edwina today?" asked the first voice.

"No," said the other. "I heard her above me this morning but I know she's gone out for the rest of the day."

There was a sound of retreating footsteps, so clearly could he hear. By this time he was already swinging down the tree—an empty flat beckoned him. He came to a spot from which he could see the back of the house with its ten stories. The flat he wanted would be on the fourth floor. He studied the back of the house.

A large stoop ran up the far side; above that was a small balcony, then a window. The climb would not be difficult; the mist was still blessedly thick. In a few seconds he stood in a small dining room. He closed the window, and tiptoed toward the door leading out of this small room. The floors, he remembered, carried their messages.

He stepped into the next room, and entered a rather luxurious bedroom, with a feather bed and bed curtains. A highly ornamented screen concealed some feminine appurtenances. He entered the living room; here again there was evidence of luxury. There was a carpet on the floor, and some comfortable chairs in front of the fireplace, and a low coffer with many pillows. He picked up a pillow and returned to the bedroom. Losing no time, he crawled under the bed and fell asleep. He slept until night had almost fallen.

Footsteps roused him; they were light and running, and he

was sure they meant that Edwina had come home. The door in the next room opened; the footsteps came nearer and into the room where he lay. They went on past him, and he heard their owner go into the kitchen. Time passed; he smelled the odor of frying meat and it tickled his nostrils. He weighed the question of asking this Edwina for some food. He had no doubt but that he'd be successful, but he wondered whether he ought to involve anyone else in this escapade. The fewer the people who knew his whereabouts, the better it might be. He lay quietly, and the meat continued to fry. He had almost forgot his resolve in the gnawing pangs of hunger when there was the sound of more footsteps. The door was flung open, and a man's heavy tread approached his hideaway.

At the same moment Edwina appeared from the kitchen. On each side of his bed, two people faced each other.

"Oh, Patrick," said Edwina, "this is a surprise, sir!"

Patrick's lazy voice answered her; he stood where he had come to a stop. "A pleasant one, no doubt. Tell me, have you been to home all day?"

"No, sir." There was puzzlement in her voice. "I just returned."

"Ah. Then you know nothing."

Edwina asked, "What do you mean, sir?"

"I mean that Lord Bothwell should be somewhere near here. Somewhere in this house." He paused, and, under the bed, Bothwell was judging his distances. If he rolled out right at Patrick's side, he could be on his feet before Patrick recovered from his surprise.

Edwina said, "Lord Bothwell?" and taking his name as a cue, Bothwell rolled over once, drew his knees up and was on his feet, facing Patrick. Edwina started to scream. Patrick snapped, "Hold your tongue!" and then he took one step backward.

"Your servant, sir," said Bothwell, keeping one eye on Patrick's left hand.

Patrick bowed. "I am delighted to see you again," he said. "Might I inquire whether there is anyone else under the bed?"

Bothwell shook his head. "I'm alone, this time. You were

quite right in your deduction as to my whereabouts. How did you know?"

Patrick said, "You have been unreported in any other quarter of the city. Therefore I suspected you had never left this building. I supposed you were waiting for night to fall."

"You are correct. And now—perhaps you will tell me why you were hunting me?"

Across the bed Edwina stared from one man to the other. Their faces were impassive, but Edwina was suddenly terrified. The tall figure of the Earl of Bothwell was, to Edwina, a combination of god and adventurer, king and outlaw.

"Don't try to stop his Lordship, Patrick," she whispered in the silence.

Patrick chuckled. "She visualizes me lying in pools of blood. Why, as a matter of fact, my lord, I wanted to tell you that I have your horse. Valentine, I think he's named. Morton's men had brought him, with some difficulty, to the palace. I was there, with James, and I expressed a desire for the animal—a magnificent creature he is, too. Did you breed him yourself?"

"His sire was Night Hawk," began Bothwell. He paused and waved his hand at Edwina. "If you'd have her bring us some food, we could talk while we eat. I have a little time."

Patrick said, "Aye, wench, you bring us something to eat."

Edwina stared at both of them. "I don't know whether I have enough," she said, weakly, but they disappeared into the living room and unaccountably they were talking about horses. She listened for a minute; then she too disappeared in search of food.

She hurried. She put every morsel of food in the kitchen on her best platters, and she was ashamed she had only wooden plates. She polished the pewter flagons and poured the ale into the finest jug. Then she put everything on a big tray and started into the living room. She could hear Patrick saying, "The idea of Hermitage Castle fascinates me."

Edwina shot a glance at him; he was lying on the coffer, and he had pushed most of the pillows onto the floor. When she came in, he got up. "Put the tray here," he said absently, and he pulled up a chair, motioning to Bothwell to do the same.

Edwina waited. She wanted to hear more about Hermitage herself; she saw in her imagination a great gray castle, deep in the Border hills, whence came tales of outlaws, the freebooters of the Border and their daring raids by moonlight.

But she wasn't asked to stay and she didn't dare intrude. She went out, with a sway of her well-covered hips, and Bothwell followed her out with his eyes.

"A likely filly," he commented, as he pulled up his chair, and Patrick grinned and said, "Satisfactory." Then they both were silent as they began to eat.

Bothwell was very hungry; he hadn't eaten since early morning. Patrick was half-hearted about his food; he was thinking, but Bothwell didn't notice his abstraction. Hearing Edwina moving around in the kitchen, Patrick was reminded of Janet. He pushed his plate aside wearily.

"Your horse is in my stables," he said, "but how do you propose to get out of this building?"

Bothwell looked up. "The way I came. Out the window, to be accurate. I'll climb the dyke and go over to the next street."

"But every close is guarded, my lord. Every one."

"Then I shall have to housebreak. I'll get to High Street through an empty house."

"High Street is patroled." Patrick's hazel eyes gleamed, and he gazed at Bothwell as though he were challenging him to find a way out of this.

Bothwell smiled. "You used a chair?" He leaned forward and pointed his finger at Patrick. "Let's suppose I use that chair. Whether or not you're willing?"

Patrick nodded. "That's your way out," he conceded; he seemed pleased that Bothwell had risen to the occasion. He said suddenly, "Where are you going, when you leave here?"

"To Crichton. Hercules is at Crichton."

"And after that? Where next?"

"To Liddesdale. To the Hermitage."

Patrick spoke abruptly. "My lord, I want to come south with you."

Bothwell put down his knife; he stared across the table at

Patrick. The image of Hermitage went through his mind; he saw clearly his own beloved Borders, the rolling hills, the moors, the swift streams, the lazy rivers. Bothwell was a Scot, but he was a Borderer first. His loyalty, his intense love, went to the Border lands which were his; his respect went to the men who were one with him. Patrick's name might be Galbraith, but to Bothwell, it was the Border name of Jardine that counted. He said, "You want to come with me?"

Patrick read more into the question than there was. "There might be a thousand reasons why I want to come but I don't see that I'm obliged to tell you any of them!"

Bothwell picked up his knife; he was still hungry. "You're not so obliged; you're quite right, except that I had no intention of asking you why you wanted to come." He smiled at Patrick in such a way that Patrick felt foolish, and he was silent as he ate. He said nothing, and Patrick began to think that Bothwell had forgot that an important decision had just been made. At last the Earl said, squinting up his eyes thoughtfully, "How many servants do you plan to take with you?"

Patrick sat up straight in his chair; excitement filled him but he kept his voice even. "My barber, my tailor, at least two grooms, a cook, and Geordie."

"Then that makes eight of us tonight. I shall be another servant."

"But we will have to smuggle you out of this street!"

"I shall be Edwina." Bothwell was pleased at the thought. "I shall borrow a cloak from Edwina, and wrap my head up in a shawl. I will be muffled to the curious gaze of the impudent soldiers who attempt to peer into the chair. If you put your arm around me, and snarl at the guards, we shall be allowed to proceed."

Patrick grimaced. "The prospect of embracing you is revolting."

"You may kiss my little ear." Bothwell raised his voice. "Lassie," he called, "come in here and bring a light cloak."

Edwina appeared with a cloak over her arm; she looked surprised, and a little hopeful. "Are we going out?" she asked, brightly, but neither man answered her question.

"Thank you, lass," said Bothwell, taking the cloak, and succeeding in getting it upside down. "Which is which?" he asked.

Edwina giggled. "Give it to me, my lord. Do you want me to put it on you?"

"Please." She reached up and laid it around his shoulders; it hung just to his knees, and Patrick nodded.

"We will cut just below the knee," he announced, and then he began to laugh. "You look odd, to say the least," he added, and went off into laughter again.

Bothwell said, "Lass, bring me a petticoat. I want to pad out the cloak; this way, if it falls open, all will be revealed." He made a face of delighted horror, and Edwina giggled again.

She ran into her bedroom and reappeared with a petticoat of scarlet hue. She slipped the petticoat over his head, and Patrick, at the sight of his boots below the crimson satin, went off into boyish gales of laughter. But Bothwell was unperturbed. He yanked the petticoat down to his hips, then he peered down at the floor. All that could be seen were the tips of his boots.

"Now for the cloak," he said, and Edwina put it on him again. He crouched down, wrapping it around him. "There. How is that?"

Patrick was still convulsed with laughter. "Other than looking hunchbacked, you are a tempting morsel."

"I'll do this then." He straightened his shoulders, bent his knees until the cloak touched the floor. Then he walked over to Patrick, who looked pleased with the result.

"That's better," he said. "Now a shawl."

Bothwell went into his crouch, and Edwina endeavored to approximate a discreetly muffled woman. She wrapped the shawl around his head twice, and flung the ends across his face. Then she stepped back and scrutinized the results.

Patrick stood up. "You'll ruin my reputation," he announced. "I assume you are ready to go, my dear?"

Bothwell waddled to the door. "Lass," he said, "the next time one of my men come into the city, there'll be a reward for you." He smiled. Edwina watched them start down the hall; she heard their retreating footsteps and Patrick's muffled laughter.

Patrick opened the street door; one of the bearers sprang forward and opened the door to the chair. It was very dark and the lights of the linkmen flickered unsteadily as they moved. Bothwell gained the safety of the chair, and Patrick climbed in beside him. The door was closed, and they began to move down the street. Bothwell arranged the cloak so that it covered his feet; he wiggled and inched it down until it touched the floor, and he turned his body sideways, toward Patrick. "Put your arm around me," he said. "Can't you be more gallant?"

Patrick obliged with alacrity, because they were approaching the end of the street. The first bearer called out to a soldier.

Bothwell's voice came muffled through the shawl. "Tell me, my dear sir, are you successful with women? You're suffocating me."

At that moment the chair was set down. They both heard the bearer say, "It's Sir Patrick Galbraith." He made a motion to pick up the chair again when the soldier grasped his arm. He had rigid instructions.

"No, you don't," he said. "Open the door."

There was the sound of a protesting voice, muffled conversation, and finally the bearer said, "But you don't know, dolthead."

"Interfere," said Bothwell, in a whisper.

Patrick obeyed; he leaned forward and rapped on the door sharply. "What goes on here?" he asked, as impatiently as possible.

The door opened, and Bothwell shrank back against the seat into Patrick's arm. Patrick leaned across him. "You impudent knave, who gave you permission to open this door?"

The bearer's face shone in the light from the first linkman; on the other side, a soldier gazed into the chair.

"Sir, he insisted on seeing the occupants of this chair." The bearer was very apologetic; he gave the soldier a nasty look.

"He did, did he?" Patrick transferred his angry gaze to the

soldier. "What's your name?" he asked, a threat in his question.

That worthy stammered, "It's my orders, sir." He backed away from the light.

"Dolthead," said Patrick. "I asked your name." At this he seemed to become aware of the shrinking figure of the woman beside him. "All right," he said angrily, "now close the door and go on." He turned to Bothwell. "I'm sorry, sweetheart. The clumsy fools." The door closed on his voice.

Bothwell relaxed in ease. "That was a very good touch. You have separate quarters? Where do you propose to hide me till we can leave the city?"

Patrick said, "The Countess is giving a dinner party. I will take you to my own chambers."

Bothwell frowned slightly, and crossed his legs; his boots stuck out under the cloak and his shawl was coming unwound. "I assume Morton will be there. I've heard he's interested in your cousin. You know," he continued genially, "if you have betrayed me, I swear I'll cut your throat before I attend to Morton."

Chapter Seven

Anne was seated next to Morton. Beyond him, at the head of the table, sat the Countess in full evening regalia. The soup of mutton and barley broth had been duly attended to, and the servant at Anne's elbow was serving her with stuffed fowl, some fat mushrooms, and French peas. The long wax tapers lit the polished board, and gleamed on the silver service and the lovely colors of the wines in their crystal glasses. Anne was trying to listen to Morton, but it was very difficult because the Countess threw remarks at her which must be answered, and, besides having Morton's obsequious smiles to acknowledge, she was very hungry.

Both she and Morton were silent for a while, and Anne took advantage of the lull to stuff herself as quickly as she decently could. Morton was wavering between the satisfaction he felt at the nearness of the woman he had already decided to make his second wife, and the gnawing thought at the back of his head which had to do with his old enemy. So far his search had yielded him nothing but a horse. Still, he was pleased with that much; Bothwell was in the city, and before long he was sure to be found. Morton thought of his many soldiers in every part of the town, and the explicit instructions they had. Certainly he could not fail to bring Bothwell to the King.

Anne was wolfing partridge as daintily as possible, and between bites her violet eyes shot appraising glances at the man to her right.

Morton caught her eye; she smiled enchantingly. He regarded her across a bridge of years. "You are so happy," he said, fatuously. "Did you enjoy your soup?"

Anne had a picture of a big black kettle hung over a hearth, a kettle which bubbled all day and from which came most meals in a French farmhouse. "Soup," she said definitely, "is just scraps of odds and ends."

Morton looked vaguely startled by such a pronouncement, and Anne changed the subject. "If they catch Lord Bothwell, will they bring him here?"

The mention of his enemy's name brought a deep frown to Morton's face. "Aye, they will," he replied. "They have orders to bring him to me first."

"I should like to see him," said Anne.

"I hope you will, my dear. I hope you'll see him bound hand and foot!"

"Oh," said Anne. "But aren't you afraid to have him brought here? Aren't you afraid some of us might rescue him?" She was having a lovely vision in which she, singlehanded, rescued Bothwell from his captors.

Morton smiled politely, and returned to his food. Anne followed his example, but under her blonde curls her head was working busily. How would she aid Bothwell, if he were brought to Morton?

There was a sudden diversion. A servant whispered discreetly in the Countess' ear, and she said, sharply, "Well, tell Sir Patrick to join us." She turned to Anne. "Patrick has just come in."

Anne smiled. "I hope he does join us," she said, and Morton tried to keep the sour expression off his face. There was another diversion; Anne could see several people talking to another servant, and then the man who had spoken to the Countess returned. "Sir Patrick sends his regrets, your Ladyship."

His tone was low, and the Countess checked an annoyed ejaculation. She contented herself with an aside to Anne. "The young man regrets," she whispered, her elbows twitching and her frown imperatively angry.

Anne said softly, "He probably isn't hungry." She glanced at Morton, and he was staring at the door. "I believe," she said, "that you are wanted. I heard your name spoken."

Morton's eyes gleamed; he rose to his feet, set down his napkin and started off. The Countess' outraged eyes stopped him. "I crave your pardon, madam," he said humbly. "There is a man at the door and I hope he has news for me."

"I hope it is important news," said her Ladyship, fixing him with a baleful eye. "It must be, for you so to lose your manners." She waved him away; she didn't wait until he was out of earshot. "It must have unnerved Lord Morton, to make just an equine conquest."

Outside the door Morton stood plucking his lip, and regarding the face of the soldier. "You say that Sir Patrick had a woman with him?"

"Aye, sir. You told me to report anyone leaving that particular close. I knew it was foolish but I came, my lord."

"You did well," said Morton absently. The retainer, recognizing his dismissal, disappeared, and Morton stood uncertainly in the hall. Finally he beckoned to another servant. "Take me to Sir Patrick," he ordered.

The servant complied. "This way, my lord." Morton's deliberate tread followed him down the hall.

Patrick was changing his clothes. In a chair by his bed, Bothwell lounged easily, and watched two servants pack clothes and help their master. The barber was hastily gathering the tools of his trade, and another man was sorting clothes. "And my sheets," said Patrick. "I must have my own linen, and my own quilts. And at least two pairs of fur-lined house shoes. Didn't you say, my lord, that Hermitage has stone floors?"

Bothwell nodded, and Patrick continued, "A dressing gown with fur, also my engraved paper." He sat down and stretched out his legs, while Geordie knelt and put on his shiny boots with their gold spurs. "You may saddle the brown gelding for me, and Lord Bothwell's horse."

The servants left the room, and Patrick started for the door. "Do you wish to lock this after me?" he asked. "I'll be in the next room writing. I must leave instructions to Chalmers, and there is one other matter which needs my immediate attention."

"It won't be necessary," said Bothwell. He was sitting next to a window, and when Patrick left, he opened the window and looked out. There was nothing to be seen but blackness. Carefully, he stepped over the sill and out into the garden; he hugged the wall, and suddenly a square of light fell onto the green grass. He stepped back hastily, craning his neck to see inside. He saw the back of Patrick's head; a sheet of white embossed paper lay before him, and on one side of the table was a book filled with figures, lines of them.

Bothwell felt guilty, even if his object had not been to spy. He had come into the garden to sound out a means of escape should their plans miscarry and his presence in the house be discovered. He started to go on, but the sight of a door opening opposite his line of vision made him suddenly sure his reconnaissance had been fortunate, for Morton stood in the doorway and his face was more unpleasant than usual. His first words were far from reassuring.

"My dear Patrick, I beg your pardon for this intrusion, but I have a very good reason for looking in on your privacy." He moved forward.

Patrick looked up from his writing. His face didn't change expression at all; his eyes were bland. "I cannot judge your reasons for their merit, Morton, since I am quite unaware of them. However, I am very busy." He bent over the table, and ran his pen down one line of figures. He gave no evidence that he listened to Morton's next words.

"A few minutes of your time is all I ask, sir." Morton lowered himself into a chair opposite Patrick and the unseen figure in the garden. Morton's eyes were sharp. Where was this woman Patrick had brought home with him? Why was he in the midst of work, if a charming and indiscreet lady were waiting for him somewhere in this wing?

"You surprise me, sir," Morton began. "One would think you were no longer a young man, that work should take your mind during the nights, when most men your age are dallying with—" he paused, waved his hands—"shall we say love?"

Patrick's face was still bent over his table, but his body stiffened a little. "Morton, you are quite aware that I indulge seldom in court life. I am a business man and I work when it suits me."

"Nevertheless," said Morton smoothly, "if I were your age, and I must admit I am jealous of your youth, I would not spend my time with cold figures. Oh, no. A lovely woman would be more to my taste. You are quite different from the Scot of my youth." He sighed, placing his fingertips together, and gazing at Patrick's face.

"If you have come to indulge me with anecdotes of your youth, pray desist, I beg of you." Patrick wrote three figures rapidly and added a sentence in his dashing Italian handwriting.

"But I trust you are not immune to Cupid's arrows? In fact, rumor says quite the contrary. The rumor has been quite explicit, also."

Patrick made no reply; he worked on, and Morton, beginning to show his anger, reddened. "It is a great pity that a man of your standing should be exposed to rebuffs by a woman like this Janet Applegate. A great pity." He clasped his hands over his stomach. Perhaps that thrust would go home.

Patrick raised his eyes. "How is Anne this evening?" he asked, absently.

This gave Morton pause; he didn't want too much outright enmity between him and Patrick, because he was quite sure Patrick had a great deal of influence over Anne. Patrick was still looking him full in the face, and Morton dropped his eyes. He had been about to leave the room; the wisdom of alienating Patrick was doubtful, and he seemed well occupied with his work, but his eyes suddenly encountered the shine of Patrick's well-polished boots. The shadow of a frown crossed Morton's face; he shot another quick glance under the table. There was no doubt about it, Patrick was booted and spurred—and where was he going at this time of night? Morton's crafty eyes studied his bent head. Was Patrick leaving last instructions before a journey, a journey undertaken hurriedly, and with no former preparation? Who was the woman he had brought home with him tonight?

"You seem to have rid yourself of your infatuation," he said. He settled back in his chair; he had been sitting forward, with the full intention of leaving.

Patrick frowned, and for the first time he was worried. Morton had been on the point of departure; his tones had been casual. Now there was an undercurrent of suspicion. To gain time, Patrick smiled vaguely. "I'm not sure that I understand you."

"No?" Morton seized on the almost friendly tone; he perceived the lack of assurance in it. "You left a certain street tonight, in the company of a woman. I would like to know the identity of the aforesaid lady." He had plunged straight to the point; if Bothwell were in this house there was no time to lose.

"My dear Morton, how very ungallant of you. Certainly you are not serious?"

"Ah, but I am. Suppose we stop fencing, sir. I want a view of this charmer. You may trust to my discretion." Morton glanced around at the door; it lay only three feet from him.

"Discretion or not, I'm afraid that's impossible." Patrick adopted a decisive and annoyed tone, as a man should in a case like this.

Morton uncrossed his legs. "Very well, then." He paused, and noted the premature relief on Patrick's face with increasing sureness that he had uncovered a plot. There was no doubt in his mind now. "You leave me little choice, sir. I shall be obliged to exercise my prerogatives."

"Morton, you speak in riddles." Patrick resumed his normal lazy voice.

"I do?" Morton smiled thinly. "Please forgive me; suppose I explain. I hold a commission form His Majesty; on the strength of that commission, which has to do with a certain outlaw, I am going to search this house!"

Patrick sat immobile and frightened. He was aware that quick and vigorous action was indicated. He thought of overturning the table between him and Morton and leaping on him, but the distance that separated them was fifteen feet at least, and Morton was beginning to rise—he stood only three feet from the door. Morton's armed retainers were within call; the house, the city, were full of enemies. Granted that he and Bothwell could flee the house, they would still be trapped in the city. Crichton would not see them tonight. Patrick's head whirled with rejected plans; three seconds passed in which his mind raced from one angle of this to another. He had bungled badly, and had been unprepared for a contingency which he should have foreseen. His guns were in the next room; the shiny dagger in his belt was useless, and he was useless.

"Morton," he heard himself saying, "my aunt would say 'the man's daft.'" As he said it, he found himself standing up, and edging around the table.

Morton showed his teeth in a smile. He had risen; he took one step backward, his eyes not leaving Patrick's face. His hand was on the door, and he threw it open. What Patrick saw kept his face unchanged; for one second he met Bothwell's eyes and the Earl grinned knowingly over Morton's shoulder. Patrick maintained his steady smile, since Morton still faced him. Then Bothwell put one arm around Morton from behind, catching his wrist in a grip that brought pain to Morton's face. A cry would most certainly have left his lips, had not Bothwell's other hand closed over his mouth.

"Walk forward." Bothwell's low voice was in Morton's ear. The pain in his twisted arm made him obey, and Bothwell kicked the door shut. "Linen, to gag him."

Patrick flew to obey; he darted from the room and returned with a bolster case from his bed. "You hold him," whispered Patrick. He had never gagged a man in his life and Morton was to be sorry for that inexperience. Even Bothwell remonstrated slightly at the amount of cloth that Morton was forced to hold in his open mouth.

"Hold on, sir, don't suffocate him," said Bothwell. "And don't wriggle, Morton; I'll break your arm. Now sit down."

Patrick finished tying the ends of the bolster around Morton's head; after staring at the trembling figure, his eyes went to Bothwell. "How did you know?"

"I was out in the garden, exploring," began Bothwell, not taking his eyes off Morton. "You finish your writing, sir; I have a bit of business!"

He drew the dagger from his belt, tossed it neatly in the air. It spun around, and he caught it with two fingers. "Watch, Morton, and don't move!" He held the haft still with two fingers; the dagger flew from his grasp and bit deep into the arm of Morton's chair alongside his arm. "Oddswound!" Bothwell was pleased. "Almost caught the cloth. I am not so deft tonight. Shall we try it again, Morton?"

Morton trembled. Bothwell was leaning over him, weapon in hand. Helplessly Morton raised his own hands. His eyes loomed large and doelike above the rough gag.

Bothwell retreated a few feet from his prisoner. "Now, Morton, I have something to say to you. First, I know that you are behind that charge of witchcraft—you and Maitland. Some day I intend to stand trial for the crime of which I am falsely accused. When I do, you will be far away." He paused, paced back to Morton, and added, "It may be, in heaven.

"The second point I wish to make clear has to do with King Jamie. I understand you have been pouring poison into his ears, and that poison has to do with my so-called attempts on his life. I have never made such an attempt and for that lie alone I should kill you now." Morton shivered violently from head to toe, and Bothwell continued, "A certain William Hamilton once gave me the lie in front of James. *Requiescat in pace*. I shall translate that for you, Morton, knowing your ignorance of Latin. 'May he rest in peace.' " Bothwell's tone was very pious.

Morton struggled to speak. He held up his hands to Bothwell, pointing to his gag, and Bothwell said suddenly, "I don't want to hear you talk! Your lying answers would drive me to murder!"

He flung away from Morton; he paid no attention to Patrick. The humor which had overlaid his remarks to Morton was but a thin veneer, and underneath he could feel the hot blood beating in his head. He swung around and with one hand dragged Morton to his feet.

Patrick dropped his pen. This eruption of violent passion made him remember how Bothwell had fought William Hamilton in a bloody duel in which he had given no quarter, even though he wounded Hamilton before he killed him. Patrick jumped to his feet; he stood behind his table. "Bothwell!" His tone was frantic.

Bothwell heard him. For a brief second the cavalier and the brute male clashed, but mercy was too new a word. He had forced Morton to his knees; he had planted his feet wide apart, and his big hands were on Morton's throat. He'd kill him as he would grind his boot on a creeping snake. "You whoreson coward, I'll open the gates of hell for you!" The moment of struggle with himself was past; his violence was cold and controlled, and he reached one hand for the dagger at his side.

Outside the door, Anne heard his voice. Ever since Morton had left and Patrick had been mysteriously absent, she had sat fussing with her food. If Bothwell were in this house, she must see him. On the other side of the door, she had knocked lightly, and because there was sudden silence within, she knocked again, said, "Patrick," and opened the door.

With incredible swiftness Bothwell raised his right fist and sent it crashing with all his strength into the side of Morton's face. Morton crumpled like a cotton doll. Bothwell's fingers released his collar, and he slid to the floor; over his fallen body Bothwell saw Anne's white face. "Now close that door!"

Anne obeyed. She sent the door banging against its frame with a backward push, her eyes never leaving Bothwell's face. She stared at him; finally she dropped her eyes to Morton—the gag on his mouth was awry and there was a split down the side of his chin from which the blood was flowing freely. She raised her heavy lashes to look Bothwell full in the face.

"Is he dead?"

"No!" The answer was like a pistol shot.

She made a motion toward Morton, and started to drop to her knees beside him. The sight of her pity sent a jealous anger through Bothwell. Reaching across Morton, he seized her arm. "Get up," he said, roughly. He pulled her to one side. "You'll stain your gown." He looked down at her. She had bent her head, and his eyes went over her bare shoulders, the soft honey colored curls; he forgot Patrick. "You're beautiful—but there's only one part of your anatomy I'd like to anoint!"

"You would have killed him," Anne said. Her mouth quivered.

"Aye, and why not?" he asked angrily, but there was defensiveness in his tone.

Across the room Patrick said not a word. He had tried to interfere before, but it was not a man's place anyway. He watched Anne.

"I'm an outlaw, madam." Bothwell was speaking. "I'm no 'varlet of the King's Bedchamber!' " His voice was bitter with mockery. "Don't compare me to those nesh gentleknights!"

"I'm not, my lord. I never should."

"Well—lassie, you know me at my worst." He held her by one arm; he could feel her shivering, and he put his other arm around her waist and lifted her over Morton's inert figure. He set her down beside him.

She put one hand on his arm to steady herself. The lace fell back from her hand; there was a gleam of diamonds on her wrist. "My lord," she whispered, "you—"

Patrick raised his eyes from the white hand that rested on Bothwell's arm. Never had he seen her more desirable. She had been frightened by the violence; she craved protection and reassurance from it. Instinctively Bothwell pulled her into his arms.

"Don't swoon," he said, hastily, urgently. "On my word of honor, lass, I hit him because I didn't want him to see you."

"You didn't want him to see me?"

"No. It would be too dangerous for you." Bothwell frowned. He said honestly, "But he was unconscious, I guess, before I hit him. He was frightened witless, the bastard."

At this Patrick couldn't repress a smile; it began in the corners of his mouth and ended in a chuckle that Bothwell heard. He swung around, still keeping one arm around Anne, and slowly his own guilty smile flashed out. "*You* were worried about the political implications, if I killed him, were you not, sir?"

Patrick nodded. "It will do your cause more good to have 'frightened him witless.'" He sighed, and he was conscious that the tension had passed. "I think there is hardly a need for formal introduction between you two."

Bothwell took his cue; he released Anne, just keeping a hand under her elbow. His tone was light, he was a courtier now, educated at two universities, master of three languages, a peer of the realm. "I fear I frightened your cousin, sir. I fear she does not have a very high opinion of me." He had turned his face to Anne. He raised one eyebrow at her, and the fingers on her arm tightened a little. "Do you hate me, lassie?"

"Aye," said Anne with vigor, sending him a look which said she understood quite well what he meant, and she put her hand to her chin.

"I'll keep it a secret," said Bothwell slowly, and he looked toward Patrick, "if you will."

"Oh, I will, my lord," said Anne hastily.

"You should have your backside warmed," went on Bothwell, his smile very slyly pleased, "if you continue wandering about gardens, I mean houses, and coming in doors unannounced. Lass, do you ever stay where you belong?"

"Oh, hush, sir!"

"You stay out of gardens—I mean doors." Bothwell grinned at her, and then he asked Patrick, "Would you fetch me some good stout rope, sir?"

Patrick disappeared, and Anne stood uncertainly gazing at Bothwell, who had dropped to one knee beside Morton and was fixing the gag on his mouth. Had he got rid of Patrick to talk to her? "My lord," she whispered, "you said gardens twice! You should be more careful!"

He didn't look up. "I should be more careful? You mean you should."

Anne took a step toward him; his dark head was right next to her hand, and she laid the tips of her fingers on the very top of his head. He was paying no attention to her, and suddenly she fastened all five fingers in his thick short hair and pulled hard.

He couldn't suppress a cry of pain and exasperation. He jerked his head aside, but Anne kept her grip; she pulled harder.

"That'll teach you!" she said gleefully, using all her strength and bracing herself.

Bothwell was still on his knees, with his head pulled forward. He yanked his head backward. Anne didn't let go, she was much too intent on doing as much damage as possible, and she flew forward at him, landing in a muddled heap on top of him on the floor. Then she began to laugh.

"You little devil!" Her head was buried in his shoulder, and she was shaking with laughter. "You took handfuls of hair!"

"You can spare it." Her voice came muffled, and Bothwell lay back on the rug helpless with laughter. He tried to talk. "Unhand me, wench. If your cousin—" The thought of Patrick's face if he came in and found them lying on the floor alongside of the unconscious Morton sent them both into gales of mirth.

"What would he think?" murmured Anne weakly.

"God knows." Bothwell ran his hand over his head, smoothing down his hair. "Unhand me!" He put his hands on her waist and rolled her over to the rug; he looked down at her face. "You always want to ravish me, you rascally wench!"

"And you know my name now," she said impudently.

He jumped to his feet, held out his hand. "Stand up, lassie. I hear your guardian!"

Anne didn't move. "Pick me up, my lord. I'm so weak from laughing."

His arms went underneath her, he scooped her up so easily. She was irrationally, intensely happy. "Oh, I laughed so," she said sighing, and Patrick opened the door.

Bothwell was on his knees beside Morton. He looked up as Patrick came back into the room and he took the rope from Patrick's fingers.

Once again Anne gazed down at Bothwell's dark head. "You're going, aren't you?" she said, wistfully.

"We're both going, lass," said Bothwell. "We'll not have any trouble leaving the city, sir. Not with your name."

Anne sighed. "Where are you going, my lord?"

"To Crichton Castle." He flipped Morton over, pulling his hands behind him.

"I wish I could go. How far is it?"

"About eight miles." As he said it, he smiled. "And if I find you behind the door when I arrive, I won't be surprised. One more thing. Morton didn't see you—if he had you would have had the very devil of a time explaining why you hadn't given an alarm. But he didn't see you, and you know nothing. Nothing! Remember that."

Anne said happily, because this was the first indication that he cared about her safety, "I'll remember, my lord."

He was binding Morton's hands behind his back. He hauled him to his feet, and hoisted the limp man to his shoulder. "Ready, sir?" he asked, already walking toward the window. "I'm going to tie him to a tree in my garden. Undoubtedly he will be delivered to King Jamie in a somewhat sad condition."

Patrick opened the window for him. "Goodnight, lass," said Bothwell, as he stepped over the sill, and Anne didn't hear Patrick say goodbye. She was listening to Bothwell's voice as the two of them walked away from her. "He will probably not be discovered before morning. Jamie should have his little gift in time for breakfast."

Part Two

Chapter Eight

JANET APPLEGATE had met Patrick Galbraith on the last Thursday in May. She had been sitting by her window, which overlooked High Street, and when a coach stopped out in front, she dropped her book and watched. She saw a man get out, come up the steps. Then she turned her attention back to her book. Five minutes later there was a loud knock on her door. By this time she had forgotten the coach. She put down her book and went to the door.

The hall was barely gray with the late daylight. The man in the hall asked timidly, and very hurriedly, "Does Master Applegate live here, Mistress? I've been up and down these bloody steps, begging your pardon, m'am."

Janet didn't have time to answer. Four flights down, the front door banged and a man's voice shouted, "Geordie!"

Geordie jumped. "I'm up here, sir," he shouted back.

"Well, what the devil are you doing, you lazy dolt? For God's sake, are you intending that I spend the rest of my life outside?" Patrick started up the steps two at a time. His head appeared suddenly, then the rest of him, and Janet stared. He came to a stop beside Geordie. "What are you doing?"

Geordie said hastily, "I asked the lady whether Master Applegate lived here."

"Does he?" asked Patrick impatiently, and transferred his gaze to Janet.

"She wouldn't say, sir," began Geordie, and Janet collected her wits.

"He lives here, sir," she told Patrick, hardly knowing what she was saying. She couldn't understand why Patrick Galbraith wanted her father, and she couldn't believe that he actually stood before her. Desperately she hunted for something to say but could not find it.

"Much as I hate to interrupt this tête-à-tête, I'm very hungry. Give me that letter, Geordie, if I must deliver it." Patrick held out his hand, and Geordie, with a sidelong glance at Janet, gave him a heavy white letter. "This," Patrick continued, "is in the nature of a request for information from Lord Usher to your father—I assume that it is your father who reads history at the University—and since I must return to Usher in a month, I shall be glad to carry the answers. If you will tell your father, I feel sure he can communicate with me within four weeks." He proffered the white, sealed paper.

Janet murmured, "Aye, sir. I will tell my father. It *is* my father," she added, her fingers feeling the letter. She still stared up at Patrick.

There, in the dim hall, her face was a white blur, and her eyes were long and green under the slanted black brows. Patrick had been about to turn away; instead he smiled. "Is your father of neuter gender?" he asked.

Janet was so accustomed to having every slip of her language corrected that she answered quickly. "I should have said Master Applegate is my father." She was very serious.

"So you should," said Patrick, just as grave. "And I should have introduced myself. Sir Patrick Galbraith, madam, and I'm charmed to make your acquaintance."

"I am Janet Applegate." She answered his bow with a quick curtsy; she started to say she knew who he was, of course, but she didn't know how to phrase it. So she was silent.

Patrick said, "If I had not dispensed with dinner, if I were not so hungry, Mistress Applegate, I should never have so far forgot myself." He was looking over Janet's shoulder into the room. "Will your father be home soon?"

"No, sir. He is away for supper, and I forgot to tell Martha, and that is why you see two places at the table. Oh!" She remembered what he had said. "If you're so hungry, sir, I would be glad—for you to stay for supper, sir. It is ready." She knew her invitation wasn't proper, but now she had done it and Patrick did not seem surprised.

"Wait for me, Geordie." Patrick turned to Janet. He seemed to expect her to precede him into the room, so she did. The door closed, she heard Geordie going downstairs in the stillness, and she was alone with this stranger. Helplessly, Janet looked at him.

"It was most kind of you, madam." He was taking off his cloak, the gold braid against its inky blackness making a splash of color on the wooden chair where he had flung it carelessly. Janet stared at the real gold buttons on his doublet and the white softness of his linen shirt. She put the letter down on her father's table. She didn't know what to say, but fortunately Martha came into the room carrying bread and a pot of honey. She stopped short at the sight of Patrick.

Janet said quickly, "Sir Patrick is joining me for supper, Martha. Is everything ready?" She fidgeted.

Martha smiled, a conspiratory smile which included both of them. "Would the gentleman like ale or wine?"

"Ale, if you please." Patrick was standing over the table and he pulled out a chair for Janet, who sat obediently, even though it was her father's place. Patrick sat down opposite her, stretching out his legs.

"Do you have any preference, sir?" she asked, shyly, indicating the platter of cold foods.

"None, madam." He smiled, and Janet heaped his plate with as much as she could get on it. Martha brought him his ale and Patrick began to eat. Janet forgot she was supposed to eat too; she couldn't believe that this had happened to her, that she was having supper with him, and a small smile of delight tugged at her lips.

"Are you laughing at my enthusiasm?" he asked.

"No, sir," she said demurely, and because his hazel eyes were on her she self-consciously took a bite of meat and picked up her bread. "I hope there is sufficient," she ventured. "My father is not so large an eater. I'll ask Martha for more bread." She took the poker which always rested against the table at her father's place and banged it on the floor, to which summons Martha responded instantly. Patrick was certain she had had one ear at the door. He was amused by Janet, by her shyness and the obvious delight that shone in her eyes.

"My uncle, Lord Usher," he said, "has written your father about a matter of history. Lord Usher is writing his memoirs, and there seem to be some points in his narrative about which he wishes to consult your father."

"He will be enchanted, sir," she said firmly. "He is completely engrossed in his subject; there is nothing he better loves than to expound on a doubtful point. I assume the point is a moot one?"

Patrick grinned. "I assume it is."

"I assume also that you know the particular difficulty?"

"Why should you assume it?"

She lifted her shoulders.

"Lord Usher probably entertained you with his problem. He must be enamored of discussing it. If you are aware of the nature of the difficulty, I might be of some aid." Her voice grew suddenly doubtful. "Sir, are you laughing at me?"

He nodded. "Madam, the big words that fall from your small mouth amaze me. And as for the problem—it is this. When the house where Darnley last lived was blown up, was it probable that the gunpowder was simply stored in kegs in the cellar?"

Janet was taken aback; she pondered. "I don't know," she said finally.

"Well, I do," said Patrick. "It's not possible. There was hardly a stone of the house left standing. Therefore, the gunpowder must have been confined deeper, perhaps in the walls of the sub-cellar, so that the explosion would force the walls to collapse. Now I could explain to you exactly why, but I doubt if you would be interested."

Janet gazed at him in awe. He was not only titled and wealthy, but she was sure he was as clever as her father. "I would be interested, sir."

She listened gravely while he told her the early history of gunpowder, its discovery, its uses. When he was finished, she said seriously, "You use big words, too."

"Was there one you didn't understand? I thought not. You are a very satisfactory listener, madam; you are that *rara avis*, an educated woman."

"Thank you, sir," she said. "Do Chinese women really wear trousers?"

He laughed. "Aye, so I'm told; I've never investigated. I see you are interested in clothes, also. I'd forgot I'd even mentioned what Chinese women wear."

"You told me everything," she said. The clock on the mantle struck seven.

"I did not talk for an hour and a half, did I, Mistress Janet?"

"No," said Janet honestly. "You ate for the first half hour."

He grinned. He stood up and pushed back his chair. "I must go, lass." She looked so disappointed that he added quickly, "I must or I would not."

She rose too, and he looked down at her. He was telling the truth; he didn't want to go, but he had been away five days. "I must be elsewhere in thirty minutes." He was still looking down at her and suddenly there were many things he wanted to know. "How tall are you?"

"Five feet and two inches. How tall are you, sir?"

"Six feet," he said, and they both smiled. "How old are you?"

"I'll be seventeen in September. How old are you?"

"Eight and twenty," he said, "and that's old, isn't it?"

"No," said Janet, "not for a man."

Patrick's eyes lingered on her face, on the smooth black hair and the white skin. He was puzzled by himself; he was wondering why he had bothered to stay with her for dinner. He put his arms around her and tipped her chin up with one hand. "Janet," he whispered, and he kissed her mouth. Finally he set her on her feet.

"Will you meet me tomorrow?" he asked urgently, keeping his arms around her.

"Where?" Her voice was breathless. "Where, sir?"

"At the Port," he said. "At ten. I'll be in my coach; I'll take you to the country."

She looked up at him. She had allowed him to kiss her, and she shouldn't have; now he wanted her to meet him, secretly. "I can't," she said despairingly. "I want to but I can't."

"Why not?" He tipped her head up again. "Why not?"

"Because it is wrong, and because you would think I was willing to—" She stopped and then went on hastily, "I should not have permitted liberties—oh, please, sir, you must know."

He said, "Was it so awful?"

"No," she said honestly. Then she realized what she had said, and she blushed deeply, the blood staining her cheeks. She could feel her heart beating. "You were teasing me, sir, and I took you literally. I am not accustomed to talking with gentlemen. I cannot come, sir."

"But do you want to come? Since you have been truthful, suppose you again tell me the truth."

"I want to come, but I cannot. If I were seen—"

"You will come," he said firmly. "On my honor, Mistress Janet, I give you my vow I shall not so much as touch your arm, if you'll spend the day with me. I'll take you to the sea."

She was waiting for him at exactly ten o'clock at the Netherbow Port, and he was on time. The coach stopped with some flourish, and Patrick jumped out. When he saw her standing there, in the shadow of the Port, with a green cape that matched her eyes, he knew he had not been wrong to spend most of the night in work—so that he might have the day free to be with her.

He took her to his house by the sea. Before dinner, he took her sailing in a deep-prowed sturdy yawl that was his pride. The Firth was choppy with a brisk northeast wind, but she didn't get sick; she was as yare as the vessel she sailed. At dinner he couldn't take his eyes from her flushed cheeks and the black hair under the tiny flared cap. Later they walked on the beach and watched the sea turn pink and gray and its colors leave with the dying sun. When he finally left her at her door, he said nothing directly about seeing her again. Instead he said, "I'll call on your father. Not tomorrow night, but the next."

He had always intended to make a rich English marriage. Jamie Stewart would some day, and perhaps soon, be the King of England. When the time came to follow him into England, it would be well and politic to have powerful English in-laws. Such relatives could smooth the way for a Scot in England. With an English wife he would be looked on as less of a foreigner, less of an interloper; with an English marriage, and his position with James, Patrick would be near to the dukedom he wanted.

But that night, as soon as he reached home after leaving her, he drew up a marriage contract. It was very simple. There was no dowry; it was only a contract between two people, and all it needed was signing. His plans were made; in the next three weeks he must call twice a week on her and her father, and then he would ask for the woman he wanted.

At eight o'clock on the night of June twenty-first, he was at the Applegate flat. He brushed by Martha, who let him in; he saw Master Applegate staring at him from his chair in the living room. Patrick looked past him, his eyes searching for Janet. Was it possible her father permitted her out at night? He frowned, then he bowed formally, for Master Applegate had risen. He was looking at Patrick with a kind of disbelief.

Patrick knew that Master Applegate held him suspect, but that had never made any difference to him. "Forgive the intrusion," he said. "Your servant, sir."

His arrogance was intensified by the polite words. Master Applegate tried to control his dislike. "My daughter has retired, sir."

Patrick nodded. Of course the old gentleman was lying, but he shrugged it off. "My business is with you, sir."

Master Applegate was momentarily amazed. Across the room he eyed Patrick in obvious puzzlement, and on the other side of the door which led to her bedroom, Janet was already crouched down, her eyes glued to the big keyhole. She had recognized his step; she had darted first to the door and then to her mirror. She had wanted to change her dress but that would take too long, so she was back by the door when she heard him say he had business with her father.

She was too well brought up to enter the room without being bidden, but not to listen and look, twisting her head sideways until she could see Patrick's head. She heard him bluntly and with no preamble announce that he had come for Master Applegate's consent to a marriage between him and Mistress Janet.

Janet clutched the door latch. "Oh, sweetheart," she whispered into the worn wood and then she held her breath, for there was dead silence in the living room.

The two men were eying each other with unconcealed dislike, and Patrick was amused. He lowered himself into a chair. "With your permission," he said, to his standing host.

There was another deafening silence. Master Applegate stood rigid; in the second that he stood there, he tried honestly to catalogue the redeeming features of such a marriage. He made his opening remark beside the point.

"Are you aware that Janet is not yet seventeen, sir?"

Patrick frowned. He wanted a yes and he wanted it quickly. "She will be seventeen in September; my own mother was married at sixteen." Patrick was bargaining for something he wanted and he was prepared to pay the highest price—that of his name. It wasn't possible that high price would be refused.

Master Applegate struggled to keep calm. "Janet knows nothing of court etiquette, nothing of what you would expect from her; she knows nothing of the way of life you lead, sir." He couldn't keep the reproof from his tone.

"She will learn." Patrick was still frowning.

"Aye," said Master Applegate, "she would learn." As he said it he made up his mind. "Therefore I suggest, sir, that Janet become formally betrothed to you, for the period of one year."

"One year!" Patrick got to his feet, his anger blazing forth. "Impossible!" Patrick was not an impatient man, usually. He was old enough, and mature enough, to know that a project begun could not be looked to for completion within a short space. He knew that sometimes one must look ahead five years, ten years, before the object in the distance could be gained. But this was different. A year stretched before him endlessly. "I don't consent to a year's betrothal! I have no intention of considering it!"

Master Applegate said slowly, "Janet is going away, sir. To my sister, in Caithness. She is going away for the summer—this year as every year. She leaves tomorrow."

"She does not!" Patrick who usually knew defeat when he saw it did not recognize it now, but in the back of his mind was a brief anger with himself for neglecting to win over this man. He had known from the beginning that Master Applegate neither liked him nor approved of him, but viewed him with deep suspicion. Patrick had considered his suspicion amusing, but now he realized his stupidity. "It isn't possible," he said desperately, angrily, "that you would refuse the honor of marriage!"

"Honor?" asked Applegate with scorn. "You do not confuse monies with honor, do you, sir?"

"I do not," was the answer. "I am speaking of the name I offer, although I fail to see why the want of monies should make those who have none of it scornful of the commodity." He was so annoyed he fell easily into a jibe that he would normally have not bothered to make. His voice grew calmer. "I have asked your permission to make Janet my wife. You equivocate."

"I would hardly call my answer equivocal. I have acceded to your demands." Master Applegate thought as he said the word that it fitted this proposal. "I have stipulated only a year's betrothal."

"You are sending her away!"

"I always do, in the summer. I would to God I had always let her live in Caithness!"

"You mean by that that then she would never have been the recipient of a proffer of marriage from me!"

"Aye, that's my meaning!" Janet was forgotten in a quarrel between these two men. "I do not consider you worthy of her!"

"Nonsense! You mouth nonsense! I—" He broke off; he'd

been about to say he loved her but damned if he would say it now. He picked up his cloak and strode from the room. Janet heard his footsteps; she heard the outer door close. He was gone.

Janet arrived in Caithness the following day. Ahead of her stretched the summer months. They would have to go by long hour by hour, long night by night. But they did slip by; the longing and loneliness and sweetness of first love went into them, and July and August gave way to cold nights and September.

Never had Edinburgh seemed such a paradise as when Janet entered it the last week in September. The smell of the city, the noise of its streets she drank in with joy, and the country she had left behind she hated with a fervent and youthful bitterness. This familiar flat held her memories of him; she had met him in the dingy hall, she had eaten with him on this table; in this room she had dressed many times, knowing he was coming.

Today she stayed only long enough to change her clothes and to put on the ones so carefully picked and pressed fully two weeks ago, when packing for coming home had been the first happiness in months. The blouse and skirt hadn't suffered in travel; she had packed them with such loving hands. The wrinkles shook out quickly from her green cape. She pulled the hood over her head and ran outside into the September afternoon. About a mile separated her from Patrick's town house on the Canongate.

The house looked just as it always had when she had passed it during the days she hadn't known him. It was a little frightening, and it was both excitement and her hurrying that set her heart to beating rapidly as she stood waiting for the echoes of the knocker to die away. After what seemed a long time the door opened, and without thought she stepped into the magnificence of the entrance hall, seeing herself framed a long way off in one of the elaborate Venetian mirrors. The liveried man in front of her stared.

"I wish to speak with Sir Patrick," said Janet hastily. "You may tell him it is Mistress Applegate."

"Sir Patrick isn't here, madam." The servant stared at her

curiously. "Sir Patrick has been away for more than two months now."

"I know," she said quickly. "I knew he had gone, but I thought—" Her voice trailed off, and then she added, "I thought he might come sometimes and you could apprise me."

His eyes narrowed suspiciously. "He never comes here, madam."

Janet's hands were fastened together. She said, "I'm not spying, sir. You fear that. Let me leave a message for him, then."

He scratched his head. "I'd let you leave a message but it would do no good. Sir Patrick never comes here, madam, I'm telling you true." He gazed at her for a minute. "You look like a trustworthy lass, but Sir Patrick never comes home any more. We don't even know when he is in the city."

Janet felt afraid; she forgot her shyness. "You don't mean His Majesty?" she whispered.

"No, madam." He shook his head. "But there are others. You know them and I know them." He grinned. "So does Sir Patrick and he takes no chances. But he might come, some day."

Janet nodded. "I'll come back then. I must see him, sir. I must!"

He smiled, a companionable smile. "You can come, mistress, if you wish. And if I see him, I'll tell him you were here."

She started to the door; she was grateful for his friendly manner, he seemed to want to talk to her. "I'll come back," she said firmly. "I'll come back often."

Chapter Nine

PATRICK was reading letters from Edinburgh that had just been brought him from the capital. He was lying on his side on one of the leather-covered benches that ran at right angles to the fireplace in the library at Crichton; the whole fireplace and its benches were in an alcove off the main room. Opposite him, on the other seat, was the young Laird of Logie, John Wemyss. Logie was talking, Patrick was trying to read, and across the rosy-tiled floor Bothwell paced, paying no attention to either of them.

He crossed to the window, avoiding the two hunting dogs, and looked out on the October countryside. He had just come today from the Hermitage.

He had done well the past three months. There had been peace on the Borders, peace while the crops were harvested, peace while the cattle were slaughtered and the beef salted down for winter. Early in the summer he and his Borderers had ousted the royal garrison from the fortress of Loughmaben—it had been a potential threat. But after that, the Border lord had demanded peace and he had got it. James should have been pleased with the quiet state of his normally rowdy Borders.

Bothwell had done well politically too, this summer, drawing to his standard almost all of the lowland nobility, counting powerful Highland earldoms as his allies, and he had come home to Crichton tonight for a very definite reason. He turned and looked at Patrick, who was still trying to read over Logie's voice. Logie was holding forth on the subject of Calvin; he continued to annoy Patrick, for although the Laird of Logie was a handsome man, his observations were hardly interesting. Patrick said, in a singsong voice, breaking into Logie's speech, "Calvin in his chamber five years taught a nun, till she was great with gospel and swollen with a son." He put down one letter and picked up another.

The staunchly Protestant Logie was offended, and Bothwell said suddenly, "Stop quarreling! Logie, you're a damned fool. You fought with Lennox on the street and earned James's anger. And you, sir, put down that letter and listen to me. I'm worried about Murray."

Patrick obeyed; he swung his feet over and sat up. "I am too, Francis," he said seriously.

Logie sat up straight too, but before he talked about Murray he wanted to defend himself in the matter of his street battle with Lennox. "Our quarrel is over, my lord," he said placatingly. "But our first Duke was coming down the street refusing to make way for anyone. Should I move?" He raised one eyebrow.

"God's death, Logie, you can confine your fighting to other than the Stewarts!"

"Except His Majesty," put in Patrick slyly and Bothwell frowned.

"We don't fight with Jamie Stewart," he said flatly.

"No, we fright him silly," said Patrick unperturbed. "Poor Jamie Stewart moves from castle to castle in fear of his mobile foe."

"The accomplished liar, Maitland, makes James live in fear of me!"

"Aye, Francis, and James fears you know his every move. Tell me, do you know where James is now?"

Logie and Patrick looked up at Bothwell, who took a letter from his pocket and tossed it on the flames. The paper caught, the sealing wax flared up redly, and as the paper crumpled they could clearly see the last line of the writing. "May Christ keep you in his holy care," and then the numerals 887; they were the numbers with which the burly Earl of Logan signed his missives.

"Aye," said Bothwell, "I know where Jamie is; he's at Dalkeith Palace, sirs, and that is where we are going tonight. Not to see James, but to see Her Majesty."

Patrick said nothing. He had thought that perhaps this would be the next move in this dangerous game of wits between monarch and subject, a game harmless so far except to a few unimportant men, like George, who had already died. Patrick stood up, looking excited, and one of the buttons on his doublet flew off; he gazed down at his chest. "Francis," he said, "I know you approve of this expansion, but I'm not sure it isn't a damned nuisance."

Bothwell grinned. "Go get it sewed on, sir. I've decided that the best way to counteract Maitland is to see the little Dane Jamie brought home with him." He was weighing in his mind whether it would be safer for Patrick to stay here at Crichton, and he decided that it wouldn't be safe for Patrick to enter Dalkeith Palace with him. Logie would be a far better guide, for probably Logie had traveled these ways before—to see the Queen's lady-in-waiting, his Danish wench with the red hair.

Against his will, Patrick waited with Gibson and the horses. The ride had not taken long; the moon was up, and Patrick was so near the palace that he could see its ivied walls as Bothwell and Logie walked away. Patrick and Gibson lay on the grass; the horses were tethered in a group of trees. The October night was still.

The sleepy guard on the postern gate let Logie in without a word; Bothwell walked along beside him, and also without a word, they separated on the castle grounds. Logie went around a side wall and into a narrow door. He asked the guard at the door one question, and slipped a coin into his hand. The guard smiled, answered, and watched Logie walk softly away, toward a set of steps. He mounted the steps, gained the second floor, turned to the right, and knocked on the fourth door down. It was opened and he stepped into the room quickly. He had passed no one but the guards.

Logie put his hand in his pocket and drew out his last gold piece. "Hello, Nannie," he said, "is Mistress Margaret in her room?" He was standing in a boudoir; the door to the other room was closed, and Logie faced an older woman in a white cap and apron.

She curtsied, took the coin and smiled. "Aye, sir," she said, and Logie went past her and opened the door. "Hello sweetheart," he said; he was laughing at her surprise. "Are you glad to see me?"

Margaret Vinstar had a blue robe flung over her petticoats, her bare feet were thrust into velvet mules, and her thick red hair was unbound. She moved toward him with a rather leggy stride. "Sir," she said warningly, "keep your voice down."

Logie grinned; he imitated her whisper. "I'll take care, madam. Are you surprised to see me?"

Her gray eyes were mocking. "Most surprised, Johnnie. His Majesty is most displeased with you, sir. Do you know that?" She looked straight at him, for she stood as tall as he did.

Logie frowned; her attitude was different tonight, as though he had displeased her. "You haven't smiled at me," he said, and he took both her hands in his. "You have the most beautiful pointed duckies, too."

Margaret dropped her eyes to her open robe. "You're an impudent knave," she said, but she did smile at him and let him take her in his arms.

"Oh," whispered Logie, "you are worth daring James."

"Am I?" Her voice was lilting with her Danish accent, for she had accompanied her royal mistress from Denmark. "I am worth the danger?" She moved in his arms. "Kiss me again, Johnnie."

Logie felt very masterful. "Only one kiss, wench, before I lock the door. I came with Francis."

"Francis?" she whispered. She let him kiss her, she was soft in his embrace, but when he released her, she said quickly,

"There's time for no more kissing, sir." She turned away. She had got to the door before he did and stood with her back against it. "I was dressing, John. I've felt poorly today." She sighed, and pushed her hair back. "But Her Majesty wants me now. Oh, Johnnie, why did you have to come tonight?"

Logie scowled, he took a step toward her and she opened the door. He made a move to take her in his arms again.

"Johnnie, don't frown at me. What can I do? Her Majesty has sent for me; I was dressing."

Logie hitched his sword belt and straightened his cap. "Ah, women. They are ever a disappointment."

She tucked her hand in his arm. "I don't want to send you away, sweetheart." She sighed, but she was leading him to the door. "Goodbye, and be careful," she murmured. Her gray eyes were narrow. "You'll imperil Francis, if you are not careful."

He nodded, she watched him go out into the hall, and she turned to her own room. She had just time for one more warning whisper. "Be careful!"

The ivy grew thick on the walls of Dalkeith Palace; it grew thick enough to let Bothwell climb with ease. Grasping the heavy vines, he made his leisurely way up to the second floor of the castle; he edged sideways until he was right beside a lighted window. He looked in cautiously, for the window was slightly open, and he heard voices.

He squinted his eyes against the sudden light; he made out the room. It was rather small. The candlelight disclosed the chairs, a big table, and the figures of two people. One was the King of Scotland and the other was Anne. Bothwell shifted slightly, moving his foot onto the ledge, and grasping the window for support. Then he listened.

"My dear," said James Stewart, "you ride exceeding well."

"Thank you, Sir." She smiled and made a deep curtsy.

James was standing close to her; he looked into her eyes. "Will you ride with me tomorrow?" he asked, his mind not on his question.

Anne looked down. "Your wish is my command, Sir."

"But I don't want to command." James paused, and Anne looked up at him.

"I would be forward if I said I was hoping you would ask me."

Outside the window Bothwell grinned. "Jamie, you are wax in her hands," he murmured to the window. He stared harder, for the King was amorously inclined—he who hardly ever paid any attention to women. James was standing very close to her now; he had to look down, for Anne was four inches shorter.

"Anne," said James, his voice very low. He put his arm around her waist, drawing her to him a little clumsily, and he kissed her mouth. For a moment they stood there, and Bothwell, entranced by this scene, almost lost his balance.

Anne put both hands against James's chest. "Your Majesty," she said breathlessly, and James let go of her reluctantly. Anne stepped back from him; her hands dropped to her skirts, and she made him a deep curtsy.

"Your Grace gives me permission to retire?" she asked, looking down as if she couldn't meet his eyes.

James was indulgent. "You have my permission." He studied her downbent face. "You may tell Her Grace that I intend to retire shortly myself."

Anne backed to the door, but he followed her; he was smiling. He took her in his arms and kissed her lightly. "Goodnight," he said, and held her hand for a second.

"Goodnight, Your Majesty," Anne said, still breathless. The door closed and Bothwell watched James come back into the room; then he too disappeared through another door which Bothwell supposed must lead to his bedroom. The room they had just quitted lay empty; he waited a few minutes, but nothing happened, so he pushed open the window and stepped noiselessly onto the rug. On silent feet he crossed the room and stepped into the hall. Near here must lie the apartments of the Queen.

He went on down the hall, came to a turn and rounded the corner. He had reached the third door down when he heard footsteps approaching behind him. In a second they would come around the turn.

Unhesitatingly he opened the nearest door and found himself in a large room with hanging tapestries and a royal dais. There was no one in this room either, so he crossed it and listened outside another door. He heard the Queen's voice. He listened still; there was more chatter, so he knocked.

He was rewarded with the sound of heeled shoes tapping across the floor; the door opened, and Alice Ruthven said incredulously, "Francis!" She stood rooted to the rug; she stared. "My lord," she whispered, and turned her head slowly to look at the Queen.

The Queen was standing in the center of the room; the sight before her eyes had brought her to her feet, but Bothwell's eyes went past her to the other figure in the room. He remembered not to give any sign of recognition, but his eyes flicked briefly over her. Then he went swiftly toward the Queen and knelt.

"Your Grace," he said low, again looking past the Queen to Anne.

"Francis!" she murmured; her voice shook a little. "Ah, my lord, you should not have dared!"

"For you, Madam."

She couldn't believe it was really he, except that no one but he would have the rash courage to intrude into a royal palace. "It might mean death," she whispered, looking down on his dark head and the very wide shoulders. "Oh, my lord." She felt the touch of his big hand on hers, and then suddenly, because he was so boldly in her rooms, she took courage, too. "Aye, and it's been months you have neglected us." Coquettishly she put one hand on his shoulder and Anne glared. Bothwell got to his feet and the Queen continued, "You've neglected us. I shall have to present Mistress Anne Galbraith, Lord Bothwell. Alice, have you closed the door tightly?"

Bothwell bowed to Anne, who swept him a curtsy; he glanced at Alice, who had started toward him with a reproachful look in her eyes. The Earl of Bothwell wished he were back at Hermitage.

"Alice, you look charming, my dear." He smiled at her, ignored Anne, and wondered how he was going to talk to the Queen.

The Queen solved the problem for him. She sat down in a carved chair. "Come sit here, Francis," she invited him; she was trembling with excitement, and she indicated a square stool with a gold fringe. It stood right beside her chair.

"I brought you a present." He sat down and opened the fingers of one hand, letting her see an intricately carved miniature dagger, with a jeweled hilt. He said, very low, "Murray gave me your message, Madam."

"It's perfect!" She took it from him, turning it over in her hands. She leaned closer to him. "I shall keep it always." She said something else, but Anne couldn't hear her. Reluctantly, Anne moved away, and Alice Ruthven, her mouth set, followed Anne.

Anne watched her; she felt sorry for her, for she knew very well that Alice was still in love with Bothwell. Everyone knew it, including the Queen. The Queen was pleasantly conscious of Alice's jealousy; every so often she would glance at Alice with a triumphant smile, and Alice would avert her eyes. Anne watched this byplay, of which Bothwell seemed unaware. She noted it carefully; she was learning quickly not to trust anyone at court, least of all the Queen and her ladies.

"Alice," she whispered, "don't let Her Grace see your jealousy, dolthead." She sent a venomous glare at the Queen.

"She'll tell everyone he paid no attention to me. I'm no fool!"

"I'd say you were." Anne looked down at her hands. "How do you expect to interest him? By scowling?"

Alice forgot her tears in her anger at Anne. "Wait till Murray passes you by, miss!"

Anne laughed. "My heaven, Alice, the way you talk." She ignored Alice, who was no threat; she had found that out easily. No wonder Alice Ruthven hadn't held her lover. Anne was pleased. "You don't scowl at men," she jibed. "You pull their hair." She smiled delightedly, remembering, and she looked over at Bothwell longingly. He was talking, he was gesturing with one brown hand. The Queen started to laugh, she put one hand over his, and he raised it to his lips and kissed it.

Anne forgot she was in the presence of her Queen; she forgot she should stay in the background. She got up, and she knew very well, as she turned her back on Bothwell, that he was watching her. Only a few feet from him, she picked up an orange from a bowl of fruit on the table.

Bothwell started to rise; belatedly he turned to the Queen he had left almost abruptly. "Your Grace," he said, "I think this may be imprudent. But I shall remember what you have said, Madam. I am grateful for your goodwill."

The Queen said seriously, "Together we will find a way. Francis, I shan't forget, either. Neither your loyalty, nor your courage." She was again aware of the danger; she had forgotten it in the pleasure of flirting with him again. "You are my gayest gallant, my lord, and I know you would never desert my cause, or Scotland's cause!"

"By my honor as a Borderer, Madam, you have only to call upon me. You have only to ask and my sword belongs to you!" He bowed, there was nothing more to say or do, and there was no time for but a word with Anne. He wanted to tease her a little.

She was still standing by the table with an orange in her hand. His fingers closed over her wrist, he didn't say anything, he took the orange from her. "You roll it like this, mistress." He proceeded to demonstrate, softening the orange in his fingers. "Then you cut a hole in it, like this—" He broke off; the inner door to the Queen's chambers had burst open. Margaret Vinstar came into the room.

Margaret remembered herself long enough to curtsy to the Queen. "Madam," she said breathlessly. "My lord." She came toward Bothwell, in her long, graceful stride. She was perfectly dressed, wearing her newest suit with its powdered gold borders, and her red hair was piled high in shining waves on her head. "Forgive me, Your Grace, but I have news." She stood in the center of the room, enjoying the limelight, taking it coolly, but her gray eyes never left Bothwell's face. "I have bad news, my lord. Logie was taken prisoner by the guards!"

The Queen let out a little scream. "Logie was with you, Francis?" she gasped.

"Don't be frightened, Madam." Bothwell stifled a healthy curse. He swung around to Anne. "Lock the door, lassie," he said, and for a moment he held her eyes, for now she looked frightened too. He went over to her and, regardless of the other women, he put a hand on her shoulder. "Don't faint, lassie," he whispered. "At least I know you won't be coming in this door." He grinned, he offered her his arm and she took it; she didn't refrain from sending a sweet, barbed smile at Alice, which the Queen didn't miss.

Bothwell was vaguely conscious that all the women were glaring at each other—all except Anne, who was enjoying it. Again he wished heartily he were back at Hermitage and that Patrick had come in with him tonight. Patrick wouldn't have got caught. Bothwell tried to visualize the place where Logie must be kept. "Your Grace," he began. "Logie was with me tonight. I have learned he is a prisoner. If I may question Margaret—"

The Queen nodded. "What do you know?" she snapped.

Margaret said calmly, "He is held downstairs, in the guard-rooms. He is being held for further questioning. Madam, it is grave, but there is nothing we can do."

Bothwell frowned. He had no intention of abandoning Logie. "You are talking to an outlaw, mistress. Is Carmichael Logie's warder?"

"Aye, my lord." Margaret took a step toward him, divining his intention. She lost her calm. "You can do nothing, my lord! It would be suicide! He is amply guarded!"

Anne's eyes were fastened on Bothwell's face. He looked annoyed at Margaret's words, annoyed at the implication he could do nothing. Anne tucked that away in her memory.

Bothwell was still frowning. "I have only Patrick and Gibson," he said aloud. "If I had but ten or twelve of my men, to create a diversion—" He broke off, and the four women stared at him, Anne thought, as though he were a god. "In a military campaign," he went on slowly, though there was not much time, "one of the first things to do is to estimate your enemy. It helps if you know him well. Now Captain Carmichael has one weak point—his head. He has the force, we have the wits; so we use what weapons we have—therefore we trick him. Margaret, I need your help."

Margaret didn't show her surprise. She tipped her head back and smiled at him. "I will do anything you say, my lord."

"Good," said Bothwell, with heartfelt relief. "Now what you must do is very easy, and I shall explain it to you very slowly. If you do not understand, ask questions, and first, know this. I will wait in the palace to see if my plan succeeds; I will be here, for you to call on. Now—" He paused for a minute occupied only with Logie's problems, and the problem of explaining his plan clearly to Margaret. Footsteps sounded in the next room. In the silence the four women and he watched the door knob turn. There was only one person who would turn that knob without knocking.

"Holy God," said Bothwell. "The King."

Chapter Ten

JAMES STEWART'S ugly face puckered with annoyance. He twisted the door knob in his hand again; there was no doubt but that the door was locked. He looked over his shoulder apprehensively; he was alone and he didn't like it. Somewhere in this palace the Earl of Bothwell was roving.

James was dressed in the same clothes in which he had entertained Anne an hour previously, except that he had changed his shoes for slippers and in his haste, had flung on a dressing gown over his shirt. His white linen collar was crumpled.

"God's son," he swore, and hit the door a crack with his fist. First the impudent Laird of Logie had been caught roaming in and out of Dalkeith Palace; then it was discovered that he had brought with him another man whose description tallied with that of an outlaw whom James had no desire to meet by himself. Thirdly he was locked out of the Queen's apartments.

He glanced over his shoulder again. Bothwell was a mobile foe, and James eyed the curtains in the empty room with distrust. He thought of Logie again, who had first resisted capture, and then refused to say who was the tall man who had accompanied him into Dalkeith. "Damned impudent knave," muttered James, forgetting his fears in his very real anger with Logie. He heard the swift patter of feet on the other side of the door, and he straightened up, ready to confront with a flood of profanity whoever opened the door. The bolt slipped, James stepped back slightly, opened his mouth to be ready for the first luckless person to face him.

"Oh, Your Majesty." Anne held the door in one hand and her skirts in another. She bent her head as she curtsied, but she blocked the entrance to the room.

"What the devil?" said James angrily. He pushed at the door; it flew open, almost upsetting Anne.

Anne said, "Oh, Your Majesty," and then backed away from her wrathy sovereign.

James turned, gave the door a hearty kick, so that his toes in the soft slippers suffered from the impact with the oaken door. "God's son," he swore again. He looked around the room; it was empty, but there were sounds of female voices in the next room. It suddenly occurred to James that perhaps the door had been locked because the palace rumors had already warned the women that there was a man unapprehended and still at large in Dalkeith. He fixed Anne with a glare. "What devilry is this?" he asked gruffly.

Anne could hardly talk. She wondered why she had been chosen to face her monarch and she was very out of breath, for first she had simply fled with the rest. "Your Majesty," she said helplessly, and tried vainly to think of some reason for the strange behavior of the locked door. "It was a jest, Sir," she murmured ineffectually.

"God's son," said James again. "Then you didn't know—" He broke off, staring at her face. "What conspiracy is this, madam?"

Anne shivered. "No conspiracy, Your Majesty," she replied hurriedly. "We," she hesitated, "we were—"

"Out with it," said James. "You didn't know Lord Bothwell was in the palace, did you?"

"No, Sir," she lied, quickly. "Oh, my heaven," she elaborated, remembering she must show amazement at this piece of news. "We didn't know that." She widened her eyes in astonishment. "That is impossible," she added, she hoped convincingly—for when James had said Bothwell's name she could see the Earl so plainly. He had picked up his cap, his half-eaten orange, and followed the scurrying women with an amused look on his face.

"Then why did you lock this door?" asked James, pausing between each word. "Why?"

"To keep someone out," said Anne desperately. It was so difficult to think with James glowering at her; he was so frighteningly moody and volatile a king. "Your Majesty," she said confidentially, "it was so silly, but we were copying a dress and we didn't want anyone to see us." She smiled, as if he should understand it was just women's nonsense.

"What? Copying a dress?"

Anne looked guileless. "Lady Atholl's newest dress, Your Majesty. It was a jest, Sir."

"Her newest dress?" James repeated, and then he began to understand. The faint smile Anne hoped for began in his eyes.

"Aye, Sir." Anne became more confidential. "And I warrant she will be surprised, too." Anne smiled bewitchingly.

"Oh," said James. "Where is Her Grace?" he asked, without further prelude.

Anne was so relieved she almost forgot where the Queen was. "Her Grace is in her retiring room, Your Majesty."

"Oh," said James again, but that piece of news seemed to be satisfactory and without another word he turned his back on Anne and she watched his figure disappear through a doorway that was hung with tapestry. She was alone.

Relief rendered her limp. Although it had been only five minutes since James had made his sudden entry, so much had happened in the meantime that it seemed like hours. First, hard on the heels of Alice Ruthven and the Queen, Anne had made for the safety of the Queen's bedroom, and behind them had come Bothwell. He had ordered Anne back to admit the King, and now she proudly realized that she had more than carried out her orders; she had held James up for at least three minutes, and by this time the Earl would be somewhere else in the drafty roomy palace. Anne picked up her skirts and made for the hall and her own room.

Marie was waiting for her. Anne's eyes lighted when she saw her face; she put her finger over her lips, motioning Marie to silence, and she tiptoed over to the door of her bedroom. For a second she waited outside, listening. She could hear his voice, low; she could hear Margaret's low answers, and she breathed a sigh of relief. She left the door and went over to her mirror.

"The Queen ordered him to take shelter in my rooms, Marie. Her Majesty thought it safest for him."

Marie came over to her and took out a jeweled comb that kept her blonde curls in place. "Hold still," she cautioned, replacing the comb with deft fingers.

Anne whispered, "In a few minutes I will see him, Marie. I thank the Lord that he is safe," she added, devoutly, "but what do you suppose he is saying to Margaret?"

Marie looked blank, and Anne paced the room restlessly. "I can't wait," she murmured, "but I don't dare disturb him; he'd hate that." She leaned against the mantle and watched the clock hands. "I've disturbed him too often, and I think he is explaining something to Margaret about what she is to do to help Logie."

Marie said, "At least he didn't ask you to do it, *chérie*. He doesn't want you in this trouble."

"No, but what can they be doing?" She went over to the door again, listening to the murmur of his voice inside. "All this time I could be with him!"

But she waited, without knocking; this time there was no excuse to come in without knocking, no excuse to come in at all. "They're even in there with my powder," she said petulantly, and finally heard Bothwell: "Then you go straight to the Queen now, and it should not be long that you have to wait. Remember, I will be here."

The door opened. Margaret slipped out and went to the door to the hall. For a second she stared at Anne, at the heavy-lashed violet eyes, the rich red mouth. Anne returned the stare, her eyes slipping over Margaret's slim figure. Margaret started to say something, but Anne said, smiling sweetly, "I'll lock the door." She gave Margaret a sidelong glance of triumph, and when Margaret stepped out, she shot the bolt with finality.

Anne ran across the room; she couldn't wait to be with Bothwell, and yet when she stood on the threshold of the little room, she could think of nothing to say except, "I hope you have been comfortable, my lord."

She thought at first he hadn't even heard her, it took him so long to answer. He was standing, he had risen when she entered. Finally he seemed to realize he should reply to her. "It's a bit hot in here, lassie," he said.

Anne looked at the fire; it was blazing up. She looked back at him and for another second there was silence. She saw he was not thinking about her.

"You would be more comfortable in your shirtsleeves, would you not, my lord?"

"I would that," he said. He began to unfasten his coat, and Anne helped him take it off. There was no other place to put it, so she laid it on the bed.

"Please sit down," she said. There was only one chair, and covertly she studied him as his long arms pulled the chair for her, turning it a bit away from the hearth.

"You sit here, lassie." He tapped his fingers on the back of the chair. Then he threw her a look which asked why she didn't obey him, so she sat down. "I shan't disturb you," he went on, absently. He crossed the tiny room to the door, scrutinized the lock and drew the bolt closed almost soundlessly.

"Are you worried?" Anne asked, twisting around in her chair to see him.

"Just a wee bit," he said. "Now put on your slippers as you always do, and forget me. It will all turn out." He was at the window, he opened the curtains. "Blow out the candles on the mantle, will you?" He waited till there was less light; then he stuck his head out the window. It was only ten feet from the ground, and he was satisfied. He let the curtains swing to again, sighed, and sat down on the stool in front of her table and mirror. "The damnable fool!" he said suddenly.

"Do you mean Logie, my lord?" Anne had put on her slippers, and tucked her feet under her. "How is Margaret going to rescue him?"

"I'd rather you didn't know."

"But I would have been glad to help!"

"Aye, perhaps, but Margaret is in love with Logie."

"Is she? She wasn't going to help him. I warrant she did it because you asked her to!"

"What?" He frowned. She knew he thought she was talking nonsense; she knew too that he would rather not discuss it, for some reason. Probably because he had to sit and wait.

He transferred his gaze to the myriad bottles and dishes that littered the top of her table; the candlelight winked on the silver and reflected itself in the Venetian mirror. "What's this?" he asked, interestedly, picking up a bottle and holding it to his nose. He made a face of rapture. "Smells like fresh salmon," he said seriously.

"It does not! That's rose water!"

"Never contradict a gentleman, lassie. What's this?" he picked the lid off a silver box and stuck his nose in it. "Powder." He answered his own question, and held up a piece of fluffy fur. "I think I'll powder my nose—if you can spare it, dear," he went on, looking at himself in the glass; he crossed his legs delicately, almost upsetting the table, and simpered at himself.

Anne burst out laughing and then quieted to hear what he was saying. "Now if you'll pour me a goblet of wine, I'll explore some more."

She poured the wine from the jug, and when she turned back to him, he had settled a blond wig on his head and was regarding the effect delightedly. Anne almost dropped the cup and he wriggled his eyebrows at her. "I look just like Elizabeth," he announced.

Anne put the cup down, and sat on the bed, giggling. "You are mad," she said, when she could stop laughing.

He took off the wig, stood up and pulled her to her feet. He was laughing too, and he said, "If I could, I'd put you on my horse, and we'd ride together tonight!"

"Can't we? Can't we, my lord?" she asked longingly, tipping her head back to look up at his face.

"You have a good grip," he said ruefully, running his hand over his hair. "I'm sure you could hang on to me all the way to Crichton, and then you could lie on the bench in front of the fire and stuff yourself full of cold roast partridge!"

"It sounds heavenly," she said. A ride through the October night was something she wanted more than anything else, ever. Was she never to be with him except for a few minutes? He was in danger; she almost said it aloud, but she stopped. He seemed to prefer that they ignore the fact that if he were discovered he might be killed before her eyes. He was still holding her hands; he was so close she could see plainly the painstakingly embroidered initials on his white shirt and the small gold buttons that marched down the front of it. Someone had woven that shirt, someone had taken extreme care in the embroidery, and Anne felt a stab of jealousy for the woman who had done it. Then she thought that it had probably been his mother and was comforted.

He was thinking too, remembering a scene he had witnessed tonight—a scene about which he was going to tease her. He said, very seriously, "Tonight I saw a playlet—I watched it from a certain window on the first floor."

He was so serious that she answered just as gravely. "A playlet, my lord?"

"Through the window I mentioned, madam, I saw a certain seductive wench entertaining His Majesty, and I must say that Jamie Stewart didn't seem equal to the occasion."

Anne said definitely, "You spy. I don't know what they say about eavesdroppers—"

"But you wish you did?" He laughed at her discomfiture. "Nevertheless, you played your part well; it was Jamie who did such a poor job."

"You think so? I warrant you could give His Majesty lessons." She looked at him over the rim of her wine cup.

"Undoubtedly. You know I am very laserly in my approach. Now if I were King, and met you, I should first ask you how you were enjoying your stay in a new land."

"You would?"

"I should use finesse. If I were King and met you, I should say, 'How do you like Scotland, lass?' "

Anne said, "I like it uncommon well, sir. What comes next?"

"Next?" asked Bothwell eying her. "Well then, we'd be done with geography and could proceed to more important topics. I don't know why this wouldn't do. 'How do you like Scotland? Let's go to bed.' "

Anne tried to keep from laughing at him but he looked so amused at the expression on her face that she gave up. "You are so practical, my lord."

He laughed. "Tell me something. I'm curious. How did a sweet piece like you ever get into Jamie Stewart's court? How did you and Patrick come to know each other?"

Anne said, almost as if she were reciting, "I was brought up in the country, in the south of France, in a chateau. My aunt took care of me; she was a most proper chatelaine, with her keys and her gold chains. I can still see myself following her up the stairs, with my eyes on her swinging skirts and her red-heeled shoes."

Bothwell smiled. "What a lovely little liar you are," he said approvingly.

Anne put down her wine cup. "What did Patrick tell you?" she asked angrily. "And whatever he said, the knave, that's no way for you to talk to me!"

Bothwell laughed at the pouted mouth. He said, nodding his head, "I like temper in a wench."

She looked angrier than ever, and he added, "If you throw anything, Mrs. Galbraith, I'll be sore tempted to beat your backside."

Anne had been taking a sip of her wine and she stopped in the middle of it, choked down what she held in her mouth and blurted, "You'd not dare!" Then she smiled at him enchantingly, and decided to find out what he really did know. "What did Patrick tell you, my lord?" she asked very properly, very sweetly.

"You're as sweet as honey," Bothwell announced gravely, intrigued by this sudden change, "and your skin is as white as snaw. Now let me see, what did Patrick say to me? He said, after he'd seen you, he was more than willing to accept you as his kin, but that he had to look through his fingers at your birth."

Anne was very quiet. She said finally, "I might have known it, truly. You see, my lord, when my mother learned that Sir Patrick was so wealthy, she sent for me. I'd been in the country, with her sister, and I used to take the milk up to the chateau on the hill, and that's when I saw the chatelaine, with all her gold chains." Anne threw this explanation in gratis. "I was sixteen, so my mother brought me to Paris, and she wrote Patrick about me."

"Your mother needed money?" Bothwell was trying to make this story come out even.

"Oh, no," said Anne truthfully. "My mother was under the protection of a Marquis, and she wrote to Patrick just for me. My mother," she cut in proudly, "was beautiful and she loved me."

"I see," said Bothwell, very grave. "What happened to your mother?"

"She died," said Anne, biting her finger, in a childish gesture. "She had the influenza, my lord. Before Patrick's letter came she was gone."

Anne's voice trailed away, and she looked so unhappy that Bothwell said, "Don't cry, lassie." He put his big hand over hers.

"She told me," went on Anne, "that she had never loved any man, truly, except my father. He was very big and blond and she had him only a few months, and then he was killed in a duel. I was born after he died." Anne's imagination made this so poignant a story that she had to blink rapidly to keep the tears from spoiling her powder and her darkened eyelashes. She brought out her lace-and-silver-embroidered handkerchief hurriedly.

Bothwell said, "Lambie, she must have been very happy."

"She loved him so much," Anne added, "that she always wore the ring he gave her, even when she had so many jewels. Much bigger, too. Like this." She fingered the emerald pendant she was wearing. "When she died, the Marquis tried to take this away from me! Imagine!"

Bothwell grinned. "I warrant he was a fool. You liked your Paris gauds better than your country cottons, too, didn't you?"

"Oh, Paris was heavenly," she agreed enthusiastically.

"They say all good Scots go to Paris when they die," he said, solemnly. "I almost went to France. Last month. To offer my services to your King."

Anne said interestedly, "You know they say he has eight and twenty mistresses, and not only that, he has a sunken bath, with steps, and he lies full length in the water while his Chamberlain stirs it."

"Certainly," said Bothwell. "I wasn't going to help him fight his war, or anything rough like that. I was going to stir water."

"If you'd gone," she began—she would never be sitting with him now. She traced her finger along his open palm. "How did you get that scar?"

"I do not know," he answered, paying no heed to her words.

"Don't you truly know?" she asked, again.

"A brawl, I suspect. I've forgotten. You are wondrous fair, wench, and I'm forgetting you're Patrick's kin, too." He said the words matter-of-factly; the unrestrained and blunt implication of his speech made her lower her eyes. He dropped her hand.

She heard him push back the stool and stand up; he went over and looked down at her fat gold watch, which was lying on the table. "I don't have much more time." He picked up his coat from the bed, noticed a lacy shawl lying beside it and picked that up also.

"Put this on," he said bluntly. "You're driving me mad."

Anne said, helplessly, "Oh," but under his eyes she took the scarf and obediently put it over her bare shoulders. He stood with his coat in his hand, watching her.

He put on his doublet, he finished buckling his belt, and he laid his hand on the sword hilt on his hip, adjusting it. He was ready to go, he was going, and she didn't want him to leave. She leaned toward him. The veneer over the brute male was so very thin. I'm mad in love with him, she thought wildly. "Before you go, my lord—"

Slowly he reached out and took her by the arms in a light grip. He shifted one hand to the back of her head and while he kissed her she stirred in his grasp so that his arms tightened and she could feel all the strength of his body, the heavy shoulders, the powerful legs. He lifted her in his embrace, so that her feet swung clear of the floor. "So I was permitted a taste," he muttered, against her mouth. He raised his head, looking down at her face as she lay back across his arm, and the fingers on one hand tightened on her shoulder in a cruel grip. "Look at that bruise, when you go to bed tonight."

He set her on her feet as he said it; he walked away from her, opened the window. It scraped a little, and then he was over the sill, standing beneath her in the dark garden, and slowly, very slowly, the curtains swung back into place.

Chapter Eleven

LOGIE blinked his eyes at the sudden light that was thrown into his room when the door was opened. He'd been asleep, his shoulder ached and one arm was numb from the battle he had fought when three guards had challenged him. He had ignored the challenge; he had fought his way past two, losing his rapier, and the third had held him at bay until the other two had cornered him again.

He sat up, still blinking, moving his shoulder to see how badly it was wrenched. He remembered vaguely that someone had told him never to sleep right after a fight; he should have exercised his muscles to avoid the stiffness he had now. But there was hardly time to reflect on what he should have done, and he looked up at the guards who had entered his room.

"What might you want, gentlemen?" he asked, mockingly. "Are you aware you are disturbing my rest?"

The two guards stared at the disheveled figure on the bed. Logie had had his coat torn off, his shirt was ripped, and there was a cut on his cheek which had bled profusely. The whole side of his face was smeared with bloodstains.

"You'll follow us, sir," one said. "Up this way."

Logie got to his feet unhurriedly. "Who wants me?"

There was no answer and he shrugged, wincing at the sudden pain the gesture brought. One guard went ahead of him, one trailed behind; and in the light of a single torch, he went up the circular stair he had descended a few hours before. He emerged into the guard room; here the light was bright, and Logie frowned at the sight of the Captain of the Guard, whom he had ever disliked intensely.

"Well, Carmichael," he said patronizingly. "What keeps you from your sleep, sir?"

The guard ahead of Logie stepped aside, revealing a feminine figure that Logie couldn't believe. He raised one eyebrow almost in the very rueful manner in which he had left Margaret Vinstar hours before.

"Sir," said Margaret, her tone distant and cool. "His Majesty desires to see you, to question you." She took her eyes from him and spoke to the Captain. "If you will escort us, sir."

Captain Carmichael looked a bit bewildered; the guards stared from Logie, who said nothing, to Margaret, who was still distant, like a being from a remote star. Without a word Logie leaned forward and opened the door for Margaret. Behind her he started down a long hall; in back of him came Carmichael, and three stalwart guards. Logie thought of speaking to her, but she hurried ahead nervously and he wondered at her haste and the awkward way she held one hand pressed into her dress. Then while he watched her, she dropped her other hand, and held that stiffly down at her side to match the first. She slackened her pace slightly, enough to make the march more leisurely as they rounded a corner and started up a wide stairway. Logie battled with the notion of sudden flight, but Carmichael was at his heels, and Logie had no doubt but that if he should make a break and run for it, he would get a bullet in his back. He sighed.

"What does His Majesty wish to ask me, madam?" he asked loudly.

Margaret jumped; she hurried on after standing still for a second at the sound of his voice at her back. "His Grace desires to know whom you brought into the palace tonight."

"God's blood," said Logie, even more loudly, and Carmichael's fingers tightened on the hilt of his sword.

"We are here," said Margaret calmly. She turned to face Logie and his warders. They all stood outside an oaken door.

"His Majesty wishes to speak with the Laird of Logie alone." Margaret's eyes rested on Logie with dislike. "His Majesty requires that Captain Carmichael and his men remain on guard outside this room. On no account are the guards to leave."

The Captain bowed. "Aye, madam. We shall remain."

Margaret said, "You shall be summoned when His Grace has done with the prisoner." She turned her back on the Captain; her heart was beginning to beat faster, and she opened the door, cautiously. Logie filed after her, closing the door without looking at it, for he expected to see James seated in a chair glowering at him. Instead there was no one in the room at all.

He frowned, and Margaret put her finger over her lips warningly. "Johnnie." She formed the word with her mouth, and held out her hand to him.

Logie's eyes widened in amazement as he saw a familiar pistol. "Bothwell's," he whispered, taking it, feeling the cold hilt in his fingers with eagerness.

She took his hand; silently he followed her across the room and without hesitation she drew apart a brocaded curtain. They were in the Queen's bedroom. It was almost pitch black; there was no sound. With her hand tight on his, Margaret drew him after her toward the square of window. Each step they took sounded loud; the floors squeaked, and when they stopped between each careful footstep, they could hear the heavy breathing of their sleeping monarch.

Margaret took the last step between her and the window. At that moment someone turned over in the big canopied bed and Margaret's heart stopped beating. Logie stood frozen, then looked toward the bed and the Queen popped her head out of the hangings. She saw the two figures framed in the light from the window, waved her hand, and disappeared again.

Logie realized then that James himself was in the bed too. His grip on the pistol tightened; he nerved himself for the noise the window would make when it was opened, and realized then that this was the second floor. He swore under his breath. How the devil was he to get down twenty-five feet in the pitch-black?

Margaret motioned to him to open the window; it was a

quick gesture, and while he obeyed with hands as careful as possible, he saw Margaret indulging in some strange convolutions from which she emerged with a length of rope. James snored suddenly; Logie jumped and waited for another reassuring snort from James.

"I hid this in my hoops," whispered Margaret. The curtains were fluttering in the breeze and Logie was already tying the rope, slip-knotting it around the leg of a ponderous wardrobe. He flung the end of the rope out of the window; Margaret knew that only seconds stood between him and safe escape.

"Francis is waiting. He will have silenced the watch on one gate."

"Sweetheart," he whispered back. He was abashed with his gratefulness to her, and there was no time for words. Even so, he tried to put his arm around her and tell her that he would never forget her help, but she stepped away, motioning him on. He obeyed, he was over the sill, and Margaret could hear him going down the rope, his feet scraping a little on the stone walls as he let himself down. She closed the window. She had still to escape from this room.

James snored on. Margaret timed her steps to his noisy breathing, she was almost at the door when the Queen's head appeared again. Margaret couldn't see her face clearly. At that moment she had reached the curtained doorway; she was out of the room. The Queen retreated under the quilts again; she gave James a shove. "Sire," she said, annoyed. "Turn over. You're snoring."

James must have obliged in his sleep; Margaret could hear no sound from the room she had just left, and she fled across it and stepped into the anteroom. Captain Carmichael sprang to attention.

"Captain," said Margaret. "His Majesty has dismissed me. He requires you to wait."

Carmichael stared at her openly. "Wait?" he asked, his eyes fixed on her face.

"Aye," she snapped. He was standing right in front of her. "Let me pass, sir." She proceeded to the door slowly, but once outside she broke into a frantic run, a run that carried her downstairs and brought her up short before a locked door. Unheedingly she hammered on it.

"Anne, let me in!"

"I'm here," said a voice. Anne stared at her visitor while Margaret drew the bolt again. "Did Logie escape?"

"Aye." Margaret felt a flush of triumph; she felt powerful, as though she could do anything. "It was as simple as Francis said it would be."

What Anne was going to say was drowned out by the sharp sounds that rent the air outside. In the silence of the night two pistol shots rang out so loud that the women were frozen, both by the noise and the implication of the gunfire. Anne ran to the window. She was hanging over the sill, her eyes trying to pierce the blackness, when there was another shot. It was farther away, and right after it, she heard a familiar voice raised in a Border war cry.

Margaret said cynically, "They announce their escape. I can't escape. I shall have to deal with James in the morning." She turned from the window and very carefully arranging her new dress, sat down in the chair. She explained what she had done, quickly. "Certainly Carmichael will tell James. If I could shut his mouth—there would still be the guards to prattle out the tale. But Her Majesty will help me, and it would help too if I might stay here with you tonight. How did you like Francis?"

Anne lifted her shoulders. "I know him so little." She yawned; if Margaret thought she would learn something, she was mistaken. Anne yawned again, and called Marie. "I'm going to retire," she announced. "Marie will help you too, if you wish, madam."

"I'll stay," said Margaret. "I need sleep, and they won't find me here so early."

She was right. She did sleep, quite late; it was almost nine when her summons came. She was calm, and Anne, eating crystallized plums and drinking a cup of wine, watched her covertly as she dressed herself. Anne was hungry and there was no time for breakfast. The first person they saw when they entered the Queen's rooms was the King. He looked virulent.

James had been up before dawn. No one had dared to disturb him during the night, least of all Captain Carmichael, who had been the first person to know he had been duped and that his prisoner had escaped him. The Captain had been disposed of; for fully an hour he had met the rage of his sovereign with bent head and a few hasty explanatory words. Downstairs now, in the guardroom, the Captain paced, not knowing what fate hung over his head, and upstairs James was ready for fresh blood. When Margaret appeared, he had another culprit.

James was standing in the center of the room. The Queen was sitting in the same chair as when Anne had last seen her with Bothwell, and from the stool on which the Earl had sat, Alice Ruthven had risen hastily as her monarch had risen.

Margaret curtsied; she noticed that James's hair was standing on end as though he had run his hands through it and even his posture was belligerent. She glanced at Anne, saw Alice and the Queen; she didn't notice anyone else. But Anne did; Murray was at the Queen's side, the Earl of Logan was also in the room off to one side with the young Laird of Burley, and with all this audience, there was still a deafening silence as Margaret made her entrance. James didn't give her time to speak; he didn't wait for the usual amenities.

"Madam!" He pointed his finger at her. "Madam, do you know of what crime you have been accused?"

Margaret stood very straight. "No, Your Majesty," she replied.

James had difficulty restraining himself; he took a step toward her and Margaret was frightened into speech. "I didn't know it was a crime!"

"Don't forswear yourself!" James's voice rose, and he took another step toward her. "God a mercy, madam, did you not help a wicked rogue escape the crown's justice?"

Margaret stood so calmly that Anne thought ice wouldn't melt on her. Margaret's voice was just as cool. "I confess my complicity, Sire," she said, low.

"Ah," said James, in a lower tone. He looked around the

room, as if to make sure that both his audience and his victim were properly aware of his royal and righteous indignation. The Queen took advantage of the momentary lull.

"Come here to me, Margaret," she said, throwing James a reproachful look.

"Well, Madam," James said, in tones of disbelief and hauteur.

"My royal lord," the Queen answered. "Margaret is my lady-in-waiting, my childhood friend."

James snorted; he waved his hand. "And does that give her the right to parade prisoners through my bedroom?" As he said the words he reminded himself anew of the enormous impudence of this conspiracy. He reddened with fresh anger.

The Queen put her hand over Margaret's. "She is not to be abused, Sir."

"Abused?" The injustice of this appalled James, and he roared suddenly, "Madam, is that Danish logic?" He muttered an oath, and the Queen turned away ostentatiously from his language. "For God's sake," continued James, "give me some wine."

Anne was nearest; she moved quickly to obey him, and her hands trembled as she poured the fragrant sherry. James picked up his cup, and addressed the Queen. "Madam, let us instance the facts. Mistress Margaret contrived to trick the Captain of the Guard, and to set loose an insolent knave whom I wished not only to question but duly to punish." As James said this, both Murray and Logan understood why Bothwell had not abandoned Logie to the King's justice. "Now there was another man in Dalkeith last night who spoke to Logie. Burley saw him and Burley knew who accompanied Logie. Burley saw fit to confess."

James continued talking. "Now Burley does not know why Bothwell entered Dalkeith. Because of your lady-in-waiting, Madam, there is no one remaining who saw Bothwell."

The room was very still, and everyone stared at James. Anne tried to look wide-eyed and innocent, and there was complete quiet when Alice Ruthven threw her bombshell into the room.

"Aye, but there was, Your Grace," she blurted. "There was

someone else who saw Lord Bothwell! I was not the only one."

For the second time silence reigned. The Queen stiffened in fear, Margaret looked slyly pleased, but Anne was suddenly sure whose name would be thrown into the room next. In the second before Alice resumed, a thousand excuses and a thousand subterfuges raced through her mind.

"Someone else?" James' eyes opened and he glanced around suspiciously. "Who was that person?" He glared at both Murray and Logan.

"Why, it was Mistress Anne Galbraith, Your Majesty." Alice smiled hatefully; this revenge was very sweet. "Ask Mistress Anne where Lord Bothwell was in the palace!"

Anne's eyes spat fire; she forgot where she was and she half raised the flag-shaped fan she was carrying and took a step toward Alice. Then, belatedly, she twisted the fan in her fingers.

"You, madam?" James rose to his feet. "You?"

Anne looked desperately at the Queen. It took only that one glance to see that Her Majesty would not help; the Queen would cross James only so far and no further. Briefly Anne thought of Bothwell; he was far away now, probably deep in his own Borders, probably lounging in a tavern eating his breakfast. And she was all by herself. There was no one who could help her, for Murray would be of no aid; he and Logan were out of favor with the King.

"Your Majesty," she said, "it is true, as Alice says. I saw Lord Bothwell."

James threw out only one word. "Where?"

"In my rooms," said Anne, very low. "He was with me."

Alice Ruthven couldn't conceal her exultation. "Your Grace, she is telling the truth!"

"Quiet!" roared James at the interruption. "I will question the lady myself." He glared at Alice and resumed. "Why was Lord Bothwell in your room?"

Anne bent her head; she wouldn't tell the truth, and fortunately Alice was so delighted at the success of her betrayal that she interrupted again. "Why was he in your room, madam?

Why don't you tell us too that you are Lord Bothwell's latest trollop?"

"She's lying, Sir." Anne stepped toward James imploringly. "Would Your Majesty ask her how she knows these things?"

James shifted his glance to Alice. How did she know? And Anne cried, "She is silent, Your Grace. She is silent because she saw Lord Bothwell herself! That is how she knows he was in my room!"

Alice grasped the back of her chair with both hands. She had forgot she would be vulnerable too. "Oh," she said helplessly.

Anne rushed on, eagerly. "Your Majesty, the truth is so simple. She saw Lord Bothwell, but she didn't say whom else she saw, someone whom only she and I saw last night!"

"Well, Lady Ruthven?" thundered the King, trying to understand the charges and countercharges that were being hurled.

"I don't know her meaning," faltered Alice.

"She knows what I mean well enough." Anne smiled. "Only perhaps she is so enamored of Lord Bothwell that she didn't even know she saw my cousin. For that is who was with me. My cousin, Patrick." Mentally Anne crossed herself for telling so many lies in one breath.

"Patrick?" James ejaculated the name. "Patrick?"

Anne nodded. "Aye, Your Majesty. He was in Dalkeith, too. He climbed in the window, and Lord Bothwell arrived later by the door. He had come with Logie, who was with Margaret." Anne knew that victory was near; she turned on Alice. "And she was there too, Your Grace. Oh, she was highly diverting. She fawned about Lord Bothwell like a hound dog!"

"I did not!" Alice was breathing hard.

Anne laughed. She fanned herself lazily. "You do not care for the truth, Alice."

Alice was so angry she burst into tears. "Lying little wench," she raged, but Murray said slowly, "Mistress Anne isn't lying, Sir."

James jumped. "Now don't tell me you were there too, Murray." Then he smiled and looked at Anne, who was as delectable as a gold doll in her gold satin bodice and her gold tissue petticoats, and he even laughed out loud to hear the next words that came from her mouth.

"Aye, Lady Ruthven, last night you had a mind to lay with him and he didn't want to be bothered!" Anne's violet eyes were mocking, she was ready to fight on, with vigor, but Logan couldn't contain himself any longer. He also burst out laughing.

"Your Majesty, and to think you and I slept sound last night!"

James grinned. The antics of his court always amused him; he was beginning to feel sorry he had missed all this. But there was one person who would suffer, and that was Alice.

"Get hence, madam," he said rudely. "You and all your kin can be gone from court! You shall close your town house; you'll not receive Lord Bothwell in Edinburgh!"

Alice curtsied. "Aye, Your Majesty." She backed to the door. She was gone, she had been sent from court. Her whole family was banished to the country. Anne felt no regret; she waited to see what would happen to her.

James said, and he sent a sly smile at Anne. "You may retire." He turned to Margaret. "You may both retire and keep to your rooms. Lord Logan will escort you."

Anne made her curtsy; with relief she gained the door, and the three of them said not a word as they walked along. It wasn't until they reached the lower halls that Anne decided she had better ask Logan now for what she wanted. She would rather have waited until Margaret was not with them, yet Logan's movements were unpredictable. She might not see him again for months. But still she hesitated.

"How did you like Francis, madam?" he asked.

"He was very entertaining," Anne said demurely. "He and Patrick set me to laughing so with their nonsense. You should have been with us, my lord."

"I'll warrant I should," said Logan regretfully. "Next time, make sure you invite me."

"Perhaps," said Anne slowly, "I'll be forbidden court, too."

Logan frowned slightly. "You're too bonnie," he decided, finally.

"I thank you, sir." Anne dimpled. "And if I am sent to the

country, perhaps you will have the kindness to take me in."

"That will be a pleasure, madam. I offer you the hospitality of Fastcastle any time you want it."

Margaret said quickly, "May I come, my lord?"

The straightforward Earl looked rather amazed at his sudden popularity. "I'd be charmed," he said.

"You have such a reputation for hospitality, my lord." Anne was already counting the days until Christmas. "Your Yule festivals are famous."

Logan recovered from his surprise. "Madam, if you would join us for Christmas, we would be honored. Of course it is news to you that your cousin and Lord Bothwell will be with us at Christmas."

Margaret asked swiftly, "Am I included, sir?"

"Certainly, my dear." Logan smiled at her, and turned again to Anne. "To be sure, you did not know Francis was coming, did you, mistress?"

Anne smiled. "Of course not, my lord."

Logan squeezed her hand; he grinned. "Mistress Anne, we shall be looking forward to your first Christmas at Fastcastle."

Chapter Twelve

"But I've been to see him at least a hundred times and he's never home!" Janet's face was as hot as the iron with which she was pressing her petticoat. "I've gone three times a week for the last months, and he's never there! I don't know what to do!" She looked as though she were going to cry and Martha clucked sympathetically.

"Now, now," she fussed. "Your father will be coming home, and you don't want him to see tears."

"I don't care!"

"You do care, mistress. And if you don't you should." Martha turned around to face Janet, a long meat fork in her hand. She pointed it. "You have made him very unhappy and he tried to do what is best for you."

"I know." Janet's face was set stubbornly. "But I love him."

"You love your father, too. You're not a wicked girl."

"I wish I were!" Janet sat on her stool with her hands over her face, and Martha rescued the pressed petticoat just in time.

"Don't wipe your face on that, miss. Here you are, going to take a nice trip for Christmas, and all you can do is weep."

"I'm not weeping! Go away," said Janet, between her fingers.

"You go to Berwick tomorrow, and you'll have a nice Yuletide." Martha folded the petticoat neatly. "It will do your father good to see his brother, it will do you good to be away. You'll come home a new lass, you will."

"I won't come home at all!"

Martha laughed, but her face was worried. She sat down in a wooden chair by the fire and contemplated first the roasting meat and then Janet. "He's never home, Sir Patrick's not?"

"No. He doesn't stay at his house."

"And Mistress Anne Galbraith? She's never home?"

"No. She is with the court. Don't you see, Martha? We are going to Berwick, and I could meet Sir Patrick if only I could tell him I was coming!"

Martha looked down at her skirts. "I feel sorry for you, I do," she confessed. "I wish I could help you."

Janet sighed. "If only, Martha, I knew where he might come when he is in the city, I could leave a message."

"A message?"

"Aye, a letter." She looked at Martha, her green eyes suddenly free from tears and very sharp. "What do you know?" she asked breathlessly.

"Me?" Martha was startled.

"You." Janet got to her feet. "What aren't you telling me?"

"Nothing, mistress. Faith, I'll warrant I wouldn't lie to you."

"Faith, I'll warrant you would!"

"I couldn't tell you," said Martha definitely. "Isna fit for you." She rocked in her chair, and then she smiled a little. "It's a lovely romance you have, dearie," she admitted.

Janet smiled. "Tell me now, Martha. I don't have much more time. I'm not going to deceive my father. I'm only going to ask Sir Patrick to come to see us in Berwick."

Martha said slowly, "I shouldna tell you this, because it won't do any good, now. But mayhap when you come back—" She frowned.

Janet was beside herself with excitement. She seized both Martha's hands. "Tell me!"

"You won't like it," announced Martha, refusing to be hurried. "You won't like it, but it's the truth, miss. Your Sir Patrick sometimes visits on the fourth floor of a tenement I know about, because I know the good lady who lives on the third floor. Ashamed she is too."

Janet said nothing but, "What is her name?"

"Edwina Black," said Martha slyly. "When you come home, you might speak to this lady I know, who could watch for Sir Patrick on the stairs. It's two streets down from my street, lass, and when you come home, I'll take you down there to see Mrs. Walter. She might help you."

Janet nodded. Her face was composed. "Well, Martha, I appreciate your aid; I'll retire to my room now." She went out, stopping in her room long enough to pick up her cloak. At her father's table she found pen and ink, and she sat only a few minutes before she began to write. "Sir: By happy coincidence I shall be in Berwick, at the dwelling of Mr. William Applegate, for the Yuletide. If you would come to the back gate at nine on the morning of the twenty-sixth of December, I might speak with you alone. God keep you, sir." She signed her name carefully, melted the red sealing wax, and left the imprint of her thumb on the seal. She had no ring to stamp it with.

Thirty minutes later, for she had to ask directions twice, she knocked on the door of the fourth floor up. There was no answer. She looked around her in the dark hall; the day was cold and the December daylight thin and misty. She knocked again, more loudly; she waited in the silence, listening, and suddenly the door opened.

Janet stared. "Mrs. Black?" she asked, thinking jealously that Mrs. Black was rather beautiful. She peered past Edwina into the room.

Edwina nodded. "What do you want?"

Janet hesitated and Edwina said, "Do you want to come in, madam?" She was looking at Janet curiously. "I don't know you."

"I know you don't madam. I came to beg a kindness from you. I should be eternally in your debt, madam, if you would so accommodate me."

Edwina's eyes widened. "Come in," she invited.

Janet hardly heard her; she was started talking now. "Madam, I have a letter here which must be delivered to Sir Patrick Galbraith. He comes here, does he not?"

Edwina frowned. "What if he does, miss?"

Janet produced the letter and Edwina looked at it belligerently, wishing she could read. "What does it say?" she asked.

"That is merely his name, madam." Janet explained. "If you would see him soon, could you give it to him for me?" Her eyes fastened on Edwina's face hopefully.

Edwina smiled. "I could, mistress, but he's gone." She put her hands on her hips and shrugged. "He's gone back to the Borders; you're too late."

"He was here?" Janet clutched the letter.

"Last night," said Edwina, sly triumph in her voice. "He's gone now."

Janet's eyes blazed with fury. "You're lying! And I wouldn't trust you with this letter!"

"So I'm lying, am I?" said Edwina truculently. "I would have given him your precious letter, much good it would do you! But now I won't! You'll never get that letter to Sir Patrick now!"

"Won't I?" asked Janet.

"Cat eyes," sneered Edwina.

Janet tilted her head. "He loves green eyes," she announced. "And he'll get this letter! Good day, madam!" She turned and walked straight into Gibson who had just come flying up the steps.

"Hello," he said, and Edwina stepped hastily into her room.

"Come in, sir," she said hurriedly, and there was such obvious haste in her voice that Janet stopped.

"I came back," said Gibson, staring at Janet. "What's the matter here?"

Edwina stood inside the door. "Nothing," she answered, smiling at him. "Why don't you come in? She was going."

"Sir Patrick left," said Gibson, "but Lord Bothwell sent me to escort Mistress Galbraith. His Lordship wants the blonde baggage delivered to him safely." He grinned. He was past Janet, and the door almost closed, when she called to him.

"Sir!" Her voice was frantic.

Gibson stopped, he turned around. "What's the matter, lass?" he asked curiously.

"You know Sir Patrick! Will you give him this letter?"

He grinned again, his eyes went sideways to Edwina. On each side of him the two women glowered at each other. Gibson's shoulders shook with laughter. "Give it to me, wench." He took it from her and looked at the writing. "And you behave." He put out one arm to keep Edwina away from the letter. "I'll give it to him," he said to Janet. "I love to carry letters from bonnie lassies. What's it say? How much you love him?"

Janet smiled at him. "If you do it for me, sir, I vow I'll never forget it! Never!"

Gibson laughed. "Ah, love. You run away now and I'll give it to Sir Patrick." He closed the door, and Edwina stepped back, eying the piece of paper in his hand. He laid it on the table carelessly. "What did you want to fight with her for?" he asked, before he took her in his arms.

Chapter Thirteen

No roads led to Hermitage Castle. Deep, deep in the Borders it lay, close to the English Marches, and for countless years its gray stone walls had guarded the Scottish side of the Border. It was set along the banks of Hermitage Water, a burn that joined Liddle Water just below the castle, and it was set on fairly level land, although behind it the glen stretched upward and the castle's cemetery and small chapel lay in the curve of the hill.

Hermitage was very old; back through the centuries its walls had endured bloody battles, long sieges, and its deep dungeons had had their share of prisoners. A moat surrounded the castle, rude boards planked it, lying across the water to the arched stone entrance, an entrance blocked by a portcullis fully twenty feet in height. Hermitage was windowless; only narrow slits in its ominous walls allowed the air, and it was a big fortress, accommodating five hundred men and their mounts with ease.

Its history was long, its masters many, famous in ballads, sometimes dark in deeds. People said there was a dread swordmill in the castle dungeons and many the shriek of the poor wretches who had been flung to its jaws, and it is true that in one deepest recess of the underground prisons there was the vestige of its remains. Hermitage had a ghost called Redcap, who paced its battlements on dark nights, a ghost that dated way back to the castle's most dreaded master, Lord de Soulis, he who had perished, so the legend ran, by being boiled alive in his armor in a great iron pot. Not far from the castle was the stone ring on which the huge cauldron had been set atop the flames, and all around stretched the Border lands of Liddesdale and Teviotdale, roadless, gashed with burns, lovely with heather, thick with forests where the deer roamed wild.

In the small village near the castle the houses were closed to the air, and the only sign of life was the smoke curling from the chimneys, for no one was abroad. It was six o'clock at night, and the short December day had already drawn to a close. Even so, a few doors opened when the sound of horses' hoofs echoed in the night, and a few people saw the mailclad riders on their way to the castle. They were riding fast, for the end of their journey was in sight. They left the village behind. Not many minutes later the huge portcullis clanked upward on its chains, throwing out the light. The sentries stepped aside at the sound of a familiar voice and the horsemen, still mounted, entered the castle.

"Was your trip good, sir?" asked the soldier who took the reins of the first horse as its rider dismounted.

"Bad," said Patrick, and strode off, his muddy boots kicking aside the fresh-laid straw that covered the stone flags of the hall. He was in the oldest part of Hermitage, the ancient keep, and he made for the narrow twisting stairs that took him past a barracks for the men, and up to the next floor, the whole of which was taken up by a vast dining hall. The doors to that immense room were heavily studded, iron-hinged. Each part of Hermitage could be defended as a separate fortress, and Patrick stood looking across the room at a sight that never failed to fascinate him. In Hermitage the centuries rolled back, and Patrick might have been standing at the board of a feudal lord of the early thirteenth century.

The huge room was raftered, its twin fireplaces were seven feet in height and wide enough to admit small trees, neatly clipped of their branches. The tables were rough-hewn, supported by tree trunks so that they might bear the weight of the massive platters and the roasted venison. There was an incredible amount of noise in the torchlit room; it smelled of unwashed men, horses, wet leather and savory roasting meat.

Patrick, from the door, saw the back of Bothwell's head as he lounged at the head of the table, a table set on a platform two steps up from the rest of the room. The Earl's chair was heavy, carved with his crest, and its ponderous arms were engraved with the Hepburn lions. He had shoved his chair back and put one boot up on the rung of the table, and he was talking to Logie and Andrew Ker, who had arrived a few days ago from the nearby Border fortress of Ferniehurst.

Patrick strode forward, avoiding the sprawled forms of Bothwell's two staghounds; he pulled off his heavy gloves as he came, threw them on the table, and sat down in his own chair next to the Earl. "How are you, Francis?" he said. He didn't wait for an answer, but picked up a tall flagon of ale and drank half of it off thirstily. "What a trip!" Then he seemed to remember that he was still wearing his helmet, so he pulled that off and tossed it to the floor where it landed with considerable clatter. "Now I'm ready for food," he announced.

He kept on eating steadily; servants refilled the tankards, cleared away the plates as they were emptied. Andrew Ker, Logie and a black-haired man by the name of Captain Ormuiston called for dice, and the three of them began to play. Bothwell himself started to join them, but decided to wait for Patrick, content now that he was safely back.

"Well, Francis," he said finally, "Edinburgh is deserted, and I'm afraid it is your fault."

Bothwell said nothing; he tipped his chair back and waited.

"The court has moved to Falkland; I don't know whether James will come back in time for the Yuletide at the capital or not. Nobody does. Your visit to the Queen accomplished two things. Maitland fears for his life and has moved again to the country."

Bothwell's face was impassive, and Patrick, studying it, wondered whether Maitland was right in his fears, but Bothwell suddenly smiled his quick boyish smile, and he looked so amused at the thought of Maitland's antics that Patrick smiled too.

"The Queen is more than ever ready to aid you, and she

has been wheedling James. To be sure, what good it does to wheedle James, nobody knows." He frowned and passed his hand over the bristles on his cheeks. "I'd say, purely as an observer, that all these moves are like the opening moves on a chessboard. You have won momentary advantages, but there is still so much room for maneuvering—and losses—that the outcome is very far off. You have won time, let us say, Francis. Time, but the checkmate is still in the future. In the distance." He was conscious of the rattle of the dice, of the other noises in the room; he leaned over and absentmindedly stroked the head of one of the dogs that lay at his feet. He regarded Bothwell a minute, and suddenly he tossed a coin, a gold coin on the table. It rolled over and lay winking in the light.

"I won that from you a couple of months ago," he said. Bothwell frowned hazily. "I kept it," said Patrick, "because the story around it interested me. It took me, while I was in Edinburgh, into a bar, where a certain Mr. Campbell spent his last night on earth."

Bothwell did not interrupt, but he sat up straighter, and Patrick continued, aware of his interest. "Unfortunately, I learned little of Mr. Campbell, beyond the bare fact that he had drunk quite heavily that night, and that he met death a few yards away, between the tavern and his home. He was discovered, lying in the street, by a neighbor some thirty minutes after he had left his cronies. But," said Patrick lazily, "that was not all I learned." He paused for effect.

"Go on, man." Bothwell picked up the coin and turned it over in his fingers. "Go on."

"Well, for some months after you had seen Mrs. Campbell, nothing untoward happened on the street. Then a tale began to be bruited about among the neighbors. The old lady was receiving money—gold pieces. She had been very careful, but such news travels fast; she was observed in the market place, and every once in a while she would change a gold piece.

"This news reached the ears of the Earl of Morton. Either that was accidental, or he had been keeping watch on her ever since she confessed you had spent an hour or so with her." He paused again. "Now let me pose a question. Why should Morton be interested in the old crone? Why should he have her watched? Was it because you had been there or was it because he knows something else about her? And if he does, what is it that he knows?"

Bothwell stared at Patrick, but again he did not interrupt. Patrick continued slowly. "To leave that for a moment, I will tell you what happened the night before I left Edinburgh. During that night, Mrs. Campbell was murdered."

"What?"

"Aye, my lord. Mrs. Campbell was murdered. She was discovered the next morning. She had been struck on the side of the head and she had evidently been killed instantly. Around her wrists and ankles were obvious marks. She had been tied. I deduced that she had been tied to a chair, probably for questioning. I deduced also that since Morton had had her watched, he was responsible for the crime.

"Now there was no use my following up Morton or his men, but there was some use in exploring. Because the kitchen was the scene of the murder, and the original hiding place of the money, it seemed possible that she had been questioned there. But you knew her. You can imagine that they would be unsuccessful in their efforts to make her reveal the secret of the gold coins. That money was more precious to her than her life, and ultimately she paid that price for it." He stopped. "As did Mr. Campbell. As did George." He stopped again and gazed at Bothwell. "Why?"

He was marshalling his thoughts. "Because of the money itself? Yet the money lay untouched for years. Or is it because the reappearance of those coins betrays a secret that someone wants kept, and kept well?

"Again I digress. That morning I went to the flat above. If Mrs. Campbell had been questioned, it was possible her questioners had been overheard. The house is not plastered, and only rough boards and rafters separate the ceiling from the kitchen above.

"The woman of the apartment was terrified to see me. As

soon as I saw her face I knew she had heard something, but the difficulty was in forcing her to talk. For an hour I questioned in vain. She had heard nothing. Threats failed, money failed, and finally the charm of your name succeeded. If you wanted to know, she would consent to tell. When I had got that far, I can tell you I was disappointed to learn she had actually heard only one sentence.

"However, she had listened for some time. It was unusual to hear voices at night from the kitchen below, especially men's voices. There were two men talking, but there were pauses during which she heard nothing, so it would seem that the old dame was refusing to answer, and might have been shaking her head. This continued for at least an hour, and the voices, while she still could not make out the words, became louder and more angry, and she swears she heard the old woman cry out, 'I have no money!'

"That is all she heard the old dame say, and right after that, just as she thought to interfere and call out to the night watch, she heard a man's voice say—and this is very important, my lord—'I don't want the money! All I want to know is where it was hidden!' That is the only sentence she caught, and after that there was silence. That is the point in time at which she was murdered, either in anger, or because Morton wanted her shut up for all time. The dead don't bite. Now, my lord, what is there that the hiding place can tell? Are you sure that the money was all that there was in the secret crypt?"

"Crypt?" asked Bothwell. "Why do you use that term?" He frowned. "It was hardly big enough for a body."

Patrick gestured impatiently. "It is only a term. But was there nothing else in the cavity?"

"Nothing. I could swear it. I reached in the entire length of my arm, and there was nothing but the poke—filled with gold."

"I have not quite finished." Patrick looked well pleased with his statement. "I remembered Alan Campbell, who had spoken to his father on his deathbed. I asked the woman upstairs if she had known this Alan. She had. Twenty years ago, he had left Edinburgh; he was going to marry his cousin, a girl who lived in Berwickshire. My story ends there. I don't know if he is still living, but if we are to follow up this search, I believe Berwickshire is our next step."

Bothwell said thoughtfully, "You are a canny Scot. Here, take this coin. Keep it. If any man can unravel these skeins that have been tangled for twenty-five years now, you can. If you could catch Morton in them—"

Patrick nodded. "I may need a week in Berwickshire," he said. He turned away and stared into the flames of the fire.

The logs were piled fanwise on the great hearth, and the soft powdery ash drifted in small piles into the room. Around him the talk went on, and he could hear the songs that the men at the other end of the room were singing, Border ballads, tales of battle, feats of arms, the conquest of women. He was struck by their similarity to the Homeric poems. Here on the Borders, where the loss of a horse was a more considerable loss than the life of a man, here for countless years the English and Scots faced each other across a narrow wavering Border. Here was the land first to feel the brunt of war; here lived a constant warrior. If his home were easily thrown up and as easily abandoned, it was because it might be burned tomorrow or the next day. If he would rather raid than farm, it was because wheatfields might be battlefields when a monarch wished it. A Borderer knew a signal fire at night meant invasion; a Borderer owed allegiance only to his lord, for the King of Scots was only the King of Fife and Lothian, nesh inland Scots who cringed to see the smoke of their own barns. A Borderer loved no man better than himself, and next to him, he had respect only for the man who lived on the opposite side of the Border, an ancient enemy, an Englishman, but the man who knew the same kind of hazardous life he did. Patrick was just as proud of being a Borderer as Bothwell was.

He yawned; absentmindedly he picked up the heavy pewter and leather tankard at his elbow, and Bothwell did the same. "To your success," said the Earl. He drained off his ale and stood up. "You know, if we want to reach Fastcastle long before dark tomorrow, we must leave at dawn."

Chapter Fourteen

Anne Galbraith stood by the blazing fire in a small room off the entrance hall at Fastcastle, her hands held out to the blaze. She was still wearing her cloak, its hood falling down her back. Her velvet gloves were lying where she had dropped them on the mantle, and she was giving all her attention to Murray, who was paternally feeding her wine from a silver cup. It was not yet three in the afternoon; dinner was to be at four, so there would be plenty of time for the long Yuletide festivities.

Anne had spent the last two weeks preparing. She had come to Fastcastle equipped with two boxes of clothes, shoes, perfumes, jewels—everything that she could think of that might be useful in charming one man. For the first time she could look forward to hours with him instead of minutes. There would be whole days and whole nights, and there would be nothing to fear, for Fastcastle was a solid and grim fortress, safe for the Border lord, far away from Edinburgh.

Anne looked up at the sound of the opening doors. There was a great deal of noise in the hall when Patrick appeared, and Anne knew that behind him would next come the man she was waiting for.

Bothwell stood on the threshold of the room, letting in the cold air, his eyes searching for Anne, and Lady Logan found her hand ignored for a second. Bothwell recovered himself quickly; he bowed, made a few polite remarks, but his eyes were straying to the fireplace. "What an entrancing costume she is wearing," he said, still staring.

Lady Logan gave a little laugh. "Anne is wearing a man's doublet, my lord. I rather think myself that it is foolish to be masculine in dress."

"Masculine?" asked Bothwell, astonished, and then he smiled. Anne's close-fitting doublet was ruffled, worn over an exaggeratedly full skirt, and from a cord around her waist she had hung a glittering looking-glass, a toy mirror. "I beg your leave, madam," said Bothwell, bowing again and, going toward Anne, he made his handclasp with Logan as brief as possible.

"Your servant, madam," he said, and Anne looked up, as if she were startled to see him.

"My lord," she said, holding out her hand. "I fear it is a cold hand for a welcome."

He ignored her words and took her hand. "Gibson brought you to me safe, didn't he?"

Anne looked at the wide shoulders right in front of her. She raised her eyes but she couldn't see past him; he blotted out the room. "Aye, sir," she said.

"You've grown taller, too, lassie."

Anne smiled. She lifted the hem of her dress to disclose the four-inch-high cork clogs she was wearing. "They are called chopines," she explained. "They give me height."

"What do you want height for?" asked another voice, and Patrick hove into view. He took her in his arms and kissed her. "Look at the envious glances I'm receiving, sweet coz."

"Oh, Patrick," she said, "I have missed you. And I've a deal of news for you, too."

"How many bills?" he asked. "I have actually been considering the purchase of a seamster's shop. Ruffs, ribbons and busk-points." He grinned. "But you can tell me the worst later. Time to dress, Annie." He glanced around. The room was rapidly emptying of people; Margaret and Logie were nowhere to be seen, Lady Logan had disappeared, and Logan was off to the kitchens to make sure about the thickness of the gravies. "Time to dress for dinner, Annie."

"Is it?" asked Anne. She could hardly believe it. But Bothwell had drawn Murray to one side; they were talking by themselves, Bothwell gesturing with one big hand, his face intent on Murray's smiling one. "No, no," Anne heard him say. "I'll speak with you again tonight. You must know that their tongues talk both ways or—" He dropped his voice and she could hear no more.

She frowned as she picked up her gloves and her muff. "I'll take my leave, sir," she told Patrick, who was edging away toward Murray and Bothwell. "A plague on both your manners, yours and his lordship's!" She turned her back. She let Burley adjust her cape, and she managed to take a good deal of time to cross the room, but when she reached the door Bothwell was still engrossed. Anne wanted to slam the door but she would have hit Burley with it. She marched down the hall and up the steps. She had reached the top and was almost to her own room when she heard flying footsteps behind her.

"Lassie, wait for me!" His voice was low as he came up to her. "This is your room?" He opened the door. She was facing him, and he lifted her over the threshold and entered himself.

"You can't come in!" gasped Anne.

He grinned. "I am in, madam. Nobody saw me; do not look so frightened. Here, Marie." He took Anne's muff and tossed it to Marie. "You put that away; I wish to talk to your mistress."

"You shouldn't have come in," Anne repeated desperately. "My lord, you must leave me now!"

"I will, lass. But only for twenty minutes. You interrupted my conversation with Murray."

"I interrupted it?"

"Certainly. Why didn't you wait? But I'll see him while I dress. I'll be back in twenty minutes."

"Will you?" asked Anne helplessly.

"Aye, I brought you something. I want to see you smile when I give it to you."

"Oh," said Anne. "But I—you said you had to go, my lord."

"So I did. But I'll be back, lassie." He opened the door cautiously and started out. Anne heard him say suddenly, "Oh, Lady Logan, I did not see you at first."

Anne's heart gave a plunge. The door was open a crack and

she peered out fearfully, expecting to see Lady Logan's terrifying and disapproving figure right before her eyes. Instead she saw Bothwell laughing at her.

He waved. The hall was reassuringly empty, and she called threateningly, "You lying knave, I'll pay you back for that!"

"Twenty minutes," he called, "and you may do your worst!"

His own room was a welter of people who wanted to see him. There were relatives of Logan's who wished to speak with the Border lord; Patrick was there, talking to Murray. Bothwell spent about five minutes with some of the lesser Border nobility, young men who hung on his words and watched every gesture while his riding clothes went off. Then he shooed them out. He could talk to Murray while he was being shaved.

"Murray, my wits tell me you're in danger. You told me you are ready to make a truce with Maitland and Huntly. God's blood, sir, it's nothing but a newfangled kind of rat trap! Now—"

"What suit do you wish, my lord?" asked one servant desperately.

"Any one," snapped Bothwell. "Just dress me. Murray, you're a fool to trust Maitland. And keep that soap out of my mouth, dolt. You're a flap-eared ass to trust Maitland. What do you say, sir?" he asked Patrick.

Patrick laughed. "Keep your mouth closed, Francis; your tongue will get cut off. Murray knows I think the same as you, my lord. I've warned him, and if he pays no heed to me—"

"Patrick's the canniest man in Scotland. Aren't you, sir? You see, he admits it, the braggart. Murray, you must promise us you'll take ordinary precautions. Keep that soap out of my mouth!"

Murray smiled at him affectionately. "Francis, be quiet a moment while I talk. I've no wish to feud with Maitland, or Huntly. They know my stand is with you, but they also know I won't hurt them."

Bothwell was silent. He looked up at Murray's open countenance; he was silent long enough to have his face dried and his hair brushed. Then he said slowly, "I fear you will go like a lamb to the slaughter, Murray, if you persist in thinking that all men are as open and ingenuous as you are."

Patrick said, "I could not have put it any better. I am of the same opinion, sir."

Murray insisted stubbornly, "I want to make peace with them! Francis, I've told them the truth!"

"You want to make peace? But have you thought what they want? Have you?"

Murray sighed. "If I could sign a truce with them, it would help you. But I'll promise you I'll stay away from Edinburgh. I'll keep to the country for a while."

Bothwell stood up. "And see that you have more than adequate guards. You've lifted a weight from my shoulders. Promise me you'll stay at Downe, you'll be safe there. Not at Donibristle, but at your castle at Downe."

Patrick repeated that. "Not Donibristle; it's too near Edinburgh." He was at the door with Murray, and Bothwell was left alone. He shrugged into his coat, scrutinized his hair as his doublet was being buttoned, looked at the clock. Just twenty minutes had passed and he was finished. His man straightened up, eyed his master as though he were a small boy he had just dressed, and seemed to decide that his choice of suit had been correct. He drew a white letter from an inner pocket.

"This message came for you, my lord. I didn't give it to you till the other gentlemen had gone."

Bothwell frowned. He ripped open the one sheet and read the few words, still frowning. Then he threw the letter onto the fire, and watched it burn. When it was nothing but ashes, he left the room.

"My lassie, it was a long twenty minutes." He closed the door behind him softly.

Anne was bundled up in a robe, sitting in front of her table. Her room was small; it was a turret room and from its windows high above the water the sound of the winter surf was plain to be heard. Anne pointed to the white velvet and fur gown carefully laid on a chair before the fire to warm. "I'm almost dressed, my lord," she said, her eyes meeting his in the mirror.

Bothwell said solemnly, "I did not expect to find you naked."

"Marie is doing my hair," Anne remarked, as though she hadn't heard him.

He came to stand right behind her. "If you leave your hair that way, you'll have time to talk with me."

"Leave it down?" asked Anne.

"I can put a pearl-embroidered net over it, mistress," said Marie helpfully.

"You find the net, Marie," ordered Bothwell.

"Don't leave, Marie! I want my hair up!"

"Mistress Anne wants what I want. You may leave now, Marie."

Anne jumped to her feet and faced him. She was about to speak when he said slowly, "Twenty minutes since I've seen you and you are always more fair than I remember. I brought you a gift to wear tonight, lassie." He put his hand in his pocket and drew forth a short chain crusted with stones.

"Diamonds!" said Anne unbelievingly. She didn't take it from him. "Oh, my lord, you should not have brought it!"

He frowned; his dark brows drew together and he tossed the piece of jewelry on her table, where it lay curled up and glittering. "It's not a bribe," he said curtly. He turned from her, walking over to the window, looking out over the sea. He stood there for about a minute before he faced her again. "Wear it or not, it's yours. However, you mistake me, mistress, if you think I consider that gift payment for possession of you."

Anne said, "My lord, Francis—" She stopped. Across the room she met his eyes. "I have never used your name before. Who christened you Francis?"

"The Queen," he said. "My godmother, Queen Mary. But since that time my fortunes have changed, you know."

He seemed so far away. "What do you mean?" she asked.

"You know my meaning. I'm a thief, lass. I stole that chain, or rather it was a ransom payment. Don't look at me so; I'm not going to make love to you."

"Are you not?"

"No, it's time for dining. You may call Marie."

Anne picked up the diamond chain; she put it on, and even though she was thinking how much she loved him, for a moment she forgot everything except that the necklace was magnificently extravagant. Her eyes shone. Then she said stiffly, "You did not let me thank you properly." Suddenly she picked up her skirts and ran to him, burying her head in his shoulder. "Please hold me, my love; don't go away from me!"

"Lambie, my own lassie, I've longed for you, too. Nights at Hermitage I've damned my lack of you." His arms were around her. "And this time I won't leave you for long hours—tonight and tomorrow and the next night."

"You brought me this." She fingered the chain, the cool stones against her throat. "I'll call Marie now, my lord. You are hungry, aren't you? You are so big, Francis. Do you remember the first time we ate together? You like mustard."

"I remember nothing but kilts. I swear I tasted nothing but knees."

"I've only five minutes," said Anne happily. "I'll have to leave my hair this way. Do you truly like it?"

"It's easier to pull."

"And you don't need to turn your back, my lord. I'm all covered."

Bothwell turned his head to look at her, in her petticoat and blouse. He smiled. "I was looking at the sea, Anne. Cursed be he who dubs me gallant!"

Anne thought that the dining hall at Fastcastle looked like a woodsy fairyland. The huge oblong room was decorated with great bunches of holly, shining ivy, and clusters of mistletoe, its gray berries gleaming waxily. Great fires blazed on the hearth, and on the long tables was a profusion of food, more food than Anne had ever seen before in one place.

In traditional fashion, the great boar's head on its massive silver platter dominated the table, but there were fat stuffed and roasted capons, wild fowl, trussed neatly, steaming from the ovens, and venison that had turned on a spit over the kitchen hearth. There were pies, innumerable pies whose flaky crusts, when pierced, emitted a wonderful aroma. One pie was so big that it required a special cart and was pulled into the hall by two servingmen. But what fascinated Anne the most was the peacock, intact with its feathers and with a brandy-soaked blazing sponge in its gilded beak. Fastcastle, famous for hospitality, outdid itself on Christmas.

Anne sat near the head of the table, because Bothwell wanted her beside him, and because he was entitled to the place to the right of his host on account of rank. Dinner lasted a long, long time. The minstrels sang the old carols; the Yule log, stripped of its bark, was dragged in, and Bothwell got up to help pull it into the room, because, as he told Anne, "It was lucky."

After dinner servants cleared away the tables, making room for the games and dancing. "How you ate," Anne whispered to Bothwell. "You ate for hours. It's late, my lord."

He seemed to be paying no attention to her. "Lassie, I'm going to leave you with Patrick, for a few minutes." The musicians had begun the opening bars of a stately dance, and Anne watched Bothwell cross the room to Margaret Vinstar. She saw him bow formally, and ask her to dance. Anne turned her back. She faced Patrick, and over his shoulder she recognized the face of another man. Patrick was talking to the man who had brought her to Fastcastle.

"Where did you get this, Gibson?" He tapped his coat, and paper crinkled underneath it.

"From a wench at Mrs. Black's." Gibson grinned, remembering.

"Christ's blood," swore Patrick. "She went there?"

"Who went where?" asked Anne interestedly.

"Nobody," answered Patrick. He started away, and Anne called, "Where are you going, sir?"

He turned back to her; he had the oddest expression of delight and disbelief on his face and she stared up at him. "Where are you going?" she repeated.

"I have an appointment."

"Now?"

"No, Anne, not now, but I've not got too much time to get to Berwick."

She studied his face. "You are going to Berwick, for an assignation?"

He nodded and she said firmly, "I don't believe you. You are going for some other reason."

He thought of Alan Campbell. It was true he had meant to leave early tomorrow morning, to continue his search for the murdered Mr. Campbell's son. But he had told her the truth; he was leaving now because Gibson had brought him a letter. He snapped at her, "Don't question me! I've told you the reason for my trip and it's my only reason! How many times must I warn you that meddling is dangerous!"

He left her standing alone. The music was playing, there was noise and laughter, and the flames leaped high in the fireplace. She stood alone, and way across the room she could see the top of Bothwell's head. Quick irrational fear took her; they should all be together, laughing. Patrick was angry with her; Bothwell was dancing with someone else. And Murray. Where was Murray? She moved closer to the fireplace and held out her hands to the warmth. She was alone and she was afraid.

Chapter Fifteen

"You received my message, my lord?" Margaret Vinstar's voice was low. "I asked you to come to my chamber."

"It is better thus, madam." Bothwell swung her around. "It is better to talk while we're dancing—and no one can hear."

"This is your dance." She glanced up at him. "This is named for you, the 'Gay Galliard.' "

He didn't smile; instead he frowned a little. "What have you to tell me, madam, that is so important that you should want me to risk your reputation?"

She lowered her eyes, tapped out a step in response to his. She said slowly, "When James had me confined to my rooms, after I helped Logie to escape—" She paused to take an intricate step.

Bothwell said, "I shall always admire your courage."

She smiled up at him. She was wearing her most daring gown; its white starched ruff and her high coiffed hair emphasized the low cut bodice. "I had you, my lord, to aid me. I knew you were there."

"You shall have all the credit; it rightfully belongs to you. Now madam, what have you to tell me?"

Her mouth set. "When I was confined to my rooms, Maitland came to see me. Lord Murray is not safe, sir. I cannot tell you more than that. Only that I know he is not safe, and that the King himself may not be innocent of plotting."

Bothwell almost stopped dancing; he held her so that he could look into her eyes. "You know that?"

"Ah, no, my lord. I cannot tell you more because I know no more. I only suspect."

"You contradict yourself," he said curtly.

"I did not so intend." She smiled at him. " 'Tis only a woman's way of wording, my lord. I did say I knew, but I only sensed danger—to Lord Murray."

"Pardon me, madam," Bothwell said formally. Suddenly he ran his eyes over her from head to toe. "You love Logie?" he asked bluntly.

Her attitude changed imperceptibly. "I risked a good deal for him," she reminded him.

Bothwell nodded his head impersonally. "He's a good lad. Madam, I thank you for what you have done. I thank you for your warning. You see it was best this way, that we should talk without my endangering your good name."

"It was most thoughtful of you, my lord." The dance was coming to an end.

"It was my privilege." Bothwell spied Patrick almost at the door, talking to someone. Patrick beckoned, and he waited for Bothwell to come over with Margaret. Then he said without preamble, "Francis, I'm borrowing that alarm clock of yours."

Bothwell said to Margaret, "Sir Patrick had the clock sent to me from France. I must show it to you someday. Or you may have it over night, and let it tell you when to get up in the morning." He had stepped back from her a little, and while he talked, he raised one eyebrow at Patrick and pointed one finger at Margaret.

Patrick's eyes swept her briefly. "Not tonight," he said, and the faintest grin went over Bothwell's face. "Not tonight," Patrick repeated, "may you have the clock, madam. I need its wakening call tomorrow."

"It's yours, sir." Bothwell turned to Margaret. "I thank you for the dance, madam, and here is Lord Murray, wanting the same pleasure." Bothwell bowed, he turned his back, and Margaret said to Murray, "I fear Lord Bothwell anticipated you, sir."

Murray shook his handsome head. "I've been waiting for this honor, Margaret. You know very well I wanted this dance with you. I made a point of asking them to play it again."

"Did you?" Her smile was very genuine. "We always get praise for the 'Galliard,' don't we?"

"And there he goes," said Murray, as Bothwell passed them, and Margaret watched him go away toward Anne.

"I wanted to dance with you, too, my lord," Margaret said suddenly. "I carry a message from Her Majesty."

"You do? A message for me?"

"Ah, sir, first give me your word that not a syllable of it shall pass your lips. I have risked so much of late. It is a frightening thing to be a woman."

Murray remembered how calmly she had faced her King, after Logie's escape. "You have a man's courage in a woman's body. I swear on my oath that no one shall know what you tell me."

"I should not have asked you," she said softly. "I know you would never prove false. Her Majesty knows of your decision to end the feuding with Maitland. Her Majesty approves of it, my lord, because you will be able to be one of us again. Her Majesty needs all your aid!"

"I know that, madam."

Margaret looked over toward Bothwell, who was standing with Anne, laughing with her. She took her eyes away from them, lifted them to Murray's face, and she said, "Her Majesty thinks that if you would stay at Donibristle, at your country home, it would be near enough and yet just far enough for safety. That is all my message, my lord, except that my mistress sends her felicitations and begs you guard you and yours." She smiled a little, seeing Logie coming toward her. "My lord," she whispered hurriedly, "I cannot talk longer."

Murray said quickly, "I thank you, madam. Ah, Johnnie, are you usurping my lady?"

Logie clapped Murray on the back. "Leave my damsel to me," he said. "Would you dance, madam?"

She was watching Murray go away from her; she watched until she could see him no longer and she turned to Logie with a small smile. Abruptly, he kissed her. "Mistletoe," he whispered, releasing her and holding up one berry. He put the berry in her hand. "My payment," he said. "Would you have something to eat, or drink, or can we leave now?"

"No," she said coldly. "Later. Much later. Now I want some wine."

It was almost twelve. Logan was presiding over a barrel of oysters that had been dragged in; they were cracked and eaten raw, along with cold pheasant and bowls of steaming punch. Anne didn't like raw oysters, but Bothwell did; he and Logan were cracking shells with gusto. He filled a cup with the hot punch for her.

"Hold it to the flames, sweetheart," he whispered, "and when it reflects the light of the Yule log, you make a wish."

"Will it come true?" she asked, firmly believing it would. She held the cup close to the burning birch log, adding a silent prayer to the Virgin. "Why did you leave me, to dance with Margaret?"

He said quickly, "Only to thank her for what she had done for Logie. It was the very least I could do, lassie."

"She is very clever," said Anne. "She doesn't buy her hair dye, she makes it herself."

Bothwell burst out laughing. "I'd as lief be bit by a dog as scratched by you, kitten."

"I wanted to dance the 'Gay Galliard' with you," she said. "I felt so alone. I was afraid."

"Afraid?" He frowned, puzzled. "There is nothing to be afraid of, Annie, my bonnie Annie." He had been listening to the sound of the surf with nostalgic ears. "Let's go outside! Let's get you some breeks and boots. Let's go outside!"

From across the room Andrew Ker launched a painted bauble. It flew over the heads of the dancers and Bothwell caught it neatly. "Come on, Ker," he shouted. "We'll play ball! Outside!"

Only the hardiest wanted to venture out into the night. It was a wild night; when the moon did appear through the scudding clouds, its pale light only made the sky and sea more ominous. In back of them the bulk of Fastcastle rose almost at the water's edge and the huge rocks against which the sea churned were crusted with blobs of ice that the waves tore loose when they crashed against the shore.

The tide was high, and Anne, in her breeches and boots, felt very small as she stood looking over the North Sea and heard the thunder of the winter surf. She began to run; it was the only way to keep warm, and she ran with the rest, the painted ball going from one person to the next, flying high, now caught by the wind, now scampering along as it eluded someone's frozen fingers.

The ball was coming in her direction, and she darted forward to catch it, almost losing her balance on the slippery rocks. "It went into the water," she shouted, scrambling down a big rock after it, but a wave tossed it high, and it was caught in the current. She kept her eyes on the floating bauble and began to run parallel with it. The waves lifted it; the incoming tide brought it toward her on the frothy crest of a wave. "Here it comes," she cried.

Recklessly she stepped into the water, it foamed around her boots and she leaned down to snatch it from the white water when Bothwell jumped down beside her. "Who got it?" he teased, reaching out one arm; he poised the ball in his hand for a minute, well up out of her reach, and then sent it flying back to one of the men.

"Thief!" She stood with the water swirling around her feet, looking up into his dark face. The moon came out from behind the clouds for a brief second; the wind whipped her hair around her face and the sea wind sent the tingling blood through her body. The moon disappeared, the water turned black and menacing, and she felt herself swung up in his arms, like a piece of Viking booty, like the captured haul from the deck of a captured ship.

Part Three

Chapter Sixteen

IT BEGAN to snow the next morning a little before nine. Patrick was five minutes early, so that by the time the back door opened and Janet came out, his shoulders and helmet were powdered with snow. For a second she stood unbelieving on her side of the garden gate.

"You came!" she whispered.

He swung the gate open. "I got your message."

She was wrapped up in a heavy unfurred cape; he could see only her green eyes and her dark brows. The whirling snow obscured the house from them and they stood alone in a small white world. "It's been six months," he said. "Six months since I've seen you. I didn't expect your letter."

"I know you didn't. But I tried to find you for so long. Ever since I came back from Caithness."

"We can't talk here. You'll freeze." He put his arm around her, drawing her down the path to the street. "I've rented a room at one of the inns."

She made no protest; she let him lift her onto his horse. Vaguely she noticed that there were two men with him; the beat of their horses' hoofs coming behind was deadened by snow. "It's not far," he said. "Don't talk till we get there." He knew she was uncertain, that she didn't know what to say to him. He drew rein in front of a tavern and he set her on the ground. "This way, Janet." He took her in a side entrance and up a narrow stair, into a room where a fire was burning.

"Come over by the hearth," he continued, pushing back her hood and dusting the snow from her shoulders. "You'll be warm in a minute. If you're not, I'll put you in the bed." He smiled, and poured a cup of wine from the jug on the table. "Here, drink this."

She took it obediently, looking up at him. "Oh, sir," she said suddenly, "I can't believe you're real!"

"Can you not?" He took off his helmet, threw his cloak over a chair. "There are many ways I could convince you," he said happily and smiled at her. "I feel very real. And I've been up since four, mistress, riding, and renting rooms, and bullying landlords into big fires. Have you eaten breakfast?"

"You're hungry," she said. "I've kept you from eating."

"I'll order food in a minute." He paused, taking in her face. "I'm forgetting things, looking at you. I told Gibson to order food sent up."

"He was the one who brought my letter. He truly brought it to you! I was so afraid he would forget!"

"I paid him well," Patrick said. "Oh, Janet, what am I talking about? What are we talking about?"

She put the cup of wine down so sharply that it spilled. "I don't know, sir," she said, her eyes filling with tears. "I love you," she whispered, "and sometimes I thought I'd never see you again."

"My darling." He gathered her up cloak and all. "My honey love." He smoothed her hair back and kissed her cool cheek and the tip of her ear. "Wee one, I love you, too. Don't cry."

Janet wiped her eyes with her hand; she smiled. "I wish you'd kiss me," she said. "You never did but once."

"An oversight on my part," he said. "But I have designs, madam, never doubt it." He kissed her, then he lifted his head. "So you remember my first kiss, do you?"

She nodded solemnly and he grinned. "Come here again, mistress, and let me show you something. God's truth, you're an innocent wench and not much good to a man yet. Now say 'I love you.' "

Janet began, "I lo— you're teasing me," she said accusingly. "I won't say it!" She jumped away from him.

"My arms are too long for you," he jibed, catching her wrist. "You went from the frying pan into the fire and back again. Now tell me you love me."

"I—won't—say—" There was a long silence during which Patrick paid no attention to the knock on the door. Finally he let her go; he walked over to the door and before he opened it he said gravely, "You're a bright lass; you learn."

Janet started to reply and he held up his hand warningly. "Not in the presence of the landlord, please, madam. Control your emotions." He laughed, and took the tray from the man at the door, brought it back to the table and pulled up a chair for himself. "I'm starving," he announced.

Janet sat down opposite him, watching him lovingly. "I'll serve you, sir," she said happily. She fixed his plate and handed it to him. Then she leaned her chin on her hand. "Do you mean to infer that after one kiss, my lessons are ended?"

He said, "I'm eating, madam. Don't disturb me."

"How long is it between lessons?"

"About fifteen minutes. Can't you wait?"

"No," said Janet. She got up and came around to him.

"Five minutes, then," he said, fending her off with one arm. "I've no time for lovemaking now. I've a deal to do this morning, madam."

"One minute," she said laughing. She took off her cloak and laid it on top of his. "Do you dare take another mouthful?"

He pulled her down on his lap. "Sweetheart," he whispered, "you lost your shyness, didn't you? What did you think I was going to do—eat you?"

"I hadn't seen you for so long. I thought perhaps you had forgot me. You are very different from me, sir."

"Faith, I hope so," said Patrick, taking a big mouthful of meat.

Janet said seriously, "I wasn't referring to physical differences. His Majesty calls you by your given name."

"I don't want to marry James."

"But sir—why I don't even know how to order food for a house like yours!"

"The problem staggers me," said Patrick. "Is it that if you have Jamie for dinner he won't get enough to eat?"

"Oh," said Janet, horror-stricken. "Would we have to ask His Majesty to dinner?"

"We don't ask, lass. Sometimes Jamie just arrives."

"I shouldn't dream of marrying you," she said softly. "It is wild and impractical and presumptuous of me, my father says. And it is true."

"Nonsense."

"Why do you love me?" she asked. "Why do you have your hair cut so short? If I had curls, I'd let them grow."

"No," said Patrick. "I refuse. Not even for you." He pushed his plate aside, and took her face in his hands. "I love you, sweetheart. You're such a little wench and you're all mine. Now tell me, if I leave you for a while will you be frightened here? It's perfectly safe."

"Leave me?" she asked. "Why, sir?"

"I had business in Berwick, but it's not pressing. I can let that rest for a few days. But I want to find a preacher, Janet, and I want to send Gibson for the keys of Bothwell's house in Jedburgh. I can take you there tonight."

"Tonight?"

"Today, I should have said," he explained. "As soon as possible, with this snow. Better that we travel this morning. We'll be alone at Jedburgh; it's the best place."

Janet said uncertainly, "I can't stay with you, sir. I must go back soon."

"What?" He drew his brows together. "What do you mean?"

"I can't stay now, sir, truly I can't!"

"Devil take it, why can't you? What is this prattle?"

"Not prattle. It is impossible for me to run away with you.

I couldn't do that to my father, sir. He trusts me. I couldn't hurt him that way."

His anger flared up. He had had everything planned concisely. "Then suppose you explain why you went to such a place as Edwina Black's, if it were for the sole purpose of breakfasting with me!"

Janet stood up. "I can't heed only your and my desires! I can't forswear my word and loyalties to my parent!"

He said curtly, "Suppose you tell me why you came."

"I came to ask you if you would see my father, and ask him again."

"Ask him again? And how many times must I offer marriage to you? How many times must I do you the honor of offering you my name?" He got to his feet and looked down at her angrily. "Janet, come with me now! I can arrange it! Marry me today!"

"I cannot," she said desperately. The image of her father was so close. What would he think if he knew she was here with Patrick, now? "He trusts me," she repeated stubbornly. "I can't break faith with him."

"You love me," said Patrick. "Every six months you'll come and tell me so, is that it?"

He turned away, and then swung back to her, seizing her arms in a strong grip. "Christ's blood, why don't you do as I say? Why must you hold me off for months? I don't come when women whistle; it's time you learned it!"

"You don't want me then?" Her voice was low.

"I want you now. Now or not at all." He let go of her arms; it was impossible that he couldn't make her do what he wanted. He would force her to. "You come with me today, or not at all."

She wanted to burst into tears; she wanted to plead with him, to make him understand. But her stubborn Scottish pride didn't permit her. "I cannot do wrong because you desire it," she said quietly. She said nothing else.

He exclaimed incredulously, "You refuse? You little fool, you refuse me?"

"Aye," said Janet, turning away to get her cloak, and he watched her put it on. "You need not escort me, sir. It is only a little way."

He nodded. He opened the door for her.

"I'll be here for an hour," he said, "if you should reconsider."

She didn't answer him. She pulled her hood over her head and went down the steps, finding the little door. Outside, the snow blew in her face and froze on her lashes, and she put her hand over her eyes as she walked along. It was not far; by the time she reached home she was ready to go back to him. It was the only way. She would tell her father and go right back. She would marry him now. She knew she would always have to give in to him; she even understood she had wrung a concession from him when he had given her an extra hour to reconsider. She shook the snow off her cape and entered the house. Her uncle met her in the hall.

"Where have you been, Janet?" His voice was sharp. "Your father's taken sick again."

"Sick?" She gazed up at her uncle. "My father's sick?" she asked, her mouth trembling.

"It's the old sickness, my dear," he said gently, regretting his first tart question. "We're bringing him down by the fire. Your aunt's fixing a couch; it's warmer down here. You can help her, Janet. But don't cry, my dear. Do not worry."

"Do not worry?" She barely spoke the words.

Her uncle was a very devout man. "All will be well, Janet, if we look to God. If we do our duties, our rewards will come. You should pray to God, Janet."

"Pray?" she said. "And would God hear you if all you wanted was a stubborn man with thick curly hair?" She whirled from him and ran to the kitchen, because she was afraid he might slap her, and she deserved it, for such blasphemy. How could she think such things when her father was sick again? "Oh, Lord," she prayed, "forgive me, and don't let him die." She sat on the edge of a kitchen stool and let herself go into a storm of weeping, and, two blocks away, Patrick picked up his cloak from the chair, flung it over his shoulders, and went down into the common room.

Chapter Seventeen

Snow fell heavily the next day and during the night. It was still snowing when Patrick left a mean lodging in Berwickshire, stepping out into the darkness of the winter morning. It was snowing and very cold, with a whistling wind off the sea, and the noise of the wind around the turret room awakened Anne early in the morning.

The wind came from the north; it came across the deep troughs and the heady crests of icy waves. It shook the small windowpanes, flung snow against the walls of Fastcastle, and whined around the tower standing high above the angry surf. The room was barely gray with light; within the curtained bed Anne could see only the outline of Bothwell's dark head as he sprawled beside her deep in sleep. She stretched luxuriously. She reached out one foot and ran it along his bare leg, then she settled down comfortably under the featherbed.

Bothwell turned over. "Anne," he murmured sleepily, and threw one arm over her, pulling her close to him.

She lay in his arms; she was so happy. "Listen to the wind, sweetheart. It must be so cold outside." He didn't answer her, so she asked softly, "Are you asleep?"

"No."

"Oh, Francis," she whispered. "I love you, I love you."

When she woke the next time he was gone. The snow had stopped, the sun was out, and the clock on the table pointed to ten. Anne sat up in bed abruptly and called loudly for Marie.

"I put your clothes out," Marie said, as she pulled back the curtains.

Anne said fretfully, "When did his Lordship leave?"

"Over an hour ago, madam."

Anne pouted; she sat on the edge of the bed with her feet hanging over. "Did he not leave word when he was returning, Marie?"

"No, madam. Do you want your robe?"

"No," Anne cried vehemently. "I want to get dressed. Where can he be?" Ignoring Marie's help she was throwing on her clothes as fast as she could. "How could he leave me, the knave? Where can he be?"

"Here," said Bothwell, from the door.

"Oh," she said. "Oh, my lord, I thought you had—I was afraid—" She stopped; she looked across at him standing in the doorway, his brimmed hat cocked rakishly and a scarlet-lined riding cloak falling to his black boots. "You are not leaving, are you, sir?" she asked pleadingly.

"No, madam. Did you order breakfast for me?"

Marie interrupted hastily. "Aye, your Lordship." Bothwell made a motion to remove his cloak and Marie lifted it from his shoulders carefully. "I'll see to the food, sir."

"Good," said Bothwell. "Faith, what a humor we have this morning, mistress. What's the matter?"

"I thought you had left!" She was fastening her bodice with trembling fingers, for she knew that tomorrow he would leave her. "I was not thinking where you had gone." She was careful to make that explanation. "I was thinking you had left me without even a farewell kiss."

He grinned. "I'd not deny myself that pleasure, lassie. I was out, at the stables. I've made a sleigh for you."

She saw he was in a gay mood; she smiled too, radiantly. "Oh, that is wonderful," she said happily. "You mean you'll take me riding?"

"Aye, madam. I had the carpenters put a driver's seat on the sleigh; we piled furs in it, and hitched up two horses. Wait until you see it. You look lovely," he added. "I like that dress."

He hurried her through breakfast. Then he put her squirrel cape around her and they left the castle by a postern gate where the sleigh awaited, and emerged into a world that was dazzlingly bright. Anne blinked her eyes against the glare; she could feel the cold on her lips and cheeks even through her mask.

"The sleigh is heavenly," she said. The horses were sleek and small and dainty, and their escort was impressively armed; the men's mail coats gleamed.

Bothwell lifted her into the sleigh and got in beside her. "It is comfortable," he said. He was boyishly pleased and proud with the results of his innovations. "It was previously used to haul wood. You little blockhead," he added. "You smell good even with furs."

"They're perfumed," she explained, seriously. "With essence of rose and English pinks."

They were passing through a small town. They went under the shadow of a church, and ran smoothly over a bridge that spanned a stream so swift running that it defied the cold and only along its banks did the ice gather.

"We're traveling north," he said.

"Toward Edinburgh?" she asked, and for the first time she realized that their escort might be needed.

He smiled; her voice had been very doubtful. "There's no danger, Anne. We are traveling toward my own lands, in Midlothian. We're going to see my cousin, William Hepburn; he has a large farm some miles from here."

"Oh," she said. "I didn't know you had a cousin on the Hepburn side."

He smiled. "Willie's not legitimate, lambie, or I shouldn't have inherited. How do you like sleigh-riding?"

"It's heavenly," she said. "It is, truly. You are so clever, the things you think of." She pulled the furs up under her chin contentedly. They had topped another hill and in the valley Anne could see smoke rising from twin chimneys on a farmhouse lying in the hollow of the hill.

"That's Willie's farm," he said. "How far you can sce today."

In a little while they had drawn up front, the doors flew open, and Anne was standing in a small hall. She pulled off her mask, acknowledged the greetings of Willie Hepburn and his buxom wife, and was then shown into a room where a fire burned.

Willie's wife, Eliza, was properly impressed and flustered. She bustled about, offering wine to his Lordship, but Anne didn't like her. "Ten years ago she was pretty," Anne thought, "and now she is a jealous old gossip." Anne refused wine; she stood near the fire, keeping her cloak on, for Eliza's eyes made her increasingly uncomfortable.

Bothwell was talking to his cousin. He was explaining, with gestures and gusto and trips to the window, just how he had had the sleigh made. There was a resemblance between the two men. Willie was listening eagerly, and nodding his head; Anne was sure he would fix up a sleigh as soon as they left. Bothwell suddenly bowed to Anne and excused himself; he left the room and Anne was alone with Willie and his wife. She endured them for a few minutes. She removed her cape, and Eliza's eyes were sharper than ever as they took in Anne's figure in the tiny jacket with its padded shoulders and the full velvet skirt. Under her stare Anne moved to a chair, her fingers playing with her silver-handled fan. She dropped that and took up the looking glass that hung from her waist, casually inspecting herself, pushing back a curl that had escaped the smooth pompadour. Willie stared too, now, and no one said a word. Finally Anne stood up, catching her cape.

"I shall join Lord Bothwell," she announced, going to the door.

Willie jumped to his feet; he got to the door first, opening it for her. "I'll show you the way, madam," he offered, smiling.

Anne was about to thank him when Eliza's voice sounded from behind them. "She can find the way, Willie. Up the steps and the first door to the left."

Anne turned, throwing Eliza a scathing look, and Eliza planted her hands on her hips and stared back. She did not wait until the door was closed; she wanted to make certain Anne would hear her. "I'll have her brat before the year's out, Willie! Mark my words!"

Anne stood out in the hall. She pretended she hadn't heard Eliza, and her heels clicked evenly as she went upstairs, but someday Eliza would rue those words. She knocked on the first door to the left.

"Come in," called Bothwell.

"Oh," said Anne. Her voice was tender and a little frightened, suddenly, but Bothwell didn't notice. He got up, with the little girl who had been sitting in his lap still in his arms, and he set her on her feet gently.

"This is my daughter, madam," he said, smiling down at the blonde head of a six-year-old girl. "My daughter, Janie. Mistress Galbraith."

Janie curtsied obediently, but her dark eyes were stormy; she didn't like this intrusion. "Daddy was telling me a story," she said, her brows drawn together.

"And he'll not stop telling the story," Anne replied quickly, tenderly, for Janie had frowned exactly as her father did. "We'll both listen," Anne went on. She motioned Bothwell to sit down as she picked Janie up and set her on his lap. "I'll sit here and listen."

Janie settled back into her father's arms contentedly and for a few minutes the story continued. Then Janie began to lose interest. She stared at Anne and finally she smiled. "Your dress is pretty," she said.

"Oh, thank you," said Anne. "Do you like red?"

Janie nodded vigorously. "Very much," she said and fell silent.

Bothwell smiled. "Do you want to hear this story, my bairn, or do you want to talk to the bonnie lady?"

She had one arm around his neck. "She *is* bonnie," she murmured, and threw Anne a delighted look. "My father brought me a new dress," she offered next. "And he brought me a little mare to ride."

"He did? Would you like to show me the dress?"

Janie slipped down from Bothwell's arms. "I'll show you," she said eagerly and scampered over to the bed. "You see?" She held up a red dress. "Mine is red too. And this is the overdress," she continued, holding up the matching overdress that resembled a fitted coat.

"It's beautiful," said Anne, getting up and inspecting the dress carefully, exclaiming at it.

Janie laid the dress back on the bed. "Last week Daddy brought me a puppy." She climbed back on Bothwell's lap, inspecting Anne from that vantage point.

Bothwell kissed the top of her head; his eyes asked Anne if she didn't think his daughter was perfect. "Now would you like to hear the rest of the story?"

"Please, my lord." She settled down in his arms, and after the story was finished, Bothwell wanted to see her writing. He had to hear her latest Bible psalm, and finally he and Anne had to inspect carefully the piece of embroidery on which she had been working. Two hours had passed so quickly that Anne was surprised when Bothwell said reluctantly that they must go.

"Oh," said Janie; she pouted a little, but she was very well behaved. "But you'll come back next week?"

"Of course, sweetheart," he said, swinging her high up in the air. "Of course I'll be back soon."

Janie transferred her gaze to Anne. "Will you come?" she asked, suddenly.

Anne said, "Could I have a kiss, too?" She dropped to her knees and hugged Janie. "Why, I'll tell you what," she went on, trying to keep her voice even and shut out the memory of Eliza's venomous prediction, "I almost forgot to give you the present I brought for you." She unfastened the cord around her waist and held that and its glittering toy mirror out to Janie. "I'll put it on you," she added, her fingers busy as she tied the cord around Janie's waist.

Janie was delighted. "Daddy would never think of a present like this," she announced; then she said quickly, defending him, "But he gave me this ring."

"Sometime," Anne said, "perhaps your father would let you come and visit me, if you would like to."

Janie's face was wreathed in smiles. "Oh, I would. I would truly. I'd be charmed, madam."

Bothwell kissed her goodbye. Anne fastened her mask and left without waiting for him. She stepped out by herself, drawing her cape close around her, letting the driver help her into the sleigh.

Bothwell appeared in a minute, looking slightly surprised at her sudden leave-taking, but he said nothing; he climbed in beside her and they began the return journey. The sun had disappeared, the landscape was gray and white; it was colder, and Anne shivered beneath the heavy robes.

"You're cold, lambie," he said solicitously, leaning over her to tuck in the fur rugs. He took both her hands in his under the robes. "Better?" he asked.

"Aye, my lord. Your daughter is perfect. Tell me who her mother was."

"There is an old custom of handfasting, here in the Borders," he said slowly. "You meet at the Eskdale fair; then for a year, you live together as man and wife. If at the end of the year, you wish to separate, that is permissible; otherwise you are regarded as married. Her name was Mary." He could see her face as clearly, in a sudden flash of memory, as it had been the time he had last seen her.

Anne was warned by his tone of voice but she went on heedlessly. "Did her mother die?" she asked.

"Aye." He frowned.

"How?"

"In childbed."

"But I do not think that—"

He interrupted. "We'll talk no further about it, mistress."

Anne turned her head to look up at his face. He was annoyed, very much annoyed, and suddenly she realized that now her whole world was bounded by him, and him alone. She took off her mask and leaned her head back against his shoulder. She put her hand up to his face and ran her finger along his brow. "Are you angry with me, my lord? But let me have your daughter after the New Year. I'd keep her in Edinburgh with me."

"It might be possible," he conceded.

Anne smiled. "I love you," she whispered. "And tomorrow you will be gone. Tomorrow night, I'll not sleep in your arms."

Under the robe his hands turned her to face him; regardless of the escort he began to kiss her. It seemed to him that he would never slake his thirst for her. "I must go tomorrow, lassie," he muttered.

"Let me go with you, then," she said. "Let me go with you."

He looked down at her face; she closed her eyes and he kissed the bluish lids. "No, Anne. No."

"But why not, my lord? Why?"

He tucked one arm around her and said lightly, "Lambie, I'm an outlaw. D'ye know anything about me, lass? I've no money. My castle of Crichton is mortgaged to the hilt; Hailes Castle—well, I could probably raise a thousand pounds on Hailes still, if I throw in the town." He grinned. "I've no money but I'm worth something dead. Jamie would reward you if you would lead me to a rendezvous. Which you could do," he added ruefully. "But, lass, let me tell you true, ever since the first night I held you in my arms and stood there in the garden with you, ever since then I've looked at no other woman twice."

Anne said, "You were faithful to me?"

He smiled, his quick guilty smile. "I did not look at any other woman twice. Is that not sufficient loyalty?"

"Oh, I hate you," she said passionately. "It's better thus—that I never see you again!" She drew away from him, pushing against him with both hands.

"You're disarranging the rugs," he said, "and you're far from strong enough to push at me. Should we part now, mistress?"

"Dare you laugh at me?" She thrust out her lower lip, and he kissed her quickly.

"I shouldn't dare laugh," he assured her. "I think it best, too. Shall I leap from the sleigh and renounce you utterly? At once?"

Anne didn't answer and he went on. "Or shall I tell you that I'd like to make you a gift of a house in Morham?"

"A house?" she repeated incredulously.

"A country house, and it's not mortgaged." He smiled at her. "It was my grandmother's house—the country mansion of the Countess of Morham. I shouldn't do this," he said gravely. "And I mean it. I shouldn't do this but I will. You will have the house, no matter what, and I'll come whenever I can."

"Oh, Francis," she said happily.

He laughed at her delight. "But you'll not know, ever, when I'm coming, so let me warn you, mistress, to practice fidelity to your lord."

Anne lowered her lashes. "What would you do?" she asked.

"Never mind, wench. And never forget that I'm an outlaw."

She said suddenly, "It will be dangerous! Too dangerous!"

He shook his head. "You'll not worry over that, lassie. You'll leave that to me, always."

It was easy for her to believe in his invincibility. "May I go tomorrow?" she asked. "I didn't thank you, my lord," she added, "and you said you were poor."

He smiled. "I'll never expect you to understand the state of my finances. And you may go tomorrow. Now you listen to me, lambie. Can you write?"

"Of course," said Anne indignantly. "But not very well."

"Your accomplishments continue to amaze me. Now the house is staffed with servants, the land with tenant farmers. You will make a list, in your own handwriting, of what you need, and I'll have those needs sent from Crichton or Hailes. Second, you will have this escort, always." He waved his hand at the men who accompanied them. "And you'll have Gibson. I'll stock the stables, and the kennels, and the first time I come, I'll bring you a pair of staghounds. You may allow them the freedom of the house."

Anne said slowly, "Will I need an escort always?"

"It's wisest."

"If I go tomorrow, may I live there all the time, with Janie? And wait for you to come?"

"That wouldn't be wise. Not till spring, lassie. During the spring and summer your presence there would be less questioned."

Anne sighed. Silently she vowed she would live there. "Oh, we're back," she said regretfully, for Fastcastle loomed up ahead of them, and she could hear the roar of the waves and feel the sharpness of the sea wind. They rounded the castle, and stopped before the postern gate. The day was over; they could not be alone again for hours.

"Tonight," Bothwell said, before he left her, "I promised Logan I'd play cards. You leave earlier, will you, lambie?"

She nodded. "I know when you are getting restless. You begin to shift your feet and ask for another glass of wine."

Patrick didn't return for dinner; Logan told Anne during the meal that Patrick had sent word he might be very late, might even spend the night again in Berwick. After dinner she sat by the fire and watched the men gamble. She tried hard to keep the concentration off her face; she was so anxious that Bothwell win, and she couldn't understand how he could be so poor and yet have pockets filled with gold.

He concentrated on the game too; it seemed as though he hardly knew she was in the room. From her chair she watched him, never taking her eyes from his, listening for his ready laugh. She paid no heed to the other women, as they gossiped about clothes, scandals and servants; she and Margaret Vinstar sat side by side, and both said little.

At ten, Bothwell looked up from the table and caught her eye. She smiled, and she saw him cross his legs and move in his chair. Obediently, she stood up and made her excuses to Lady Logan. For thirty minutes more Bothwell stayed at the table, and Margaret watched him leave too. Her gray eyes followed him from the room, and then they shifted to Logie, who was busy with his cards.

" 'Snails," he said petulantly, "I've lost a fortune to the Border lord. I'll see if I can win some back from you, Murray." He filled his wine cup to the brim. "Francis walks off with the money, and the mistress Anne, too."

Margaret dropped her eyes to her lap; she smiled a little, but Murray frowned. "Hold your tongue, Logie," he said sharply.

"What?" asked Logie, annoyed.

"There's no call for your words, sir," said Murray, curtly. "You've drunk too much."

"Damn the knave who says I drink too much!" Logie stood up uncertainly.

"That's why you lost so heavily, sir," Margaret put in, deliberately irritating him. "Lord Bothwell stays sober while he plays, and takes the money from the wine-bibbing fools."

"And takes the wenches from the court gallants," said Logie, looking at Murray. "Strong arms instead of soft words." He grinned mockingly.

Murray stood up. "I asked you once to hold your peace!" His blue eyes were full of anger, and the room was very still.

Logie went over to the fireplace; he drained off his wine and set the cup down on the mantle. He looked over to Margaret. "It's the truth," he said to Murray, drunkenly earnest. "She's lain with him for these two nights!"

Murray took a step toward him, one hand on his sword, and Logan leaped to his feet. "Apologize, sir!" Murray's voice was low. "God's blood, you'd not say that to the Earl of Bothwell!"

Logan interrupted. "He's drunk, Murray." He motioned to two servants, who came to stand on either side of Logie. "You'll seek your room, sir," ordered Logan. "Now!"

Logie swayed; he leaned against one of the men. "I'll go," he said sullenly. "I've no wish to defend a whore's honor. Let Patrick Galbraith do that when he hears this little tale."

Chapter Eighteen

THE next day was so cloudy, so dark, that Anne had lighted candles to dispel the gloom. She stood by the small window, alternately watching the heavy mists roll in off the sea, and watching Marie pack.

"I have no patience," she said fretfully. "I do wish you'd hurry. You'll not be ready within the hour."

"But I will, madam." Carefully Marie laid a satin robe in the square trunk.

"He loves the sea," she said, leaning against the window. "He rode off along the sea route."

"You'll watch him ride off many times, mistress. Better that than watch him sail away."

"Aye," said Anne practically. "But like as not, someday he'll be off on a voyage. If you do not hasten, Marie, you'll not be ready! Gibson will be waiting on the hour."

"I'll be ready, madam." Marie said this for the tenth time.

They were both silent. Anne paced the room; she was all dressed for her trip, her trunks were almost packed, and her fur cape lay ready. "I think I'll have a little wine before I go," she said. "I'll pour it," she added, and she was standing by the fire sipping the Malmsey when the door flew open and the tall helmeted figure in the doorway banged it closed. Anne almost dropped her cup at the clatter.

"Patrick," she said, staring at him, for she had never seen him look the way he did. He was booted and spurred, and he was very wet, his feet heavy with mud and his mail coat shining with rain drops, but it was his face she stared at. "You intrude, sir," she said bravely, trying to keep her courage at the sight of him. "It is only customary to knock at a lady's door."

He bowed elaborately, taking off his helmet, but he said nothing to her; he spoke to Marie. "Leave us." His voice echoed in the small room, and Marie backed away from him in fear. Marie had a healthy respect for a gentleman's anger, and she closed the door gently, and put her ear to the keyhole carefully. "Little fool," she heard him say. There was a brief silence, and then his voice went on, lower. "Suppose you tell me whether or not the gossip with which I was regaled this morning is true!"

Anne's face went white. "It's true, sir," she blurted. "It's true, Patrick, and I beg you not to be angry with me! Patrick, if it please you—"

"I should have taken a whip to you, to teach you manners!" He caught her by the shoulders with hands that left their mark. Then abruptly he released her. "You are almost ready to go?" he asked. He glanced around the room, noting the filled trunk, not looking at her.

"Aye," she said.

"You will go straight to Threave." He turned now to watch her expression.

"I'm going to Morham," said Anne.

His smile was unpleasant. "You are going to Threave, if I must use force. I have a country house; the same cousin who brought you from France is living there. You will take up residence with her."

"I'm going to Morham," Anne repeated desperately.

He shook his head. "No, my dear, you are not. You are not going to your lover. You will stay in the country till this scandal dies, till I find you a husband who will overlook your generosity because of your so obvious charms. I want to warn you now that without me, you have nothing. I want to warn you now that my Edinburgh residence is closed to you."

Anne said wildly, "I need naught from you! I have a house,

and I am going to take Lord Bothwell's little daughter with me. And I do not need a town residence. I have rooms at the royal palace! Perhaps you've forgotten?"

He eyed her with amazement. "God's blood," he said. "You have rooms in the royal palace." He couldn't believe he had heard the words. "And I suppose you think that James will be glad to welcome not only Bothwell's whore, but his bastard daughter. Holy Jesus, mistress, have you lost your mind?"

"Aye," she sobbed. "What if I have? I love him, sir, I love him!"

In answer he walked across the room and picked up a small but heavy case. "And I'll keep this," he said mockingly, "so you'll not be inclined to disobey my orders."

Anne jumped to her feet and flung herself at him. "Give me that!" She grasped his arm in both her hands, digging her pointed nails into his hand. "Give it to me," she raged, struggling to pull the case from his grip.

He took both her wrists in one hand; she kicked at him, but he laughed at her efforts to hurt him, for his boots were heavy rawhide. Suddenly he gave her arm a twist that stood her straight and rigid; he pushed her back into her chair. Anne buried her face in her hands.

He stood over her; he had put his helmet on and he seemed immensely tall. He said, "You are the kind of woman who defies a man up to a certain point, and then collapses like a house of cards. You will do well to remember that you have no weapons against me. You will go straight to the country; I've made all arrangements for your trip. I shall expect to hear from you in about a month. Then it will be, 'Oh, Patrick, I'm so sorry; when can I come home?' " He picked up the case again and went to the door. "But it will be two months before I allow your return. In the meantime, you'll not try running away. It is very cold in the country now, and very lonely. They might not find your body before spring. You'd be an unlovely corpse by that time, mistress."

"He'll kill you for this!" she burst out at him. "Aye and I hope he does!"

Her words brought the image of Bothwell right into the room. Patrick stared down at her bent head; she was crying disconsolately and she was murmuring, "I love him." She raised her head, and she said pleadingly, "Let me keep the necklace he gave me. Let me keep that."

Patrick's hand tightened on the case of jewelry he held. His anger at Anne was suddenly swept away, and if he had been angry before, it was as nothing to the violent rage which filled him now. "I'll give it to him, myself!"

Anne stopped her crying instantly. She held out her hands to him; slowly she got to her feet. Her voice trembled. "I pray you, sir, I didn't mean what I said!"

"No?"

"You'll not fight with him! Oh, Patrick, you'll not fight, you and he! You'll kill each other!"

"Will we?" His eyes gleamed.

"Aye, you would. You might both die!"

"You'd find another man, quick enough." He turned from her; she ran to him, catching his arm, but he shook her off and shut the door with finality.

He took the same set of curving steps that Bothwell and Anne had used the day before, and emerged into the open by the gate. His men were waiting, and he swung up into the saddle without a word. He had a fresh horse and he spurred ahead of his riders, following the old sea route to Dunbar. With the sea to his right, he was riding into the north wind.

It was near dusk when he passed the ruins of Dunbar Castle. There the road turned from the sea, veering off toward Edinburgh. It was nearly dark when he approached Hailes, so that the bulky shape of Traprain Law, which rose like a humped whale in the center of the Hepburn lands, and the pile of Hailes Castle at its foot were one mass of snow and gray stone.

The castle was surrounded on three sides by a moat, and on the other side the lazy waters of the Tyne lapped at its walls. The road to Edinburgh ran right past; travelers had to splash their way across the river at the foot of the castle walls. It was the oldest castle of the Hepburns, having belonged to them for centuries, for the earliest titles in the Hepburn family had been those of the lordship of Hailes, and the surrounding land was their first land. Legend had it that a Hepburn had saved the governor of Dunbar Castle from a savage horse, and thus earned the first gift of land, and from this came the crest of the horse's head and neck bridles, and from this too, came the emphasis which the lords of Hailes, and later the Earls of Bothwell, put on their reputation as horsemen.

Patrick and his escort clattered into the courtyard; the great door opened, set as it was in nine feet of stone wall, and Patrick entered a hall that was lighted with flickering torches.

"Follow me, Gibson," he said sharply, and strode off down the hall to a big door. He flung it open; Gibson trailed him uncertainly into the room, and both men looked down at the top of Bothwell's head, as he lay on the floor with a cushion pushed under his elbow. He was shaking dice, talking to them.

"Come on, now," he said, and threw. He looked up at Patrick. "Put your money in, man," he invited, moving his legs.

Hercules was lying bulkily on his stomach, his chin in his hands; Captain Ormuiston and he both smiled at Patrick. Patrick hardly acknowledged their greetings; he was letting Gibson divest him of his wet mail, and suddenly Bothwell looked up again. His eyes fastened on Gibson, then they shifted slowly to Patrick's face. Bothwell didn't move. He said slowly, "Sir, how did you find the hunting in Berwickshire?"

Patrick said, "I found it good!"

"Ah. Then perhaps we should have a word together, alone, should we not?" Bothwell heaved himself to his feet; already he and Patrick had forgot there were other men in the room, but Bothwell didn't speak until they were alone. Then he said, his eyes never leaving Patrick's face, "How did Gibson get here?"

"I countermanded your orders! You scarce expected that, did you?" His hazel eyes were narrow and he was taking off his coat.

Bothwell took a step back. He was going to fight for his life in a few moments and he knew it well. But first he wanted to know one thing. "Which of my men told you, sir? 'Fore God, you tell me true, sir, or I'll hang every living one of them!"

"None of them," said Patrick thickly. He was thinking of Anne as he had left her; and he had come in and found Bothwell playing at dice! His voice was roughened with anger. "Since I have the honor to challenge you, my lord, which weapon do you choose?"

Bothwell was thinking of Anne, too. Only a few hours ago he had held her in his arms and promised that soon he would come to Morham. He had asked Patrick which of his men had given her away only because he had wanted to protect her. He took another step back from Patrick. He would not only have to fight for his life, but he would have to try not to inflict a mortal wound. He glanced down at his belt. "I have no dagger," he said. "I left it on the dining-table." He could see the knife clearly, as he had left it, on the table in a room down the hall; it had then been covered with blood from the rare beef. He shot one glance toward his table; there was a pair of dueling pistols in a box, but Patrick was too angry to notice them. Bothwell decided to test his anger.

"I'd prefer to use the rapier," he said mockingly.

Patrick's face whitened with rage. Although he'd been fencing for months, he was still far from the swordsman Bothwell was, and he was well aware that Bothwell knew it. "You whoreson coward," he snarled. "Your father's bastard blood shows up strong in you!"

Bothwell laughed at the insult. He drew the rapier from its sheath and put one thumb on the end of the shining blade; the length of steel quivered and arched itself between his hands. It was a murderous weapon, and Patrick already faced him with the same supple sword.

In that second Bothwell knew he couldn't fight. It was too dangerous. Patrick was too angry, too reckless; Bothwell had to think for both of them. And he had to think quickly. "I wager you a hundred pounds, sir," he said, jibingly, "that I'll not draw blood. Aye, why should I fight you?" There was one chance and he took it. He flung the rapier in his hand across the room; he hooked his thumbs in his belt and regarded Patrick.

"I'm going to give a call, sir, and have you put downstairs to cool your heels till your sanity returns!"

His words had just the effect he hoped for. Patrick took one step forward, sword in hand, toward the unarmed Bothwell; then Patrick stood stock still, his arm outstretched so that the point of the rapier was about three inches from the Earl's chest. "Try to call anyone!" Patrick tossed the weapon to one side and lunged at Bothwell with all the force of which he was capable. They crashed to the floor, taking a table with them.

They didn't hear the noise but in the hall a frightened servant scurried to fetch Hercules; in the hall there gathered quickly a small group of men who listened to the noises from behind the closed door. A particularly loud crash sounded as Hercules came running with Gibson and Ormuiston right behind him. He came to a dead stop and listened.

"God's foot," he whispered and turned to look at Gibson. "Man, what started this?"

Gibson grinned. "What always starts a fight? A wench."

"We cannot interrupt." Hercules slowly came to that decision.

Gibson was amused, and besides, he had taught Patrick the art of wrestling. "If you're thinking that little Jock had his back broken last week, I'd not let it worry me, Hercules. His Lordship and Sir Patrick are well-matched. Sir Patrick has learned how to fight; he wants to see how well he does."

But Patrick was not doing so well. Years of training were telling over months. Patrick's breath was short, and although he had inflicted heavy damage, he knew he couldn't last much longer. He grappled with Bothwell, close in, because he was afraid another blow would finish him. He succeeded in getting his foot behind Bothwell's, and again they went to the floor, locked together.

There was very little light now. The candles on the large table lay on the floor beside the overturned piece of furniture, and the tapers on the mantle were the only ones left burning. In a whirling medley of arms and legs they rolled over toward the fire, and as they struggled, each for a vantage point, there was no sound except their breathing. They wrestled silently, Patrick desperately, for he knew he was losing and he couldn't prevent it. He was lying on his back; Bothwell's shoulders pinned him down, and his right arm was caught and twisted in an iron grip. The taste of blood was in his mouth; the pain from his arm set the muscles stiff in his face. Bothwell tightened his grip mercilessly; he shifted his weight slightly and lifted his head, staring down at the face of his antagonist. "Will you surrender?" he muttered.

He left himself unguarded, for he had moved a bit, freeing Patrick's left arm. Viciously, Patrick brought up that arm in a blow that caught Bothwell under the chin and numbed Patrick's elbow by the force with which it struck. Bothwell slumped forward. Patrick felt his arm released, and he twisted away, but his arm was still pinned down by Bothwell's shoulder. Painfully Patrick extricated himself; he rolled over, his head on the floor, his body stretched out. He saw the edge of the table, the blackened ends of two candles, and his discarded sword. He licked the warm blood off his lips and closed his eyes. He slipped gently into unconsciousness.

Outside the door the sudden silence was startling. It was so complete a silence. Gingerly Hercules took hold of the latch; he opened the door a crack and peered in. By the light of the remaining candles and the low-burning fire, he saw both men lying amidst the wreckage of the room. Their faces were hidden, and there was no sound from the group of men who looked in. Without a word, Hercules closed the door. "We'll not go in yet," he said.

Gradually Patrick came back to consciousness. He shifted his body and turned his head, lifting it from the floor with some effort. Bothwell was still lying on his face, and while Patrick watched, his legs moved, he heaved his shoulders and struggled to a sitting position. Slowly Patrick sat up too; they sat opposite each other, their boots almost touching. Both of them looked down at the small space between their feet.

Bothwell said slowly, "Is your arm broken?"

"I think so," muttered Patrick, low.

"I heard no snap," said Bothwell, just as low. The blood dripped down onto his shirt. "You won your battle," he added, matter-of-factly.

Patrick didn't answer and Bothwell continued. "I wanted to apologize before but there was scant time. I should never have gone to Fastcastle; I should never have involved Anne; I should never have promised I'd meet her in Morham. There is only one amend I can make now. I shall not see her again. I think that there will be little scandal, sir, for what involves her up to this point is merely rumor."

"You did not attempt to deny it."

"No. Not to you. But to anyone else I stand ready to—" He stopped.

Patrick smiled a little. "You stand ready to defend her," he ended the sentence. He raised his head and looked at Bothwell. "Francis, there was only one way for me to fight and that was this way." This time it was Bothwell who was silent while Patrick talked. "I've never been in such a mad rage as I was tonight, when you threw that sword away. Did you not realize that I actually might have killed you?"

Bothwell's dark eyes shone with sudden laughter; he pointed one thumb at the fireplace poker. "I was standing right alongside of it, man," he said.

Patrick laughed. "Oh, that hurts. Francis, I'd like to campaign under you."

"Thanks," said Bothwell laconically. He picked up his coat and sat forward on his heels. "Let me see your arm." He felt along the bone. "It's not broken," he said, and deftly he knotted the sleeves of Patrick's doublet to make a rough sling. "Let it rest in that." He stood up, pulled a fur rug nearer the fire, threw on a few logs, and stretched out wearily. His chin ached, his whole head ached, and the ragged split under his chin stung badly. "What are you doing?" he asked Patrick.

Patrick was on the other side of the room. "I'm getting some whiskey and water," he said. His lips were swollen. He came back to the fire, lying down on his side because his arm hurt. "I couldn't bring water. Too much trouble. You pour the stuff, will you, Francis?" He sighed deeply.

Bothwell complied, filling the cups brimful, and Patrick swirled the liquor around in his mouth to take away the taste of blood. "I wish Alan Campbell could have told me a longer tale."

Bothwell set his cup down half empty. Suddenly he remembered that he had asked Patrick about his hunting in Berwickshire and Patrick had said it had been good. Bothwell said, "You found him, did you not? I used that ruse to get Hercules out of the room. What did you find out, sir?"

Patrick repeated, "I wish he could have told me more. He did speak with his father before the old man died, and this is what he said, 'I couldna write, son; I dinna ken what to do but what I did.' "

Bothwell frowned; he put his head down. "What does that mean?" he asked.

Patrick forgot how tired he was. "Why, I thought about it long. I think it means, or rather it implies, that he did something. It makes me think that somewhere in that kitchen is a message. Are you sure that there was nothing but the money in the crypt?"

"Crypt? Why do you always call it a crypt?"

Patrick filled the cups again. "It's a term. But if there was nothing in the wall, perhaps it is the hiding place itself which is the message!" He moved to sit up, and hurt his arm. "Do you see what I mean? He was highly paid for a midnight task. Perhaps in a room in an unknown castle, there is a wall with a crypt that corresponds to the one in Mrs. Campbell's kitchen! Perhaps, as hers was, it is two and a half feet off the ground, the third stone up from the fireplace! How else would Campbell leave a message? How else but in his own handiwork?"

Bothwell said wearily, "Would he have wit enough?"

Patrick considered that. "He had to hide the money from his wife's cupidity. I believe he slyly thought to fix in his own mind exactly where he had opened a wall, and later replaced a stone—because I think that's what he did—for someone, somewhere, in the dead of night, and in a castle that remains mysteriously unknown."

Bothwell put his head down again. "Morton knows something."

"Aye," said Patrick. He yawned. "Morton knows a deal about this."

"We'll see what he knows. Later."

"Aye, Francis." Patrick settled himself so his arm rested comfortably. He yawned again.

Hercules came into the room about midnight. The candles on the mantle were guttering, the whiskey jug was empty and so were the cups. Hercules threw a heavy rug over both sleeping men, he put more logs on the fire, and then he went softly out, closing the door behind him gently.

Chapter Nineteen

THE kitchen in which Janet Applegate worked was cold and drafty except very near the hearth. The first week that she had been home in Edinburgh had been a very cold week. She took the lid off a big black pot that hung over the fire and peered in at the stewing fowl. The water was bubbling, the broth was getting thick, and she replaced the lid, took off her apron and went to her father's door. She knocked.

"Come in, my dear." Master Applegate looked up at her affectionately as she came into the room. "Bishop Spottiswood and I have been talking."

"I heard you, father," Janet said.

"I've been brought up abreast of the news. I heard all about Sunday's sermons and their repercussions."

The Bishop sat up straight. "I told your father, Janet, that after the sermons, some of the preachers were summoned to Holyrood, and His Majesty asked them why they preached in favor of Lord Bothwell."

Janet's eyes widened. "What happened, sir?"

"One temerarious man pled that it was the spirit of God that had purposed his sermons. His Majesty was so enraged he could do naught but repeat, 'the spirit of God!' "

"You see, Janet, King James is dealing with not only a man, but a political and popular force. And his Borders."

The Bishop said pontifically, "All Teviotdale runs after him, too." He paused a moment. "And I put just those words into my history of Scotland. You know, one night early last April

—a Tuesday night it was—Lord Bothwell came to see me. I took him into my study. Ahem." The Bishop coughed. "I talked to him very frankly. I said, 'Your Lordship, you must beware of spending your youth in riotous living!' "

Master Applegate had heard this story before. "And two nights after that, he had—uh," he paused, and shot a glance at Janet, "we heard about his Lordship's flirtation with the Lady Ruthven."

Janet hid a smile, but the Bishop was not daunted. He went on. "But as I said to your father, these are troublous times. This week—in this week alone—we have witnessed a comet, which the vulgar call a 'fiery besom'; and hailstones the size of doves' eggs have rained down on our roofs. These are portents, my dear, perchance ominous ones. There are storms coming."

Janet thought of Patrick; she gazed at the Bishop as though he might tell her the future. "Storms?" she asked.

"This is the lull, before the thunder, I fear. Your father is one with me in thinking thus."

Janet said quickly, "I hope you are wrong, sir. Could it not be that these are natural phenomena? I have read of such. Eminent men believe 'tis absurd to fear portents. Do they not, sir?" she asked her father.

Master Applegate smiled. "Aye, Janet. I agree with Bishop Spottiswood because Lord Bothwell is also a natural phenomenon. A Scottish one, shall we put it? It is also natural that when His Majesty and Lord Bothwell battle there will be storms."

"Oh," said Janet. "But Lord Bothwell is so strongly placed." She put her faith in Bothwell completely. Patrick's safety lay with the man he called so easily, "Francis." She could hear him saying, "I'll ask Francis for the keys to his house in Jedburgh." Janet wondered what it looked like, and then she remembered that there was no time for dreaming now.

"I'll do my errands," she said. "I'd prefer to go now, sir, for your medicine." She gave one last look at her father before she went. He did seem better today; he hadn't coughed so much. But it was so cold. She tied a red plaid shawl over her head and went out into the bitter gray afternoon . . .

The short January days went by. One ran into another and hurried the month along to its close. On the Canongate the town houses of the Earl of Bothwell and Patrick Galbraith stood side by side, alone and shuttered. In the gardens, the branches of the pear and apple trees were limned sharply against the winter sky, and some days, when Janet walked by, the Edinburgh haar obscured even their outlines. Snow piled the walks and lay heavy on the bushes and the steeply sloping roofs, and farther south, in Liddesdale, Hermitage Burn idled along between snow-covered banks. Patrick stayed at the Hermitage, making but few brief trips during the month. He had followed Bothwell's example, and adopted a grayhound which followed him even to his bedroom at night and slept before the smoldering fire. This was the room where once Mary, Queen of Scots, had sat beside the bedside of James Hepburn, as he had lain wounded by the two-handed sword of little Jock Elliot, whose peel tower still stood solidly where Witterhope Burn met Hermitage Water. Patrick spent his days fencing in the huge paved hall, and teaching his hound the arts of the chase. He named him Lupa, and he had made a bet with Bothwell that Lupa would outgrow the Earl's own mammoth hound.

Bothwell himself was restless, and for him, moody. The thought of Murray coping with Huntly and Maitland continued to worry him. He felt far away even though he received news daily and a stream of adherents and visitors touched at the Hermitage, and very often stayed weeks. Night usually found him gambling, but dawn saw him up and out, and sometimes he would be gone for two or three days or more. He visited Bewcastle in England and stayed with the Captain of the English Marches; the next few days might see the two of them fighting. One time he traveled far north to see the Earl of Atholl. The trips he made by himself proved to him that he could roam the country with impunity. He never mentioned Anne; he never spoke her name, but Patrick watched his usually good-natured host turn restless and impatient, and on some days the soldiers of the garrison walked with care, for their lord's inflammable temper was something to be reckoned with. And Patrick watched with apprehension; among Bothwell's allies were the Ormuistons and the Kerrs, the Douglasses, and the rest of the lawless Border. Across the land the King moved from castle to castle in fear.

In Edinburgh there was strife and discontent. Maitland and the Queen were open enemies; the Earls of Logan and Atholl and Gowrie numbered themselves as friends and kinsmen of the outlawed Bothwell; the Master of Gray, Lord Ochiltree and the Duke of Lennox were in the same category, and the preachers of the Kirk inveighed every Sunday for their champion, Bothwell. Who else could drive the Catholic Huntly from his strong position at court?

In Edinburgh intrigue followed intrigue, and enemies on one day were friends the next. Huntly's friendship with Maitland was one of narrow suspicion, and the Court eyed it with misgivings and mistrust; no good could come of such unnatural allies. Spain and England both thrust interfering fingers into the affairs of Scotland, and behind closed doors agents of both countries wrote long letters to their sovereigns and paid out gold to the men with whom they dealt. From her southern throne Elizabeth watched the career of the Earl of Bothwell with a smile of satisfaction. The Border lord was the Protestant "lamb" and good luck to him. At the same time she wrote James: "And as for Bothwell! Jesu! Does any ever muse more than I that you can put up with such temerity!"

James took this with his customary sour silence. He knew very well that Elizabeth would employ Bothwell as an ally if suitable terms could be arranged, and was not his outlawed kinsman welcome on the English Marches? He implied this in his return letter. It was a game; between these monarchs there was little or no trust.

On the sixth of February Bothwell rode north with one hundred horsemen. Patrick had not liked to see him go; such an escort boded ill. But Patrick stayed at Hermitage until the next day. It was the seventh of February, 1592.

At Aberdour, on the coast of Fife, across the Firth of Forth from Edinburgh, the Earl of Murray was at his residence of

Donibristle, as part of his plan for his truce between himself and the Earl of Huntly. This was the day he was to meet Huntly, but when he arrived at the ferry he was told that His Majesty had ordered that no boats cross the Firth that day. Murray turned home, puzzled. He and his sheriff came back to the house which stood almost at the water's edge. His wife and his children were staying with him, and he and Lady Murray talked long that afternoon, speculating on the turn of events.

That morning, the Earl of Huntly set out on a hunting expedition of sixty men. From the palace windows James Stewart watched him go; from another window Maitland saw the last man ride out of sight, with slyly satisfied eyes. He turned from the window. "He is at Donibristle," he said.

Margaret Vinstar didn't move from her chair by the fire; she had not bothered to watch Huntly and his men clatter off. She frowned a little and said impatiently, "I had given Lord Murray the message on December twenty-fifth. It is now the seventh of February. More than six weeks have passed."

"The lapse of time was regrettable," conceded Maitland, placatingly, "but quite unavoidable, madam."

"Much could have gone amiss. I have a small neck." She put her long hands to her throat, and then she rose. "The next time I brew a pot for you, you shall have it thicken more quickly, sir."

Maitland rushed to open the door for her. "It shall be as you say, madam." He hesitated.

"It shall be in March, then. Perhaps." The word hung between them, and he stood looking at the door she had passed through, his smile gone, his eyes thoughtful. "A man's a fool who places his trust in traitors," he murmured to himself. He crossed to the fire. "Especially if they walk with the shape of Eve."

Earlier that morning, much farther south in Teviotdale, the maiden Lady Galbraith, sixty years of age and Patrick's cousin, had left her country home of Threave on a two weeks' trip to a neighboring mansion, lying some twenty miles away. At the last minute Anne had not been able to go. Anne was sick. Lady

Galbraith had first assured herself it was nothing serious, and Anne had begged her not to change her plans. Anne would be safe and comfortable by herself; she had Marie, and perhaps in a few days, when she had recovered, she could join Lady Galbraith as they had originally planned that she should. With some reluctance, the elderly lady set forth alone in an uncomfortable litter, and she reached her destination before sunset. Upon arrival, she took advantage of her years and insisted on bed. After she had crawled under her quilts, and sipped the last drops of her hot wine toddy, she thought rather guiltily of Anne, who had certainly seemed to feel wretched that morning, and who was now all by herself in a lonely country house.

But Anne was not sick that night as she sat by the fire in her bedroom; she was not sick, but she was thoughtful. Her needlework was thrown aside and she was thinking of the letter she had written last night, a letter which by now should be in the hands of the man to whom it had been sent. She tried to visualize Patrick's face as he read the uneven carefully-traced lines, and she wondered whether he thought the letter had been difficult to write.

It had not, for Patrick had been right. Not that she regretted her storm of anger against him; she was permitted that, but it was impolitic and silly to keep on with the quarrel. It was not only silly, it was insane, for this drafty old house was frighteningly lonely.

Anne went to the window and peered out past the curtains; in the moonlight the gently sloping hills stretched far and wide, with only the occasional outline of a tenant farm to relieve the bareness of the farming country. The last snow had melted somewhat, but still on the hills the moonlight shone on white patches. Besides that, there was nothing to see and nothing to hear except the howling of the winter wind as it whistled unhampered over the frozen brown earth. Anne let the curtains close again; there was nothing else to do, so she went to bed.

The eighth of February dawned cold and misty. Anne woke slowly to see the pale gray day, and she lifted her head experimentally. Marie was in the room, moving softly; the fire was blazing up. On a stool by the hearth were Anne's clothes, neatly arranged to warm, and when Anne sat up in bed, Marie slipped a warm robe over her shoulders. She watched her mistress carefully.

"How do you feel this morning, *chérie*?"

Anne stirred, pulling the bolster up behind her back. "Why did you wake me so early?" she asked. Her eyes were on the hands of the clock; they pointed to eight.

"The messenger," said Marie, quickly and with eagerness. "The messenger you sent to Sir Patrick. He is here."

Anne said incredulously, "Patrick is here?"

Marie shook her head. "Oh, no." She was sorry she had given the wrong impression. "Just the messenger. He is returned."

"Oh." Anne leaned back against the pillows. "Send him in then, Marie. He will have news for me; he will have news."

Marie had kept the messenger right outside; now she ushered him in. He twisted his cap in one hand and in the other he held a letter. "Mind your boots!" said Marie sharply, for he had almost touched the rug beside the bed with his muddy footgear.

He stopped short. "Aye. Good morrow, madam."

Anne said, "Tammie! Is that letter for me?"

"Aye, madam." He nodded and held it out helplessly, for he had been forbidden to step on the rug.

"Dolt," said Marie, taking the letter and giving it to Anne.

Anne took it in her hand eagerly; then her expression changed to one of incredulity and disappointment. "Why, this is mine. This is the one I sent you with. Why?" she asked, almost tearfully.

He said, "Sir Patrick is not at Hermitage. He is at Usher."

Anne threw the letter down on the counterpane. "Why did you not go there?" Her tone was angry.

He looked amazed. "To Usher, madam?" The thought of it rendered him momentarily speechless. "I dinna ken the roads, madam. It is miles and miles. Way up in the Highlands," he continued, trying to make her understand how inaccessible were the Highlands, now deep in snow, bitter with cold, and no place for a man to travel unaccompanied, especially a man who had never been farther north than the next town.

Anne looked at the unopened letter. "You may go," she said, but when he had half-turned she asked, "Why didn't you give the letter to Lord Bothwell, then?"

"He was not at Hermitage either, madam." He fidgeted with his cap; there was something he wanted to say, but he stood silent.

"Not there?" Anne repeated.

"No." He hesitated a minute and then blurted, "There is terrible news, madam."

Anne's face went white; she stared at him. "Lord Bothwell," she whispered. "Is it Lord Bothwell?"

"Oh, no." His voice was firm, and Anne was so relieved the color came back to her face till one name brought her up short.

"Murray! Go on; tell me!" And she heard him repeat, "He was murdered, madam. Murdered. Yesterday."

Anne gasped, "Are you sure? Is it true?"

"Aye, I'm sure, madam, but . . . it's true. They say it's true at Hermitage."

"But who did it?" she cried.

"Lord Huntly," he said, "and that is why Lord Bothwell has gone north. To catch the Gordon, and everyone hopes he will kill him, mistress! Everyone looks to him to see justice done!"

"No!" Anne cried. Fear swept her; she forgot Murray was dead. "Godamercy, you'll force Lord Bothwell to his death! You and your talk! Oh—you may go, Tammie." She put her hands over her mouth and sent an agonized appeal to Marie, who shooed Tammie out and was back by the bed in one second.

"Get the pot; I'm going to be sick again," Anne wailed. She lay on her side, her head over the edge of the bed. "I shouldn't have eaten so late last night. But I didn't know it would matter."

The retching took her again, and Marie made vague clucking noises which were meant to be sympathetic.

"I think I'm done now," said Anne weakly. "Give me a towel."

Marie dipped a towel in warm water and sponged off her

face; she fixed the pillows again. "Now lie still," she ordered.

"I am so hungry at night," Anne said. "And Lord Murray is dead. I know it's true. He is dead." Her eyes filled with tears; she turned over and buried her head in the bolster, and the waves of nausea assailed her again. She picked up the linen sheet and wiped her eyes. "Whatever am I going to do?" she cried despairingly.

Marie looked at her in silence. Anne's face was white; her eyes were almost closed, and the heavy lashes made shadows on her cheeks. Marie sighed faintly. "You are so fair," she murmured. "I should not fret, if I were you. Once these next days are past, you will find a man to help you."

Chapter Twenty

"Aye, he was murdered, my lord." Patrick was pacing the floor, back and forth, in a big bedroom with windows that overlooked a mountain loch cradled in the surrounding mountains.

The Earl nodded. He was accustomed to Patrick. He knew paced to and fro so restlessly. "Tell me the whole tale, Patrick," he said. "I know you are anxious to be gone, but you can spare me a little time, sir."

"You wish to bring those memoirs up to February '92," he said. "Well, my lord, the tale is simple; bloody and simple. It reeks of treachery and trust, both." He paused, remembering how he had warned Murray to stay at his castle of Downe. "Francis and I, sir, tried to make it so plain! And he promised us he would stay up here, in the Highlands!"

"Another noble Highland name has gone." The old Earl folded his hands carefully. "Pray continue, Patrick."

"Lord Murray did not stay at Downe, sir. For some reason, some inexplicable reason, he went to Donibristle, and from there he intended to pass over the Firth; he meant to meet with Huntly and sign a truce. He started off on his mission, and he was turned back. James Stewart had ordered that no boats cross the Firth!"

The Earl nodded. He was accustomed to Patrick; he knew he was to remember this part of the story; it was a significant part.

"So, Murray turned back; he went home to Donibristle, and in the meantime, Huntly had crossed that Firth, with sixty men.

He was out hunting; he was hunting human game. Now Murray had no adequate guard, but when Huntly and his men surrounded and attacked the house, Murray and his servants barred the doors and got the muskets ready. But Huntly, not wishing to spend his own blood, and knowing that Lady Murray and the children were within the house, set fire to the dwelling. Simple, my lord, is it not?"

"Murray came out then," said Lord Usher slowly, "to spare his family?"

"You anticipate the tale. He came out, through the flames, and he fought like a lion, sir. He fought his way through a circle of men, and escaped them, running toward the darkness beyond the eerie light of the burning house. He ran toward the darkness and the security of the beaches where the northern surf surged against the rocks. He fought his way past Maitland's hired murderers, and he would have been safe, sir, he would have been safe but that the fire betrayed him. An errant spark—somehow the long tassel of his helmet caught fire, and they found him.

"There's very little more to tell. They surrounded him at the water's edge, Huntly amongst them, and they forced him down against the rocks, tore off his helmet, and Huntly himself drew his dagger and stabbed him in the face. That is when Murray spoke to Huntly. He had been already mortally wounded by gunfire. 'Ah, George,' Murray said, and he smiled—you know his smile, sir—'you have spoiled a better face than your own.' Thus he died, sir."

Lord Usher lifted his eyes to Patrick's face. "You expected it, didn't you? But why Murray, Patrick? Why the 'bonnie Earl'?"

"He was of our party. He was loyal to Bothwell, beloved by the common folk, beloved by the Queen."

"So Jamie Stewart is part guilty?"

"Aye, sir."

"His mother would say he is no Stewart! His mother marched openly against her enemies!"

"Aye, my lord. But she is dead."

"I thank God," said the old Earl. He held out his hand and Patrick took it in his firm grip. "You will be off soon, Patrick. God guard you and keep you. Remember that you too walk in danger. Remember I have no other heir. Patrick, before you go, why did you not marry Master Applegate's daughter?"

Patrick looked down at his boots. "Master Applegate did not approve the match."

"What?" exclaimed the Earl angrily. Then a reason occurred to him. "You mean he deemed his daughter too low-born?"

"Aye, my lord. He feared for her happiness."

"Ah, well, Patrick, that is understandable. You should have insisted. Certainly you loved her. She would have brought you no dowry." He grinned at Patrick knowingly, and Patrick smiled back. "Nephew, you are a stubborn man. You let a lass get away from you?"

Patrick said suddenly, "You are right!"

"You'd not admit defeat yet, would you?"

"No," said Patrick. "I do not, my lord."

"A man is never defeated till he has ten daughters." The Earl laughed. "And even then there is hope. Now you may go, Patrick. Get south to Lord Bothwell, as I know you wish to do. I'm too old to help you, but I wish you good hunting!"

All during the long ride south, the image of Janet's face was in front of him. When he stopped in Caithness to have the horses' shoes cocked against the snow and ice he saw her face in the dancing flames of the forge. This time, when he saw her, he would speak to her father, too. She had been right before. He must try to remember how she felt about her father; perhaps someday he would know himself, except that he didn't want daughters, he wanted sons.

He passed through the wide lands of the Gordons. He saw the destruction; he saw for himself how Murray's clan had wreaked their vengeance on Huntly and the Gordons by terrible burning and pillage. Village after village lay smoldering, looted and abandoned.

This sight brought the other riders close, but Patrick rode on. "Hurry them," he ordered Gibson, who was riding abreast, saying nothing, his jaw set stubbornly. "Hurry them; this is no time for talking."

Gibson turned in the saddle, barking out orders, and he spurred ahead to catch up to Patrick. He threw him a look that Patrick answered. "What is there to say? Next time, it may be Bothwell."

Gibson frowned, creasing his eyes against the glare of sun and snow. "I'm no bag of guts, sir, but this hits hard, it does."

Patrick was silent; he was concentrating on speed and only speed. "We must reach Hermitage. In Edinburgh—" he broke off. He was trying to frame quick words to Janet's father. Master Applegate would have to be persuaded to let Janet ride south with him tonight. Crichton would be safe; he could leave her there. He must make Applegate see that Edinburgh wasn't safe for Janet. Tonight she would have to ride with him, and trust him, and if Crichton were not safe, she could come to Hermitage.

"There's Queen's Ferry!" he shouted at Gibson. "We've made time. And Lord Bothwell will want news from the capital."

"He will and that's true, sir."

"We know nothing yet; we'll learn more." Patrick was already sure he'd have Janet with him tonight and he was concentrating on the problem of what was happening in Edinburgh.

"This will make Jamie more unpopular than ever!"

Patrick smiled a little. Gibson was probably thinking of revolution. "A monarch begins with such prestige, Gibson, it cannot be overcome by licensed murder, I fear."

Gibson grimaced, digesting the words. He had great respect, no matter how unwilling, for Patrick's mental processes. "But his own clan, sir. The King's own clan!" Gibson shook his head; he couldn't understand.

Patrick's smile was cynical. "Kings have no clan. Kings often dip their hands into the nearest kin's blood. Do you know any history, Gibson?"

Gibson nodded defensively.

"Then ponder it."

They left the ferry behind. They had crossed the Firth, and daylight, the brief winter daylight, was almost at an end. They would just make the capital city before the night. Gibson hadn't spoken a word for miles now; they were in the city riding up High Street, and Patrick drew rein before a tall stoop. "Wait for me, Geordie." He was standing beside his horse, and little Geordie was holding the reins.

"There's a tavern just past Stinking Stile." Gibson pointed up the street. "I'll go there." He sat motionless in the saddle, watching Patrick's figure leap up the steps and disappear into the door to the common stair. Then he turned and rode slowly up the street.

The fifteen men who were Patrick's escort followed him. It was night, but there was not the quiet that night usually brings. Instead, a blanket of darkness covered a tense and waiting city. There were bands of men on the street; torchlight illumined their faces. Gibson was going only a block from where he had left Patrick, and even in that short distance he had to use his riding whip on two men who attempted to stop his horse. By Stinking Stile a group of citizens had gathered; they were well armed, some in armor, and Gibson was pleased at what he saw, for perhaps Patrick had underestimated the temper of the city.

It was wild tonight. Doors were tightly closed, windows shuttered and fastened securely. In the shops, where lights still burned, Gibson could see that the proprietors had gathered a few friends each, with their hagbuts and swords, in case of trouble.

Gibson dismounted in front of a small tavern; he left his men outside, but before he could open the door the night sounds were rent by sharp screams, a woman's screams, and then a volley of vituperation was laid on the head of her malefactors. Gibson jumped to the entrance of a narrow close beside the public house. Just up the street, several men were trying to batter in the door of a private house. Gibson shrugged; it was no affair of his, but he motioned his men to wait in the close head, rather than on the wide High Street. Then he went into the inn, leaving the turbulent night behind him.

There were few people in the room. Gibson chose a table

far back in the room. It was near a small window that opened onto the close. It would suit very well. He sat down and waited.

While he waited, he loaded two pistols, laying them across his knees carefully. He was wishing he had never come to Edinburgh, but since he was here, the least he could do for Bothwell was to secure information. Although he was momentarily disappointed that instead of a pretty wench, an older woman came toward him, he decided she might tell him more.

"Dame," he said without preamble, "what goes on here tonight?"

"Trouble, sir," she said briefly, but her eye lighted, and Gibson knew he was in luck. She looked like a garrulous dame.

She was. She brought him ale, and she talked rapidly, in bursts of sound. Even now, Murray's body lay in Leith, unburied, brought there by his mother, the Lady Downe.

"The Lady Downe, sir, she took three bullets from his bowels, and she had his picture painted, as he lay there dead. She gave the picture to His Majesty, and she gave His Majesty one of the bullets. One she kept, and she said about the third bullet, 'I shall not part with this, till it be bestowed on him who brings justice!' "

Gibson was very impressed. "I'll warrant you Lord Bothwell gets that bullet!"

The woman clasped her hands together. "His Lordship," she whispered, and she glanced around to see if anyone had heard Gibson. "The town is gone mad, sir. Why, it's not safe to venture the streets tonight, with Maitland's soldiers mutinying for want of money!"

"His soldiers mutinied?"

"Aye, sir. Some say they have been paid, now, but they are all over town, making trouble, and Maitland says Lord Bothwell is coming, and that is why they are all over town, doing harm. There's plenty of people who'd like to see his Lordship ride into town!" She stopped to look apprehensively at some newcomers.

Ten men crowded into the inn. They were talking loudly; they were Maitland's soldiery, but they weren't drunk, and they seemed in good spirits.

"They say this will kill Lord Murray's mother, sir; they say she'll not live a week longer, with her son lying dead on his bier and the King forbidding her even to bring his body to the Regent's tomb to be buried. I feel sorry for her, puir ladie and her puir laddie, with his bonnie face all torn by Huntly's dagger. And who's to have justice when Jamie Stewart himself is guilty?"

Gibson muttered, "Bothwell, dame."

Her eyes shone. "The King has turned against his ain. And now Morton and Maitland are going to ride against Lord Bothwell in the morning. That's why they paid the troops; that's why they're in the city tonight, and the gates closed, sir."

To conceal his surprise, Gibson drank off all his ale and ordered two more tankards. She leaned close to him before she left. "If ye're one of Bothwell's men, sir, you be careful. They'll not want news carried to the Borders tonight!"

She moved away. He muttered his thanks, and he sat facing the door. This was no time or place to meet Patrick Galbraith, for that well-known face would be spotted the minute he appeared. Gibson shoved back his chair, stood up, and suddenly he sat down again. It was too late to leave now; there in the doorway was framed a tall figure.

Patrick pushed past the men in his way without even seeing them. One man he shoved aside with a muttered curse. He noted Gibson, and came across the room to him. He slipped into a chair without speaking.

"What's the matter?" Gibson's voice was low; he eased the pistols on his lap.

"Janet's not there!"

"What?"

"She's not there, she's gone!" Patrick was remembering the last time he had seen her. "I went to find Mistress Applegate," he said bluntly. "She has gone. Her father died; she has gone, and no one knows where she went!"

At this revelation Gibson scratched his head and looked amazed. "Holy God," he said, inadequately. "Did you ask the people in the apartments?"

"Certainly!"

"Well, what did they say?"

"That she had gone. Her aunt came back from Caithness for the funeral, and she was to take Janet back with her, but Janet disappeared and no one can find her. The aunt left the city yesterday. Somewhere, in Edinburgh, in this city, she's alone!"

"This city," repeated Gibson. "I was wondering when you'd notice that, and I'm also wondering if you know that you've been recognized." Gibson's gray eyes were wary as he looked over Patrick's shoulder. "I have something for you, sir; just take it under the table and mind the cock."

Patrick let his left hand slip over the hilt of the weapon; he swung it gently away from Gibson until it dangled between his knees.

"Now turn a little in your chair, sir. I do not like your back to them."

Patrick followed orders. He shifted the heavy pistol slightly, raised his right hand to feel the reassuring sword hilt at his hip. "Now what do we do, Gibson?" His hazel eyes rested on the men who were obviously watching him; they were between him and the door, and Patrick felt a rising excitement that sent the blood beating in his throat.

"Nothing, for a minute. Let them make the first move."

"But I have nothing to fear, Gibson. The worst Jamie would do to me is to shut me up in the castle for a while."

"If you weren't killed first. By mistake, sir." Gibson smiled blandly. "And we have messages to carry. That's why they will try to stop you. There are orders out for a royal army, for the purpose of taking the Border lord, in his own Borders." Gibson snorted. "So we must get to Hermitage—to take those messages. Maitland and Morton start tomorrow."

Patrick said nothing; it was Gibson who had the news. "The city gates are closed, sir; we'll have to spend the night in the city. It may be two days before we reach the Hermitage."

The men who had been watching them were talking together in whispers, and suddenly one of them stood up straight, and the men around him broke out of their semicircle.

"Now!" said Gibson. "Mark the window behind us. Pick up your ale and do what I do."

Patrick lifted the heavy pewter tankard, but he had one order to give himself. "You first, Gibson, because I doubt if they'd dare kill me." He stopped, every muscle in his body tense, and he eased back his chair so that he could get to his feet without bumping the table. His hand was still tight around the handle of his ale. The men were coming closer. In another five seconds he and Gibson would be surrounded, and then everything happened so quickly that later Patrick couldn't remember exactly what he had done.

There was only five feet between them when Gibson gave the signal. The heavy tankard in his grasp flew from his hand into the face of the nearest man. The action was so unexpected that it was successful, and Patrick's tankard followed as quickly, catching a big bearded man on the side of the face. Patrick jumped to his feet. He heard Gibson say, "The table! Save your powder!"

Like automatons, working together, they lifted the heavy table and sent it crashing against the approaching men, and it created such confusion amid the shouts that now filled the room that Patrick shouted, "The chairs!"

His quick brain had caught Gibson's way of defense. A small room, too many men, and much confusion. They could get away under cover of the confusion. It seemed no effort at all to scoop up a chair in one hand, to send it flying at the scramble of men so near him. At the same moment Gibson fired his pistol at a man who was raising his to shoot, and almost at the same minute he had knocked out the window behind him with the butt of the discharged weapon.

The maids screamed loudly, and the acrid smell of gunfire hung over the oaths that came in an unbroken stream from the fallen man, who was trying also to shout orders. Then Patrick was by himself, next the window; Gibson was out into the street below and Patrick could hear his voice.

"Save that shot, till you're in the window!"

Patrick swung one leg over the sill—the window was so

small. There were so many things he had to do, so many hands and arms to watch. Which of them was raising a loaded weapon? His eyes swept the small table and the figures of the men close to him, reaching, stumbling over the table and chairs, over the hunched body of the man Gibson had wounded. Patrick tried to wriggle sideways and get his other leg up without turning his back, and he felt a ragged cut against his leg from the glass that still clung to the lower pane. He swore, never taking his eyes from the scene in front of him.

"Get back!" He shouted, his tones heavy with authority, and it stopped them momentarily, all except one man who smiled, and raised his pistol carefully, taking his good time to aim.

Patrick saw it just in time. He'd never shot a man before in his life but he did so this time, with determination, with a sudden atavistic desire to hurt. He dropped from the window the instant after fire and smoke had belched from the pistol in his hand.

Gibson seized his arm as he came down. "This way." He jerked him around and the first thing Patrick saw was Geordie's scared face and his own horse.

"Why do we not fight it out?" he muttered, mounting at the same time, thinking that now they had enough men.

Gibson grinned. "We have no time for pleasure, sir. We have to hide. All night. And then we have to get out of the city, sir."

Patrick slipped the pistol into his saddlebag; he was disappointed. "Is that all, Gibson?" he asked.

Chapter Twenty One

THE town of Hawick lay on the Liddle River about ten miles from the English border. It was a small town, but not small enough so that unfamiliar riders caused heads to turn, and the two horsemen who clattered over the bridge and through the streets were never noticed. The pair had entered Hawick at ten o'clock; a few minutes later they had left the town behind—they were following the river into Liddesdale.

The day had dawned clear, although the winter sun was pale, and in the distance they could spy the towers of Branxholme Castle against the sky. They were still within sight of the castle when by mutual consent they drew rein in a wooded glen. The path ahead was starting to descend.

Anne looked around at the thick trees. "How far is Hermitage from here, Tammie?" she asked.

He frowned; he didn't know the distance in miles. "We'll be there afore dark," he said, making the best answer he could.

Anne straightened her cap, settled her cloak around her shoulders, and lifted one hand to touch the shining well-brushed hair that fell into a thick roll. She glanced down at her polished boots and the trim breeches.

There were no roads to follow, but there was a trail through the deep glen they were descending. The trees clustered close around them, brushing at the flanks of the horses. "There are caves over there," Tammie said, pointing toward the side of the hill.

Anne didn't answer; she wasn't sure of the wisdom of talking.

Voices sounded so loud in the wilderness, yet it was a wilderness that might suddenly disgorge mounted men, coming up from every side to investigate two lonely travelers. Suddenly they emerged onto what looked like a level plain.

"Be careful," said Tammie from ahead. "We skirt these bogs." The small, agile, Border-bred horses they rode were trained for this type of country, but Tammie had slowed his pace, to allow Anne to keep up with him. He had time to send more anxious glances upward at the sky; although Anne was too preoccupied to notice it, Tammie began to be afraid of snow. It was just a few minutes later, when they had left the bogs behind, and traveled up to the crest of a hill, when the first flakes came drifting down into their faces.

"It's snowing!" Anne cried out from behind him, and he turned in the saddle quickly at the sound of her voice.

"It may not last long," he called, for he was some distance from her. "Follow me closely."

She obeyed rapidly; the thought of losing him was terrifying. "We cannot go back," she said tentatively.

"Perhaps we had better go back." He stopped a few feet from her and turned around again.

"Oh, no, Tammie!" If she went back, she would never have the courage to come again. Now that she was halfway to Hermitage Castle, she must go on.

Tammie said nothing else; he didn't remind her that the hardest part of the trip was yet to come. He went on, and she followed close behind. The snow was light but it fell steadily and slowly. Gradually she forgot her fright and she began to wonder only what the end of her trip would bring her. What would Hermitage look like and what reception would await her there? She did not think of either Patrick or Bothwell; she thought instead of Bothwell's little daughter and Eliza Hepburn. "She'll get no brat of mine," muttered Anne to herself. "The fat witch!" And Eliza occupied her mind when she suddenly realized that it was snowing hard and that the whirling flakes were almost a curtain in front of her. She forgot everything else but fear.

Up ahead of her Tammie whispered his *Ave Maria;* it was said of Borderers that they always pattered their prayers when they rode off on a Border foray, and this was worse than a raid, much worse, because Tammie was afraid he was lost. But he kept on; there was no use in returning now. They might see another rider, they might even be taken by outlaws, and Tammie would have liked nothing better than to see a group of bearded, heavily armed men right now. Anything was better than the trail-covering snow. He was still murmuring his prayers when out of the trees behind them came the unmistakable sound of another horse.

Tammie wasted no time; he raised his voice in a shout which quavered in the winter stillness. "Hey! Hey, there!"

The answering shout was the result of his prayers, he was sure. He reined in; Anne came up alongside, trembling with the cold and the unexpected voices. Both of them peered into the snow, and suddenly another horseman came up to them. He was no more than a boy.

"Who are you?" he asked, his voice muffled, and he drew closer, eying them with both suspicion and curiosity.

"I'm Tammie Elliot. We come from Teviotdale. We're lost."

"Oh, I come from Teviotdale, too, and I'm not lost." This prod was accompanied by a grin. "I'm young Jamie Telfer."

"You are?" Tammie was impressed. "I've heard about your father, I have."

Jamie nodded. "And where are you going, lad?"

Tammie said meekly, "We have a message for Lord Bothwell."

"You're on your way to the Castle?" Jamie spurred his horse ahead importantly. "Follow me, then, lads. I'll show the way, because that's where I'm going, too. Who's he?" he asked, indicating Anne.

Tammie stuttered a second, then remembered his instructions. "He's a French page belonging to Mistress Galbraith. He's carrying a message to Lord Bothwell."

Jamie went on in silence; he did know his way, snow or no

snow, and his pace was fast for Anne. She jogged along, her head bent; she concentrated on keeping up to Jamie. She was lost in a daze of fatigue by the time she saw ahead the looming walls of a great castle.

It looked like a ghost castle. It was all gray and square; it was formidable and frightening, and she said uncertainly, "Is that Hermitage?"

She craned her neck to see the rising walls in front of her; in this secluded valley Hermitage dominated the scene. It was so very big. She dismounted and, taking a clean linen towel from her bag, she stripped off her gloves, using handfuls of snow to wash her face, toweling vigorously until her cheeks and nose were pink and clean.

Jamie watched her with increasing astonishment. "What's he doing?" he asked, and Tammie didn't answer because it was obvious what she was doing. "They say Frenchies are all mad," continued Jamie. "His hair is long, too." He was walking toward the moat, leading his horse, and Anne and Tammie followed him, under the archway. They were in an immense hall.

Anne's heart was hammering so loudly she was sure Tammie could hear it. She saw nothing but the back of his head; she didn't feel the stone flags beneath her feet, she didn't hear the noise of men's voices until she came to a sudden stop behind her two escorts. In front of her was an open door; in the small apartment it revealed Captain Ormuiston lounging at his table. He looked up as a man said, "It's young Jamie Telfer, Captain. His father sent him."

These words meant something to the Captain, for he nodded his head, smiling at Jamie. "We expected you, laddie," he said. "You may see to your horse, and we'll feed you afterward."

Jamie said smartly, "Aye, sir. Thanks, sir." He turned away and Anne watched him disappear into the inner court, for she was still in the outer defenses of Hermitage.

"And this lad is Tammie Home, Captain. He was here before."

The Captain frowned hazily. Then he seemed to remember,

and he shifted his eyes from Tammie to the figure standing beside him. "Who's that?" he asked, laying down the pen in his hand and pointing with his finger.

Anne stared down at the tips of her boots. Her cloak covered her whole body; the soldier stared, and Tammie said finally, "It's a French page. He has a letter from Mistress Galbraith for his Lordship."

"Where is the letter?" asked the Captain, his eyes on Anne.

Nothing happened and the Captain repeated his question. "Do you understand me?" His voice was sharp.

Anne mumbled, with a thick accent, "*Oui*. Aye. Here it is." She held out a white letter, sealed with red wax that was stamped with the letter G.

The Captain said, "Give it to me." He waved his hand at the trooper but Anne drew back.

"*Mais non*," she said desperately. "My lady, the Mistress Galbraith, said this letter must be put into his Lordship's hand." She pointed to herself. "I, I must bring it to him."

Captain Ormuiston stared at her; he cocked his head on one side but he couldn't see her very well and at last he shrugged. "Women," he said, to all of them. "God's me, women." He picked up his pen again to point with. "Gregory, take these lads up to Lord Bothwell." The thought of the correspondence that had to be delivered personally amused him. "I hope the wench has written a letter that will improve his temper."

Anne followed Gregory down a hall; they passed a large guardroom with a circular fireplace, and then they began the ascent to the dining-hall. The narrow steps cut into the stone twisted around; Anne caught a glimpse into one of the barracks for the men, and as they left that behind she could smell the odor of food, of meat cooking. She was almost there.

"What did the Captain mean?" she asked Gregory, who was climbing ahead. "Is Lord Bothwell in bad temper?" Gregory twisted his head around; he was smiling. "You would not call it bad," he said. "It's worse than that. M'lord did not catch Huntly."

At the top of the steps there was a small hall, only big enough for two doors to open on it. The two guards stepped aside, the doors opened, and at first Anne saw nothing at all—the whole huge room was a blur. On the threshold of the hall she stood paralyzed, the letter in one hand, her cloak drawn around her figure. She realized Tammie was right beside her and she looked at him imploringly, but he was taking in the hall; his nostrils quivered at the smell of the meat, and his eyes were round as they went over the sturdy, hardened soldiers, with their bad table manners. But most of all Tammie was staring at the back of Bothwell's head; he had never expected to see the Border lord so close. Anne stared, too, at the so familiar dark head, and she didn't know whether she wanted him to turn around or not.

Gregory went slowly forward the few feet that separated the head of the table from the door. "My lord," he said, a bit apprehensively.

Bothwell didn't move. "Well?" he said.

"There is a letter for you, sir. From Mistress Galbraith."

"Give it me." Bothwell held out his hand, and behind him Gregory motioned Anne to give him the letter.

In desperation she walked two steps to Gregory and put the letter in his hand. He in turn gave it to Bothwell, and the Earl tipped back his chair, set down the tankard of ale. He began to open the letter.

Anne had come closer to him and suddenly Gregory noticed she was standing right behind the Earl's chair. Her head was bent; she had wrapped herself in her cape. Gregory frowned at her attitude; he eyed her sharply. "What are you doing?" he asked harshly.

She retreated from him, recoiling from his look of suspicion, and Gregory came toward her slowly, so that she backed to the door. "All right," said Gregory, still harsh. "You saw Lord Bothwell get the letter. Come along."

Anne said involuntarily, "Oh, no." She stood her ground, but Tammie was fearful. He reached out to take her arm, to pull her. "He said to leave," he whispered, but Anne couldn't leave. She couldn't go downstairs with these men; she must speak to Bothwell.

At that moment Tammie was edging out the door. Gregory still had suspicious eyes on Anne—he wanted to tip her head up so he could see her face—when suddenly, from the head of the table Bothwell roared, "Hold there!" He swung around in his chair. "Who brought this letter?"

There was complete silence in the whole room. The two guards at the door froze to attention; Gregory stopped dead, and between them Anne was trapped. Bothwell threw down the letter; he stood up and his dark eyes flicked past Tammie and came to rest on Anne.

"Christ's blood!" Incredulously he stared at her bent head. She was here. In this familiar room, where he had never expected to see her, she was here.

Only a second had passed, but before Bothwell could speak, Gregory was spurred to action. He seized Anne by the shoulder, pulling her around to face him. "Who are you?" he growled.

She cried out, "Release me!" She raised her hand and jerked away from him violently; her voice was sobbing and Tammie responded to the appeal. He drew his knife and, at his action, the two men near the door leaped forward toward him.

Bothwell covered the ten feet that separated him from Anne and Tammie in two long strides. With one arm he sent Tammie backward out of danger; Tammie stumbled and fell, his head striking the stone floor with a thud.

Anne ran to him, falling beside him on her knees, gazing down at his face. She pushed the hair back off his forehead. "Oh, Tammie," she wept. "You've killed him," she said, turning her head to look up at Bothwell who was standing over her, and she was about to burst into tears when Tammie stirred.

"Godamercy, he's alive!" She had been so sure he would never move again. "Oh, Tammie," she whispered, "open your eyes!"

"Stand up," muttered Bothwell. "I ought to beat you!"

Anne got to her feet slowly, taking as much time as she could. She had lost her cap, her cloak was lying on the floor, and in her short doublet and hose she looked very small. Her hair was falling to her shoulders; after the wet weather it was curling around her face. She took a step back from Bothwell and stood framed in the doors.

The silence was broken by a low whistle from the back of the room. "By Jesu," said a deep voice, "it's a wench!"

The nearest men jumped to their feet; they crowded closer, and those in back climbed on the trestles, the tables, the better to see. Their faces wore delighted smiles; there were more whistles, and one man called, "Did you bring a friend?"

Bothwell gave no indication he heard anything. "Hand me her cloak," he ordered the amazed Gregory, who stooped to gather up the cloak but never took his eyes off Anne.

"Here it is, my lord," he said, eying Bothwell.

"And her cap," ordered the Earl. He was still frowning deeply and Anne smiled. She planted her feet wide apart, hooked her thumbs in her belt, and smiled.

"And see that the lad is taken care of." Bothwell put the cloak over Anne's shoulders; his back was to the room. "I will beat you," he murmured, and stood aside politely for her to precede him.

There were a few parting injunctions shouted to them; there was a great deal of laughter, and then they were alone on the stone steps.

"This way," said Bothwell impassively, putting a hand under her elbow and guiding her down the steps.

"Where are we going?" she asked meekly. "Oh, Francis—"

"Patrick is not here. You were well aware of that, were you not?"

"Aye," said Anne; she hung back. "Francis—" She stopped on the stairway; she was two steps above him and her face was level with his. "You'll not beat me, will you?"

"You need it."

"I'm so hungry," said Anne, uttering the first words that occurred to her. She put her hands up to his face; she leaned forward until her lips touched his.

He didn't kiss her; he didn't move except to turn his head and when he did her soft hair brushed his cheek. "This defense renders any man helpless, is that it?"

"Marry-go-up, my lord, it does!" She stood straight and flung the words at him. Then she smiled. "I warrant you're too much a milksop for kissing!"

"We'll test that soon enough. And 'tis no place for talk—this stairway. Take my arm."

They went on down the steps, emerging into the hall. Anne walked as slowly as she could, toward the apartments in the left wing of Hermitage. At their entrance the servant in the room jumped to his feet.

"I want a tray of food, some wine, some ale." Bothwell turned aside to inspect the brightly burning fire and it seemed to meet his approval.

Anne glanced around her. There were two big chairs by the hearth, the stone floor had no rugs, and the bed was the biggest bed she had ever seen. It was fully fourteen feet wide.

"This is your room?" she asked haughtily. "I would rather be elsewhere."

"And where did you expect to be entertained? In the reception room? Well, I'm sorry, madam, but Hermitage does not boast a gallery."

Anne stood just inside the door. "Art angry with me, Francis?" she whispered.

He turned, and started toward her, then he went over to the fire and leaned against the mantle, putting his foot on the fender. "I suppose it has not yet occurred to you that your Tammie was almost killed. Not by me," he added quickly, "but by the other two."

"It was not my fault," she said defensively.

"Was it not? You give the lad scant credit for aiding you. And also you are not aware that you have acted like a little whore."

She flushed, her violet eyes darkening with anger. "And do you care, my lord?"

He said evenly, "I? Why no, madam. To tell you true, there's no one I'd rather see in my room tonight than a leaguer lady." He was still leaning against the mantle and she burst out, "You'll not dare—"

"You'll be quiet," he interrupted, because there was a knock on the door, "till we are alone again." He watched her, from his vantage point, while a servant brought in the food and drink Bothwell had ordered. Then he bowed to her. "Now you may continue."

"I did not come to lie with you!" She spit the words at him. "You can sleep alone in that bed. I did not come for that!"

"No?" He bowed again. "You desolate me, madam. Why did you come then? Suppose you enlighten me?"

Anne whirled; her cloak flew around and her wet boots made marks across the stone as she marched to the door. "I am going home!" she announced, over her shoulder.

He did not move. "No, you are not."

She said, as though he hadn't spoken, "You may provide me with an escort!"

He shook his head. "No. A woman's whims are not sufficient reason to send any of these men out into a storm."

His calmness infuriated her, unshed tears glistened in her eyes, and she cried out against him because she was so helpless. "Oh, I hate you! I came all the way here—" Her voice was shaking; she broke off but she wouldn't give in to him, and blindly she seized the door latch and opened the heavy door.

"Close that!" His voice was sharper and he took a step toward her.

"No, I'll not!" she snapped back at him, leaping into battle vigorously now that she had aroused him. She turned, leaving the door open, putting her hands on her hips and letting her hair swing over her face as she looked at him defiantly.

His inflammable temper soared up. "You shall close it!" he ground out.

"Will I?" She laughed at him, then she languidly pushed the blonde curls away from her forehead. "Will I?" she repeated lazily, giving the door another push with her feet.

"Aye, you'll close it! Patrick expects you to behave like his kin, and not like a cheap trollop! D'ye want every man in the castle to hear you?"

"Aye!" she shouted. She had planted her feet wide, her lower lip was thrust out belligerently. She fastened her eyes on his belt, then rebelliously she kicked the door shut with a loud bang. "You ass-eared ape!" she cried, whirling away and picking up a heavy cup from the tray, which she launched at him with all the force she could summon. Bothwell ducked his head; the cup flew past and landed on the hearth with a clatter, rolling over the stones.

She retreated from his advancing figure hastily; in anticipation of what he might do she laid both hands on her hips. "Oh, Francis," she gasped out, "oh, my lord, I closed it! You'll not hurt me! I came to tell you I am with child!" She threw herself into his arms. "I am going to have a child." The words came to him muffled in his coat, and he tipped her head back with his hand.

"What did you say?" he asked incredulously.

"Pick me up," she pleaded. "I'm so weary." She felt his arms go around her and lift her so easily, and she closed her eyes and sighed with contentment. "I do love you," she whispered. "By heaven, I do. Why were you so fierce with me?"

He sat down in his big chair with her in his lap. He too gave a long sigh, and then he smiled. "You wench. Why didn't you tell me right away, lassie?"

"You would not let me."

"How illogical you are." He put his hand up and pulled at a thick curl, twisting it around his finger. "How fair you are," he said softly. "But are you sure about the bairn, Anne?"

"Aye, Francis." There was silence, in which she endeavored to read his expression. "And it's a boy," she added, firmly.

"What?" He stared at her intently. "How do you know?"

"Because I'm so sick in the mornings," she said, still very firm. "I know it's a boy, and he will look just like you. Marie says it's a boy, too."

"Holy God," he said. Then he asked, "Are you so sick in the mornings?"

"Marry-go-up," she said happily, "I'm helpless all morning; if I sit up in bed, I start to be sick." She looked very pleased with herself.

He said wryly, "You might be carrying a little bitch just like yourself." He raised one eyebrow at her but his tone warned her.

"I have not acted like a lady, have I?" she asked tentatively. "But I never was a lady till a year ago," she added, eying him.

He burst out laughing. "And you'll never learn, either." He studied her face for a minute. "Small difference, lass. You have more lure in one finger than any other two women rolled together." He was silent for a while. He was trying to compute what this would cost him; some land would have to go, or else another mortgage could be piled on Hailes Castle. Thinking of Patrick, he didn't notice her silence.

Finally she said, "You think we can keep people from knowing?"

It didn't occur to him to lie. "No," he said bluntly.

Anne put her arms around his neck. "Francis," she whispered, "first tell me you believe it is your child and none but yours."

His answer was to kiss her. He meant to be tender, but with her in his arms he forgot that, forgot everything but his driving desire for her.

"Francis," she murmured, "you haven't answered me."

He raised his head. "Lassie, I know it's my bairn."

"Please, I'm so hungry."

He buried his head in the curve of her throat; he let go of her reluctantly. "I'm hungry too. I'll keep away from you for the space of ten minutes." He grinned, pulled the table nearer to the big chair and carved off a piece of breast of fowl, putting it in her fingers. "Eat fast, wench. It's not hot, either."

"Doesn't matter," said Anne, her mouth full; she ate with gusto and Bothwell carved her another piece. "And some beef, too, Francis."

She ate in silence, not only because she was hungry but because she needed time to think. Evidently it had not occurred to him that he might marry her, and she realized that her very actions had precluded such thoughts. Earls married ladies; they didn't marry the women who came to Hermitage Castle. She thought of the knowing stares of the men, and she wondered desperately how she could have been so foolish as to think he would marry a woman who had brazenly let his men shout at her. He turned aside to pour her a cup of wine and she studied the angle of his face so intently that when he turned toward her he caught her look.

"Perhaps you should have milk." He smiled then, the charming guilty smile that lighted his face, and she was suddenly sure that her baby would look just like him. He would be just like his father, and she would name him Francis, but he would not be Lord Francis Hepburn, as the eldest son of an earl should be; he would not be heir to an earldom, nor would his picture ever hang in the gallery at Crichton. Another woman's son would have that place, a mealy mouthed son of a mealy mouthed lady. "Godamercy," Anne said, her mouth still full, "I'll warrant no one ever had the troubles I have." She licked off her fingers and sighed lustily.

Bothwell laughed. "Isn't there enough to eat?"

"It's not that," she said gravely. "Although I'd like an apple." Her face brightened at the idea. She bit eagerly into the apple he handed her. She sighed again, thinking that at least she was with him now. "Oh, sweetheart," she said, "do you want a bite?" She held the apple to his mouth and he took a big bite. "Will you take me back tomorrow?"

"I must." He frowned slightly. "I'll have a horse litter fixed for you, so that you'll be more comfortable. You shouldn't have ridden here; you might have lost the baby." He frowned again.

She said, "That would be just as well, my lord."

He took that up immediately. "Is that what you think?" His voice was sharp.

"Aye," she said defiantly. "D'ye think I want a nameless brat?" She turned away and threw the apple core into the fire.

"You'll not be bothered with my child, madam. I will take care of him." He was staring into the flames.

"You will take care of him? Here?" Her voice was mocking. "Will you bring a suckling brat to Hermitage?"

"Lady Logan will take him for me, and he'll be well raised." Bothwell stood up and set her on her feet; he pushed the table away and sat down in the other chair. He began to take off his boots.

"Mayhap you'll even bear him for me! Or mayhap your precious Lady Logan will. I'd thank her kindly for it, that I would! And I warrant you mean that he will be better raised by Lady Logan than if I had him, do you not?" She was glaring at him.

"That was my meaning," he said, with no inflection. They had both convinced themselves they were arguing about a boy.

He stood now, without his boots, and started to take off his jacket. Anne watched him in silence, and suddenly she said, "Well, you'll not have him! He's mine, and I'll take care of him myself! Why, I warrant I could get myself a husband before six weeks are out!"

This statement made him stand stockstill. "It might be a way," he conceded, nodding.

She misunderstood him. She thought he accepted the idea easily. She set her mouth so she wouldn't say anything too quickly. "I could marry," she insisted.

"I doubt it," he contradicted. "After a ride to Hermitage Castle, there's not a man in Scotland would have you. Who wants a wife that's already carrying an outlaw's brat?"

"But you said first—"

"I know I did, but I forgot how fast news travels. But if I could get you to Patrick's house early enough tomorrow morning—" He broke off; he sat down on the edge of the bed and was thoughtful.

"In the morning?" she asked. She came over and sat down beside him, swinging her feet over the bed. "I'll not go," she vowed silently. She had so much. She was here with him; he was bound to her by a child. She had all tonight, many hours, hundreds of minutes, and tomorrow—well, she could look to tomorrow when it came.

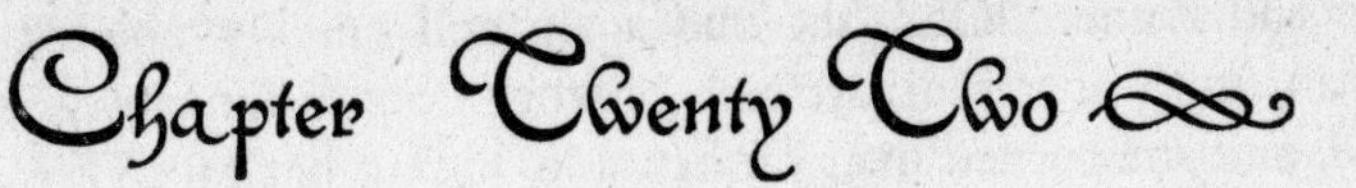

Chapter Twenty Two

WHEN Anne woke up in the morning, the first thing she saw was the top of Bothwell's head and shoulders. He was sitting in one of the chairs by the fireplace, and she rolled over on her side to see better, peering around the edge of the bed. The flames in the fireplace were roaring up the big chimney; Bothwell was dressed, and someone, she didn't know who, was putting a pair of newly polished boots on his feet.

"Good morning, m'lord." She sat up in bed, clutching the quilts around her.

He turned, smiling at her. It was good to hear her voice in the morning, and he stared in pleasure at her tousled yellow curls and her white shoulders. He stared, and his servant stared too. Bothwell picked up one of his own shirts and tossed it to her.

"Better put this on, lassie."

"It's a bit large." She looked around the room which was deep in gloom, for there were no lights but the fire, and the narrow slit of a window showed the sky to be gray and menacing. "Is it going to snow?" she asked, with an air of innocence. There was nothing she would rather see than a heavy snowstorm.

"I think not." He stood up and came over to her.

"I've lost my hands," she called, gaily, waving his shirt sleeves at him, but she was afraid of what he was going to say next. Was he going to tell her he was taking her home?

He was. "I doubt if it will snow, but even so, lass, the sooner we start the better."

"Oh," said Anne. "Oh," she said again and quickly pointed at his man, with an air of extreme horror. "Send him away," she cried, and she turned over on her side, hiding her face. She didn't move until the door was closed, and then she raised her head, and her eyes were full of tears. "I'm going to be sick," she wailed.

"Good God!" It didn't occur to him that this had come on rather suddenly.

"Get me something, m'lord," said Anne, hiding her face in her hands again, as though she were choking.

He grabbed up a linen towel and a basin; he took her by the shoulders and hauled her over the side of the bed. "I'll hold your head, lassie," he said comfortingly.

"No," she said desperately, "no!"

"But, Anne—what's the matter, sweetheart? I'll stay with you."

"I don't want you," she sobbed. "I want you to leave."

Uncertainly he got to his feet, looking down at her commiseratingly. "You don't want me to stay?"

She shook her head from side to side. "You have breakfast." She sounded as though the very thought of food choked her. "Go 'way, my lord, and I beg you, do not come till I call you."

He went to the door. Anne sighed with relief, but before he had quite left the room, she remembered something else. Her clothes. "Would you have my shirt washed and ironed, and my boots polished?"

He looked amazed, but he gathered up the articles in question. "I'll be back soon, lassie."

"No," she called, "do not come soon."

Left alone, she rolled over on her back, putting her hands under her head. The clock was ticking noisily, its hands pointing to nine. She was very delighted with herself. Now all she had to do was go to sleep. She put the pot on the floor, threw the towel after it, and closed her eyes.

A knock on the door wakened her. She sat up, rubbed her

eyes, looked at the clock. It was almost three in the afternoon, and not only that, it was snowing. She could hardly see anything but snowflakes through the window.

"Come in," she called, happily, wondering who it was, for it couldn't be Bothwell; he would have walked right in.

"Oh," she said, seeing Lawder's face and her clean clothes over his arm. "They look very nice," she said, approvingly. "Now you may bring me lots of hot water for bathing, some fruit, and a light wine. Do you have any sherry?"

He looked nonplused. "I'm not sure, madam."

"Well, then bring wine, and some cool water. And the fruit. Hurry, now, don't stand there. Where is Lord Bothwell?"

"Away, madam."

This pleased her, and she yawned contentedly, relaxing in the featherbed until her wants should be supplied. At five o'clock she was standing by the window looking out, sipping her watered wine while Lawder put the room to rights and removed the big wooden tub she had used for her bath.

She saw Bothwell come. She had had to stand on a chair to see out the high slit in the stone wall, and she watched until the last man clattered over the planks. She jumped down from the chair just as he came in the door.

"I thought you were never coming." She was in his arms, ignoring his wet leather coat.

"I thought you were never going to wake up!"

Anne smiled impudently. "I did not get much sleep last night, my lord. And take off your wet coat, Francis. I've another warming by the fire for you."

He stood with his back to the fire, looking at her.

"Francis, I took an old shirt of yours, and if you wish, I'll keep it as a pattern, and I can weave you more. I'm very clever at a handloom." She stopped and asked, imploringly, "Do I have to go home now?"

He grinned. "You're a Border wench." He took her face in his hands and pushed back the curls. "Now hold still; I've something for you."

Anne waited impatiently while he put an earring on her ear;

it took a long time. "Oh, you're clumsy, Francis. Let me see it!" She pried open his fingers and extracted the mate. She looked down at a sapphire. "It's beautiful," she cried happily.

"A bauble for a Border wench." He put his hands in his pockets and surveyed her with approval. "Here's a mirror," he said, extending a polished metal square.

Anne twisted her head from side to side. "What a mirror, Francis," she said commiseratingly. "How ever do you manage?"

"Oh, it does well enough," he said gravely. "Except when I pluck my eyebrows."

Anne was thoughtful. "Patrick told me that Borderers are very vain about their women. He said they always bring their wives a present from a raid."

Bothwell nodded solemnly. "Patrick is always right." He looked down at her. "And I have something to be vain about, with you. Shake your hair back so the baubles show, wench; I'm taking you to dinner with me."

He seated her beside him at the head of the table. The men gaped. Captain Ormuiston was obviously delighted: his black eyes sparkled with merriment. The Hepburn led captains grinned at her, and she was struck by their resemblance to their lord. There were only two men at the table whom she knew, Burley and the adventurous Laird of Nidrie. Anne seated herself as though she were at a banquet and Bothwell, from the corner of his eye, watched her intently. He was curious to see how she would behave. He introduced her quite formally to the men she didn't know, and when that was over, there was a brief silence during which the rest of the men in the room stared, whispered, and nudged each other, sending envious glances toward the master of the castle.

Across the table from her, Captain Ormuiston regarded her closely. He couldn't resist one jibe. "I notice your accent has improved since last night, madam," he remarked.

Anne said benignly, "I'm quick at learning, sir."

Nidrie cut in quickly. "And after your arduous ride, madam,

I hope you slept well last night." He was sitting next to her, and shot her a look.

Bothwell's face was expressionless, and Anne saw he wasn't going to come to her rescue. She returned Nidrie's stare with interest, and she said, demurely, "Oh, how kind of you to think of me, sir. I had an excellent rest, and, sir, I wonder if you'd lend me your knife?"

Nidrie pulled the dagger from his belt and handed it to her. Anne thanked him, and began to attack the beef on her plate.

Bothwell grinned. "Hungry, lassie?" he asked, approval in his voice.

"I'm starving, my lord."

"And will you have wine or ale, lassie?" He was smiling at her in such a way that her heart turned over with joy.

"Wine, if I may." She heaved a little sigh, but they weren't through with her yet.

Burley said challengingly, "Perhaps Mistress Galbraith would like her wine laced with brandewine. Like this." He poured a generous quantity of brandy into his own cup.

Anne hesitated, and this time Bothwell intervened. "Not till after dinner," he announced. Anne sat in silence, listening to their talk on politics, about the King, about the Borders, and the latest raid. One of Bothwell's bull hounds sat with his head resting on her knee, and she fed him scraps from her plate. The food was coarse, the bread black, the beef salted and tough—but never had she been so happy.

"Now you may have the brandewine, lass." Bothwell fixed her cup for her. "Have you ever thrown the dice, Anne?"

She hadn't, but she had watched many times. "Aye, m'lord."

He pushed her the box, and she rattled the dice in it with what she hoped seemed like expert fingers. Her throw was high, and Bothwell shoved out many coins.

"She'll beat that next time," he said.

"The devil she will." Nidrie took up the bet.

Anne threw again, hopefully. "It's higher," she said, happily, looking at Bothwell as though he were a wizard.

"You cannot win on that, lassie." He smiled. "That was a

wager betwen Nidrie and me. Now you throw again; I'll show you what to do."

"This is fun," she announced, after she'd won what was a lot of money to her. "Only, I don't count very quickly, my lord," she murmured aside to him, and he burst out laughing, and filled up her wine cup for her.

"That's a lot of brandewine," she said, doubtfully. "Will I get drunk?"

"Certainly." He was still laughing.

"But you are used to it."

"I'll drink two for every one of yours. How will that be?" He looked so amused, that determinedly she picked up her cup and drained it.

"Then you had better hurry, sir," she announced. "And, by heaven, I was cold, but now I am nice and warm—inside."

Inside Hermitage, inside the bare stone walls, it was cold. Outside the snowflakes whirled; the whole Border was deep in heavy snow, covering the moors, the marshes, the bare hillsides, the bogs. Outside, the wind howled with increasing intensity; winter, drawing to a close, was having one last fling. Through the storm a small company of riders plodded their way, trying to make time against the storm and the news they carried.

"It'll be midnight before we reach Hermitage." Patrick shouted the words to Gibson, who was ahead of him.

He could hardly hear the shouted but muffled reply; he concentrated on keeping Gibson in sight.

"Much farther?" he finally shouted again.

"No!" Patrick could hear that. He brushed his glove against his face, and wondered if perhaps beards were warmer than a clean-shaven face. He would have liked to roll out of the saddle and go to sleep; instead, he bent forward in the stirrups, doing his best to keep up with Gibson.

It was almost midnight when Anne realized that she had had too much to drink. The dice kept blurring in the oddest fashion, and it was so hard to concentrate that she gave up, and leaned back in her chair with a sigh of contentment. "I feel heavenly," she declared, and started to pick up her half-filled cup when Bothwell shoved it away from her.

"No more, lassie." He said it absently; he held the dice in one big hand. Suddenly there was a noise that everyone recognized. In the distance were faint shouts, and then the rattle of the winches as the huge doors downstairs were opened. Bothwell flung down the dice; he pushed his chair back, got to his feet. Then he changed his mind, sitting down again, but turning, so that he faced the doors.

"Who could it be?" asked Anne interestedly.

He shrugged, but he was frowning. "Wait and see," he answered briefly.

Anne could hear steps now. The door opened, and there stood Gibson, soaking wet, with snow clinging to his shoulders and boots, and, behind him, Patrick. Anne thought he looked even wetter than Gibson.

Bothwell jumped to his feet, strode over to the door. His eyes were on Patrick, and the two men conversed in low tones, so that Anne couldn't hear what they were saying; but it must have been important. She caught the words "soon," "already."

Bothwell nodded. He and Patrick were staring at one another, but evidently Patrick said nothing about Anne, even though Anne knew he had seen her when he had first come in. She rose, stood a little unsteadily, and then walked over to the two men.

"It's my fault, sir," she said, without waiting for him to speak to her.

She lurched, and Bothwell put an arm around her, steadying her, and over her head his eyes met Patrick's. Neither man spoke, and Anne rushed on quickly, "Please forgive me, sir—"

He interrupted sharply, "Francis, if you'll send her downstairs . . ." He inclined his head toward the door. "There's not much time to be lost."

She straightened up, and she smiled very formally at both men. "I'll leave you, sirs," she said.

Bothwell offered her his arm. Patrick, by his words, had

abandoned her, and she was his now; she belonged to him.

"I'll take you myself, lassie," he said gently. "Sir, you may expect me back in a few minutes; you'll want food."

Anne looked up at him gratefully; she put her hand in his arm, and she didn't forget to say a proper goodnight to the other men. But when they got back to the room on the ground floor, she burst into tears.

"He hates me," she sobbed, holding tight to Bothwell. "And if he only knew that he is the one person in the world I love, besides you, my lord."

"Sweetheart, Annie." He tried to comfort her. "Don't cry. He blames me, too."

"No, he doesn't," she contradicted. "And it wasn't your fault. If you had taken me back this morning, no one would have known. I mean, he wouldn't have known."

"You couldn't help being sick."

"Oh," she said, guiltily; she dropped her eyes, and wiped them with her handkerchief. Then she cried, "I think I'm going to be sick now."

"I was afraid of that; I gave you too much." He set her in a chair and dived for the basin, placing it on her lap. "Do you want me to leave?" he asked, remembering the morning.

"No," she sobbed. "I want you to hold my head. Oh, I am going to be sick!"

He scooped her up and laid her on the bed, with her head hanging over the side. "Don't leave me," she gasped.

"I won't," he said grimly, "and you weren't sick this morning, were you?"

"No," she confessed, hanging onto his arm. Then she sat up. "I'm better now." She stared at him; she was frightened out of her nausea. "I guess I will be all right, and you may go now."

"May I?" She did not see the twinkle in his eyes. "Shall I use this belt?" he asked her grimly.

Anne scrambled backward across the big bed, away from him; she sat on her haunches protectively. "I'll never lie to you again! I'll never lie again, I swear it! Francis, I beg of you!"

He dived across the bed at her; he was laughing. "Beg me

some more," he said. "Oh, lassie, you are sweeter than honey. I told you that once before, did I not?"

"Aye," said Anne, remembering the first night they had ever really talked together. "I loved you then. So much."

He was silent a minute and she wondered what he was thinking. Then he pushed her away. "Unhand me," he said. "Patrick is waiting for me, Annie."

Patrick had brought bad news. It was very bad news. He recounted it baldly, monotonously, point after point, and alongside of him, Bothwell listened in silence, nodding his head every once in a while to show that he had taken in the precise import.

"All men between sixteen and sixty," he repeated Patrick's words. "A euphemistic statement. Just how many men do you reckon will respond to that call?"

Patrick tapped his fingers on the table. "Impossible to judge, my lord; there's great disquiet in the city—some mutinies. But let's say four thousand may respond to the royal orders."

"And James will march himself—against me. It seems I'm the only man can move Jamie Stewart to battle."

"Jamie is commanding the foot; Maitland and Morton the horse."

"And the foot will stay behind. That's where James belongs." Bothwell sighed, rested his arm on the table, started to take a drink of brandy, and then thought better of it. Instead, he transferred his gaze again to a large map spread out on the table before him, and idly he traced a line, from Hermitage, across country to Kelso, from there to Dalkeith, to Leith.

He was silent so long that Patrick said, "What are you doing that for, Francis?"

"Because that's our line of march, man." He picked up a pen and traced the line roughly. "How was the weather before you entered the Borders?"

"Not so bad; there was no snow in Edinburgh, but there may be now."

"The wind's lessening; the snow's stopped." Bothwell smiled again. "The wind's veering to the south, and I think that will do as well. So James had Murray killed, and now he wants me

He's taking his own sword and dismembering his own body."

Patrick nodded. "His own clan," he agreed. "But just what do you intend to do?" He watched Bothwell's face. He was surprised at the Earl's reaction to this news. He had expected him to be bitter; he had expected that inflammable temper to burst forth in rage; he had expected anything but this. But, really, there was little or nothing to do. To combat the force which James had summoned by a call to arms, would take the whole Border, would be tantamount to civil war. Even if Bothwell could raise the force, and Patrick thought that he could, what could ever be the outcome of open rebellion? There was nothing but death ahead that way.

Patrick said, "Maitland and Morton should be in Kelso now. That Border town was their first objective. What are you going to do? Are you going to quit Scotland?"

"No," said Bothwell bluntly.

Patrick frowned. "Well?"

"I showed you our line of march, and my troops are right here, peacefully sleeping now."

"You're going to ride against James with four hundred men?" Patrick couldn't believe his ears.

There was a flash of temper in Bothwell's answer.

"Man, should I run? From Maitland? And with four hundred Borderers, would I be afraid to tackle James with ten times that many? Besides," continued the practical Border lord, "James may not be able to raise that many troops, and he'll lose some in line of march. They won't be well enough provisioned. I know them, man, from practical experience. When I used to be the one to lead the royal armies, and when I counted on Morton—the fool!" He swung around to Ormuiston, and his voice was low as he issued the first orders. "Each man to be provisioned for four days. Salt beef, oatcakes, and water. Thank God my Borderers can do without their ale. They aren't Englishmen! Each man to carry either a hagbut or pistol, whichever he is best equipped to use, and a light axe in the saddlebow. All those with rapiers, will wear them. See that the horses' shoes are well cocked. Later, I'll show you our direction. And send me Graham. I've a commission for him." He grinned so diabolically that Patrick and Ormuiston both wondered just what was the nature of the "commission." Bothwell watched Ormuiston leave, he turned to Patrick again, and he said, "There's just one more thing I want to talk to you about. Anne."

Patrick's face was inscrutable. "Yes?" he inquired.

"I want you to stop blaming her. Although she came here to me, I pursued her first." He thought he was speaking the truth, but Patrick, knowing Anne, also knew how she had got her invitation to Fastcastle.

"You pursued her?" he asked, blandly.

"Aye, and that's the truth. I almost took her the first night I met her."

"And why didn't you?"

"Because there wasn't time."

The blunt answer made Patrick grin.

"So she rode here." Patrick half smiled and he said, "I think she's kin to me, Francis. God knows she can stick to one purpose, regardless of consequences."

Across the table, Bothwell regarded him closely. It was true, they were alike, especially in the curly yellow hair, the wide-spaced eyes. There was a resemblance in the brow and the carriage of the head. "You are alike, for cousins, for man and woman."

Patrick said, "My father and her father were twins, my lord. Mine was the eldest." He was suddenly impatient. Why were they talking about women, at a time like this, when the royal orders had already gone out, when even now those forces were in the Borders? He said as much, curtly.

"You have more important problems, Francis, haven't you? You may not live much longer."

"That's why they're important, man. Anne came here to tell me she's going to have a wee bairn. Mine."

Patrick stiffened; he drew in his breath carefully, and committed himself to nothing. "Yes?" he said.

"Yes. That's why I'm approaching you. It's time I had an heir. I want to marry her tomorrow."

Chapter Twenty Three

It was a strange wedding. Very different from the wedding of Bothwell's father and his mother, the long-legged Jan Hepburn; very different from that wedding which had been celebrated at Crichton, with the Queen as the most honored guest and a host of nobles in attendance.

Anne and Bothwell were married in the ancient chapel up the hill from Hermitage. Through the deep snow they'd ploughed their way, past the tumbling Hermitage water. The little chapel was dim with antiquity; alongside of it the headstones of the graves in the cemetery were buried beneath snow already melting in the sun, but inside the sun's light could barely filter through the arched windows.

Bothwell held her hand in his; even in her boots she scarcely came to his shoulder. Her face was very white, her eyes solemn, and she looked straight ahead, so that only his warm fingers clasped around her own, and the occasional murmur of his voice told her it was really he who stood beside her.

She hardly heard the words of the preacher fetched so hastily from the nearest kirk. This was a church. Its tiny size seemed to accentuate its consecrated purposes, and the light that did come through its tiny-paned windows was holy light. Anne bowed her head. Eight months ago she had, at Patrick's insistence, joined the Scottish church, and she had done it to please him, because he had asked her. She had tried to understand that religion and politics were closely knitted, but this was too revolutionary a lesson to learn quickly, and Anne had continued to kneel at her prie-dieu every night, to make her devotions. Yet this ceremony was different from paying lip-service to another church. This was marriage.

Anne prayed silently; she confessed her sins, that were so many. She had disobeyed the dictates of her church; she was being married outside its arms. "Holy Virgin," and she formed the words in her soft native tongue, "I do it for him whose hand I hold, and for my babe. And tonight," she ended, "I will make a proper prayer."

The ceremony was over; Anne looked up at her husband. Surely she had been wedded to him in the house of God; surely the Holy Virgin had blessed this small church whose stones had been laid before anyone had even heard of a new kind of faith.

She put her hand in his arm, she gazed up at him worshipfully. "I love you," she whispered.

He winked; he was in a far from reverent mood. He strode out of the little chapel so fast that Anne had to run to keep up with him, and out in the sunlight and the valley and the smell of the new snow, he smiled broadly at her, squeezing her arm.

"It's beautiful," Anne breathed. She stopped, turning back for a last look at the chapel, and her breath came as white as the white of the hills and the lazy branches of the trees that hung like woven webs over the brawling Hermitage water. "It's the most beautiful church I've ever seen, my lord."

He turned to look too. "It is lovely," he conceded, rather surprised. "But you'll freeze standing here, Annie."

"I might never see it more," she said, wondering then if she would ever stand here with him again.

He grinned. "I might not either."

He seemed so unperturbed that she asked solemnly, "Don't you have any religion, Francis?"

" 'I will no priests for me to sing but ae bagpipe to play as spring,' " he quoted, laughing at her. "God love us, lass, you're not expecting me to ride to my death today, are you?"

"No," she said, and she shivered. "Oh, I am cold."

"I'll not have it; not you and my bairn!" He picked her up in his arms; his boots squashed deep into the snow as he ran down to the small back gate of Hermitage. "Listen, lass, and you'll hear the bagpipes even now! They're playing for you!"

The garrison had done their best to please their lord and his bride. Large bunches of holly and pine branches festooned the walls of the dining hall; the great tables were scrubbed well, decorated with ivy, and red-cheeked apples and nuts. The cooks had outdone themselves, for there were pastries and white bread, roast venison, and wild fowl, gamey and strong. Red wine filled the cups to overflowing, and on the hearth the ale warmed.

The wild skirling of the bagpipes filled the air, so that the birds nested high above in the rafters, the goss-hawks and the merlins, mewed shrilly, flapping their wings and shaking their bells, while the dogs barked, and the men's voices shouted out boisterously, "A bachelor again he'll never be!"

The ale wasn't warm enough for a toast, so Anne seized a red hot poker and thrust it into the brew until it hissed and foamed and was poured into the cups still frothing. Bothwell set her on the table, and they raised their glasses to the Border bride.

"It's best to see them in breeches afore ye marry," said one Hepburn to another, wisely, "or ye find ye've bedded a bow-legged lass."

They looked at her and approved of her. "She came through a michty bad storm the lass did. She got what she wanted," continued the Hepburn who, like his lord, valued courage above everything else, "and a braw bairn she ought to have of his, too."

They wanted to please her. They sang her songs of the Border; they sang her the song of the outlaw Murray.

> "There an outlaw keeps five hundred men,
> He keeps a royal company!
> I would know of whom ye hold your lands,
> Oh man, who may thy master be?"

Anne looked at Bothwell as he lustily gave the answer to the ballad's question.

"'These lands are mine!' the outlaw said,
'I ken no King in Christendie!'"

She couldn't keep her eyes from his face. She put her hand over his big one, and Bothwell smiled at her and picked up her hand, looking at the heavy gold ring on her finger. It was etched with roses, and it boasted seven diamonds, and it fitted her perfectly although it was rough where it had been melted and rejoined for her this morning in the castle's forge.

"I'm sorry I couldn't buy you a new one, lass." He lifted his shoulders helplessly.

"I want nothing but you," she whispered, and tried to smile because it was almost time for him to go.

It was time. She watched while his armor was buckled on. She would have wished it far heavier, for all he wore was light sleeveless mail, over his leather jack, and a tasseled helmet, polished until it shone. "Heavy armor is nothing but an impediment." She had heard him say that to Patrick. "The value of cavalry is in its speed. The fight always goes to him who moves fastest. It always will."

She went out into the huge entrance hall, feeling the stone flags again beneath her feet; she watched his men ride out.

They wore their leather coats, and bright scarves wound round their necks, their only protection against sword thrusts. Their light axes were slung in the saddles, along with the heavy pistols, and their saddlebags bulged with provisions that were to last for at least four days.

They were all assembled in the hall. Anne stood back in the corner. She couldn't take her eyes off his tall figure. She was so proud of him, and she listened to his deep voice as he addressed his men.

"I have here," he began, "a proclamation which we are going to post in Leith. A copy to be sent to the ministers meeting at Dunbar." He eased his shoulders a little, and hooked one thumb in his belt. "I am going to read you part of it. 'Whereas, we are forced, for our safety, to admit into our company Borderers, which perhaps may be fearful to the common people where we travel, upon our honor we promise that none of them shall take violently from any person not my enemy, and, if they chance to transgress, it shall be on the hazard of their life!' "

He paused; there was complete silence. Bothwell rolled up the parchment, handed it to Patrick, hooked both thumbs in his belt and surveyed the faces of the men in front of him. "In plain language then, any one of you caught pillaging, despoiling, robbing or laying hands on a woman violently shall either be shot at once, if it is expedient, or brought back to hang at Hermitage. Is that clear?"

There was no answer except the nodding of heads and a few reluctant smiles. "There'll be no march-treason this time, my lads! Because I've promised by my faith as a Borderer!"

His faith as a Borderer! There was not a man in the room who did not know and solemnly believe that such a pledge could not be broken. Once made, it could never be retracted, and the sturdy soldiers of Hermitage knew that their lord would not budge one inch if any of them were caught robbing; not one of them doubted but that if Sir Patrick himself were found guilty he'd be shot as soon as "it was expedient."

The first troop clattered out of the hall, their banners waving, their trumpeteers sounding the horns gaily, the reckless notes echoing to the rafters. Standing alongside of Bothwell, Anne watched them go. She pondered all she was learning about these Borderers, responding to their way of life, wondering if it were possible that any men but these had ever been so gallant, so reckless, so virile. Along with their ruthlessness, their lusty brutality, there was a gay humor and charm—all this spirit and lust for life exemplified in the man beside her—the Border lord.

"They are wonderful," she cried, compressing into that one word their ready eagerness to challenge any foe at all, regardless of his strength.

He said lightly, "They're my 'lambs.' And now it's time to go, sweetheart."

She couldn't help it, she ran into his arms and begged him to take her with him. He held her away from him gently, and he said, low, "Anne, I want you to take care of my wee bairn. You have an escort to Crichton; I've ordered a horse-litter for you."

"But when will you come?" The words came out in a rush; she held his arm, running her fingers over the smooth leather.

"Don't fret, sweetheart. I'll come. Take care of our bairn."

"I will, my lord; I swear I will." She put her hand over her heart, on her crumpled doublet. "By my faith as a Borderer."

"Good lass!" He squeezed her shoulder, took the reins of his horse, and swung up into the saddle. "This is Valentine," he said. "I don't know whether you've ever met him before."

Anne kept her voice steady. She said, "He's magnificent, sir."

Bothwell looked down at her standing there, and there was something else he wanted to say. "We'll have moonlight again." He said it as though he were reminding her, and he repeated it, gaily, the slogan of the Border. "We'll have moonlight again!" He waved his hand, and was gone, out the big archway. Anne waved too, running toward the doors, standing on tiptoe in the arch until she couldn't see him any longer, until she couldn't even see the last rider, or the floating banners, until even the sound of the horns had ceased to come echoing over the Border hills.

Part Four

Chapter Twenty Four

THE town of Kelso was crowded. It was a small town, and it had been augmented in the last three days by fifteen hundred horsemen, gathered under the royal banner, come to the Borders in search of a notorious outlaw. The town was crowded, its inns were crowded, so that in the paneled room at the best inn in town the men were shoved and pushed against each other as they tried to quench the thirst gained in the four days' wait.

"What's your name?" The speaker was a man of consequence. He was a captain of the guard; he wore a highly gilded corselet, and over his arm hung a coat of buffalo hide.

"My name?" The man addressed took a long pull at his ale, wiped his mouth with the sleeve of his leather jack, and said, "Graham, if it's any of your business."

"It is. Where do you come from?"

"England. And if you mean, where have I just come from, why, then I'd tell you Hermitage, and 'twouldn't be no lie, either." He hunched his shoulders—and they were powerful shoulders. "What's your name?"

Captain Home didn't even hear that question; he was staring at the suspicious character he'd spotted the minute he had entered the inn. Now his suspicions were proved correct too. He felt a flush of triumph. "You admit it, do you?" He set his glass down sharply. "You can come with me, knave. God's blood, the impudence of you!"

The other frowned, looking puzzled. "Why, sir," and his voice was meek, "I'd no call not to tell the truth. I escaped from

Hermitage two days ago, because they were busy raising men, from Liddesdale."

"What?" Captain Home looked puzzled now himself, and then he nodded his head a little, and spoke his thought aloud. "I didn't think you'd admit coming from Hermitage." He surveyed the man in front of him, and added, "You can come with me, anyway." He was still going to have a small triumph; whether this was one of Bothwell's men or not, much could be learned from him.

"But I ain't done nothing." Graham hung back, his face ugly.

"You can explain to other than me." Captain Home was already shouldering his way out of the room. "And try no tricks, Graham, if that's really your name."

"Why would I lie?" Graham slouched along, obviously reluctant, at the side of the impeccable Captain. Ormuiston would make mincemeat of you, with all your feathers, he thought, as he walked along, wondering what was next.

The Earl of Morton and Maitland were next. Captain Home escorted him right to their presence, in one of the burgher's houses that they had commandeered for themselves during their stay in Kelso. Graham was brought in to them, and he looked around curiously. He'd seldom been in so fine a house before, except on an errand of thievery.

"Rugs," he said, interestedly, kicking at the nap. He was rudely interrupted.

"Look to your manners, rogue." Morton spoke sharply, and turned to Home. "Who is this rascal, sir?" His eyes swept Graham from head to foot.

Graham curled his lip downward, and muttered his name, whereupon Morton roared, "Hold your tongue!"

"It's my name." Graham shifted from one foot to the other.

"Quiet, gallows bait!" Morton's temper had been rising for four days. "Who is he, Home?"

"He told me he'd just escaped from Hermitage. I thought he might have useful information, sir. I hope I did right."

"You did." Maitland's calm voice entered the conversation, and he added, "I'll question this man, Morton."

Morton pouted. Graham lowered his eyes to keep Maitland's shrewd gaze from piercing his thoughts, and Captain Home was respectfully silent. Maitland said slowly, "You escaped from Hermitage? When?"

"Two days ago, sir. The snow held me up, and my horse is aweary, sir."

"Ah! And how did you escape from Lord Bothwell? Why did he hold you prisoner?"

"I was took a month ago in a raid on Carlisle, sir. And I escaped because Lord Bothwell is busy raising men, sir."

He made his "sirs" come thick and fast, and his simulated meekness kept his eyes on his boots. He was remembering Bothwell's face as he had said almost those very words to him.

"Busy raising men?"

"Aye, sir. Lord Bothwell asked everyone, and me too, if we'd join him; he's paying high, sir. And I said I would, and then I took a good horse, and out into the snowstorm I went, sir. I'll see England again, sir, devil doubt it!"

"See England again? Then why did you come this way?" Maitland's gray eyes were menacing.

Graham said plaintively, "First I got lost, sir. Then, I didn't want to see Liddesdale again, so I landed for Kelso. I knew I'd be safe here, sir."

Maitland nodded; he was apparently satisfied. "Bothwell would try to enlist every rogue in the Borders," he said to Morton, "whether or not they were English." He rubbed his chin reflectively. "Do you know how many men Lord Bothwell has raised?"

Graham said nothing. But when Maitland repeated his question sharply, he kicked at the rug again, and muttered, "I didn't know you were talking to me, sir. I thought you meant that gentleman." He pointed his dirty finger at Morton. "I would reckon, sir, that his Lordship has got about two thousand horse, sir, already, before I left."

"Two thousand!" Morton started up from his chair, but Maitland waved him back. "Why, that's impossible."

"Not at all, Morton, not at all. That would not be all the

thieves of Liddesdale. Unfortunately it's not at all impossible. However, we must assume that this rogue's estimate is bound to be incorrect in some degree." He ran his eyes over Graham in such a way that Graham was moved to spit lustily, regardless of rugs, and his aim was good, for the spittle reached the toe of Maitland's house shoe.

Maitland's narrow face wore a look of extreme horror and disgust. He wiped his shoe off on the rug, and he said, coolly, "There is no breed of men I so dislike as Borderers, English or Scot. Would you swear, Graham, that Lord Bothwell has two thousand men?"

"Aye, sir, that I would. And he's not satisfied with that number, news having reached him, sir, that many were after him. But I know something else I ain't told yet."

Maitland raised his head. He said curtly, "Out with it, then!"

"His Lordship plans to be at Kelso the fourth of March, to exercise and run the horses."

"The fourth of March?" Maitland and Morton exchanged looks, and Morton burst out, "That's day after tomorrow."

Maitland nodded. He thought of his fifteen hundred men, already dwindling, grumbling, wanting to return to Edinburgh, because they were cold and out of money to spend at the taverns for food and drink. He thought of the heavy guns of Edinburgh Castle, and he sighed a little.

Graham said eagerly, almost too eagerly, "His Lordship expects to catch you in Kelso, sir."

Maitland smiled thinly; he sank down into a chair. "Take him out," he said, "before he repeats any of his nauseous behavior. I must say, rogue, that I'm vastly surprised that you are not one of Lord Bothwell's company."

Graham began, injured, "Why, sir, I'm—" But Maitland cut him short, waving his white hand in a tired gesture, and Graham was ushered out into the street.

Left to himself, Graham looked up at the windows of the house he had just left, and muttered, "I'd no idea it would be so easy, for all my lord said it would." He scratched his chin, fingered the coins he'd been given. He had walked only a little way down the street before he knew he was being followed.

He was prepared for that, but he knitted his brows trying to remember exactly what his instructions had been, in case he was put under observation. He could see the Earl plainly, leaning forward over the table at Hermitage punctuating his words with gestures of his big hands.

"You're to do, Graham," Bothwell had said, "exactly as you would if you were suddenly free, and with some money to spend. Remember, you've had a hard ride." Well, it had been a hard ride, and he did have money, so he went to the nearest inn. He ordered dinner, paid his one shilling and four pence, and had a shilling for bed and bedding. But while he ate, someone watched him, and it took the edge off his appetite. He finished his meal, and racked his brains. He had some notion of fleeing, but he remembered just in time that his horse was tired, and Bothwell had warned especially against flight.

He looked around the room. The soldier following him was still there. What would he do next? If he weren't so nervous he could think better. Fortunately for him, the flick of the maid's skirts showed him the right way.

Five minutes later, Graham, from an upstairs window, with the wench on his knee, watched his pursuers ride away.

Graham woke early the next morning. It was the third of March, the day was unseasonably warm and, even with the customary lack of sun, the snow was melting rapidly.

He rolled out of bed, donned his boots, and put on his jacket. Then he took a seat at his window, and there he waited for what seemed to him the whole day; but in space of time, he sat watching for exactly five hours. At the end of that time, he made his way downstairs and out to the stables, paid tuppence for his horse's board, and tipped the stable boy with his last penny. He rode in the direction of the English Marches, and he cantered along slowly; he had plenty of time.

The country he traveled through was bare and bleak, and it seemed by its very topography to show that it was no man's land, the boundary area between two nations which had been at war too many times. There was a lack of trees; there were no forests, just empty stretches of country which truly no nation could want, but which had been fought over for centuries, as the border surged from one side to the other. Graham traveled almost to Northumberland; then he turned across the face of the moor, galloping swiftly now, running his horse with eagerness, feeling the damp, warmish mist in his face, hearing the familiar thudding of the horse's hoofs with recurrent satisfaction. What was a Borderer without a good mount?

He could see the Cheviots now, low-lying hills with their rising tops shrouded in fog, and he slowed his pace, for the snow lay deeper here, patches of it concealing the roughness of the terrain. There were more trees now, more cover; he splashed through a lazy stream, and entered the first wooded slopes of the Cheviots. He didn't ride much farther.

He was far from being an imaginative man. He had done his job, it had been surprisingly easy; that had been his reaction yesterday, and it was still his thought. But now, with his journey ended and his task done so well, the first excitement of success and accomplishment pervaded him, his heart started to beat in an amazing fashion, and his hands were so damp that he tried to wipe them on his already wet jacket. He came to a sudden stop, pulling up sharply to the figure waiting for him, there in the shadow of a tall pine.

He blurted out his story; he even told how he had spit at Maitland, and the deep brown eyes of his master crinkled with amusement.

Bothwell listened in silence as the tale unfolded, and when it was ended, he said, "You're a good lad." That was all; then he dropped two gold coins in Graham's fist.

"Ten pounds!" Graham's face lighted up. "Why, that's two and a half months' wages, my lord."

Bothwell said, honestly, "It's small enough recompense, Graham. I'd triple it, if I could." He looked rueful. "Spying's dangerous business, man. You might have been hanged, you know."

Graham gazed at him with fondness. The Border lord never minimized, never overemphasized what you did for him; he returned honesty with honesty.

"I wasn't afraid of that, my lord."

Bothwell laughed. "Were you not?" Graham's stolidity amused him, but he sobered quickly. "You'll join Ormuiston again. That way." He pointed, and both men wheeled, and with the ability of Borderers, disappeared into the trees.

Patrick was waiting for him. His face under the steel bonnet looked rather grim and forbidding, so Bothwell composed his face and looked grim too.

"We're for Kelso," he said, curtly, and gave the order for the trumpets to sound the march. He said nothing else; he waited for Patrick to remonstrate.

Patrick had a difficult time. He visioned Kelso swarming with soldiers, and here they were, at the head of four hundred men; but he restrained himself and spurred his horse. He wondered what the men were thinking, for they knew they were outnumbered four to five times, and here they were riding right into a rat's nest. Patrick shot a glance over his shoulder; the sun was trying to come out, and as they crossed the moor, its rays shone briefly, touching the steel bonnets of the men. The pace was even and rather slow, so Patrick could keep looking back; at least it was better to be riding, than to wait as they had this morning—all day in fact, up to now.

"These horses need letting out." Bothwell's voice broke into his thoughts. "We're here to speed and exercise the horses; by my word, we are." He smiled. "I'll race you across the moor, sir."

"Oh, certainly," said Patrick, "let's play games." But he took up the challenge eagerly enough.

The terrain changed; it was hilly again, and bleak, and cold. The mist was thicker, but now, through it, he could see the outlines of the town ahead. He expected Bothwell to slow his pace; but the Earl gave no indication whatever that he had any such plans, and, with Bothwell slightly in front of Patrick, they galloped into the town in clouds of dirt and dust and thundering hoofs.

Patrick couldn't understand what he saw, but there was truly no doubt about it at all; there was no one in Kelso who should not be there—no one at all. It was deserted, empty. Maitland and his soldiers had gone.

Bothwell drew rein in the courtyard of his favorite inn; through the town, in back of him, had come his four hundred men, and doors and windows had flown open, as the townspeople had watched their progress. In the courtyard, Bothwell dismounted in a leisurely way; Patrick refused to give him any satisfaction, and refrained still from any questions. Bothwell looked around at the men, and he spoke to Ormuiston, so that all could hear.

"Maitland didn't expect us until tomorrow; he was apparently reluctant to meet us at present, due to a slight misapprehension. He was under the impression that we had quite a few more men than we actually have. This was furthered by one of you who went ahead to spread the rumor. So, since he has conveniently left us in complete possession of this town, we shall do as I expected to do for the balance of the day. We shall exercise and run the horses." He looked around the first ranks, and motioned to one man. "Graham," he said.

Patrick stared, beginning to realize just what Graham had done; and Graham himself, far from being sheepish, was all too conscious of his importance. "Aye, my lord?" he said.

Bothwell handed him the reins of his own horse.

"You may take Valentine, and see that you do this job as you did another, more dangerous one. That's all." He turned, and the inn door almost banged in Patrick's face, because he was still thinking deeply about something else.

He slid into a chair opposite Bothwell.

"Any questions, sir?" asked the Earl gravely.

"Devil take you, Francis. No! I'm only thankful for this tavern, and its beds."

Bothwell grinned.

"But I fear you'll sleep on the ground again tonight. I'm not billeting these men on any town. We're too few to be apart. I'll feel safer in the hills."

"Such caution," Patrick teased him gently. Then he added slowly, "It's the mark of a good gambler to take the best chances, and guard against the ones that might be costly, yet of which the guarding against costs nothing but wariness."

Bothwell looked puzzled, and Patrick said dryly, "You do it by instinct; you don't reason it out." He was ready to expound his point, but he was interrupted by noises outside, and he twisted around in his chair to see who had come into the yard. The inn door flew open and both he and Bothwell stared in some surprise.

"Ochiltree!" Bothwell pushed back his chair and stood up, his dark head almost touching the rafters of the low room.

A few affectionate oaths flew around the room and when greetings were over, Ochiltree sat down, still smiling. "I heard you'd not be here till tomorrow," he began, as a preamble. "I might have known you'd be either late or early."

Bothwell said seriously, "I couldn't meet Maitland in a pitched battle; I'd have lost too many men. I wanted him to retreat."

Patrick leaned back in his chair and listened to their talk about the situation, both political and military. Patrick was weary, but he was content with himself. It crossed his mind how odd it was that he, and Ochiltree too, could, with such equanimity, talk of taking up arms against their monarch. Both of them knew that James had a good deal of personal liking for them, and James, in his own way, would understand how they felt about Murray's death. Guilty or not of the murder, James wouldn't blame them for seeking revenge. He was human enough to have tender fondnesses for those he liked; it made Patrick wonder whether he wasn't human enough to have a spiteful hate that would not let Francis Hepburn ever have peace.

"Do you desire peace, Francis?" He broke into the conversation with his wry humor. "Or would it bore you?"

Bothwell was never quite sure when Patrick's vagaries had a real bearing on the subject; he frowned a little. "Are you listening, sir? Did you hear we have allies in the north?"

Ochiltree had mentioned the names of powerful Highland earldoms, and Patrick replied, "I was listening, my lord."

Ochiltree asked impatiently, "You have allies here, on the Border, certainly?"

Bothwell smiled. "'All the impoverished sons of Border nobility.'" He mimicked what Maitland had said about him. "But some I sent home, sir. A few are in the field this afternoon, doing some maneuvering on a kind of cavalry charge."

"Then what is your plan, Francis?" Ochiltree lowered his voice. "I brought fifty men with me."

"Tonight we spend here—I think with safety. Tomorrow we ride to Dalkeith, and on to Leith."

Bothwell put his chin in his hand; he seemed to be staring straight ahead at nothing. He knew very well that his plan was a reckless one; he would be following Maitland almost to the capital city of Scotland, almost to the walls of the city where James was in residence. But there were two reasons why he thought this was the best plan. It was just possible that he and his four hundred men could cross the Firth, and slip north into the land of the Gordons, and so catch the man who had murdered Murray. It was just possible, too, that Maitland might straggle north so that the swift Border horses might catch that rear guard, as another generation of Borderers had caught the English at Ancrum Moor. Bothwell knew all the details of that encounter; his grandfather had been one of the leaders of it. And then, there was the most hopeful of all thoughts; perhaps Maitland would avoid battle, perhaps he would retire without fight, and so jeopardize his prestige that he would be compelled to retire from his position at court. It was sadly jeopardized now, by his initial retreat from Kelso. His complicity in the death of the Bonnie Earl had already earned him the contempt, the hatred of the people. Chancellors must be wary; had Maitland overstepped his mark? Bothwell frowned. He gazed at Patrick, then at Ochiltree, and while he looked at Ochiltree, his mind registered the fact that he had brought fifty men with him; Ochiltree was always prepared for feuding.

"So, tomorrow," continued the Border lord, "we ride for Leith."

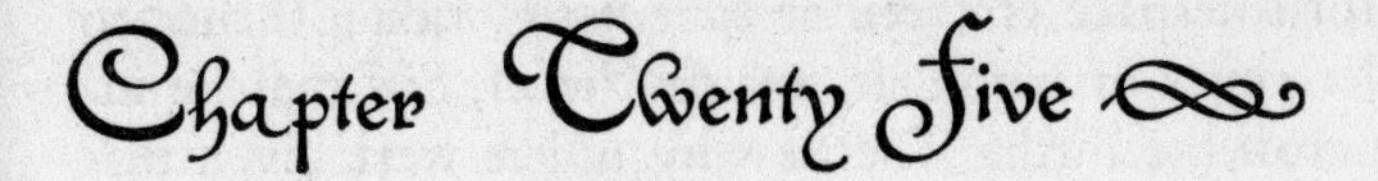

Chapter Twenty Five

THE royal army made a very neat picture. There were two thousand foot, commanded by the King himself; they had marched out of Edinburgh early in the morning on the fifth of March, and they were reassuringly accompanied by trundling guns, taken from the Castle of Edinburgh, and now planted in formidable array on the Lipperhouse, to back up the marching troops.

Ahead, the cavalry of Maitland and Morton rode in simple formation, their gear clanking, the armor glittering in the sun, for it was just ten o'clock in the morning.

James felt the fresh warm air, unseasonable still for early March, with a great degree of aplomb. He was proud of the army so hastily recruited when it was learned that Lord Bothwell was impudently riding on Leith. This morning, very early, he had been to church; he had made his devotions. He had made an impressive speech in which he had announced royally, "I desire none of you to stand only so long as ye see me stand"— And now he was riding, out of the city, toward a rash foe. He felt wonderfully confident; in back and in front of him, and on all sides, was an army which outnumbered the Border lord's many times. James rode on.

The royal forces stopped just short of Leith. They were stopped by the vanguard, and both Maitland and Morton came riding to James, their faces alight with importance. But Maitland controlled himself, and he spoke dryly.

"Sire, we have ascertained that Lord Bothwell arrived at

Dalkeith last night at five o'clock, having left Kelso at nine hours in the morning. He and his company refreshed themselves at Dalkeith for the space of three or four hours, riding thence to Leith under cover of night. It was my belief, Sir, that he intended to cross the Firth. That is why orders were given that no boats shall cross today, and for that reason all sails and rudders were confiscated from any boats that might be expected to disobey Your Majesty's command."

Maitland paused, and James nodded. "Continue," he said.

Maitland essayed a small bow. "Therefore, I have given the order to march toward the south, cutting off his retreat, Sir."

James almost broke into praise at so smart a move. Then he remembered that he should have thought of it himself. "Very good," he offered, benignly. "Very fine strategy, sir. We shall march to the south." The three men exchanged smiles, and Maitland and Morton rode off again. The only thing they forgot was that perhaps Lord Bothwell might think of this maneuver himself.

On the southwest side of Leith, the ground sloped gently upward to a low-lying hill. There were few trees; the visibility was excellent. To the north lay the town, behind the hill was Restalrig Castle, and beyond it, the village of the same name; and in the hollow of the hill, four companies of Borderers were drawn up neatly in battle order. They had been there since nine o'clock.

Under the spreading branches of a still bare tree, Patrick waited. He was wrapped in his heavy cloak, lying on the ground, half asleep. He had had two hours of rest like this last night, then more riding, and then another few hours of sleep, for he had slept, heavily. The rest of the men had slept too, except for a few who had paced the improvised camp, walking to and fro, their hagbuts over their shoulders. They had all slept after the full day and part of the night of riding—all except Bothwell, whose restless energy had kept him wakeful.

He had sat most of the hours in which the rest had slept, with his hands clasped around his knees. The moon had been full last night. From the rolling countryside he could see the sea, he could hear the crash of the waves on the shore as the full tide flung itself against the sandy beaches. There was his outgate; there, before him—the sea. The first Hepburn lands had never been without sight or sound of that sea; it was as much a part of him as his hands or his legs, and what was there about it that moved him so strangely? Why did he miss it so, shut up there in the walls of Hermitage? Even the Border hills had no power over him such as this. Sometimes his longing for even the sound of those waves—for the sharp salty smell—sometimes the longing became a physical hurt. And while he sat there, that March night, it was not the battles that he remembered. Exciting as they had been, he didn't even think of the capture of the Spanish barque that had put those new lovely wings on Crichton. He thought of the deep green wash as it came over the heaving decks, he thought of the sails bellied out to the wind, and the sounds in the rigging.

He thought of distant ports, the coast lines he knew so well, the islands lying north. The last trip he had made had been to the Orkneys. The harbor was as clear in his mind as the puffs of smoke of the guns from the fortress that had greeted his arrival. He had been bullied by the weather that voyage, so that a gale had taken him north of the harbor, along the treacherous coast where the reefs lay ready to rip the keel from the stoutest vessel. What a wind that had been! It must be like, just a wee bit like, the gales that whistled through the Straits of Magellan. And he thought to himself that as soon as he got to Crichton, he must read again the book Patrick had given him, a book on navigation of the southern seas.

The moon was waning, the tide dropping. Bothwell rolled over on the ground and put his head down, finally to sleep to the slow murmur of the surf.

He wakened the men early. There was no time to lose this morning, for they were in a trap, here at Leith, and even Maitland would see it. He had let them have as much sleep as he could, and then it was time for food. He felt relaxed and easy this morning, with the sun bright on the water.

"A good day for golf," he said to Patrick, who looked amazed.

At eight he had started his troops south. The going was easy, almost slow. "So that the beef settles." He knew this country so well. He had already picked the spot where they would await James—a gentle hill southwest of Leith, the hill that concealed the small village of Restalrig that lay behind it. He divided the Borderers into four companies, giving Patrick and Ochiltree the Liddesdale men. Patrick had no fear now, only a sort of vagrant curiosity about what was going to happen next. At nine they had reached their vantage point, and there they had waited, for the space of one hour, and Patrick took advantage of it by almost falling asleep again on the hard ground. He sat up when he saw Valentine in the distance, galloping up the hill with Bothwell astride. Horse and man came up with an eagerness that Patrick was far from feeling himself.

"Get up, man, and you'll see a sight!"

Patrick heaved himself to his feet, dragging his cloak; he stared in the direction from which Bothwell had come, and he didn't smile. "Jesus," he said briefly. He neatly folded his cloak, putting it in the saddlebag, and swung into the saddle. "How many men do you reckon them to be, Francis?"

Bothwell squinted. "I'd say their cavalry would make two to three of us, and the foot is about two thousand." He rubbed his freshly shaven chin; he'd allowed himself that luxury this morning.

"But we can't meet them!"

"I should say not. Jamie is forcing me to retreat. We'll wait here only about ten more minutes, so that they have a good chance to see us." He yawned, and surveyed his men, drawn up, as they were, in four companies. Ochiltree and Ormuiston came riding up, and there, in plain sight of the royal armies, the four men listened in silence as orders were given.

In ten minutes the retreat would start. First by the castle, through the town, and continuing to the height of a passage called Restalrig Lone. From there to Waster Dudingstoun. Patrick heard his orders; he was commanding a troop of one hundred men, and he was first to go. He galloped off, remembering the line of a book he had just read. "A retreat is the most difficult of all military maneuvers." His company moved off in good order, Gibson alongside of him, and they had reached the village of Restalrig before the last company of Borderers quitted the field. James saw the whole maneuver plainly; the last troop of Borderers moved off, the sun ceased to glint on their weapons and bonnets, and the hill lay empty.

Patrick's orders had been brief, but they were strict, and they fretted him. This was so slow a pace, but the horses were not to be tired, and Patrick almost captured the illusion that they were out for a morning's canter. Some distance behind him, Bothwell was thinking the same thing, but he had quite a different motive. He was pondering the problem of whether or not his strategy would be apparent; his movements were so slow. But it could not be helped; this was the only strategy he had. He was so near the royal forces that a swift charge would overtake him. Still Maitland knew not so much about swift charges; he didn't employ cavalry that way. But some of his captains were more experienced. Bothwell damned them, briefly, and continued on his way.

When he reached Waster Dudingstoun, there was more distance between him and Maitland's vanguard. This pleased him, and he sent a horseman ahead with messages. They were to keep on this steady pace, easy on horses and men, until they came to the town of Noodrie Marshall; they were to pass through the village, and up onto the hill. That was all.

Bothwell was still in the rear. Although he himself had left the last town behind, he was a good deal behind his other three companies. And the King's armies hadn't seen him for the space of two miles now; they were quite far back, the foot having held them up.

At the head of his troop, Bothwell spurred forward a little more swiftly. He wanted to disappear now, for quite a while, and the Borderers behind him were glad enough to ride faster. Nevertheless, it was an hour before they reached the village of Noodrie Marshall. Ahead of them the other troops were mounting the hill on the far side of town. The whole South lay open to them now; they had gained their point. The lines of communication with the South could hardly be cut off now, unless there was quick action on the part of their adversaries.

Bothwell came up the hill at full gallop, letting off steam, and he and Valentine pounded up to within a few feet of Patrick and Ochiltree.

"Scatter," said the Earl briefly. " 'Tis as good a place as any." Good? It was perfect. He looked down the hill in front of him. There was nothing to be seen yet. And the hill was shaped like a cup; it was called the mote of the Weymat. On all sides the hill sloped downward, and around its lips were thick forests, bushes, undergrowth.

Bothwell called out a few names. The men rode forward, and even while he called those names, the rest of his Borderers disappeared into the trees. In two minutes there was nothing to be seen of them.

Bothwell dismounted; the various captains crowded around him in a circle, along with Ochiltree and Ormuiston. Patrick, forgetting himself, crowded in too, expectancy making his face eager and excited. Bothwell reached up and broke off a long bare branch. Standing there amidst his men, he drew a rough circle on the ground, a circle exactly like the rimmed hill on which they awaited James, and at four different spots around the rim of the hill he drew four X's.

"One hundred men to take each of these positions under cover." His voice was low, and no one spoke. Patrick heard himself being given the Liddesdale men, and he thought he knew why. They were the aptest and most ruthless fighters. They would make up for his own inexperience, he thought ruefully, wondering now not about the outcome of this particular venture, but about acquitting himself well in front of the critical Borderers.

Bothwell's orders were so simple. 'Twas so simple a ruse, that now Patrick was a bit worried—until he reminded himself that simplicity was the essence of cleverness. All Patrick had to do, all each captain had to do, was wait until James's cavalry intruded itself unprepared into this cup-like hill. Then they would use the fast cavalry charge that Bothwell had been practicing.

"Use all speed," ended the Earl dryly, "with much benefit of gunshot." He stopped, threw aside his stick, and looked up from the drawing on the bare ground, as if to ask if there were one who did not understand. Patrick was silent, as was everyone else, and Bothwell threw him a brief smile, a speculative smile. The circle of men drew apart, wondering if a circle made up of four hundred cavalry men would catch in it the royal cavalry.

Bothwell and his few men slipped back into the nearest cover. They were the watches, left to spy northward, left to see if the royal troops would fall so neatly into this trap. He hitched the reins of his horse to a small tree, and flung himself flat on the ground, and he inched forward slowly, scraping along until he lay almost at the edge of the cover.

"They'll come soon." He whispered the words to Gibson, who lay only a few feet from him.

Gibson nodded. "I could do with a spot of ale," he volunteered.

"In fact, you'd prefer to wait in a tavern." Bothwell grinned, and rested his chin in his hands. "One thing I want to make clear, Gibson. If this trap works, and if they send men up the hill, I do not want them shot and taken. I want them put to flight. There is nothing so catching as flight."

Gibson nodded again, and he inched his way off a little; Bothwell could hear him moving from one watch to another, relaying those orders. By the time he got back, crawling on his stomach, the first company of the King's guard had moved into sight.

They were at the bottom of the hill; they came to a full stop, and pretty soon they were joined by another cavalry unit.

"That's all the horse." Bothwell's voice was low, tense with excitement. "And there's Morton; even from here I can't miss him!"

Gibson was silent; he watched while the foot marched slowly into view. They looked tired. The day was hot, and their pace had of necessity been fast. But evidently something had been decided on, for the foot assembled behind the cavalry for protection, and then several men rode forward quite a space.

"They're talking this over," whispered Gibson.

"Too bad they can't talk to you." Bothwell raised one eyebrow. "But I wager you ten pounds they think we've fled. Watch!" The foot was moving again now, toward the south, as though they hoped to cut off a retreat. But they didn't move far from the protective horsemen, and there was still the cavalry, right ahead of the watching Earl. Suddenly the troops divided into two, the cavalry, thus separated, fanning out on each side of the hill. Bothwell couldn't resist an exclamation of delight and Gibson swore under his breath. He glued his eyes on the men in front of him, down the hill, and he lay so still that two squirrels investigated his boots.

"There's Jamie Stewart." Gibson barely breathed the words. Plainly they could see the King, with his own guard, and they could see the four horsemen who rode up to him. There was a space in which nothing happened, while James pointed to the brow of the hill. There was more talking, evidently, and the three horsemen galloped off; they were coming straight at Bothwell and Gibson.

"Let them come," muttered the Earl. He didn't move from his position for three minutes; then he leaped to his feet, and was in the saddle before Gibson could follow.

The three horsemen came up the hill slowly; they were well armed, but wary. Of course, there was little possibility that any men were concealed in the thick belt of trees that rimmed this hill, but even so, it was expedient to reconnoiter with care. They fanned out a little, but kept close enough together to protect themselves. And there seemed to be no one there.

"I think it would be well enough to give the order to ride," the first man spoke to the second.

"I warrant it's safe enough." The answer came back quickly. They had reached the top of the hill by now, and they saw no one there.

The first rider raised his hand; that was to be the signal in case there was nothing to be feared. At the foot of the hill the first cavalry troop spurred their mounts and came forward, at a good pace, because their King had ordered them to overtake and cut off the outlaw Earl of Bothwell. That first troop was halfway up the hill, when Bothwell gave the signal.

The first to be caught in the vortex were the three horsemen. They would never know what spared their lives, for out of those woods, the dense woods, on all sides, there came an avalanche of horsemen, riding at breakneck speed. There was only one thing for them to do, and that was to flee, at top speed. They veered their mounts, plunged downhill toward their own company, horror-struck, as the woods disgorged their shouting foe.

The Borderers attacked with vigor. They let out their war-cries with high glee, for this fast cavalry charge suited them. Hunched in the saddles, they gauged their distances so that their pistols seemed to ring out point-blank in their opponents' faces; and they used their two-bladed axes with fearsome dexterity. The light glinted on the wicked blades, and that first company of horsemen, which was halfway up the hill, was caught and surrounded.

They tried to fight, but it was useless. On each side their men fell, their horses cried loudly, plunging beneath their riders, and on all sides, everywhere, were those yelling Borderers, reckless as only they could be, swinging their axes with savage skill, hacking their way through to the center, spitting gunfire.

Patrick and Ochiltree had led that charge. Never in his life would Patrick forget it. Never would he forget the lust for battle in which he was caught up, for victory was so sweet. His men moved like seasoned troops. Speed, which was the overword of the Border raids, was what worked the miracle.

Down the hill, the second company of King's cavalry was fighting valiantly. Separated from their allies, surrounded in the bottom of the cup, they were beset by two hundred men with the Border lord at their head. Valentine came charging up to the foremost riders, past whom already frightened men were fleeing, and plunged into the thick of them.

The gunfire was deafening, as Bothwell had wanted it to be. The Border lord himself used a two-bladed axe, his long arm reaching out to knock a man from the saddle with an arm or leg hanging useless and bloody.

Four hundred Borderers? There seemed to be thousands. The foot soldiers fled in terror. They could see nothing but that their cavalry was ripped to shreds, caught up in a melee of men and horses, pistol shots and yells. They fled incontinently, regardless of their King, forgetting their tiredness, throwing their weapons aside to make movement easier. What good was armor against a mounted Borderer, who rode at you point-blank, swinging his axe with a motion that cut down two men at a time? They fled while there was time, while their helpless cavalry was being annihilated; they fled while the horsemen were still the object of attack.

Bothwell was in the thick of that attack. He had tried to find Maitland, but he had not succeeded; he had had the satisfaction of seeing Morton hit, his ribs stove in with a tremendous blow from none other than the ubiquitous Graham. But Morton had got away, pulling his horse toward safety. He fled, with the rest that could get away, the ones who weren't surrounded too completely. Bothwell had lost his axe, buried in the side of one unfortunate man, and it was not the duty of the Border lord to round up prisoners. He wrenched his sword from its sheath; there was not so much room now, but room enough to charge on a man with the bare blade in his right hand, room enough to come up alongside, and deliver a sudden thrust. He drew back sharply, tearing the sword from his enemy's arm; it was not a fatal blow, but it was enough, for the man rolled out of the saddle, and Bothwell watched only briefly as his horse was confiscated by a greedy Borderer. Then he turned.

The fighting was almost done. His dark eyes swept the field with an eye to booty. There were loud cries of surrender; already the Borderers were having to stop their battling to accept prisoners.

There were just a few of the King's cavalry still ready to give battle, and two of them suddenly saw, right before their eyes, the black horse and the glittering mail of the Border lord. Their weary animals were spurred forward.

Gibson saw it from a distance. Bothwell had wheeled his horse. Out of the melee two men came at him. He swerved to one side, galloping forward, trying to pass between them. As he did, he reached out with the sword, using it almost as a knife, slashing at a face he barely saw, using his speed to carry him safely through.

It almost did. He would have been safe if Valentine hadn't stumbled over a rabbit hole. His foreleg crumpled; Bothwell went forward in the saddle. At the same time he felt the pain in his shoulder. Horse and man went down.

Bothwell had been thrown clean of Valentine. Both the lance, which had struck through his shoulder, and the horse's stumble, had contrived to toss him neatly over Valentine's head; he sprawled on the ground, rolling over once, losing consciousness only briefly, knowing immediately that his right arm was useless. He lay on his stomach for a second, but he must turn over; he was helpless this way. He used his left arm to roll himself over, dragging the twenty-four-inch dagger from his belt in the same gesture. The breeze was cool on his bare head, for he had lost his helmet.

He heard the thud of a man dismounting. He made himself use his right elbow to lift him from his supine position and he waited until the man above him was very near. Then the hand with the dagger came upward swiftly, the blade buried itself, and Bothwell gave it a vicious twist that would bring his opponent down on the ground beside him.

"Are ye dead?" he muttered, rolling over, so that his body lay across his adversary. There wasn't any answer, so Bothwell looked at the face beneath him. He'd never seen the man before. With a long sigh, he pushed himself up to a sitting position.

Valentine nudged him gently, nuzzling his face; the reins hung loose, slapping at the side of the horse. "Good lad," Bothwell murmured, "just a minute." He ran his left hand over Valentine's leg but there would be no swelling yet. He tried to move his shoulder, and clumsily, using his left hand, he eased the light mail coat off, and opened the neck of his leather jack. Sitting there, on the ground, he suddenly became aware of the circle of boots that surrounded him, and at the same moment Gibson dropped down on his knees beside him.

Without a word, Gibson drew his slender knife and cut apart the linen shirt. "It went all the way through," he announced. "The opening in front is small, but you can see it's ripped your shirt and jack on both sides." He opened the saddlebag and drew out a length of linen.

"Just wad it, man, front and back." Bothwell was endeavoring to move his right arm a bit.

"Keep it quiet, my lord; you'll hurry the bleeding." He stuffed the linen close to the gaping lips of the wound, and carefully fastened the leather coat to hold the padding in place.

"Good. Now give me a heave." Bothwell held out his left hand, and Gibson pulled him to his feet. He stood a bit unsteadily, and he motioned to Graham, who was standing near. "I need help," he said simply.

Graham leaped forward; he bent down, cupping his hands, and Bothwell put one foot in them, resting his good left hand on Gibson's shoulder. He was up and in the saddle with dispatch, and he looked down and smiled. "I saw you get Morton," he said to Graham. He tucked his right arm across his waist, and hooked his thumb in his belt to support it, and from his vantage point he surveyed the man he had dragged down with a twist of his long dagger. He saw the gleam of a ruby ring on his finger. He pointed. "Hand me that," he ordered. "My lass will like that. Devil take you, lads, it's a wonder he's not stripped of his gear by now!" He tucked the ring in the pocket of his jack. "Now, follow me, lads!"

There was almost no fighting left to do. In the cup of the hill were only Borderers and their prisoners, and those were off, apart. Beyond them fled the men who had escaped the trap, some wounded, some terrified for their lives. Bothwell spurred Valentine on; pursuit and capture of some of the fleeing men meant money, horses and armor. In full cry, after the defeated, went the Borderers, hot on the trail, now eager for booty.

The miles went by fleetly; each mile saw the overtaking of some luckless stragglers, and they were stripped and shoved to the rear as fast as their pockets could be emptied. The route they had followed in so leisurely a fashion this morning, was eaten up by the fleet-footed Border horses; the hard, still frozen winter ground echoed to the thudding hoofs, and only a mile separated them from the racing foot soldiers.

They overtook the rear quickly, rounding up the prisoners; ahead of them lay Edinburgh, and to the south, the royal fortress of Craigmillar. The foot soldiers were cut off from Edinburgh; they raced for the safe walls of Craigmillar, pell-mell across the fields, with the King and his few horsemen right in the middle of the flight.

Bothwell galloped on. He could feel now the warm wet blood trickling down his side and back, and he looked down at his coat; at least he couldn't see that the wound had bled enough to leak through his coat. He himself now could see Craigmillar. Its walls rose in the distance, and only half a mile separated him from his King.

He looked back; his Borderers were either following him, or else were momentarily occupied with the taking of prisoners. The banners of the King's forces still flew around a motley group of men with the King. Bothwell drew up sharply, Gibson to one side of him. All sorts of thoughts were chasing through the Border lord's head. He could take Edinburgh. With four hundred men, he could take the capital; he could probably capture James. Absently, he tucked his hand inside his jacket and moved the wadding a little.

"If I were sure of taking Maitland—" His voice trailed off, and Gibson nodded. Maitland was probably far away by now; he was no man to stay around a lost battlefield. Suddenly Bothwell made up his mind.

"Sound the retreat," he ordered, and Gibson said smartly, "Aye, sir," and wheeled off.

The trumpets blew. The soft air carried their sounds to the spot where James was standing, just half a mile away, almost at the gates of Craigmillar, in this fair ley field where the sun shone. The trumpets blew, and each Borderer turned his mount, obeying the command. They assembled quickly, forming their original troops, except for the few men who were guarding the prisoners and the horses.

"D'ye see this, cousin Jamie?" muttered Bothwell, as he surveyed their neat maneuvering, as he watched his troops coming together, lining themselves on the plain, in good discipline. He was proud of them! He rode to the head of the lined-up companies, held up his hand in greeting. For a minute he stood there, taking in their formation, and he cast one last look at the huddled defeated group in the shadow of the big castle. His smile was rueful, but he turned, leading his men back toward the south again.

This victorious retreat was as leisurely as the first had been. Bothwell led his men as far as the gentle slope southwest of Leith, where he had stayed this morning for an hour, before they had seen James. There, on the hillside, he stopped them; the prisoners were gathered together in one spot, many of them hurt. But his first attention was to his own men.

Who was missing? Who was hurt? Bothwell himself sat motionless astride Valentine, while the captains checked rapidly on their individual commands. They finished quickly, came to report to Ormuiston, who relayed the news to Bothwell.

Ormuiston said proudly, "None missing, my lord. Ten wounded. All can ride."

Bothwell smiled, a smile which made Patrick, who was beside him, clamp his lips shut so he wouldn't show his emotion. But Bothwell only nodded. "See to the wounded," he ordered, and he himself turned his mount, riding over to the group of prisoners.

There were many. He was amazed that there were so many, and he reckoned quickly that, therefore, few had been killed. He was satisfied with that too. He had no desire to leave a field with many dead; it would have reacted against him politically. He rode up to the improvised camp where only a few heavily armed Borderers glowered at their captives, stretched on the ground in various attitudes.

The guards prodded their prisoners into attention; those who could, were forced to stand. "His Lordship's here," growled out the Borderers, looking up at their lord with admiration. He'd wrested victory for them.

Valentine danced a little, and then stood quietly while Bothwell surveyed the defeated men. He transferred his gaze to the ones badly hurt. "They are to be freed," he commanded, and the men looked up at him with sudden gratitude. Everything that had happened had been so swift, so miraculous, and this was the final miracle. Some of them started right off, regardless, and Bothwell frowned. What lack of discipline!

"Stay them!" he ordered. "First they will look to their hurt comrades. See that that is done." Lord, he didn't trust them with their own; they'd leave their companions-in-arms half-dying on the field.

He grinned as he watched his men prod the unhurt captives with their muskets; he grinned when he heard some of the language used. The scene amused him, and he forgot the weakness that he had been feeling. In front of him the prisoners were binding up the wounds of their fellows, and the air was thick with the coarse jibes of the Borderers.

Patrick rode up; he was almost at Bothwell's side when he stopped short, turned to Gibson, and said, "He's hurt!"

Gibson frowned slightly. "Aye, sir, I know it, but it's a clean wound, right through the shoulder."

Patrick said, "He's losing too much blood, Gibson. It takes a lot of blood to come through and soak that leather." He went right up to Bothwell. "Francis, let me look at that injury."

Bothwell put his hand inside his coat, moving the linen again. "It's just bleeding," he said. "The only thing, man, is that I don't know how much farther I can ride." He frowned, but Patrick saw that his tanned face was drawn. Patrick wanted to give orders, but he couldn't, not here. He wanted to say, "The devil with these prisoners, let them all die," but he didn't. He waited in silence; finally Bothwell was satisfied.

"Start them marching," he ripped out the words impatiently. "They are to go in the direction of Leith." He had no doubt but that his commands to the defeated foe would be obeyed; they were frightened enough to do his bidding, and he wanted them straggling through the streets of the port. He wheeled his horse again, trotting back to his men.

"Ormuiston," he said, low, "I don't know how far I can ride, but you are to take the men home. To Hermitage. You will ride to Dalkeith, and there refresh both men and horses. Push on as soon as possible, unless there is any difficulty—but there won't be any." He left behind him only the pitiful remnants of an army; there would be no pursuit for days, weeks, perhaps months. He had demonstrated to James that he, James, was not equipped to deal with his cousin on the battlefield. Not only that—James would have a time finding men who wanted to face the Border lord.

Ormuiston said, "Aye, sir."

Patrick had extracted a water container from his saddlebag. "It's whiskey, Francis," he explained, holding it out.

Bothwell took it gratefully, drinking freely. He said, "I needed that, sir," and handed it back. Thirsty as Patrick was, he refrained from drinking himself, and he put the liquor back.

"Are you sending them all to Hermitage?" Patrick put forth the question tentatively. "Francis, we need a few men." Whether or not James's army was defeated, it was far from safe for Bothwell to travel by himself, in this state.

"Reserve ten, then." That was all he would concede. "I want them to get back safely," he added, stubbornly, irritably. The pain in his shoulder was knifing through him even when he was motionless. He could feel the blood, already crusted, lying against his ribs and the hollows of his back and stomach. But still he waited, motionless on his horse, watching the men start off, and it wasn't until the last of them had disappeared over the hill that he gave the order to march.

By this time, Patrick was in a fever of impatience. Not so Ochiltree, who had campaigned with the Earl of Bothwell many times before, and knew it was useless to fret. Then they, with their scant ten men, galloped off in a southerly direction. The fields of Leith were empty, but for the dead.

"And where now, Francis?" Patrick put the question with an assurance he did not feel. It should not be necessary for them to go far. He shot an anxious glance at Bothwell's face. "Where now?"

Bothwell frowned. His hand was still hooked on his belt to ease his shoulder, and with his fingers he could feel the ring in his pocket. "I have a lass," he said. "I'm going home."

Chapter Twenty Six

Bothwell stopped only once between Leith and Crichton. He stopped because of Valentine, and while the horses were looked to, he sat close to a fire, his boots almost in the drifting ash. He refused food; he drank some hot raw whiskey. Then it was time to go on again.

He spoke not a word as the miles went by. He needed every breath, every ounce of energy. Now the pain seemed to be not only in his shoulder but all through him; it seemed as though he had been riding for long, long hours. His big saddle was suddenly too large; he wound the reins about his good left hand, and hunched himself forward.

"Only two more miles, my lord." Graham's low voice pierced through his consciousness. Bothwell reflected hazily that Graham's accent was almost like his own; sometimes it was impossible to tell an English Borderer from a Scot.

"Graham," he said, hoping his voice would carry, "you know when Jamie mounts the throne of England, we will not be the Borderers any more." He didn't know why he said that, but he must say something to cover his weakness.

"The devil we won't." Graham was startled by the thought. "I warrant, my lord, that we'll call ourselves Borderers hundreds of years from now."

Bothwell smiled inwardly at the heatedness of Graham's tone. He tried to say, "Perhaps you are right," but his voice was so low that Graham couldn't hear it, and the Englishman rode closer, peering through the dark.

"Are you . . .?" He broke off, hesitantly, and looked over at Patrick who was on Bothwell's other side. "Sir—" he began.

"Here's Crichton, Francis." Patrick made his tone sharp. "Here we are!"

Bothwell had let go the reins; he was guiding Valentine with his knees, and he was groping for the bridle to steady himself. He grasped his high pommel instead, and let himself gently forward. There were lights now, streaming from open doors; torches flickered in the stone courtyard, and beneath his horse's hoofs there was the sound of flags. He slipped out of the saddle, because he couldn't hold himself steady any longer, and he forgot there were men who would help him. He looked through the big open doors; the steps were shallow, and he could mount them well enough. He was surprised that he could. The doors were open. There was the hall, arching up gracefully; there was the staircase, rising like fluid stone, with its famous balustrade etched deep with the Hepburn roses. And she was there too, coming down toward him, her hand on the balustrade. Then she was running toward him swiftly, her gown flying behind her, her hands outstretched.

"Lassie!" He smiled, and said, "You look as beautiful as though you were expecting me! And I brought you something." He dug his good hand into his pocket. He remembered, later, seeing the flash of the ruby ring; he remembered her quick murmur, "Lean on me, my lord." After that, there had been nothing but a velvet blackness.

Anne dropped to her knees beside him. She was crying noiselessly; she was trying to unfasten the blood-soaked jacket. She felt a hand push her to the side, and Patrick was kneeling beside her, his knife in one hand. He slit the leather neatly, and Anne heard his low voice.

His calm tone made her glare angrily at him; then she whirled and started up stairs.

"Up here," she said, and then she burst out, "Oh, Patrick, will he die?"

"Who? Francis?" Patrick grinned. "He's as weak as a horse.

Anyway, lass, you'll see him brought home, feet first, more than once."

Anne said, "He walked in, sir!"

When Bothwell woke up, the first thing he was conscious of was an unfamiliar smell. He turned his head a little, opened his eyes, and closed them again. There was that smell again. He moved slightly, feeling the cool linen sheets; they felt so cool because he was so hot. He lifted one hand and pushed back a smooth quilt, and he sniffed experimentally; he opened his eyes again. He saw Anne.

She was sitting beside the bed, and she was pulling the quilt back over him. He pushed it away stubbornly, and he said, "I smell like a rose; that's what I've been smelling."

Anne faltered; she was so unnerved at his sudden waking. "We washed you with my soap, my lord."

"A rose," he repeated. She had pulled the quilt up over his chest again, and he gave up. Underneath it he moved his left hand and touched his shoulder experimentally, feeling the bandages that criss-crossed his entire chest and back.

Anne's eyes filled with tears; he was suffering, and he wouldn't say so.

"Does it hurt so much, sweetheart?" she whispered.

He did not seem to have heard her; at any rate, he didn't answer her question. "I'm hungry," he said. "Lass, I'm starving. And I have a fever, don't I?"

"Aye, my lord, you do."

"Well, then, bring me some wine."

"Wine?" Anne repeated, horrified.

"Aye, lass, wine. That cures a fever. And some meat. I'm hungry," he repeated, louder.

"Meat?"

He rolled over on his side, his good side, and put out one arm, grasping her wrist. He grinned at her.

"D'ye think I'm dying?" He closed his eyes, and Anne went to the door to send someone for that extraordinary order, and also for Patrick. She needed Patrick. She came back to the bed; she thought Bothwell had fallen asleep again, and she took his hand. She put her cheek against his, kissing the corner of his mouth and the hollow underneath his cheekbone.

"Oh, that's nice, lassie." His good arm went around her, and he smoothed her hair.

"You're awake again," she said, accusingly.

"Do you kiss me only when I'm asleep?" He opened his eyes and asked, "What time is it?"

"It's ten o'clock, m'lord. You slept all last night and today." Anne thought of the vigil she had kept all those long hours.

"Well, then, no wonder I'm hungry. I haven't had any food for almost two days. You feed me, lass, and I'll be up tomorrow."

But he wasn't. The next day the fever was worse and, when Patrick changed the bandages, the edges of the wound were leaking, not healing. "Infected," he said, brusquely. "It won't heal till the pus drains out. It's a matter of a few days."

"But isn't there anything you can do?" Anne knelt by the bed, her hand on Bothwell's burning forehead.

"Nothing," he said. "We don't know what to do for infection. Only let it drain, and pray, and be glad it's not a bullet hole. They're worse."

He tried to send her to bed, but she refused. "I'll sit by him," she said stubbornly. "Oh, Patrick, he may die."

"You've not slept for two days," he said impatiently. "Let me stay with him, then."

"I'll not leave him!"

He went to the door. "I cannot give you orders," he said.

Bothwell opened his eyes as the door closed. His eyes glittered with fever. "What is it?" he muttered.

"Oh, my darling," she whispered. "Go to sleep again."

"I was not asleep," he said. He looked up at her, bending over him. He frowned. "Patrick told you to go to bed."

"How do you feel? Do you want some wine?" Anne asked, ignoring his words.

"Take off your dress and get in bed." He closed his eyes again and Anne watched his face. He seemed to be asleep. But when she sat down in her chair by the bed, he looked at her again.

"Did you hear me?"

"Aye, Francis."

He smiled a little. He pushed the quilts back and caught her hand in a strong grip. "Did you like the bauble?" he asked, drowsily, for she was wearing the ring he had brought her. "Well, lassie, do as I say then." When Patrick returned in the morning, they were both still sound asleep.

Bothwell insisted on getting up the next day, and the following day he insisted on getting dressed, even to his heavy boots. He went outside to inspect the sprawling stables, the servants' houses; he walked about the fields and orchards. Anne went with him; she trotted along beside him in a daze of happiness, while hurried whispers preceded them. "The lord and his lady are comin'!"

But when they entered the huge hall again, he was tired, visibly. Anne started on upstairs, hoping he would follow her, so she could induce him to stretch out in front of the fire after his walk, and she had almost reached the top step when she heard voices below her in the hall. She descended a few steps and peered curiously over the banister. She heard Bothwell's voice.

"Why, Isobel, I'm glad you came!"

Anne went down one more step so that she could see better. She saw a figure in brown velvet riding habit, the shoulders so padded that her waist seemed infinitesimal, and there was a tiny cap perched on her dark hair.

"Oh, Francis," she was saying, "we did so want you to have supper with us tonight, you and your countess. My congratulations, my lord."

Anne heard Bothwell hesitate; she knew how tired he was. But what he said was, "Isobel, I regret very much that we cannot come tonight, but Lady Bothwell is not well. You understand—the events of the past few days—she hasn't slept well."

Anne's eyes widened. She almost contradicted her husband from her particular vantage point; instead, she was extremely quiet, so that she could hear every word.

"You know how the lass would be," continued Bothwell's deep voice. "I had a bad shoulder, Isobel, and—" He left the sentence unfinished.

Isobel said, "I'm sorry, Francis. Please convey my regrets to Lady Bothwell. We are all eagerly awaiting the pleasure of meeting her. I am glad your wound was nothing."

So he had told her his wound was nothing? He must have, for he said, "It didn't bother me at all, Isobel. I hardly knew I had it, but my lassie was worried."

Then they argued about when they would see each other, with Bothwell insisting that Isobel come to Crichton, since she had already invited them. Anne went on upstairs and waited for her husband.

"I heard you," she said, accusingly.

He shifted his feet. "Why, I—" he began, and then grinned, looking sheepish. "I didn't want to tell her I was—" He broke off again, and sank lazily into a big chair. "Get someone to take these boots off me, will you, lass?"

Anne said, "There's no crime in being sick, my lord."

"Is there not?" He sighed; he hated to admit he wasn't always feeling full of life, and he said, "Rub my head, lass, will you, and undo this belt?"

"You bairn," she said, lovingly. "You're so proud of being big and strong, that you won't ever admit you don't feel well." But he will admit it to me, she thought, hugging the idea gratefully. At this very moment he seemed to belong to her more than she had really ever hoped. He had married her because of the child she carried; she had got him because she had schemed and planned and lied to him, when he had wanted to take her home from Hermitage.

She looked down on his dark head; his eyes were closed, his big hands rested loosely on his knees. Suddenly he opened his eyes, and stared into the flames of the fire. She dropped down on the floor, putting her head against his knee.

"I love you," she said, happily. "Will you always tell me everything?"

He smiled, running his hand over her blonde curls.

"Everything? There is plenty a wench shouldn't know, especially about her husband." He was thinking that the raid on Leith had been a success; he smiled when he thought of it, and he was wondering whether his decision to leave James alone that day, had demonstrated to James that he, Bothwell, had no designs on the life of his monarch. But that was something only time would reveal. In the meantime, Maitland was out, hiding in one country house after another; the Stewarts were back at court, in all their flamboyant glory. What difference this would make to his fortunes, again only time would tell. Politics was a dangerous and unstable game. He said, almost peremptorily, so that she knew he meant it. "And there are some things, Anne, that you must never dabble in. There are some things I don't desire you to know."

Chapter Twenty Seven

There were parts of Edinburgh that were far from savory. Although it is true that the wide and well-paved High Street excited the admiration of foreigners, there were parts of the city where the refuse stood in stinking heaps, where pigs squealed in the cellars; there were streets called Thieves' Row, and other names equally fearsome, and in these streets the inhabitants lived, as Hercules put it, "like ants in a dunghill."

Thieves' Row itself was a twisting alley near the Flodden Wall, a battlement that had been thrown up by amateur hands almost a century before. The houses were crowded so close together that at their tops they almost met; usually there was dingy wash hanging over what balconies there were, but, in the back, each house boasted a tiny plot that was filled with empty barrels, some bee skeps, garbage, and the remains of butchered pigs. The street had its tavern, its bawdy house, and you could hire a man to slit a throat for only ten crowns. Janet Applegate had lived on Thieves' Row for almost two months.

Janet lived in the third house down from its entrance on Candlemaker's Row. She lived in the fifth flat up, and the only thing different about this apartment was its cleanliness. She lived alone with Martha MacGregor, for one of Martha's boys was a butcher's apprentice who slept in the shop at night to keep watch, and the other boy was in service with the Ruthvens.

Janet slept in the kitchen because she preferred it. It was a large room; its hearth and well-scrubbed deal tables and chairs made it the most pleasant room in the apartment. She had stored her books in the big cupboards; she had put up hooks for her clothes. She could sit at the window and look out into the street as she read or sewed. She had been sewing when she saw Martha coming down the street; when Martha entered Janet already had her cape on.

"I'm going out, Martha," she said.

For the first time in weeks she sounded happy. Martha smiled at her. "Going out?"

"Aye. I wanted to wait for you. Malcolm just came; he brought the meat you wanted, but he had to get back to the shop quickly."

"And where are you going, miss?"

"Walking," said Janet. "The sun is shining, Martha. It's April and the sun is shining!"

Swift happiness poured through her, and yet there was no reason why she should be happy; today was no different from any other day. For two months now she had hardly ever walked out, except on the day when so many people had gathered on the streets because Lord Bothwell might have ridden into the city. It had been only four weeks ago, and it seemed much longer than that. "Martha," she said suddenly, "I'll tell you what—I'm going to buy some material for a new dress, and maybe enough for a new petticoat!"

Martha was pleased. "But the money?" she asked, diffidently.

"I have plenty of money. I have three hundred crowns!" A slight frown crossed her face; she had got the money from the sale of their furniture. "I kept the books," she said, "and at least I did not go to Caithness! To marry the first long-bearded farmer that asked me!"

"What's wrong with beards, miss?"

"Nothing," said Janet. She smiled. "Except that I like men without beards."

"Oh. I see. Our lady has her likes and mislikes. Well, let me tell you something, miss. That money will not last you long. 'Tis not much money; you'd best buy a ribbon for your hair."

"I'm going to earn money," Janet retorted. "Today I'm

going to walk to the palace and see if Lady Gowrie and the young Earl have returned yet."

Martha snorted. "They've not, lass. My Willie is in service with the Lady Gowrie and he will come to see us as soon as they come back."

Janet said, "Rumor hath it, dame, that they will be permitted the city soon. I know Lady Gowrie; his lordship studied with my father at the university last year. I'm sure she will recommend me."

Martha was busy taking off her cape and adjusting her cap. "You take my word for it, miss. You buy a ribbon, and forget about dresses and such. If you wait for your man without a beard, likely you'll have gray hair."

Janet laughed. "You daunt me not, dame." She waved goodbye, stepping out into the filthy street where the April sunlight shone so bravely. Wrapped in her gayest cloak, she started down another twisting alley to High Street.

It took her an hour to walk to the royal palace, but it took only a glance to see that the town house of the Ruthvens was still closed. Janet retraced her steps slowly, for it was all uphill going, and besides she passed Patrick's house. There was obviously no one home there either, at least no one of importance, for the house looked vacant, and from only one chimney came a lazy curl of smoke.

She walked back up the hill to the city. She thought only of the day when he could return, for certainly soon the city would be safe for him. She bought silk, for the first time in her life, and she bought enough of the shiny green material to make a full petticoat. She topped it off with a length of satin ribbon, and she walked into Thieves' Row with her arms full.

"Why, Mistress Janet." She was halfway down the street when the words made her turn, and the man who had spoken bowed deeply.

"I greet you, sir," she said properly, and smiled a little, preparatory to turning away again.

"Your servant, madam." He bowed again, very gallantly, and almost he would have passed for a gentleman, his dress was so smoothly elegant. "May I have leave to walk with you?" His eyes were on her intently. "I swear you have avoided me, madam; you cannot deny it."

"I have been very busy, sir."

"Then might I have leave to carry your bundles?"

"No, thank you," said Janet swiftly. She tried to go past him, but he held his ground unobtrusively, and he was about to speak again when from behind him came another voice, and a heavy hand was laid on his arm.

"Is he bothering you, Mistress Janet?" The speaker towered truculently over the figure of Janet's admirer.

"Oh, no, Johnnie," she said, but she looked up at the red-haired Johnnie gratefully.

"I'll see you home," he announced, "in a minute." He turned to the other. "You leave before I wring your neck, Pritchard."

Pritchard ignored him. "Goodday, madam. But I trust you and I will talk again. It's been a pleasure." He bowed and sauntered away, casting one backward glance at them.

Johnnie muttered, "He's a murderer, he is. You want to be careful of him; he's lower than a dunghill puddle, take my word for it."

"Oh, I do, Johnnie, but I did not want trouble."

"Trouble?" He did not think a street fight was any trouble.

"Aye," said Janet. He had taken possession of her packages. "Your arm is healed, is it not?"

"It is that, although my pockets are not." He smiled ruefully. "It's a foolish Scot will go off to battle with any siller in his pockets. But you know I lost my horse, that day at Leith. God's foot, those Borderers, they even took my boots! All the way from Leith I walked, without my boots!"

"But you should not fight against Lord Bothwell," said Janet gravely.

"God's foot," he repeated. "I'm a soldier. I ride when I'm told. But I'd rather shoot the big cannon," he added, thoughtfully."

"Why don't you, then?"

He sighed. "I'm not versed, mistress. I cannot write nor read the numbers."

"You mean that if you could write—" Her voice trailed off; she was thinking how much he had done for her in the past weeks.

"All those books I helped you bring," he said, "you read them, do you?"

Janet giggled. "Aye, but you would not like them much."

"I like you better," he announced.

"Oh, Johnnie, you have helped me so often. I wish I could return you a favor." They had come to her house; they were standing at the bottom of the dark stairwell that twisted its scarred wooden way above them. "I could help you learn to read and write."

Johnnie raised his brows. "You truly could?"

"Aye. It would not take so long."

Johnnie digested this. "If I could only read the numbers, only read them, I would be fit for a higher command. Mistress, did you mean it?"

"You have my word on't." She held out her hands and he put the bundles into them.

"It would be most kind of you," he said formally, because that was what she had said to him a number of times. He smiled, his teeth flashing in his bearded face. "I'll come tonight, with your permission." He stood for a moment watching her ascend the stairs, then he put his hands in his pockets and strolled away slowly, whistling as he went.

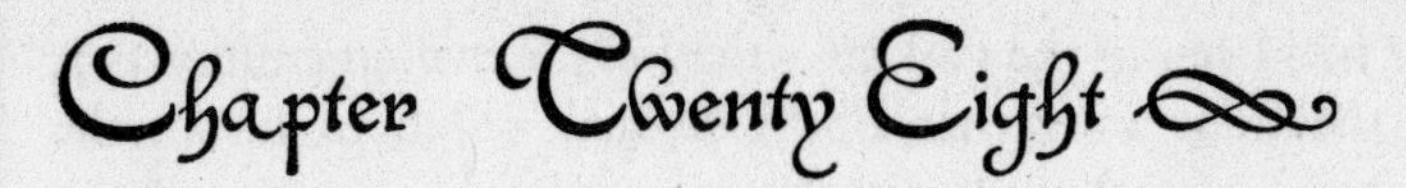

Chapter Twenty Eight

"You should have served me a pair of my own spurs tonight for dinner, Anne. Instead of the neat's tongue." Bothwell's dark head had been bent over a long list of figures that lay before him on his table; the results of his addition were hardly satisfactory. "The silver spurs would do," he added.

Anne was lying on one of the fireside benches in the library, watching him as he worked. "What do you mean, sweetheart?"

He smiled ruefully. "When a Border wife wants money she serves up a pair of her husband's spurs, as a hint that he should ride out on a foray." He laid down his pen and frowned at his list. "We're poor, madam."

"Are we, my love?" she asked dreamily, relaxing again, pulling the pillows under her head. She didn't think they were poor. She had acres and acres of land, huge dwelling places; she had a master of household, a master of horse, a bailiff; she had a castle garrison, housed in the keep, commanded by a Captain David Hepburn. At least so Bothwell had told her in the last few hours, interspersing his labors with numerous instructions on what was to be done in his absences, on who was responsible for the collection of rents, and when, and so many things her head swam. When he was gone would be time enough to tend to her duties. When he was gone, she would see that the long unused apartments were properly aired and furnished, the huge linen closets emptied and their contents washed and laid in the sun to bleach. When he was gone—but she wouldn't even think about that now. Instead she watched him contentedly and thought about the conversation she had had with Patrick that afternoon.

They had been in the gallery—the long Venetian gallery that was in the new wing that Bothwell had added to his castle. Patrick had been telling her the names and achievements of the men who had sat for the various portraits on the walls.

"This man," Patrick had said, "was the third Lord Hailes, the first Earl of Bothwell."

"Was he?" said Anne. "Patrick, if a child is born in handfast, is she legitimate?"

"What?" He was annoyed. He hated to be interrupted; he believed that it reflected on his ability as a teller of tales. "Is who legitimate?"

"Francis' daughter," she explained. She put her hand on his arm and looked very appealing. "I'd like her to live with us, here."

"What?" he said again.

She hurried on. "Patrick, you have done so much for me, giving me such a dowry, so that Francis could clear the mortgages from Crichton. I am so grateful," she continued, very serious, "that you suggested that Francis settle the castle and its towns on me. That was—"

"The usual arrangement," he cut in. "Very usual. But now what do you want?"

"His daughter."

He stepped back from her, regarding her with amazement. "You'll have children, Anne." He lifted his hand and tugged at his curly head. "Dozens, probably," he added.

"Aye, sir—oh, no, not dozens, but as I was saying, I am so grateful for the dowry. Fifteen thousand crowns is so much money. And all I want to know is if his daughter couldn't be legitimate, because she was born in handfast."

"What happened to the mother?"

"She died, Patrick. She died in childbed."

"That happens," he said. There was silence.

"She is a darling, Patrick. You should see her." Anne pursued her advantage. "If she could just be declared legitimate, she could live here with us, instead of with that hateful toad Eliza. Oh, I'd like to take a whip to her, I would!"

Patrick grinned. "Is that the reason you want the child? To spite Eliza?"

"No, sir. Truly it's not."

"What's her name?"

"Janet," she answered. "Janet Hepburn."

"Without the coat of arms," he said cynically.

"She was named for Francis' mother," Anne put in.

"Janet," he said slowly. He didn't speak for a minute. "I'll do it," he said finally. "I'll try."

Anne hunted for something to say, and nothing was adequate. "You'll find her, sir," she said, low. "I'm sure you will find her, someday."

"Aye, someday." He turned away impatiently. "And when I do, it may be too late."

"Ah, no, it will not." She stopped. He did not want to talk about it, and suddenly she said, "Patrick, who is that beautiful woman?" She pointed to a painting across the room.

"Where?" He followed her finger. "She was the wife of the second Earl."

"She is lovely." Anne walked over to get a better look, and he trailed behind her listlessly. "What was her name?"

At her question he came to life. "She didn't have a name. Only Agnes. She was the bastard daughter of Lord Erskine; she was the mistress of James the Fourth, till the Earl of Bothwell saw her, and fell in love with her."

"And he married her?" Anne stared up at the beautiful painted face.

He was too preoccupied to give her the tale he generally would have related. He said only, "The Hepburn married her."

Anne said firmly, "She is the most lovely of them all. I've a mind to hang her picture over the mantle in my room." She laughed, and he cut her laughter short brusquely.

"D'ye imagine you are two of the same kind? Well, let me tell you that she—Agnes—lost her husband, just some months after she married him. She was left a widow with a squalling brat, and he lay dead on Flodden Field, alongside of his dead King!" He was rewarded by her look of horror. "I've warned you so many times! Francis should not be here now; you keep him here!"

"I do not!" She was near tears. "I did not ask him to stay!"

"You did not ask him to stay!" He mocked her tone. "He thinks he ought to stay; it's spring, madam, and he's running acres and acres of farms. For you. And you want to meddle in his affairs. How do you know he wants his daughter here?" He swung away from her, then turned back, and he put one hand on the back of her head, his fingers in her curls. He tipped her head back. "You did not ask him to stay! You draw him like a lodestone; aye, and you'll draw him into danger. And when you do, come not to me whining, because that's one time I shall not be able to help!"

She remembered those words when she woke early the next morning. Bothwell was sleeping with one arm flung over her, and she lay beside him contentedly, knowing he was safe. She gazed at the outlines of her room as she listened to his regular breathing, and suddenly she remembered the way Murray had died. He had been with his wife too, and probably she had thought him safe. Anne moved restlessly; she tried to forget Murray. She lay quiet as long as she could, then she got out of bed and pulled aside the curtains. Almost fearfully she scanned the now familiar landscape.

There was nothing to be seen but rolling fields, budding trees. She let the curtains fall back into place; she was shivering with cold, and she hopped back into bed and pulled the quilts up under her chin.

Bothwell stirred sleepily. "Are you sick?"

"Oh, no. Go back to sleep; it's early."

"What's the matter?" He yawned. "What's the matter, lassie?"

"I'm afraid," she blurted. "I'm so afraid something will happen to you!"

He was relieved; he laughed, and he said comfortingly, "Nothing ever happens to me, lassie."

This understatement was hardly reassuring. "Everything happens to you," she said, gulping out the words. "Everything."

He grinned. "Including you."

"Including me?" she whispered. "But I love you; I'd never do anything that would ever harm you. I swear it, Francis."

"Are you jesting?" He didn't know what she was talking about, and he shrugged away her words. "Go to sleep, lambie. You make the pleasantest pillow."

That night Crichton had visitors. From nearby Borthwick Castle, Lady Isobel Borthwick and her husband and their always present house guests rode up in the early evening. They made quite a cavalcade; when Anne descended the wide stairs to greet them, the hall below seemed full of people. Anne's eyes swept past Isobel, just noting the tall slender figure. They swept briefly over Alice Ruthven and her mother, Lady Gowrie; they came to rest on the red hair and white face of Margaret Vinstar.

Anne lifted her fan lazily; she came down the rest of the steps, and regardless of the people in her way, she went to Bothwell and stood beside him. From there she threw Margaret one scathing look before she smiled at Lady Gowrie.

"We're charmed to welcome you, madam."

The evening began very propitiously. It was warm enough in the gallery; the fires in the handsome new chimneys were enough for the big room. Lord Borthwick, who fancied himself as a mixer of drinks, spent his time concocting a punch, sending the servants hither and yon for the ingredients he wanted. Logie, Burley and Andrew Ker were staying at Crichton; the handsome Hepburn who commanded the garrison and the adventurous Nidrie made the women's eyes jealous as they rested on their hostess.

The time grew later and later; this was Bothwell's last night at home, and Anne watched the hours go by. At twelve she was fretful; unlike her guests, she hadn't drunk much. And now, just at twelve, someone started to play the bagpipes. There were three of the instruments, and Bothwell was playing one with gusto; their noise made Anne's head swim.

"Hateful sounding things," she said to Patrick.

He looked at her surprised. "You are not enjoying yourself, are you, Annie?"

"Do not call me Annie!" She glared at Logie, who was performing a dance by himself to the tune of the whirling pipes. "I wish they were all fifty miles from here! Why don't they go home?"

Patrick raised one eyebrow. "They are enjoying themselves. Take my advice and smile a bit. You look like a small storm."

"That Borthwick woman! Bringing all her sisters over here." Anne blew out her breath. "Look at her and Francis. What does her husband think she is doing?" Anne transferred her glare to Lord Borthwick.

"Isobel Borthwick has been friendly with Francis since their cradle days. She is a charming woman and you're a fool to make an enemy of her."

"Oh, I am, am I? Marry-go-up, sir, but you know a deal of everything. What else am I doing wrong?"

"You're doing poorly as a hostess. You're scowling. I suggest—"

"Pooh," said Anne, interrupting rudely.

Patrick laughed. He bowed politely. "I'll leave you to your tantrums. Only it's my guess you'll not have them long. I thank God, your Ladyship, that now you have a husband."

"I'll show you," she called after him. She stood by herself, then she walked slowly toward Bothwell, swinging her fan. She came to stand beside him. "Francis," she said softly.

He turned to look up at her, for he was sitting, his legs stretched out. He was strumming his lute, and chanting a poem. He stopped playing. "Well, madam?" His cup of punch sat half empty, and Margaret reached over and handed it to him.

"Since Anne interrupted you, my lord, have this before you finish the song for us."

Isobel said quickly, "Francis has such a memory for verse. You have remarked it, have you not, madam?"

Anne preserved a silence, and Lord Borthwick said heartily, "Francis has a memory for verse and terrain. Did he whisper poetry to you, my dear?"

Isobel laughed. "He must have bewitched her, the sorcerer! How else would she have married the knave?" She tweaked Bothwell's ear, and he caught at her hand.

"Now be seated, my own countess," he said to Anne, moving over on the small bench. "I'll show them how I won you."

"I know what you'll sing!" Isobel clapped her hands. "I wager you ten pounds, Francis, that I know the poem!"

"Done!" Bothwell beckoned to Lord Borthwick to bend over, and he whispered in his ear. Borthwick smiled delightedly; he nodded his head to Isobel.

"Well, madam?" he said. "What's your guess?"

Isobel said slowly, "It's one of the Sir Philip Sidney love poems, is it not? Why, you used to quote them often, Francis."

Bothwell grinned. "You owe me ten pounds, Isobel. Tell your lady, sir, what I just whispered to you."

Lord Borthwick laughed. " 'The reiver, he stole fair Annie!' You owe ten pounds, my dear. Bothwell, look not to me; the lady owes it."

"What is a reiver?" inquired Anne icily.

"A pirate," said Bothwell; he gave her a long look and stood up. He offered her his arm.

Anne drew back. She looked up at his face. Then she looked to Isobel, who lowered her eyes, and turned away to her husband. She said something, but Anne paid no attention. She took Bothwell's arm.

"Are you ill?" His voice was low.

"No!"

He was walking her slowly toward the doors. "And how old are you?"

"Seventeen! You know it."

"You are acting like a dried prune. I'd warrant you to be sixty."

Anne's eyes blazed. But she kept on walking. "So you know so many love poems!"

"Poetry gives me pleasure. I have a memory for it. Why have you not ordered any food, or more wines?"

"Because it did not please me."

"I see. But your guests are hungry. I'm hungry."

"I hope they starve," said Anne.

They were at the doors; he propelled her through them, and out into the halls. "And now, madam, you'll seek your room. I shall make apologies for you; later you can make them in person." He motioned a passing servant. "Take her Ladyship to her room," he ordered, and then he stepped back into the gallery.

For a second Anne stood in the hall where he had left her; she was trembling with anger. She marched down the hall and she banged her door behind her with such violence that Marie shrieked and jumped to her feet. Anne said, "He sent me to bed! Just like a child!" She hurled her fan across the room, and began to pace back and forth, her skirts swirling. "The whey-faced wench—fawning around my husband!" She flung herself on the bed, her heels in the air. "I'll fix her. You'll see."

Marie had not said a word. She was just about to inquire, to satisfy her curiosity, when the door opened and Patrick sauntered in. He surveyed the scene for a minute, then he laughed and strolled over to the bed.

"Well," he drawled. "What a temper she has."

Anne sat up, tucking her feet under her. "Be gone." She spat out the words. "What do you want?"

"I wanted to inquire about your health. I heard it was poor, so poor it necessitated your retiring."

"You came to gloat. I hate you too!"

He burst out laughing. "Why do you not return to the party?"

"Because if I did, Francis would be like to send me back again and lock me in. And that she-goat Isobel would laugh at me." Her face puckered, and she looked as though she were going to cry.

Patrick rubbed his chin with his hand. "How do you like marriage?" Then he said seriously, "One word, Anne. Everyone in Scotland is aware you rode to Hermitage to see Francis. Everyone suspects you will have an early-born child. Remember that, lass."

"And they think that's why he married me?"

He nodded gravely. "That is the rumor."

He thought she would be angry again. Hence he was surprised when she said, "But I did marry him, did I not?" She smiled, and he leaned over and kissed her lightly.

"I'll drink a toast to you, Anne. But know one thing more. You have nothing to fear from Isobel. You are venting your spleen on the wrong woman."

He waved his hand, and went back to the long gallery, making his way to Isobel. He liked her; he enjoyed her company.

"We are only a mile away, you know, sir." Isobel was flattered, but she was very fond of her younger sisters, and she was a bit sorry that Patrick did not seem interested. She sighed a little, and then gave her attention to him completely. If her sisters couldn't compete— She ate her supper with him, at one of the small tables that had been brought in.

"You must be careful of women from Borthwick." Bothwell stood over both of them.

Isobel smiled; she had a lovely smile. "We tangle men from Crichton in snares," she told Patrick.

"Aye, sir; she speaks the truth. You know Borthwick Castle has a tall tower that overlooks the entire countryside. She will lure you to a midnight tryst; then she watches from the tower, and instead of the fair lady, you meet a number of angry gentlemen." Bothwell laughed; he turned to Margaret Vinstar, who had come up beside him. "As God's my witness, that happened to my grandfather."

Isobel regarded her hands. "We are guileful, sir."

"But what happened then?" asked Margaret slowly.

"An irate husband shut my duped grandfather up in the tower for a few days. It's not a romantic story, madam. There was no duel, and no loving." He smiled at Isobel. "I've always been terrified of her, since I was told the story."

"Who told it to you?" Patrick asked.

"I did," said Isobel sweetly, and Patrick grinned.

"She is a true Border wench," said Bothwell approvingly. "She has the best seat on a horse of any woman I know; I taught her."

"Perhaps Lady Isobel could teach Anne," said Margaret.

Isobel stared at her. "If Lady Bothwell would only share her dressmaking secrets, I should be charmed."

Bothwell and Patrick were both silent; they eyed each other, and Isobel continued, "Lady Bothwell has the most beautiful clothes."

Margaret moved away, toward Logie. Bothwell looked down at Isobel with a smile. "Thanks, lass," he said. "That red-haired wench annoys me." He drew his brows together. "Someday I'll slap her," he ended, and Isobel said quickly, "Do not, Francis."

Bothwell did not hear her; he had gone off, and Isobel continued to Patrick, "She is mad in love with him."

Patrick shrugged. "She will recover."

"Aye, but recovery is ofttimes painful. You would think, sir, that Francis would know of her love for him."

"If and when she interests him, he'll know it, madam. Before that, why should he bother?"

Isobel laughed. She rose. "Now I must take my charges home." She corralled her two sisters; she maneuvered it so that, out there in the moonlight, Patrick had to lift one of her sisters into the saddle. "Goodnight," she called to him.

Isobel was deep in her thoughts about him; all the way to Borthwick she was remembering the way he laughed and what he had said, and when she reached her own room, she undressed in the dark, letting the moonlight make quite plain the cushioned window seat where she laid her clothes.

She got into bed, but she was restless, and she went again to the window, curling up on the seat to look out.

She couldn't see Crichton. Only the tops of the new thick chimneys were visible. Yet that was where Patrick was now, and suddenly she went out into the hall, and up a narrow set of stairs. She emerged into a dusty passage with a barred door at one end.

She was cold. She had run up without her robe; her feet were bare. She stopped; she was about ten feet from the door when she came to a standstill. "Isobel," she said aloud. "You are a matron. And what is worse, your feet are filthy." She stood in the hall for a moment longer, then she turned, ran downstairs, and lighted her candles. Before she got in bed, she would have to wash her feet.

Up in the tower, Margaret Vinstar watched her lights snuff out, one by one.

Chapter Twenty Nine

THE following afternoon Anne drove the short distance to Borthwick. She was unattended and she drove a cart pulled by a ram, a cart so low that her skirts almost touched the ground. It was a sight that was to become very familiar to the farmers and tenants of Crichton; later they would watch for her and her slowly-plodding ram. But it was a very demure Anne who entered Borthwick Castle at four o'clock in the afternoon. She was pleased that everyone she had met the night before was there.

The men had just come in from riding. Hunting dogs sprawled around the small room; Anne had to step over them to enter. Everyone was talking and laughing, but Anne seated herself during a surprised hush. Isobel put a cup of wine in her hand, and Lady Gowrie, who sat next to Anne, anticipated Isobel.

"Why, we're so happy to see you, dear. We were so sorry you were indisposed last night. Now you are evidently fully recovered."

Anne caught the look that passed between Margaret and Alice Ruthven. Anne sighed a little. She looked straight at Isobel and from her to Lord Borthwick, who cleared his throat hurriedly. "You must be quite recovered, as Lady Gowrie says. We are much honored by your visit to Borthwick, madam. Did you ride over?"

Anne said sweetly, "Lord Bothwell does not like me to ride."

There was a second's complete silence in which she stared at Margaret. "Francis fixed me a small cart; he hitched up a ram to it. You know how Francis is, madam," she continued to Isobel. "It amuses him to make things. My cart has even a cushioned seat."

"It does?" asked Isobel weakly.

"Aye," said Anne. "We go very slowly, but Francis thinks horses are too dangerous for me."

Isobel gasped. She had never expected Anne to admit openly that she was having a child. She finally recovered. "I must congratulate you, madam. I vow I must; you have quite taken my breath," she said suddenly, and she smiled.

Anne smiled back, pleased with Isobel's response, but Lady Gowrie was astonished. "Are you sure, my dear?" she asked cautiously.

Anne nodded. "Quite sure, your Ladyship." She had kept her cloak over her shoulders and now she threw it back.

Isobel stared at the magnificent heavy diamond necklace Anne was wearing, even though it was quite unsuitable for an afternoon's visit. "How beautiful those stones are, madam," she said, with detached envy.

"Francis made me a present of this," said Anne, touching the chain with her fingers. She looked straight at Margaret.

There was another silence until Isobel's sister chimed in. "Madam, ever since I was tiny I've loved your husband. It must be wonderful to have a husband as gay as he. I warrant he keeps you laughing all the time."

Anne smiled but her violet eyes were cool. "Sometimes he is angry, though. Last night he was very angry with me."

Margaret stared, she hesitated, then she said, "Lord Bothwell was angry with you?"

Anne said gravely, "Francis was most disappointed with me, and I have come to present my apologies to all of you. Last night I promised him I would apologize in person for my lack as a hostess. My indisposition rendered me unable to stay the evening with you."

Margaret said cuttingly, "Is Lord Bothwell still angry?"

"Oh, no," said Anne. "It was his last night at home."

Margaret turned away, her jealousy like a sharp pain. Then she asked, softly, "When did Lord Bothwell leave today?" She tried to shove everything out of her mind but the movements of this band of men. "When did he leave for Hermitage?"

"Not till two o'clock. Lord Bothwell slept late." Anne sent one final barbed glance at Margaret; she was finished with her.

At this Lord Borthwick drank off all the wine in his cup; he surveyed Anne, and he muttered to his brother, "The battle-field is safer than this room." He filled his cup up to the brim. "We'll drink a toast to Bothwell, madam. To his health and his continuing good-fortune."

Anne was pleased. "I'll tell Francis," she said; she watched Isobel drink and put her cup down. She abandoned Margaret; now she could talk to Isobel about clothes and children and food.

"You'll have to wait for a good sunny day for the linen," Isobel said, after listening to Anne's domestic problems.

"I know. But the last time we had neat's tongue—and Francis is so fond of it—he said the gravy was too thick, like pea soup."

"Well, you must tell the cooks right away, so that they remember. I know he hates pea soup, too."

Anne sighed. She did not want to go, but it was time. Isobel walked outside with her, and Anne forgot she had ever called Isobel a whey-faced wench. "Some day perhaps you might stay a while at Crichton, madam. It would be a great honor to have you."

"I'd be charmed, truly." Isobel couldn't resist one question. "Has your cousin left with Francis?"

Anne nodded. "Indeed he has. All the gentlemen have left, except Logie. I haven't seen him today." She glanced at Isobel, speculatively. "But Patrick—and Francis—will be home soon. When they do come, you must join us, madam."

Isobel smiled; there was a twinkle in her eye. "And no doubt you'll last the whole evening through. This afternoon, you came out with all the honors, madam."

Anne said demurely, "Thank you. After all, Francis is my

husband." She flipped her fan open with a gesture of one hand and snapped it closed again. "My regards, madam, and I do look forward to your visit."

On her way home she was thinking of Isobel. The path wound around the lazy Tyne River; on both sides the valley went upward. It was comforting to know Isobel was so near; Isobel knew all about babies, she had two children, and she would come soon, if only because Patrick might turn up. Anne smiled, thinking of Patrick. The path turned sharply, the ram plodded on, and then suddenly he stopped; Anne screamed, and the knot of men who had gathered about the river bank whirled to face her.

"Your Ladyship," cried David Hepburn. He had been kneeling beside a figure on the ground. He leaped to his feet; he ran toward her, as Anne got out of the cart and stood staring at the weeds, the mud, and the trodden bank.

"Do not look!" He was at her side, and he took her arm.

"I saw him," she sobbed. "It was Johnnie!" Her face was white with fear and terror. It was Johnnie!

"The Laird of Logie is dead, madam," he said softly. "We only now found him; they just summoned me. Madam, your Ladyship—"

Anne whispered, "I'm not going to be sick. Who is the other."

"A lass he met. I warrant that he met her."

"Is she dead, too?"

"Aye." He stood for a second uncertainly, then he picked her up in his arms. "Lean your head back, madam," he said unnecessarily, for Anne already had. He strode rapidly toward Crichton, whose walls rose very near, not more than a few hundred yards away. He carried her all the way to her own apartments. He laid Anne on her bed.

"Her Ladyship swooned," he informed Marie, who was already filling a cup with wine.

Anne raised her head from the pillows. "Thank you, Captain," she murmured. "It's that I—" She broke off and he nodded at her solemnly.

"I know, madam."

"You'll inform Lord Bothwell?" Anne's lips trembled.

"I have already sent a messenger to Hermitage. There's been treachery, madam. Some whoreson traitor—I beg your pardon."

"It's granted," said Anne, with a return of vigor. She sat up in bed. "Who was the girl, Captain?"

He frowned. "A lass from Borthwick. There is one thing that puzzles me, madam."

"What?" asked Anne; the color was back in her face. "What puzzles you, sir?"

He still frowned. "She was not bonnie, madam. And Logie had an eye for the wenches. This lass, she was not bonnie."

Chapter Thirty

LOGIE was buried in the cemetery at Crichton. Both Patrick and Bothwell had arrived that night at Crichton, riding hard from Hermitage. Both were tense, uncommunicative, and they had talked all night in the library. Anne had gone down once, at four in the morning, and they had sent her back upstairs brusquely. Two days later they had laid his body in the little cemetery, and then they had ridden off again. Neither one had told her anything but that his murderers had not been found. "Yet," Bothwell had added, and Patrick had nodded his head.

"They were many, then?" Anne asked fearfully.

"Aye, lassie. But you must not be frightened," he said quickly. "Anne, you must not be frightened."

But it resulted in the fact that she was never permitted to ride out alone. Not unless she were traveling right around the castle, in the stretching fields where there were always men at hand. So the day she rode over to get Bothwell's little daughter, she was accompanied by a troop of forty riders, with David Hepburn at the head of them. They made an impressive cavalcade.

Willie's farm looked very different from the way it had in winter. Now, in the last days of April, the trees were budding, the fields were soft brown and furrowed neatly, and there was the sound of birds in the dovecotes of the farmhouse.

Eliza's small eyes were blacker and more malignant than Anne remembered. Eliza came from the house with Janet trailing behind her, and Janet's face was flushed with excitement; she looked from Anne to the man who was carrying her boxes.

"There is only one more box, madam," she said, smiling, her eyes alight; she remembered to curtsy.

Anne leaned down and kissed her. Eliza's two daughters were watching this scene from the doorway; they edged down the steps and sidled closer to Anne, who noticed them with an uplifted eyebrow. The last box was in the coach. "Say goodbye to the little girls, dear," Anne reminded Janet; she turned to the daughters. "And you may say 'Goodbye, your Ladyship.' You must learn your manners better." Anne had Janet's hand in hers, and she turned toward the coach, but not before both girls had obediently repeated, "Goodbye, your Ladyship."

Eliza wrinkled up her nose at hearing her children obey Anne, but she remembered in time that this was Bothwell's wife. She made her curtsy too and Anne acknowledged it haughtily. With a flip of her skirts she was in the coach with Janet beside her. The coach started off, the horsemen with it wheeled about, and clouds of dust rose in Eliza's face. Anne smiled delightedly. "I hope the old bawd chokes."

Every morning during the spring and summer Anne drove out with Janie in the small cart. She liked to play her role as mistress of this vast estate, its orchards and tilled fields stretching around in every direction. She liked the admiring glances of the men; she would ply her fan, make her suggestions, and be sure again that everything was done on time.

When the noonday sun was high in the heavens, she would retreat to the coolness of her stillroom, and there she pored over the old recipes for marmalade, taken from Queen Mary's own royal recipe, and spicy jams, and sweet-smelling perfumes. There she watched the roses crushed, the alcohol added, and she herself would watch the brew carefully, spooning in the sugar, smelling the finished product with delight. Then, in her childish round hand, she would add her own recipes for perfume to the old ones that had been written by the women who had preceded her at Crichton.

Sometimes she went over her accounts. Four pounds a month

for every soldier in the garrison. Rents were carefully collected and itemed, and debts were paid. Two bells of wheat and two of corn went every year to the family of the Cockburns, who a long time ago had rescued an earl of Bothwell from his pursuers, and hidden him in their kitchen till danger was past.

Crichton was so peaceful. The cool summer breezes fanned through the lovely halls and gallery; there were always guests, and the sound of laughter and hurrying feet always in the halls. In the afternoons, Anne sat outside, under the shade of the big elm, watching the pall-mall, drinking cooled sherry. When she walked in the sun, she kept her mask over her face to protect her skin from the sunshine; she wore embroidered satin gloves so her hands would not lose their soft whiteness.

Sometimes, only sometimes, she would have Bothwell near her, lounging at her side; or else she would watch him on the tennis court, so hard to beat because of the great length of arms and legs that seemed to encompass the whole court. After he had played, he would fling himself down on the grass at her side, mopping the sweat off his face, consuming quantities of ale brewed right at Crichton's brewery.

He arrived at any time of day or night. One time he came in her window at midnight; she hadn't known he was in the room until she felt his hands on her shoulders. She had been sitting at her table, writing, and he said, "A lady should not write, except to her lord."

"Oh, my darling, I was," she said happily.

He bent over her to see the letter. "So you love me," he said softly; he turned her around to face him. "Ah, sweetheart, it's been many long nights that I've suffered from lack of you."

But Crichton was not the world, even though it seemed so to Anne. Beyond its confines, and only some two hundred and fifty miles to the south lay the summer palace of Nonesuch, residence of the English Queen. Anne didn't know that the same August day that she herself had received a letter from her husband, another letter had traveled southward from the Earl of Bothwell to the Queen of England. Elizabeth was reading that letter now; it lay on the table in front of her, and suddenly she pushed back the white sheets and looked over to Lord Burghley.

"You may continue," she said.

Burghley had been reading aloud from another letter, although he had really been thinking about the next one. "The Dean writes," he began, "that Lord Bothwell is a nobleman of wonderful wit, and has as wonderful volubility of tongue. He possesses agility of body, on foot as on horse. He is competently learned in the Latin, well-languaged in French and Italian, much delighted in poetry. And he is of a very resolute disposition both to do and to suffer." Burghley smiled at the Dean's choice of words. "The Dean goes on to say, to use his own words, that Lord Bothwell is 'nothing dainty.' "

Elizabeth smiled, but seemed disposed to say nothing; so Burghley went on. "That is the Dean's exact estimate of his Lordship, who so recently spent a week with him. But I have another, more important correspondence, one that has immediate bearing, Madam. I have your leave?" He rustled among his papers and brought out one. He was thinking of the lawless Border, its many complaints, and also the very many requests for monies for damages, and for Her Majesty's garrisons on the English Marches. It took monies to arm, and keep armed, those Borders. "This letter is from Lowther. I shall read it. 'Bothwell is come again into the opposite Borders. He means to hold house at Hermitage in Liddesdale, and to essay the drawing of all Borderers to partake with him in his fortune. He will give good satisfaction of his soundness and devotion to Her Highness, and will abide trial of all matters heretofore done.' I suppose," put in Burghley, "that he expects complete forgiveness." He sighed, and resumed his reading. " 'If not accepted, and himself well-entertained, I fear the Border will fall into such disorder as will not be easily settled. And therefore I crave your Lordship beforehand to take Her Majesty's pleasure on how I shall deal with the same when it comes to my handling.' "

Burghley finished and waited for the explosion, which was surely coming. But he had to know how to answer this letter. If Lord Bothwell were not well-entertained, "I fear the Border will fall into such disorder as will not be easily settled."

"It's like a threat!" she burst out, and Burghley had no doubt but that she would box Bothwell's ears for him, if she had him here.

"I doubt if his Lordship meant it as a threat," he said smoothly. Any temper tantrum his Queen had was less violent than when it was due to requests for money, and agreement with Bothwell would save money. "No man has more credit with the Liddesdale men than Bothwell, Madam. No man can control them so well. What shall be my instructions to Lowther? How does Your Grace wish to handle Lord Bothwell?"

"You speak as though his Lordship were a fowl I wanted plucked." She gripped the knobs of the chair arms in her long fingers. "And how will you have him, Madam? Roasted or boiled?" She had mimicked Burghley's voice. "By God's body, I can but muse forever on that mad land of Scotland! They are a pack of fools and knaves, and James is worse!"

Burghley kept a judicious silence; he sighed a little, for it was very hot, and almost no breeze was coming in the window opposite him.

"We shall accept Lord Bothwell's allegiance," she said, suddenly. She pulled her chair nearer the table again, looking down at the bold writing that crossed the pages. "We shall also ask him about the status of the Protestant party. I shall put him the question as to the number of the Catholics in Scotland, and whether or no the two parties could be reconciled."

Burghley tried to keep the vague horror from his face. Whence came this mad scheme to reconcile the two religious parties in Scotland? He knew with certainty he would never be able to predict his Queen's next moves.

"Your Majesty will take Lord Bothwell's word for it?"

"Aye. I would and I shall. His hand is like Essex's," she added. "So you might tell Lowther we would not take it amiss should he decide to entertain Bothwell, at the risk of displeasing the crown." She glanced down at the last line of the letter she had received. It had ended with a flourish. "I kiss your heavenly hands." Elizabeth looked at her hands and smiled. . . .

Miles to the north, the capital city of Scotland lay bathed in mist. The wind off the sea was cool, although it didn't dampen the ardor of the flies that buzzed over the slaughtered animals in the Grassmarket, and it was warm enough to make the stenches in the meaner streets rise thickly from the refuse piled in them. In the royal palace the windows were open to the air, and James, sweaty and smelling of horses, was stripping off his clothes after the morning's ride. He was about to have his nap, and he was not half-listening to Morton's voice droning through the remarks tossed out by the King's chamber gentlemen.

"What, Morton?" he rasped, rudely. "You mumble."

Morton said, "Does Your Majesty realize how truly dangerous he is? That he will sooner or later make an attempt on Your Majesty's life? Aye, he needs only the abetment of Elizabeth, and he will get it, Sir. You mark my words."

"God's son, Morton, I've marked your words too often. You weary me." James scratched his ear with his fingernail, and then inspected it to see the results of his digging. "So my kinsman is dangerous, is he?" He swung around and his gaze fastened on the young Laird of Cessford.

"Cessford," he rapped out sharply. "What's this tale I'm told of your battle with Bothwell?"

Cessford was not quick enough to perceive the sneer in James's voice. He answered proudly. "We fought for two hours, Your Grace. Two hours." He let his eyes go around the room to appreciate better the admiring expressions that he expected to see on the faces of the other men.

"What commendable fortitude," jeered James. "You fought with Bothwell two hours, and where are your wounds?"

Cessford rubbed his cheek with his hand tenderly. "Here, Sir," he admitted honestly. "The visor of my helmet was knocked askew. The lance came too near my throat for comfort, Sir."

Everyone stared at the still livid scar that marred Cessford's cheek near the jawbone, but James said nastily, "And where are Bothwell's wounds, sir? Where are they?"

Cessford lost his smile. "He did not have any." Then he added quickly, "We fought on horseback, Sir. I was attended by one man, and Lord Bothwell by a man named Gibson. At first I could not believe that it was he, riding so unconcernedly and almost alone, in Lothian. I challenged him, and I will say this for him." His blue eyes swept his audience. "He was eager for a duel. I challenged him, and he said, 'Cessford, we'll have a wee bit of sport,' and I could see that smile of his. And if there were ever four tired men, it was the four of us, after two hours. To say nothing of the horses."

James's expression was not only sour but enraged. "By God's son, ye knave, why did you not run his animal through and deal with him on foot?"

"We were ahorse, Sir. We fought on horseback."

"I know it, fool. For the love of God, was ever a man plagued with fools as I am! Why did you not thrust at his horse?"

Cessford flushed; he faced James. "It was a point of honor, Sir." He was for a moment silent, and then he blurted, "It would take a strong man to have the courage to thrust at Valentine."

"Ah," said James. "Here we have the truth! We have only your word for the two-hour battle, sir. Only your word. And the same for your honor."

Cessford's face was white, and the jagged scar showed deeply red. He bowed briefly, and he was angry enough to leave the room without waiting for James to dismiss him. "Your servant, Sir," he said, at the door; and to his surprise, the Laird of Burley accompanied him. Together they stood in the hall and examined each other with level eyes.

"His Majesty and honor." Burley spoke the words in an undertone. He had actually said nothing harmful, but he kept a quizzical expression.

Cessford didn't answer; he was afraid of saying too much, so he was silent. He walked on down the hall and Burley said, "I'm going to Crichton, sir. Why do you not join me?" There was laughter in his voice.

Cessford set his jaw firmly. His face was still white with repressed anger; he could still hear James grinding out his accusations in the repetitious way he had. He came out into the court hard on Burley's heels.

The men waiting outside for Burley were trim; drawn up

two abreast they waited patiently, and one man brought the young laird his mount. Burley swung up into the saddle; with his hands resting on the pommel he looked down at Cessford smilingly. "Are you sure you'll not come, man?"

The brief flicker of summer sun turned Cessford's head bright copper; his blue eyes shone. In the court the wind stirred the banners, and the south lured beckoningly. Behind him was a crossgrained monarch, who knew nothing of fighting; in front of Cessford was the pull of adventure. He said, "Bothwell looks like Satan, till he laughs."

Burley smiled. "He's ane guid mon," he said only. "Will you ride south with me, sir?"

Cessford's head nodded suddenly. "I'm coming, man," he said, and when he was astride his horse, he spurred ahead until he and Burley were riding side by side. "I'm coming," he repeated, "and even Francis Hepburn will be surprised to see me! Let's make it in an hour!" And even though they had the city yet to travel through, they covered the eight miles between Crichton and Edinburgh in less time.

Bothwell wasn't at the castle. Just before Burley and Cessford arrived there, Anne was in the library talking to Patrick. He was ready to ride; he had been pacing the room, his booted feet ringing on the tile floor.

"He hasn't been here for almost a month." Anne pouted, threw down her needlework, and looked to him as if for confirmation.

"I know it," he said, and came to a stop at her chair. "I know it, lass."

"But what is he doing?" She stood a bit clumsily, searching his clean-shaven tanned face.

He shrugged. "Hunting," he said shortly. "And we've been in England."

"He does not come and I know why," she said angrily. She looked down at her figure.

Patrick said placatingly. "Politics took us to England, Anne. That's where Francis is now, and that's where I'm going as soon as Gibson is ready to ride."

"England?" She threw a glance at him but his face was impassive. "And who is in England, sir? You men think a wife is someone who stays home by herself while you go off and bed another wench." She turned away from him angrily. "And more oft you are cuckolded than you know!"

He laughed. "I'll not deny it, lass."

"I'm going to tell Francis he'd best be careful, or I'll do the same to him!"

"I would not tell him, if I were you. You had better keep it secret if you truly intend your words, madam." He walked over to a table and picked up his helmet.

"You are leaving now?" Her voice had lost its anger, and now she was only sorry that within a few minutes neither Patrick nor Bothwell would be at Crichton. She followed him down the hall. "I wish you were not going," she admitted.

"I came to see if there was any news from the capital," he said honestly.

She knew he meant news from the inquiries he had instigated for Janet Applegate. "And there was no news?"

He shook his head. "Nothing, Anne, nothing. None of her father's friends have seen or heard from her."

She was about to be sympathetic when the huge doors opened and the servants attending them ushered in two dusty figures who came toward her across the wide expanse of hall. Nearer now, they both bowed; she recognized Burley.

Burley kissed her hand; he explained he had presumed on the hospitality of Crichton once more, and this time to bring a friend. He presented Cessford, and Anne was puzzled by the twinkle in Patrick's eyes. She shot him a questioning glance while she acknowledged Burley and his friend.

"I see you are recovering from a wound, Cessford." Patrick's voice was delighted.

"Oh," said Anne. "I do hope the air at Crichton will benefit you, sir. Were you hurt lately?" She smiled at him.

She was surprised to see him redden. "A scratch only, madam. Sir Patrick exaggerates. Truly it is nothing to warrant your concern."

Burley was afraid of Patrick's caustic tongue; he was not sure what Patrick would say next. "If we have leave, madam, we shall make ourselves presentable." He bowed, and Anne could hardly wait for the two to leave so she could question Patrick. No sooner were they out of earshot than she whispered, "Patrick, why did you smile like that?"

"Because of the way Cessford was wounded." He laughed, clapping his helmet on his head. "And now I must take leave of you, my dear—"

"How was he wounded?" Anne interrupted.

"Dueling with Francis." To tease her, he started for the big doors, and she scampered after him, catching him by the arm.

"Do you mean to tell me he dueled with Francis?"

Patrick nodded gravely. "For two hours, I understand, madam."

"And he has the gall to appear at Crichton?" She whirled about and made for the steps. "I'll call David," she announced, with the full intention of having the stalwart Hepburn teach this Cessford a lesson. "How dare Burley bring him here? How dare he?" She stamped her foot. "I'll help him recover, I will!"

Patrick said from behind her. "Are you going to have him cast into the deepest dungeon, madam, or do you intend to employ the gallows?" She didn't answer, and he continued, now serious, "Take my advice, Anne, and welcome him. We may have drawn an erstwhile enemy into our ranks. If Cessford can forget, I know Francis will. I know not what's happened here, but James may have driven Cessford from the royal camp by His Majesty's usual ineptitude."

Anne had been standing quite still, listening. "I'm not sure I can be pleasant to the knave. He and his wounds."

"My dear, you can be pleasant to anything in breeches. He's young, he looked very ready to be impressed by your charms. Now you can help Francis, and enmesh him firmly in the cause of the Border lord."

She smiled; she was thinking of Bothwell. "Tell Francis that Cessford is at Crichton, and tell him to come home. Tell him I love him." Her voice was very soft. "Tell him to come home."

Chapter Thirty One

POLITICS had taken Bothwell to England. At Bewcastle, Captain Musgrave, warden of the English Marches, was glad to receive his Scottish guest, and at Bewcastle, in between the hunting, drinking and gambling, Bothwell had seen to his rising political fortunes, fortunes now enhanced by the goodwill of Her Majesty, Elizabeth of England. But it was a puzzling turn of events, none the less.

At first it had seemed so reasonable that if he had lost the favor of one monarch, he should seek it of another. If James of Scotland were his enemy, then Elizabeth might be his friend. But now he did not know whether the interest of the English Queen would be help or hindrance; these past weeks he had been suddenly unsure of pursuing this course, a course that might mean treason. He fretted in England. He was restless now that his letters had been answered with such promptitude.

He had promised to keep peace on the Borders. That was an easy enough promise to keep. When the English had questioned his newly spoken allegiance to Elizabeth, they had reminded him of his previous willingness to take up arms against her. He had answered that query with the blunt truth.

He had been willing, five years ago, to fight for Scotland's imprisoned Queen. He would have eagerly, he admitted, sought to free her; he would have been pleased to fight the English. But his own monarch had deemed peace more desirable than honor, and Lord Bothwell could not go against the expressed wishes of his King. He had ignored, in his reply, the terrible raids that had been made that summer, after Mary's death.

But Elizabeth was evidently willing to forget those raids, too. She accepted his blunt reply. Bothwell knew that if Patrick had been there he would never have let him make such a reply, but now it was done, and strangely enough, the truth was accepted as such. It really seemed as though the truth had enhanced her opinion of him. That night, he said to Sir Simon Musgrave, "You know I've very little left of my earldom, sir, but my motto." He didn't need to tell Musgrave what it was; the Captain knew very well that it was "Keep Faith." Bothwell went on dryly, "I do not intend to lose that; a man hangs onto his last gold piece till there's a good trade for it."

Captain Musgrave was silent. He rubbed his chin and asked, diffidently, "What does your Lordship think of the question of the two Churches? What answer would you give Her Highness as to the position and possible reconciliation of the Scottish and Catholic?"

"You asked me that yesterday. Let me say that the multitude of the one may, in time, and that soon, wreck the other. The Presbyterians are fewer in number. Reconciliation would mean that the Catholic party would rule the King."

"I did not realize that the Catholics were in the numerical majority."

"Ah. Well they are." Bothwell thought of Anne, and he smiled ruefully. "Understand me, sir. I believe in religious freedom, but politically you know I stand with the preachers and the Kirk, against Huntly and the Catholics. With England, against Spain." He frowned a little; his hopes lay in his leadership of the Presbyterians. They were powerful in England; they must be powerful in Scotland. That was how he could help Elizabeth; that was why she would help him. He said strongly, "We must fight to keep the upper hand."

"Quite so." Musgrave nodded. "I think it would be permissible for me to say that Her Majesty will be pleased with your sensible answers. I think she will be pleased with your course, my lord."

"Her Majesty is very gracious," said Bothwell, his tongue in his cheek. He was thinking that he had only one thing to fear. In finding a friend, had he perhaps discovered an ally who might forever close the door between him and James?

He had been at Bewcastle three weeks. His restlessness was mounting; even the hunting this morning had been poor. It was late August, the noonday sun was hot, and lazily he and the last rider dropped behind the rest. "You look weary, my lord," his companion murmured.

He pushed the cap off his head and mopped his brow. "I'm hot, madam," he said shortly. "I'm far from weary, I'm hot." He was annoyed. "A morning's hunt does not tire me, mistress."

Margaret Vinstar frowned; she said softly, "Why is it I always say the wrong thing to you, my lord?"

"I do not know, madam. Why is it?"

She laughed. "Do not scowl at me, Francis."

He turned his head to look at her; there were tiny beads of moisture on her upper lip, but her hair was as shiny and smooth as it had been when they had started out. Suddenly she reined in. "I'm so thirsty," she said. "Could we stop here?" She pointed with her riding crop at a swift flowing stream only a few yards away. The water bubbled over the rocks. "It looks so cool."

Instantly he drew rein. He helped her dismount, and they walked over to the burn, pushing past the thick bushes to the grassy bank. He was surprised to see her put her hands in the stream and clap the cool water against her face, and she drank eagerly. "Aren't you thirsty?" she asked, for he was standing motionless.

"Aye." He knelt, and put his whole head into the stream, coming up with his hair dripping. He brushed it back with his big hand. She leaned back on her elbows, watching him.

"I'm going to take off my shoes and stockings."

He got to his feet. "I'll tether the horses, then." He disappeared, and when he returned, she was sitting with her feet in the water; she had taken off her hat, and was leaning over, splashing the water with her hands.

He sat down, stretched out his legs, and then lay full length on the soft grass, his hands under his head. The trees made a curtain through which he could see the sky, and he sighed with sudden contentment. "Look, a wood throstle," he said, breaking the silence.

She turned her head to look at him. "Francis, you amaze me sometimes."

"I do?" He was still watching the bird, as it moved on the limb of a tree near him. "Why do I amaze you?"

"It amazes me that you know the name of any bird."

"I recognize many."

"I suppose you mean you know all of them."

"Not only that, but I'm good at fish." He smiled. "Are your feet clean yet?"

She said, reprovingly, "They were clean."

He regarded her for a long time. "I'll warrant you polish your toenails, too."

"I've always spent a lot of time making myself lovely, Francis," she said truthfully. "Ever since I was a small girl."

"Well, you are most fair," he conceded.

"Thank you, Francis."

"And after all, it is a woman's duty to be as fair as possible."

Margaret laughed. "A man speaks," she said.

He nodded. "How much time," he asked, curiously, "do you spend on yourself? How much time, would you say?"

She turned again to look at him. "Why, Francis, I truly cannot tell you in minutes, or hours."

"Try," he urged, frowning at her.

She pondered. "About three hours a day, then. Perhaps."

"Such equivocation, mistress. Three hours?"

"Aye. Would you give that much time if you were a woman?"

He considered this point. "That's a long time," he said finally. He picked an ant off his arm, and spat out the blade of grass he had been chewing.

"And that does not count the long hours given for choosing

clothes, seeing that they are fitted perfectly." She rose, and came over to him, sitting down beside him. "Besides clothes, Francis, there are perfumes—and so many other things that when I begin to enumerate them all, there must be dozens." Her voice trailed away idly. "Would you give that much time if you were a woman?"

"Holy God. I didn't answer that question the first time because I'm content with my estate."

She laughed at him again. "Why do I make you angry, sometimes?"

"You do not anger me."

"Francis. Then I annoyed you."

He chose another blade of grass to chew. "You seem so mocking, at times, mistress. I dislike irony, in a woman. I think I do."

"You are very honest, my lord."

"I'm honest, now. I should never have told you that, if I had not found you different from my old conception of you."

"Irony is cool and detached," she said.

"Aye. I used to think you that. Underneath you challenged me."

"I knew that. I tried to—" She broke off, and she said suddenly, "I used to love you." She watched his face. "You do not seem surprised, Francis. Have so many women loved you?"

"No."

"You are lying, now. You are unnecessarily modest. You can always tell me the truth."

He did not answer, and she said, "Why do you think so many women love you?"

"Wench, we'll stop talking about me."

"Will we, Francis? But aren't you even going to ask me if I still love you?"

"That's exactly what I was going to ask. We'll talk about you." He raised himself on one elbow. "Do you love me?"

Margaret smiled. "I had avowed a previous affection. Then I hated and despised you. It made me cruelly unhappy, and I knew it was wrong to hate you so much. . . ."

He lifted his hand and took her by the chin, meeting her

eyes. "You are making a great understatement," he said slowly, dropping his hand, "but I do not know what you mean."

"Well, my lord, 'tis very simple. I wanted to hurt you."

"How?"

She looked away from him, toward the swift stream. "You had hurt me, you see, Francis. And now I know I am making you uncomfortable by speaking thus. My intensity—you prefer lightheartedness, laughter."

"You are wrong, mistress. There are some things you do not know about me."

"But if I could just make you understand I love you every way. I like nonsense too, Francis. I like to feel alive, and laugh. I know if I could just be with you sometimes, like this, that is all I can ever have, and all I really want. It's worth waiting for. You are."

"You might change your mind."

"I might," she agreed, still watching the water foam over the rocks.

"Then quick, before you change it, give me your hand."

She put her hand in his, and he encircled her waist with one arm, drawing her over beside him on the grass. "Oh, Francis," she whispered, "I love you."

It was the next day that Patrick arrived at Bewcastle. He ate first, then he went in search of Bothwell, and he was directed to the gardens, where the guests were playing pall-mall. By the time Patrick arrived the play had stopped, but he spied the Earl's dark head, and Margaret was with him. Patrick hardly spoke to her.

He said, "Francis, there is a little surprise for you at Crichton."

Bothwell took a step forward. "Anne," he said urgently. "You mean—"

Patrick laughed. "No. I did not mean that. Cessford's at Crichton."

"Oh." Bothwell felt a surge of relief, but he was suddenly aware that he should be at home. Then he remembered what Patrick had said. "Why is Cessford at Crichton?"

"I do not know. Perhaps it would be best for you to discover that, unless he has already fallen in love with Anne."

"In that case, perhaps it were better Francis did not discover it." Margaret smiled, but she was puzzled. Why was the Laird of Cessford at Crichton Castle? A quick fear went through her.

Bothwell paid no attention to her remark. He had made up his mind to go home. "Are you ready to ride to Scotland, sir?"

Patrick looked down at his boots. "I seem to be."

Bothwell nodded. That was settled then. "How is my countess?"

Patrick hesitated, and Bothwell fidgeted in the silence. He didn't know whether there was something wrong or not. Finally Patrick said, "Anne is well. She had a spell of her old trouble, but it passed."

Bothwell smiled. So she was annoyed with him, was she? "Nothing was hurled or broken, was it?"

Patrick laughed. "Nothing irreplaceable."

"I'll dress." He started away. "I'll be back in a few moments."

Patrick watched him go. "I'm rather surprised to see you, madam," he lied.

"Are you, sir? Shall we walk?"

"Well, then, I'm unsurprised, Diana."

"The huntress," she said slowly. "Why do you bother to ask questions when you've already answered them?"

"Because I'm always asking myself whether those arrows of yours are deadly." He watched her carefully, but he could observe no change of expression on her face.

"I would they were," she said lightly. "I should aim at you."

"I'm flattered. Especially since I should follow Francis."

Her eyes blazed with anger. "I accord you no favors," she snapped at him.

"You may later, madam."

She turned, ignoring him, but he turned too, and they walked back toward the sprawling house. "Why be angry?" he asked, matter-of-factly. "My words are in the nature of a compliment."

She walked beside him in silence, and his hazel eyes were

intent on her. He was sure she would have liked to run from him; he was certain she was somehow afraid of him.

"Here is Francis," she said, quickly, and he heard the relief in her voice.

Margaret looked up at Bothwell. He was leaving, she had known he would leave her like this, but perhaps—"You'll come back, my lord?"

"I'll return," he said curtly. He must return; his business was still unfinished.

"Goodbye, then," she said, sending a mocking smile at Patrick. "And do give my compliments to Anne."

Patrick bowed. "We shall," he said. "We most certainly shall."

They arrived at Crichton late at night; even the upper halls were in darkness. Bothwell strode along to his own rooms, battling with the notion of waking Anne. He should not, she needed her sleep now, but he wanted to see her. He had just about decided to rid himself only of his boots before he sought her, and Lawder had just begun to light the candles when both men perceived the figure sleeping in his bed. Lawder withdrew discreetly.

"Oh, Francis," Anne whispered drowsily. He had tiptoed over to her side, and Anne pushed back her curls and smiled at him. "You do not need to be quiet; I'm awake."

"So I hear." He sat down on the edge of the bed, picking up her hand.

"You've been away so long."

"I know. But how do you feel, lassie?"

"It was better in here, in your bed," she said. "I was not so lonely."

"Oh, my darling, I'm no kind of husband for you!"

"You are," she contradicted.

He sighed. "I warrant you thought otherwise many times during the past weeks. Now I am a reformed man, and I'll stay home for a while, so tomorrow night we'll celebrate and have a party."

"Oh, Francis."

"And I brought you something." He dug down in his pocket and came up with a long, intricately carved gold chain. "Now you may say 'Oh, Francis' again." He suddenly felt less guilty.

Anne looked at the chain with delight. She put it on, and he seemed so surprised she said, "I wanted to see how long it was, when it was on. It's beautiful, Francis."

He laughed at her. "You are so wonderfully practical. Now do not cry, lassie; tell me something. How do you like Cessford?"

Anne smiled. "Oh, he is very gay, Francis, and very gallant always, to me, and very polite. He is quite handsome, too."

Bothwell was bending over, taking off his boots; his dark eyes were thoughtful as he listened to her chatter about Cessford. "So you like him," he said finally. "I warrant you've impressed him, lassie. But I'll judge him for myself tomorrow."

The next day he and Patrick spent almost all their time with Cessford. It was at the party that night that Bothwell first noticed the young laird's preoccupation with Anne; even with Bothwell constantly at her side, Cessford was usually there too. "Are you enjoying the party for my countess?" Bothwell asked him.

Cessford replied unhesitatingly. "It's an Anne-party, my lord. We have them every night at Crichton." He was plying Anne's fan for her because she had said she was warm.

"You do?" Bothwell eyed him sideways.

"We surely do, my lord."

"Perhaps you think I should come home and enjoy them myself more often."

Cessford agreed with him. "You surely should. The only disappointment now is that Lady Bothwell will not dance."

Anne acknowledged this by putting her fingers on his arm. "You must stay another month, sir. Then I shall dance with you the entire evening."

"You go too far, wench," Bothwell put in. "I'll have the gentleman out on the field of honor." He caught Cessford's eye, and they both smiled.

"I'd hesitate, my lord. Once is enough."

Anne remembered the duel; Cessford had told her all the details of the encounter. "I'll never understand men," she said reprovingly, and Bothwell replied, "Madam, you underestimate yourself. If you do not understand them, who does?"

And she did understand him well enough to be certain that in England he had been unfaithful to her. From his account of his stay there, all the women had been nondescript; he told her of the different men he had met, the letters he had received, and it was only at the end of the week, the night before Bothwell planned to return to England, that Anne, alone with Patrick, began her questioning.

"And who else was there at Bewcastle? Besides all you have named?"

Patrick was apparently searching his mind. "No one else."

"Not anyone else?" Anne's violet eyes met his.

"I think not," he said. "Oh, Margaret was there. Did I mention her before?"

"You did not!" Anne stood up and threw down her fan. "And why did you not confess she'd been there? Why? The bony goat!"

Patrick grinned. "Enough, madam," he begged. "I've done nothing and neither has your husband. You're dreaming, Annie, I swear you are."

She sat down again, picked up her fan. "D'ye suppose I'm an utter fool, sir? You'd carry no tales. But tell me this, Patrick, truthfully. Will she be at Bewcastle when you return tomorrow?"

Her calm surprised him. "She said she would." He spoke the truth this time. "At least I honestly received that impression, that Margaret would wait for us."

Anne smiled. "Francis is hardly interested in her now, I'm sure of that, but I dislike to see him return there, especially since she is expecting him. I've a mind to disappoint her; I've a mind to keep her waiting longer."

Patrick said earnestly, "Anne, he must return. You cannot stop him."

Her smile was very sweet. "Can I not, Patrick?" she asked.

"Can I not?"

He remembered that the next morning, when he tried to find her. He went literally from room to room, from her bedroom to the morning-room, to the little stillroom where she concocted her perfumes. Nowhere could he find her, and Bothwell and he were leaving at noon. Puzzled, he sought out Marie, and she could tell him nothing either, only that her Ladyship had dressed very early, and that she had gone out in her little cart, as she often did.

"His Lordship rode out after the countess," she ended. "I should not worry, sir. Lord Bothwell will find her."

But Bothwell had been as much worried as Patrick was. He had set out at ten, on horseback, without breakfast, and he was lucky enough to find someone who had seen her go.

"Her Ladyship went in the direction of Fala Moor," Bothwell was informed.

He spurred away in haste. It had rained the night before, and it was easy to follow the tracks of the cart. But why had she gone to Fala Moor? He could not divine her purpose. It was a hot day, the sun was out and the landscape shimmered with heat. Hatless and coatless, and with only a dagger thrust through his belt, he galloped on, expecting to see the cart as he topped every hill. He had gone halfway to Fala when he saw her ahead of him, coming toward him, and she wasn't in the cart, she was walking.

She was walking briskly, her bonnet shielding her face, and in one hand she held the reins. The ram walked docilely beside her, and in the distance, when she caught sight of the rider coming at her at a fast gallop, she moved off the road, leaving ample room for the approaching horseman. He slowed his pace, not wanting to rein in suddenly and frighten her, and he waved. When he reached her, she was as surprised as he. For a second they stared at one another, and then he jumped down beside her.

"Where have you been?" His voice was rough with anger. "How many times have I given orders that you're not to be out by yourself? How many times, Anne?"

"It's a fine day for a walk, my lord," she answered stiffly.

"Look up at me! Curse that bonnet!" He tipped her head up. "What's the matter?"

"Nothing, my lord." Her eyes were huge in her white face.

"There is something the matter! There always is when you speak to me thus. Why are you walking?"

Anne's lip quivered. "Do not talk to me so." She looked up at his tanned face; there were beads of sweat on his forehead and his white shirt clung to his shoulders. "Do not frown at me," she whispered.

"Why are you walking?" He spoke each word measuredly.

Anne stamped her foot. "Because I want to have my baby now!"

"What!"

"And I will have my baby today, too! And you cursed at me!"

"I did not!"

"You did. You cursed my bonnet. I suppose you're angry, because if I have your son now, you cannot go back to England to visit your latest wench! And you shan't go either, because I'm having pains right now!" She burst into tears.

"Lassie," he said gently. "My own darling, I have no latest wench to return to." He was knotting the reins of his horse to the back of the cart as he spoke. He picked her up, setting her on the cushioned seat; he started the ram walking, then he pulled her over into his arms so she could recline. "Give me your hat, Annie," he said.

She gave it to him, and he set it on his own head, so it shaded her, and she could relax against his shoulder. There was momentary silence.

"It is more comfortable this way," she said very low. "I can put my head down."

"Is the pain bad?" he asked.

"No, Francis, truly it's not."

There was another long silence. Finally Anne said, "I hate her, Francis. I'd like to cry but I will not."

Her face was white and she had closed her eyes; the blue showed through the lids, like a child, he thought. "Anne," he said steadily, "I love you. There is no one else but you, and there never will be. I shall not swear it because there's no need for swearing."

She turned her head into his shirt. "Now I will cry."

"Do not, lassie. You must know I love you, or I'd not wear this hat. God's blood, madam, I have my masculine pride. Look at me, Annie." He stopped the ram for a minute, and he took her face in his hands and kissed her. "Look at your fine husband."

"My love," she said. "You look beautiful."

"And if Patrick sees me I'll never hear the end of it." He snapped the reins over the ram, urging it on. "You go to sleep, Anne. Try to sleep."

She did. She dozed in his arms until the walls of Crichton were right before them. Bothwell carried her to her own room. Then he looked wordlessly to Marie for help.

Anne smiled at him tenderly, for now he did not try to mask his concern; he looked helpless and bewildered. "Do not fret, Francis." She repeated the words while Marie deftly loosened her dress, drew the slippers off her feet. "You leave me, now, Francis."

He stood in the center of the room; certainly he should do something. "I'll fetch Isobel," he said suddenly, with great relief. "I'll be right back, sweetheart, I'll come right back." He disappeared out the door, colliding with two hastily fetched maids whom he brushed out of his way with a curse, and he was back with Isobel in twenty minutes. Isobel had lost her usual calm.

He hurried her up the steps, and into Anne's boudoir. "I'll go in first for a minute," he said hastily, and left Isobel alone in the room with the startled Patrick.

Isobel shook out her skirts, and tried to catch a lock of deep brown hair that had come loose in her mad ride. "Francis would not let me ride my own mare," she said to Patrick, over her shoulder, for she had found a mirror and was repairing some of the damage to her hair. "No, I had to hang on in back of him because Valentine is the 'swiftest horse in the Borders!' "

Patrick smiled, and Isobel went on, "I think he expects his son to come as fast as Valentine."

He laughed and came to stand behind her, watching her face

in the mirror. "Do not look at me," she said, "when I can see myself at the same time. Then I can have no illusions as to how I look to the beholder."

"Turn and face me," he said.

Isobel lowered her eyes. "I am a matron with two children."

"You are three and twenty," he said. "Six years younger than I am."

"Patrick," she said, "I wish you would not. And do not ask me what I mean!"

"Women from Borthwick," he said. "Isobel—"

The door opened before he could say more. "He's not born yet," announced Bothwell. "Anne wants you, Isobel."

She smiled. "Francis, have you eaten yet?"

"Eaten?" He had forgot food entirely. "How could I eat now?" he asked incredulously.

"You could," said Isobel. "Patrick, will you take him away before he drives me mad? And feed him; give him something to drink." She went into Anne's room, then she put her head out the door. "And, Francis, we need candles, when you return."

"But it's not dark!"

"No, Francis, but night comes, you know." She closed the door.

It was ten o'clock in the evening when Anne's baby was born. Bothwell heard the initial cry. He stood close outside the door and waited; he had to step aside to let Isobel enter the room.

"How is she?" he asked. "Isobel! How is Anne?"

"You cannot go in," Isobel cried hastily. "Aren't you going to look at your son?" She held the baby in her arms, and all Bothwell could see was a tiny face. He stared.

"It's a boy?"

"He's a boy. He is Lord Francis Hepburn. Now Scotland has two of you, God help us all."

"Can I see Anne now?" He edged toward the door.

"No. Look at him, Francis. He's a beautiful, big boy!"

"Big?" Bothwell looked at Patrick and Patrick peered down at the baby too.

"Congratulations, my lord," he said, nodding his head. "Is he big?"

Isobel sighed. "He is three and twenty inches long. That means, my lord, that he has only four feet and some inches to grow. I imagine he'll manage it."

"Given time," said Bothwell. "But when can I see Anne?"

"Now," said Isobel. "We're glad to get rid of you."

Bothwell stepped into the room. It looked just as it always did; the candles were burning on the night table, and the rest of the room was in shadow. He tiptoed over to the bed; he remembered belatedly he hadn't shaved, and he was wearing an old shirt, and Anne looked beautiful. He was afraid to sit on the edge of the bed, so he knelt beside it. "Lassie," he whispered. He lifted one of her hands. "I love you, lassie."

Anne opened her eyes. "Isn't he beautiful, Francis?" She sighed. "Isn't he wonderful?"

"I don't know," he said earnestly. "But you are. I love you." Clumsily he smoothed her hair.

"You said that before. I remember."

"I know. When we were riding. And then I told you to go to sleep. You must go to sleep now, too."

"I will. But I'm glad. I'm so glad you told me, Francis, before the baby was born."

Part Five

Chapter Thirty Two

"This is the night the witches ride in the Lammermuir hills," Patrick murmured. He drained the liquor in his cup. "Some call you Black Bothwell, Francis, versed in the blackest of the arts. What do you think—that she is a witch?"

"Of one sort, at the least."

Across the wide room she was coming toward them, her head high, the torchlight glowing on her red hair. And in this vast and shuttered hall she looked strangely out of place.

The hall at Hailes Castle was very old. Over its windows the shutters were fastened close, and its hewn rafters were blackened with smoke from the great hearth which extended right into the room.

Patrick said quickly, "Allow me, Francis."

She had come up between them; she stood at the fireplace with a man on either side of her, and the hum of laughter and voices from the rest of the room seemed to recede and leave them standing on a small island of silence. Her first words were commonplace.

"It's been a magnificent hunt, Francis. You've well repaid the English hospitality."

Bothwell's dark eyes were on her. For almost the whole week's hunt he had avoided her, and she had been as aloof as though he had never once utterly possessed her. "Hailes Castle is old and crude, mistress."

"It suits you," she said softly. Today they had had five

hundred beaters to drive the deer, and two hundred Irish hounds; Margaret had watched Bothwell, armed only with his dagger, follow his favorite hounds into a glen where the deer had been driven. Eighty of the animals had been killed, and tonight his Borderers had supplied kids, fresh salmon, pigeons, grouse, and ptarmigans; there had been ale and sack, whiskey and the powerful aqua vitae. "The English were impressed," she said proudly. Then she added, " 'Tis a pity Anne was not able to join us."

"Anne is at Crichton," Bothwell said. Why did she talk about Anne? Anne did not even know where he was; he had moved about often in the past four weeks, but tomorrow he planned to return to Crichton, and tonight was all he had left for Margaret. "There is Captain Musgrave," he said, and he turned and left Patrick standing alone with her.

"I regret I was not hunting with you today," Patrick said, "but I was mining in Haddington."

"Mining?" She was thinking of Bothwell. "Do you mean you truly went into the pits?"

He nodded. "I've been there since dawn, madam; I was supervising the installation of a mine car I invented."

"And what is a mine car?"

"A mine car is a vehicle on wheels; it descends into the pits and returns by way of a set of pulleys. It obviates long hours of manual labor."

She was gazing at him with amused admiration. More than the fact of his invention, she was impressed with his energy and the idea of a gentleman descending into the filth of the coal pits.

"Do you know what night it is?" he asked. "It's All Hallow's Eve. You have your cloak on, come with me."

She drew back instinctively; then she changed her mind and took his arm.

"I'll take you to the battlements, madam, and you may watch the night. Perhaps you can see the witches ride." He led her down the hall, and up a long dark stairway; he opened a narrow door, and a gust of salt wind blew into their faces.

"Oh," said Margaret involuntarily, for the door banged shut noisily. Her fingers tightened on his arm and he put one hand over hers.

"Afraid?" His tone was light. He drew her over to the breast-high walls; they could walk around the castle here, high up on its battlements.

"It is a little terrifying," she whispered. The wind caught at her cloak and blew it away from her figure, enveloping her in the chill October night. Above them the sky was ragged black and way below them the waters in the moat lapped at the stone walls menacingly.

"Terrifying? Madam, so much blood has been spilled in these walls, these moats, these dungeons, that this night, All Hallow's Eve, should not frighten you."

She had caught her cape around her; she leaned against the stone barrier. "I am fanciful, then," she said.

"So may I be, but this is the time for fancies."

"I have not seen him for two months."

"Why did you come?" he asked briefly.

"He is magnificent as a hunter! Tonight I wish I were a witch; I would feed him magic potions, and lure him to a trysting-place." Her hood was flung back and her face was white in the darkness. "Oh, why do I tell you this?"

"Because you are not a witch, but human." His tone was dry. "I'm the only one who knows he was your lover; I'm the only one to talk to. And what would you do, Margaret, when that magic potion had been digested and was no more?"

She said low, "I'd brew a pot and poison him and let him die."

"Would you?"

"No," she cried. "I'd let him go again! Oh, Patrick, help me!"

He said abruptly, "I cannot help. I'll take you down to him." He said nothing as he guided her down the stairs and back to the big hall. The torches still burned brightly, there were still the laughter and the insistent hum of the men's voices as they talked about the hunting.

"But it is just as cold here," she said.

"Come over by the fire," Patrick said, walking along beside her.

"The smoke will sting my eyes."

"The smoke will veil you in gray; you will be a wraith." He

smiled, and then he added, "But, madam, *do* not meddle. I warn you, do not meddle, more than perhaps you have already done."

His cup of liquor was right where he had left it, and he picked it up empty, twirling it in his fingers. She made no reply for a minute, then she realized that she must pretend to misunderstand. She looked toward him calmly.

"I shall meddle, sir, between Francis and Anne. If I can. And if you'll look toward the door, you will see that 'tis not I who am meddling this time."

Patrick had turned his head as she spoke. "Anne!" He swore softly, for she stood in the doorway, not looking at him or Margaret. She had already passed them by. She was standing, waiting for Bothwell to see her.

She was dressed in black satin and lace, and a black lace collar fanned out stiffly behind her head, leaving the bodice of the dress cut deeply to show the white shoulders and breast. The dress was cut and worn without hoops, so that it clung to her figure in the style of the Italian Renaissance. Dressed in black also, Cessford was at her side, and she kept him waiting too until across the room Bothwell saw her.

She moved toward him then. When she walked, her dress, split up beyond the knee, showed the flouncing lace petticoats beneath it. The dress was too daring, and the way she had taken Cessford's arm was daring also. But Bothwell didn't move until she had come up to him.

"Madam," he said, and he bowed formally, ignoring Cessford. "You surprise me."

"I've no doubt of it, my lord! I've no doubt I intrude, also!" Her eyes flashed at him, he saw her familiar pout, and she tilted her head back. "Will you present me?"

He offered his arm, but she affected not to see it. For a second she thought he would seize her hand, and she was a bit sorry when he didn't. She leaned on Cessford's arm. "I'll speak to Patrick first, and Margaret."

"This is a delightful surprise, madam," she said. "I do hope you have enjoyed yourself at Hailes!"

"Oh, I have, Anne." Margaret smiled. She pretended to study Anne's necklace, for she had known instantly where she had seen it before. "What an unusual chain, my dear. It reminds me of a piece of jewelry owned by an old friend of mine."

Bothwell frowned guiltily, but Anne said, "How odd. I should certainly be curious to see her necklace."

"Unfortunately she lost possession of it. She used it to purchase her honor from a Border brigand." Margaret glanced sideways at Bothwell.

"Truly?" Anne smiled sweetly. "But I didn't know one could purchase honor." She kicked aside her train with her foot and a movement of her hips, and rested her gaze on Patrick. "Your servant, sir, and I warrant you are surprised to see me too."

"I am that, madam." His tone was as controlled and distant as Bothwell's and she was taken back.

"I warrant you mislike my dress," she murmured, over her shoulder, as she turned her back on him.

Patrick stepped over to Cessford, whom she had left behind momentarily. "Did you bring my cousin?"

Cessford tore his eyes from Anne. "Aye," he answered.

"But why, man?"

"She wanted to come. I stopped by Crichton and told her Lord Bothwell was at Hailes. She asked me who made up the party, and when she learned the names, she asked me to bring her."

"Anne asked you where Lord Bothwell was?" Patrick broke off sharply. "When did you arrive?"

"About an hour ago."

"It would take an hour for her to make an appearance girded for battle." His tones were light. "We'll watch the fireworks."

Cessford did not understand him, but he was not curious and he moved toward the fireplace, edging in to Anne, who was regaling the party of men with the latest Edinburgh gossip.

"Truly," she said, "I swear it. The first time Lord Home attempted the abduction, he was driven off. But that didn't dampen his ardor for the lass."

"But what happened then, madam?" Captain Musgrave didn't know whether it was the story or Anne that interested him so much.

"Then Lord Home returned the next day, and this time he

had enough men. Lord, he blocked off the whole of High Street, and carried off his prize in his arms!"

"A method that has its merits," said Bothwell's voice suddenly. Anne jumped. Patrick was on the other side of her and the conversation lapsed.

"It's too bad you did not use those tactics, sir," said Anne, loudly. "Poor Patrick, always yearning for his Janet."

Patrick looked down at her with eyes as angry as her own. "You'll have the goodness, madam—"

"Some day you'll find her," Anne interrupted airily, waving her fan. "A lovelorn male is a pitiable sight, is he not? And now, will you forgive and excuse me, my lord? I promised to show the Laird of Cessford the oubliette where the martyr Wishart was kept prisoner."

Bothwell's eyes met hers in a steady look. He bowed, and both he and Patrick had odd expressions.

"You'll both excuse me, sirs?" she repeated, less assuredly, but she turned her back on them defiantly.

"By heaven, I hate them both," she muttered angrily. Her skirts swished as she went down the hall. "This is the keep," she said absently, not even caring what she said to Cessford now that they were alone.

"I'm not sure of the wisdom," he began. He was looking around; down the hall he could see a guardroom toward which her hurrying steps were carrying them. "I'm not sure," he said again.

Anne paid no attention. "Bring a torch," she ordered, to a man who had come forward. "We go this way."

Graham did as he was bidden; in the light of the torch he carried, they descended steps carved from the stone, and as they went down the air grew more dank, and there was the smell of decay and wet stone far beneath the earth.

"To think how many wretches were confined here—" Cessford broke off as the steps stopped, and they emerged into a small room. Here the walls were mottled and sweaty with water; there was a heavily barred door at the end.

"More steps," said Anne. She wished she had not come; carefully she lifted her skirts and trod gingerly after the stolid Graham and his torch.

The second flight was not so long. Fifteen feet further under the earth they stood again in a level space. "The river and the moats must be above us," Cessford said.

Graham threw open another barred door. Beyond a narrow walk were the deepest dungeons, the oubliettes, dark holes into which many a prisoner had been flung and forgotten. Cessford peered down into the nearest one; the torchlight shone on the wet walls but could not pierce its depths; the light frightened the rats and their feet made pattering noises as they scurried for the darker recesses. Cessford drew back, and he went over to Anne, who was looking through from the door.

He held out his arm for her to take on the journey back, but as they started off Anne slipped, her feet going out from under her on the slimy rocks. Quickly he caught her. They were alone in the room, concealed from Graham by the door, and Cessford forgot whatever caution he had had. His arms went around her and he began to kiss her. Anne struggled in his grasp and he started to say how much he loved her. He wanted to tell her that he was mad with love for her, that he wanted to marry her when she was free, and that he had really come to Crichton today to tell her so. But he said none of this. Under the sudden flood of light ahead of them, he straightened up and thrust Anne away from him.

"Francis," Anne gasped.

Bothwell did not speak. He stepped aside to allow two more men to come into the room. Hercules entered, and behind him Gibson, who first barred the door and then waited silently, holding his torch high. The three of them looked across the fifteen feet of space that separated them from Cessford.

"A neat trap, sir," said Bothwell. His eyes flicked over Cessford while Graham closed the other door. "There is no escape, as you've noticed. There are four of us, and one of you."

"Francis!" Anne cried out. "Oh, my lord—"

"You'll not speak, madam." He did not look at her. "This is a rat trap, Cessford, with a woman as bait."

Cessford put his arm around Anne protectively. "You lie, my lord!"

Anne cried, "Do not say that! In the name of God, unsay it!"

"No, madam. You lie, my lord. I'll never believe that Anne has betrayed me!"

"You are not asked to so believe." Bothwell stood quietly, letting Gibson divest him of his coat.

"But he is guiltless, Francis. Punish me, my lord; it's my fault!"

Bothwell took a step toward her. "We'll talk later!"

"You brute," Cessford snarled. "You black renegade!"

Bothwell laughed. "Save your breath, sir. Think not of your little Anne, but of yourself."

He came toward them, and Anne sobbed, "My lord, I entreat you. He's not my lover. Francis, I pray you believe me!"

Cessford quickly put her behind him. "Do not touch her," he cried, helplessly, for Gibson and Graham had seized his arms and he struggled uselessly against them. Bothwell watched the scene with satisfaction before he suddenly seized Anne's wrists and half-tossed her to Hercules.

"A pity you must witness this, madam. But I've warned you often. Release him," he said in a matter-of-fact voice.

Cessford shook off his guards. "You'll hang for this, my lord. Aye, you'll hang for this!"

"You'll not ha' the pleasure of watching me kick my legs," said Bothwell. "Now, Cessford, I could put you in that oubliette in which you were so interested. And I'm not sure but that it would not give me more pleasure than a duel. But we have an audience, sir, so play up; unsheath that sword and we'll make short work of this. The lady is shivering."

Cessford shouted, "If you harm her, I'll kill you!"

"By my honor, sir, you've lost your head as well as your heart to my wife."

"Your honor?" Cessford drew his rapier as he spoke. "You and your Borderers have never known the meaning of honor."

"I acknowledge the compliment. Therefore I deem it only fair to tell you that, should you kill me, my men have orders to hang you on the gallows here at Hailes. They shall not waste time taking you back to Hermitage to hang."

"No, Francis," Anne sobbed. "He is innocent."

"Good. Then he may meet his maker with equanimity."

"Holy Mary." She folded her hands. Then she started forward, but the sudden flurry of steel made her shake so that she couldn't move. The torchlight shimmered on the crossed swords, the ring of steel was loud in the stone-walled room, and she trembled with the wet cold. She remembered that it was her fault that Cessford had kissed her.

The duelists circled and Anne found herself staring at Cessford's face. His hair was curled up at the ends, just clearing the white ruff he was wearing; his blue eyes were narrow and intense, and there was an expression in them that Anne did not understand. She thought wildly, "He'll die because of me."

"Stop it!" she cried, and made a motion to seize at Bothwell, but Hercules caught her arm.

"Be quiet," he muttered.

"Francis, Francis." She whispered his name. "I swear by Mary that he only kissed me, and it was my fault. Punish me, my lord. Francis!" She stopped on a cry, because a shimmering blade had darted at him, and Bothwell had parried the thrust just in time.

He had heard her calling him. "Francis, Francis." He made a sudden lunge at Cessford, getting under his guard, but Cessford eluded the riposte gracefully, moving to one side with the ease of a practiced fencer. But in the movement, he slipped on the uneven rocks and fell.

Anne was paralyzed with the unexpectedness of an incident that had left one combatant sprawled on the floor defenceless. Hercules' hold temporarily slackened; she wrenched from his grasp, running the few feet to Bothwell.

"My lord," she gasped, "I pray you fight no more."

He shoved her away. "Put your hand over her Ladyship's mouth, Hercules." He watched Cessford get to his feet. "I want not that my wife's chatter should hasten your death, sir; I want to deal fairly, even though you scarce deserve it."

Cessford shifted his rapier to his left hand and wiped the palm of his right hand on his shirt. "I acted according to my own lights, my lord."

The swords crossed again, and though she had been warned, Anne started to speak. She had hardly opened her mouth before Hercules' huge hand clamped over her lips, and she was helpless in his grip. There was no use fighting against the giant strength of Hercules' arm; she was too frightened to bite his fingers.

The water dripped insistently from the stone walls, the torches gleamed on the wickedly sharpened blades. Cessford was fighting desperately now; he was attacking with all the skill he could summon, but it was not enough. Even Anne could recognize that it was not enough. Every time he gave way a little, the narrow steel had come closer. With her free hand she twisted the heavy chain she was wearing, and she prayed silently; it was Hercules' arm that kept her standing.

The torch flickered suddenly as Graham shifted it higher. The light made Bothwell's rapier look like a shiny strip of glass as it leaped forward, catching Cessford's shirt at the shoulder, ripping the soft cloth. Beads of sweat stood out on his face, his shirt hung open, and he circled away so that Anne could see his face. The sight made her struggle wildly against Hercules; she struggled so desperately that Hercules was forced to loosen his hold to get a better one, and she managed to cry, "No, no," but then it was too late.

The shining point of Bothwell's sword had gone through Cessford's guard; there was a moment of utter silence, startling after the stamp of their feet and the ring of sword against sword. The deadly thrust had done its work thoroughly; Bothwell drew his blade back and Cessford fell at Anne's feet.

"You've killed him!" Anne would have gone on her knees beside him but Hercules still held her tight, drawing her back from the fallen man, and from the blood which was spreading slowly across his chest, down onto the uneven rocks. She could not believe it; she could not believe that the man who had just ridden to Hailes with her, who had just kissed and held her—could be dead.

But he was. His blue eyes were closed, his lips were parted slightly, as though he still might speak, might whisper, "I love you," as he had whispered to her. She remembered how kind he had always been; she remembered his kiss, and she remembered how he had sought to protect her from Bothwell.

She looked down at his still face with a flaring of love for him. "Poor laddie," she whispered, and again she tried to push Hercules away. Dimly she realized there was nothing more to do for Cessford; she turned her violet eyes to Bothwell. "You've killed him," she repeated incredulously. "You."

"Aye, madam." Bothwell looked down at him. "There's no need to stop that blood. There'll not be much more of it anyway—he's gone." Silently he held out his hand for his coat, and Gibson handed it to him, but before he shrugged it on, he wiped off the sword still in his hand, sheathed it, and hitched his belt into place.

"You bring him, Gibson. You and Graham. I'll take that torch." He had his coat on, he took the torch, and Anne drew back from him fearfully.

"Do not touch me," she gasped, turning to the door blindly.

Without a word he picked her up, throwing her over his shoulder like a bundle, and he started up the stairs, mounting them quickly. Behind them came the steady tread of Gibson and Graham with their burden. Anne did not know whether she lost consciousness, but suddenly Bothwell set her on her feet in the hallway upstairs. The hall looked just as always; it was the same hall she had left some thirty minutes before. She grasped the newel post for support and she could not keep her eyes from Cessford's body. "What are you going to do with him?" Her voice was low with her pity.

"We've reverence enough for the dead." Did she think he was brute enough not to care decently for Cessford? He said, almost as if he were forced to, "The hands which take care of him will be gentle."

"He loved me." She put her hands to her face to hide the tears from him, and she felt him take her by the shoulders and turn her around. His hands were strong and angry.

"Go upstairs!"

She did not move. "Go upstairs, madam. You may weep in solitude!"

At his open anger she stopped her crying. "I'll weep where I please!" She was standing on the second step and their eyes were level.

He released her shoulders, trying vainly to control the rampant jealousy. At his look she raised her fan.

"You devil," she raged suddenly, "I'll—"

He wrenched the silver-handled fan from her grasp, and broke it between his big hands. He threw the pieces down on the steps. "Get up there!"

She turned to obey; she was frightened, and she stumbled over her train. Impatiently, he waited until she had composed her skirts, and she went upstairs as he had bidden. From the foot of the steps he watched her go, and then he could not send her away, and he bounded up after her. As he entered her room, Anne turned to face him.

"My lord," she said pleadingly.

He said abruptly, "I did not kill him because he was your lover!"

"But he was not, Francis. Oh, why did you kill him, then?"

"Why?" He stared at her loose blonde curls; he saw he had ripped the black satin from one shoulder. "Because he was a spy, madam. Because he lied to you and me, or rather to me. He wanted to marry you, once he had succeeded in betraying me."

The full impact of his explanation hit her hard; for a few seconds she stood very still, taking in the two sentences that said so much. If they were true, they explained so very much.

"He never deceived either Patrick or me, although we made him think we believed his story. He thought we believed he had deserted the King. But he never had. He was going to prove his loyalty and worth to James."

Bothwell was thinking of all the ways Cessford had given himself away, but the worst mistake he had made was in bringing Anne to Hailes. No one had known Bothwell would stop at Hailes tonight; no one could have known unless he had been spying. Anne had wheedled this information out of Cessford; for the while Bothwell could let rest who had relayed the news to the dead man. And Anne—he had been so much in love with her that he had dared to bring her. Bothwell thought ironically that he had reassured Cessford too well, and he remembered Cessford's last words, "I acted according to my own lights." Well, so he had, and he had taken too big a chance on the roll of the dice.

"Scots do not give up feuds so easily, madam." In those few words he told her of the hatreds and violence that had plagued Scotland.

"He was a spy?" She could not take it in completely.

"Aye; he deserved hanging. But I'm a generous man. And he loved you. I'm not wrong about that either."

"No, you are not." She spoke the truth baldly. "He loved me."

"He'll get his reward in heaven. Are you regretful, madam, that I did not defend your honor better than you defended it?"

He had turned on his heel and sudden fury raged in her. "So now you bring your trollop to Hailes! And you dare to talk to me!"

He said truthfully, "I did not know she was coming. In fact, I did not know you were coming."

"But women follow you, do they not? You dare to bring your whore to Hailes, and you dare to talk to me about defending my name!"

He laughed. "I dare, madam. You have brought events to an unwelcome climax. Jamie is not going to take kindly to Cessford's death. You have forced my hand; you will force Jamie's. I could thrash you till your buttocks were pink, but I shall not. I have other more pressing business tonight, and it may occupy me for a couple of weeks. Until then, we shall postpone our talks."

Anne's face grew white with dismay. "Francis," she pleaded.

"Patrick is waiting for me." He took the big key from the door and his tall figure blocked the entrance. "One more word, madam. You are never to wear that dress again."

At three in the morning she finally got into bed. She had been sure when he left that he would not return, but still she had waited, and she did not sleep until very late. She was up early, but it was not early enough. Bothwell had left Hailes at dawn with Patrick and the hunting party, and he had left instructions to Hercules. Lady Bothwell was to stay at Hailes until she was sent for. Anne was a prisoner in her own castle.

Chapter Thirty Three

IT TOOK Anne six weeks to escape from Hailes. The first days she had passed in crying and sleeping. When she stopped her weeping, she slept deeply.

Hour after hour she spent at the window, looking out, expecting Bothwell to ride into view. She rehearsed innumerable conversations—what she would say to him, and what he would reply.

"If only he would come." Over and over she repeated the words, leaning against the window, watching. But the days passed, and he didn't come, and there was no word, nothing.

At the end of the third week she asked Hercules if she might have a mount, might ride out into the country. Confined like this, she was increasingly restless, increasingly miserable.

Hercules said that he doubted if his Lordship would want his wife exposed to the weather. The weather was so bad now; November, and already it was very cold. But he would inquire of his Lordship. To please madam, he would send a messenger to Crichton.

"Lord Bothwell is at Crichton?" She couldn't believe it.

"Aye, madam." At Hercules' answer she whirled away, up the steps. He was at Crichton, with her baby, and he didn't want her. For a month he had kept her shut up at Hailes while he stayed at Crichton. Anne could see her lovely rooms. Her room at Hailes was bare, bitterly cold. And he was with her baby, her little son. How long was she to stay in this freezing hellish castle? How long was she to endure Hercules' solemn guarding, covered though it was by respect?

But she waited still, until there came a letter from Crichton in response to the one Hercules had sent. Evidently the Earl had not troubled to answer it quickly, for it was ten days before the courier from Crichton arrived, and then it was a flat "no." Lady Bothwell would do well to keep to the castle, for fear of endangering her health. This was no weather to go abroad in. And as for Lord Bothwell, he was going that day to Hermitage, there to stay the month out, so that Hercules should expect no further word from him until the middle of December.

Hercules told her this with the faintest smile on his face. Anne was so angry when she heard the contents of the letter that she almost burst into tears. She had a difficult time keeping the rage from her voice. That voice was so sweet it should have warned Hercules.

"Very well, sir," she said coolly. "But I do think I shall step out around the castle for some air." She had her cloak around her shoulders, as indeed she needed it in the icy hall, and Hercules didn't object to her walking out; after all she could not go far.

She didn't go far; she sauntered around the moat, peering down into the water, and later she idly stopped by the stables, looking over the few men there, picking out a man who would suit her particular need. The third day she walked out, she had decided on a young man. He was about sixteen, a boy who would be amply suited. It took her three days to be sure he would do as she wanted.

Thus for two more weeks she went out each afternoon, late, so that it was dark when she came in. Every day she was dressed the same, in boy's clothes, because she explained almost tearfully to Hercules that she must go out, and still be warm enough. The clothes she had brought with her weren't warm enough for the December days. Not for the weather outside.

On the ninth of December, late in the afternoon, she was dressed and ready. Carefully, she lowered from her window a packed box which held her precious clothes and the jewelry she had brought. She had no money. Then she went for her usual walk.

Everything happened as scheduled. She sought out the stables, after she had promenaded the moat. It was almost dark. There was no one about, and in the stables she met her accomplice, her most willing but apprehensive accomplice. She donned an old cloak, stained and smelling of horses and sweat; it fell below her knees, and quickly she tucked up her hair under an old cap.

"Ready!" she whispered excitedly, and she didn't wait to be helped to mount. She was in the saddle and starting out the door before young Adam could change his mind.

In a hurry he was up and after her. They came to the gates and Adam flaunted a letter Anne had prepared. "We're for Crichton," he announced, and the gates opened. They were free from Hailes.

"This way," said Anne, her voice low and shaking with exuberance. She turned toward the river, and before Adam realized it, she was in the middle of the river, fording it with aplomb, splashing ahead of him.

He was more than startled. After her, he and his horse went into the icy water, and he didn't catch up with her until they had forded the stream. "Your Ladyship—" his dark eyes were frightened and astonished—"this is not the way to Crichton. This is the way to . . ."

"Edinburgh." She laughed, her spurs jingled, and she bent over the saddle urging her nag to greater effort. "They might have seen us," she explained. "Hurry!"

"But, your Ladyship." He was trailing her again, and he galloped alongside, peering through the dusk at her face. "Not Edinburgh?"

"D'ye think I'd go to Crichton?" Her voice was full of mockery. "D'ye think I would? M'lord can come hunting for his wife, aye, let him hunt. By heaven, lad, I'm no bitch that comes running home with her tail between her legs." As she said this, she spat lustily and pushed her cap to an angle. "Nay, it's Edinburgh for us." The air was tonic and she threw back her head drinking in the cold air and blowing it out in long white streamers. She was warm with exercise, and felt against her body the knife tucked in her belt.

"Are ye armed, lad?" She wasn't afraid; she asked the question just to show him that she was unafraid of the worst.

"Aye," he replied reluctantly. He had a sudden vision of Hercules, and he shivered at the thought. "Oh, Holy Mary," he muttered.

"There'll be no trouble, lad," she said reassuringly. "We'll be in the city and in our house. D'ye think ye can climb in a window?"

"Aye," he said again, forgetting to address his mistress properly. He wasn't worried about their trip; he had far worse worries than that. The vision of Hercules followed him all the way into Edinburgh. At any moment Hercules might discover their disappearance, perhaps already. Indeed, now, surely pursuit was coming.

Alongside of Anne he went through the city gates up High Street and into the Canongate. The city was noisy, men were abroad, and lamps burned in the shops. But at the town residence of the Earl of Bothwell it was very dark, frighteningly so. He and Anne stabled the horses. They crept cautiously around the side of the dark house, neither saying a word. At the first window Anne stopped.

"Try it," she whispered.

He obeyed with shaky hands. He didn't like any of this, and he wished he had never agreed to this wild plan. He wished he'd never seen her before. "It's locked," he murmured helplessly, hoping she would repent of her foolishness in time.

He was immediately disappointed; a locked window was nothing of a hindrance to her. "Break the pane nearest the lock. Well, break it, I said."

Timidly he took his knife and the shattering glass made him jump back. There was nothing to do now but obey her, because they must spend the night somewhere. He reached in, and slowly the casement window swung open.

"Help me in." He gave her a healthy push, and she was in the window. He jumped in beside her, remembering to close the window, and the first thing he was conscious of was the cold and the smell of the musty long-closed house.

Anne didn't give him time to think. "Find me a candle; find some wood." She was peering around the big kitchen in which they stood. She could see the outlines of the large fireplace. "I think there is wood in the basket."

With his numbed hands he busied himself with both requests. He heard her moving about the room, and while he was piling logs on the hearth, she took up the candle and disappeared. She didn't come back until the fire was blazing up, and he was eying the bright flames gratefully.

Anne stood holding her hands to the heat. "It's a lovely house," she announced, pleased. After all, it was deeded to her. She was thinking that tomorrow, in the morning, she must go to the money lenders. "Now if the fire is well, you may get my box, and I'll show you where you may light another fire. I've picked out my bedroom."

He stared. It was just occurring to him that this was most improper. He said feebly, "I'll sleep in the stables, madam."

Anne looked appalled. "You will not. You'll sleep in the room next to mine. Now get my box."

She was still waiting for him when he returned, this time via the door. His face was white and scared, for now the vision of Hercules had been replaced by the imaginary face of his master. Adam stood in the center of the room, her box in both hands. "Your Ladyship," he began, timorously, "his Lordship . . ." His voice trailed off.

"Pooh to his Lordship. Are you afraid of him?"

"Aye." Adam nodded solemnly. They stared at one another, and finally Adam, emboldened by her confidence, said, "And I'll warrant you are too."

"Pooh," said Anne, this time less certainly. Her voice dropped, and she asked, "Would he flog you, Adam?"

Adam shivered; the fire was less comforting now. "He might. He might do anything when he gets angry, madam."

"I'll not allow it." She was very decided, but her eyes were speculative. "Come on, I'll show you the way." She picked up the candle and preceded him down a long hall, past closed doors, and up a wide stairway that sounded ghostly beneath their cautious tread. Above the ground floor was the gallery, silent and empty, stretching along the whole front of the house, and behind it was the room that Anne had picked out.

Its tight-shut window rattled in the wind, and shadows lurked in the dusty corners. Adam put her box down, and disappeared again for wood. But even after the fire was lighted, the room was still icy, musty and very dirty. Cobwebs hung from the ceiling, dust lay thick on the furniture. But Anne was tired. She crept into bed, without sheets, but with heavy blankets, and she slept in her clothes, with her knife under her bolster. She slept heavily, and in the next room the youthful Adam succumbed to sleep too. For a while his fears were forgotten and no dreams disturbed him.

Anne hardly knew where she was when she woke in the morning. Her room, herself, both looked so different in the young daylight that filtered through the dirty windowpanes. She sat up in bed, hugging the quilts around her. The fire had died, only ashes littered the hearth, and the gusts of the north wind stirred those ashes with invisible fingers so that the smell of them was in the room along with the smell of must and cold. On the chest at the foot of the bed the dust lay so thick that it seemed inches in depth, and on the bedposts and canopies the cobwebs fluttered long and trailing. Opposite her line of vision an old mirror showed her the small figure huddled in the bed. For a long time she stared at her image. Her hair was a mass of tangles, and she was smeared with dirt.

"Faith, I look a fright." She swung her legs over the side of the bed, and even through her thick stockings the floor felt like a piece of ice. She raised her voice as loudly as she could, for it suddenly occurred to her that Adam perhaps had gone. He might have been too frightened to stay. "Adam!" she yelled. There was no answer, and she ran to the door and out into the hall. The door to the bedroom he had used stood open and there was no one in the room.

"Holy Mother of God," she murmured, wringing her hands.

Was she alone then in this huge ghostly place? "Adam!" she called again, her voice quavering, and she heard her voice echoing with awful misgiving, so that when he answered her from downstairs she was breathless with relief.

The top of his head appeared up the steps and he was carrying something. It was not until she saw the steam that she knew what it was. "Water," she cried with delight. "Why, Adam, if I were queen I'd knight you for this, lad. By heaven I would." She backed into her own room and he followed her, staggering under the weight of the huge black pot he was carrying.

"I couldn't find anything smaller," he explained, setting down his burden with a heavy sigh of relief. "I spilled some."

Anne put one dirty hand into the pot. "There is plenty to scrub what shows," she said, practically. She turned toward him, now obviously thinking of what she had to do this morning. "How long have you been up?"

"About an hour, your ladyship. I have the fires started in the kitchen, and I washed, too." He exhibited his clean hands and face with proper pride.

Anne scrutinized him gravely. "Then wash your neck, Adam. You'll be my page this morning, and you'll have to serve until I find—" She broke off because he looked disappointed. She continued, "You'll have to serve until I find decent clothes for you. Perhaps you can find something in the house. You look while I dress."

He nodded, not unpleased with the thought of finding himself some nice clothes, perhaps even a pair of shoes, and he backed out of the room, closing the door behind him. Anne lost no time. She washed her face and neck, her hands; she did her hair, and from the box she took a velvet dress, matching gloves, and her heavy cape, lined with fur. Thirty minutes later she was coming downstairs, looking exactly like a countess dressed for the city streets. She caught a glimpse of herself in the long mirror on the wide landing, and she stopped, noting every detail of her appearance. She sniffed experimentally, and decided that her scent covered up the lack of a hot bath. Then she stared at herself again. Going out into the streets of Edinburgh was like walking out onto a stage. No one expected to see her, no one would quite believe it was she. She was well aware she had no small shred of reputation left now. People said she was lucky not to have a bastard brat; she could have lived that down, in fact, she almost had, until her husband had killed a man and then shut up his wife in one of his castles.

Still, it was an intriguing reputation she had, and she wasn't ashamed of it. She still stared at herself, and decided she needed one more little touch to her ensemble, and she pondered the need all the way downstairs, until she stood at the door of the library.

"I know!" She brushed by Adam, who had found himself another pair of breeches and a coat, but who had to be satisfied with his own boots, no matter how worn. She searched for only a few minutes among the dusty books to find what she wanted. She cleaned it off on an old jacket that someone had thrown down many years ago and had never stopped to pick up again. She came to the door and stood very demurely, her hooded cape thrown over her blonde curls, both of her hands clasped decorously over an old Bible. "I'm ready, Adam," she announced, in a tone as sweet as her pious appearance.

A bit astonished, Adam followed his mistress out the huge doors, under the carved lintel and down into the street. Quickly they left the house behind them. Anne walked neatly and as though only the cold morning hurried her at all, and Adam trailed behind, trying to imitate the very correct pages he had seen attending their various mistresses.

A light snow had fallen during the night. It was powdery underfoot, and lay delicately on the housetops and on the steps of the houses that lined High Street. It was so familiar a scene that Anne forgot herself as she drank in the gray city.

She walked uphill; ahead of her the huge Edinburgh Castle frowned as always. She passed through the square and almost under the shadow of the Town Cross. She was on her way to "Jingling Geordie,"—George Heriot the royal goldsmith, the money lender.

Geordie transacted business in a small krame hardly seven by seven feet, that lay almost in the shadow of St. Giles Cathedral. Anne left Adam standing outside. The tiny room she entered was paneled in wood, a coal fire burned in the grate and although the room was stuffy and hot, it felt delicious to her frozen feet and hands. She removed her mask unhurriedly.

"I greet you heartily well, sir."

Geordie blinked, rose to his feet, and bowed. "Your Ladyship." He said nothing else, but he kept staring at Anne, and in the back of his mind was the fact that he would have a good bit of gossip for his King, should Jamie Stewart drop in today for another loan.

"I am on my way to church," said Anne, demurely.

Geordie permitted himself a smile. "Naturally, your Ladyship." He was tempted to ask if this was purely a social visit.

"However," Anne went on, "I have business with you first, sir."

"Honored, madam. Will you sit?" He indicated a chair; he pulled it toward the fire for her, and she sat, carefully arranging her skirts. Geordie sat down behind his table, eying her, wondering how much money she would ask for, wondering too if it were safe to lend it to her without incurring the wrath that both Lord Bothwell and Patrick Galbraith would undoubtedly feel for any indulgence of her whims.

"Now my security, sir," Anne continued, "will be my town residence."

"Ah." He pondered this disclosure, and he frowned. "How much?" he asked bluntly.

"One thousand pounds Scot." The answer was just as blunt.

He shook his head slowly; it was too much, too much money. Why did she want it? "I fear I am unable to accommodate you, madam."

"Why, sir?" she asked airily. "I must open my town house, and for that I must have money. However, all that you give me will be put back into your security."

"True." He nodded his head, but he didn't believe her. Once she had the money, she would be off up the street to buy velvet and a few lengths of satin, to say nothing of a jewel or two.

He said suddenly, "Madam, I cannot possibly lend you money. But I can give you some advice gratis. You had best leave the city; you had best return to Crichton. Madam, this is dangerous for you!"

Anne stood up. "Dangerous?"

"Aye, madam. Very dangerous. Lord Bothwell cannot know that you are in the city. What would his Lordship say if he knew it?"

Anne set her mouth and looked stormy. "I need no puling advice, sir," she began, and she would have said more if the door hadn't opened suddenly. A man stepped into the room, began to excuse himself and stopped short. "Anne," he said incredulously.

The Duke of Lennox bowed elegantly; his eyes sparkled as he took in her face. "You look charming this morning. Do you realize that this is the first time I have been able to congratulate you as my new kin?"

The Duke was a Stewart; he was related to Bothwell, but Anne wasn't sure just what the relationship was. "Thank you, sir."

The Duke noticed Geordie for the first time; he seemed to become conscious of just where he was. "You are on your way to church, madam?"

"I've just come from church, sir." Anne was trying to remember the name of a money lender whose reputation was none too good. She would ask the Duke.

Lennox said, "I'm at your disposal." He almost hurried out the door, and he deposited her in his chair without ado. "You should be at home, madam," he said shortly. "I swear I forgot in the pleasure of seeing you, just how hazardous this is for you. Madam, does Francis know you are in the city?"

It was too much. "No," cried Anne. "A plague on Francis. And I'm going to stay here too!"

The Duke hardly heard her. "Put your mask on, Anne. For God's sake, cover your face, and pull your hood over those curls. I'm going to take you home."

Chapter Thirty Four

"I'LL not help you, sir," said Margaret quietly. She was sitting in a deep-cushioned chair in front of a bright coal fire.

Morton stopped his pacing. "She is in the city! She was seen as she came from Geordie's. God's body, she wore no mask, even!"

"You say Lennox was with her?" Margaret's gray eyes took light from the fire. "Bothwell will not like this, sir."

"It matters little whether he likes it. She is here, and she will trap him, if we are clever enough."

Margaret said, "You are not, Morton."

"Ladies do not run away," Morton said definitely. "Not from their husbands."

Margaret laughed. "You are so stupid," she said flatly. "Obviously Anne did. Though why she would want to—"

"She wants him to come after her. And he will."

"Will he?" asked Margaret. She laid her hands carefully on the chair arms. "Will he, sir?"

"Madam, let's not speak in riddles." He turned away impatiently. "If you'll not help there are other ways. More obvious ones."

Margaret said slowly, "I'll not help you this time. I must wait. I must wait and see the outcome of this." Then she thought she should give a more apparent reason for her refusal. "It is too risk-filled, now," she ended.

Morton went to the door. A plan was taking shape in his

mind, but Margaret had said he was not clever enough. He was pondering that as he left her . . .

The Duke had already deposited Anne at her door and escorted her into the dusty house. He was still remonstrating.

"Madam, you cannot stay here!" He waved his hand at the hall in which they stood. "Impossible! Incredible that you could conceive of such an idea!"

Anne had remembered the name of the money lender. "It's way past noon," she said.

"God's blood, madam, what matter the time? Except that every minute you stay in the city it is more dangerous!"

"You are right, sir," she said, suddenly docile. "I'll leave."

"I'll send an escort," he announced, turning for the door.

"No," she cried. "No. I'll not have it. I'll go as I came, with Adam. We shall be safe."

He hesitated. "You'll leave now?"

"Aye," she said quickly. "As soon as I dress."

"Perhaps it would be best that way. I fear you have been seen; an escort of my men may be more hindrance than aid. You came disguised?"

She nodded. "And I'll go disguised. You leave me now, sir."

"Perhaps it would be best." The Duke fidgeted; he did not know which plan would be more feasible. But he did go to the door. "You should reach Crichton this afternoon, before sunset."

"I shall," Anne called. She stood in the door until the Duke's chair had disappeared down the street. Then she summoned Adam. "We're going to another part of the city," she announced, as she gathered her cloak around her, and went down into the street again.

Their journey this time was longer. They followed a devious route; where Thieves' Row joined Candlemaker's, Anne stopped. She looked around herself uncertainly. "You may wait, Adam," she whispered.

Adam sighed. "Aye, madam." He stared at her imploringly, but she turned her back and slowly entered the small door before which they had both stopped. Anne started to close the door behind her, but another woman had appeared. Anne gave her a brief look; she was glad that someone else shared the small room with her, but she had no intention of relinquishing her prior entrance. She walked forward, and the man who emerged from back of a thick curtain eyed her with surprise.

She didn't remove her mask. She did not know how to proceed, so she said quickly, "I am the Countess of Bothwell."

The man bowed, and Anne rushed on. "I need money."

The answer was as swift as her demand. "Madam, I cannot lend you money!"

Anne's eyes through her slitted mask met his. He was well enough kept, in his dress. He was not at all what she had expected from the tales she had heard about him; she had thought he would be more menacing, and more eager to lend her a few hundred pounds.

"What do you mean—you cannot?" she asked imperiously.

"I mean that I cannot lend you money. I should never get it back."

Anne said stiffly, "Mind your manners, rogue!" She saw clearly that she would not be able to stay in the city in her own house, without money; but if she had a little, she might at least rent a furnished place, and buy food. She lifted one hand and released one of the gleaming sapphire earrings that Bothwell had given her. "How much for these?" she asked haughtily, extending her hand.

He shook his head wordlessly even as he examined the stone in her palm. "Nothing, madam."

Anne drew back from him, clenching her fist over the earring. "Why?" she asked finally, despairingly; she looked at him in fear.

He wet his lips and glanced hurriedly over his shoulder to the other woman whom Anne had forgotten. Anne turned too, so that Janet Applegate said, "Madam, I beg your pardon but—Master Lang is affrighted to lend you money on your jewels."

"Why?" Anne cried.

The dusty little room was silent again. Janet gazed at Anne

in awe, and with some astonished pity. "Madam," she said, "Master Lang knows Lord Bothwell; Lord Bothwell buys his smuggled golf balls here, I know."

"And he is afraid of Francis—of Lord Bothwell?" Anne asked, in a very solemn tone.

Janet smiled. "Master Lang is afraid that if he took your jewels, Lord Bothwell might come in here and demand them. But that is not the only reason. Only two hours ago—" She hesitated.

Anne made an effort at calm. She began to refasten the earring. "Only two hours ago—what?" she inquired coldly.

"His Majesty summoned all his resident nobles, and their retainers, to attend him in a ride to the Borders!"

Master Lang said hastily, "Your Ladyship, heed Mistress Janet!"

"The city is not safe for you, madam!"

These sentences came almost at the same time. Anne said, "I thank you for your help." She felt utterly alone and she wanted to cry. She thought of Bothwell, of grim Hailes Castle and Hercules; she thought of Patrick. Then she remembered the name that Master Lang had uttered.

"Who are you?" she said to Janet.

"Janet Applegate, madam." Janet suddenly emptied the contents of a small purse on the worn table. "Count that, Master Lang. You will find it correct. My debts are paid." She turned to Anne, who was regarding her with appealing eyes. "Let us go, madam. We can talk better on the street." She opened the door, and Adam's friendly face appeared again.

"You are Patrick's Janet?" Anne asked incredulously. She stood just outside the door.

"Aye, madam. I am. I hope I am."

"Godamercy! And what merest chance brought you here, now?"

Janet smiled; her heart was thumping fast. "If you knew how I'd prayed for such a chance as this! But, if it please you, we should not stand here. We should—"

"I know!" Anne interrupted. "We'll go to Crichton. That

is where we'll go." Anne could see the walls of the castle, rising so safe, and not so far away, either. "We have horses. Two horses."

"I am small. I can ride with your page."

Anne was walking rapidly, casting glances at the girl beside her. "God was good to send you to me," she said. "But I did not expect you to be quite as you are."

Janet's green eyes gazed at her questioningly. "No?"

"No. I had thought you would be more retiring."

"Adversity teaches well," Janet said wryly.

"How have you lived, mistress?" Anne asked curiously. "Patrick was fearful for you. He said this wicked city would eat you alive."

"It almost did. Till I learned to bite. And as for how I lived, first I had to borrow from Master Lang. Then I gave lessons in reading and writing, and I kept accounts. Today I repaid the last of my debt."

Anne was silent, and Janet said, "Oh, madam, do not fear. Do not be afraid!"

"But I am," Anne cried. "I'm shaking."

"Have you eaten?" asked Janet practically.

"No. But what else do you know of His Majesty's plans?"

"Nothing. Do you know where Lord Bothwell is now?"

"No. All I can say is 'no,' " Anne gasped.

"But where do you think he is?"

"At Hermitage."

"He will be safe there. And we shall be out of the city soon."

"But Francis may not be at Hermitage. You do not know him!"

"I think I do, somewhat," Janet said. "Madam, your husband, they say he belongs to all the lasses in Scotland."

Anne shot her an angry glance. "What mean you, mistress?"

Janet laughed. " 'Tis just a saying. And forgive me for laughing at you. I am so happy!"

"And I have never been so weary. I expect you are happy, and not so hungry as I am."

"My poor lass," said Janet commiseratingly. "We are almost

at your house, and we shall be at Crichton before two hours are gone." She took Anne's arm and led her down the Canongate.

"This is not the way to the stables," Anne said, as they went up the walk. "We might as well go around."

"I think you should have some wine, first. Certainly there is some here." Janet had opened the door, and she pushed Anne into the first chair she saw. "Wait for me."

"No," Anne exclaimed. "Send Adam. You find me a little wine, Adam, or anything that there is." She leaned back and closed her eyes. "I shake," she whispered.

Janet frowned. She thought that she should have first found Anne some food, and she blamed herself. But now they were too far from any shop. "Hurry, Adam," she called, to his retreating figure. "Madam, you can ride with him; it will be easier for you."

Anne kept her eyes closed. Janet pushed her hood back and massaged her head. "The wine will aid you," she whispered. She was cold herself; it was icy in this house, and the winter afternoon was already throwing its shadows in the hallway. She adjusted Anne's cape, so it covered her knees. "The wine will aid you," she repeated softly, in the stillness, for there was no sound in the house; she could not hear Adam's footsteps any longer.

Anne opened her eyes suddenly. "Where is he?" she asked, low.

Janet raised her voice in a shout, and the echoes of her voice were eerie in the long-closed house. They died away. There was no answer.

Janet called again. "Adam! Where are you?"

Both women looked down the long hall that sheered off the center hall. The doors were shut ominously. "I'll find him," Janet said determinedly.

"No!" Anne seized her arm. "Do not go to the back of the house! I heard something." She had jumped to her feet. She pulled Janet toward the library door and when she had bolted the heavy door behind them, she glanced around the room to make sure there was no one in it. Janet went over to a window.

"Madam, we can leave this way." She pointed to the casement.

Anne was still standing with her back to the door; the bolts pressed into her hips. "Do not go," she whispered, gazing past Janet at the black square of glass that Janet was trying to unlock.

"We must. We're trapped here."

"Adam's gone," Anne wailed. "They've killed him. Don't go."

"I must and you must." Janet had the window open; it looked out into the side gardens, and it was almost dusk outside. She put her leg over the sill and dropped down. "Now, madam," she said, and moved away, to one side.

Anne's fingers seemed icy and useless, but she clutched her cape and laid the other hand on the window when suddenly the whole casement was ripped from her grasp and over the sill she saw a long sallow face. She gave a scream of terror.

"Hold your tongue. There's no one to hear you." The face was nearer; it moved with its owner out of the dusk, and a man stepped into the room. He leaned out the window and said calmly, "Give her to me."

Anne watched Janet being hoisted in the window; her eyes were closed, and Anne forgot her fear. She rushed at the figure of the man who had handed Janet in the window, and she went so fast that she accomplished her mission. He tumbled from his perch astride the sill, and Anne bit hard into the hand that was trying to disentangle her from him.

He seized her roughly and dragged her to her feet. "Here, here, none of that, madam." He let go her hands. "You're not to be hurt," he muttered, massaging the hand she had bitten.

"Fat beast," she gasped at him. "Filthy fat beast." She whirled away from him to the other man who held Janet. "If you hurt her badly, I'll, I'll—" She broke off, lifting Janet's hair away from the side of her head, where a big lump was rising. "Lay her on the floor, gently," she ordered.

The fat man said, "Do as her Ladyship says. Lay her on the floor. Then you may go tell the men to saddle up."

Anne dropped to her knees beside Janet; she watched the

other man leave the room, and then she took both of Janet's hands in hers. "Open your eyes, please," she implored frantically.

Janet did not move, but she looked at Anne through slitted lids. Anne did not understand, so Janet opened her eyes. "I may swoon again," she murmured weakly.

"Holy Mary, I wish you wouldn't." Anne tried not to cry, and Janet closed her eyes again.

"She cannot possibly ride," Anne said. "Who are you?"

"My name is Sym," he said, "and she will be able to ride, by the time they are ready. It will take a few minutes."

"But where are we going? What are you going to do with us?" Anne got to her feet and faced him, eying him sharply, wondering if she could successfully launch another attack.

"No, madam," he said warningly. "You are not to be hurt. You are to be in Lord Morton's care, that is all, your Ladyship."

Anne looked pathetic. "Why?" she asked. "Sym, I'll pay you well, very well." She lowered her voice. "Sym, Sir Patrick will pay you much more than Lord Morton. He'll pay you much more!"

"I shouldn't dare," he said frankly.

"But," said Anne, "but, why not?" She came close to him. "Sym, you do as I say, and—"

He shook his head. "No, madam. I could not if I would. And you'll come to no harm."

Janet sat up slowly, frowning at him. She leaned back against her hands. "Why do you want Lady Bothwell?" she asked calmly.

"Lord Morton is offering the Countess his hospitality," Sym said.

Janet was quiet a minute. She looked so thoughtful that Anne said nothing either. Finally Janet said, "Sym, this is more dangerous than you think. If Lord Bothwell should follow his wife, and find her here with you, he'd kill you, Sym."

"If Lord Bothwell comes into the city tonight, he'll be caught."

"Has he ever been caught, Sym?"

Sym paled a little. "No, mistress," he admitted.

Anne said, "His Lordship will not come tonight, Janet. He'll not come after me. He'll be too angry with me. But you know who will come, Sym?" Anne smiled wickedly. "Hercules. And Hercules could break your neck with one hand!"

"Let us out this window," Janet continued where Anne left off. "We shall reward you. Well." She rose and took two steps toward the window. Sym stared at both women.

"Come, Sym," Anne whispered. "It is not yet too late to save ourselves. All of us."

There was a minute's silence. Sym started toward the window cautiously. "There are six of them," he muttered, both to himself and them. "Six."

"We have time." Janet tried to fight off her dizziness. "It is already dark in the gardens, Sym."

Sym said suddenly, "No, I cannot. There is no time. Listen!" His eyes sparkled with the thought of betraying Morton, for a lot of money. "Perhaps later, I can help you. Later," he whispered. "And be careful."

Anne said, "You coward!"

Janet put her fingers to her lips; Sym went past them to the door, and she said to Anne, "He may help us."

The footsteps were right outside. "Now ladies," Sym said, and he winked at Janet. "If you will go ahead."

The door flew open; there was a tall man standing on the threshold, and he had hooked his thumbs in his belt, for he knew very well what he would find. Janet stared, and Sym stared, and then Sym gave a cry of alarm. He backed off in fear.

"She is not hurt," he burst out. "I was going to help her, my lord. Later!"

Bothwell said, "I should not dirty my hands with you, rogue. Take him out, Graham, and search him." He did not look at Sym, he paid no attention to Janet. He was thinking that although he had a reputation as a constant gambler, he actually indulged himself not so often, preferring sometimes to stake a good deal of money on one horse, or one dice game. Tonight he had gambled once more, instinctively. He said dryly, for his impatient anger at her flight was not yet dispelled, "Mine seems a timely entrance, madam."

Anne said, "I did not think you would come. For me," she added.

He raised one hand to smooth back her hair, and he sighed. "Lassie, Hercules informed me last night that you had fled. I would not have come, Anne, for a runaway wife."

"Francis," Anne said. "I was coming home, now! I truly was not running away!"

Bothwell laughed. "Were you not? Where were you going, then?"

"I was—I was coming home later," she said defiantly. "When I was very ready, my lord!"

"Are you ready now?"

"Francis! Do not use that tone to me."

"I asked you whether or not you were ready," he repeated. "A civil and proper question."

"I'm ready, my lord," Anne said meekly. "But please do not send me away again!"

He frowned. He said quickly, "You know it was scarce politic for me to follow you, do you not? But I knew there would be trouble. I've been waiting for trouble over Cessford's death. I hardly expected—although perhaps I should have—that you would be the spark to set things off."

His tone was so matter-of-fact that Anne cried, "But where are you sending me?"

"To Crichton, lassie. With David Hepburn." He shifted his gaze to Janet, who was listening with wide eyes. "Who is the lass, Anne?"

"She's Patrick's Janet," Anne answered, just as Janet said her name, too.

"God in heaven! Your servant, mistress. Well, you shall go to Crichton, also."

Anne started for the door unwillingly. "But where is Patrick?"

"He's here. We'll be along later."

"But Francis! You should not stay here! You may never get to Crichton!"

"You are quite right. That's why I want you there. I've been rather a fool, as Patrick was telling me while we rode. You ken, Mistress Janet, that Patrick has quite a way with words." He grinned, his eyes swept Janet, judging her swiftly. "Jamie has the dice now, and it's his throw. That's another way of saying that it's my turn at a room in the Castle. That's why I am here, because it makes small difference where I am caught. However, my good fortune is holding yet, while Jamie hugs and fondles those dice. I'll be along, after I've concluded to-night's business. It is something, you know, to catch these retainers of Morton's. Patrick and I—we have been looking, for a long time, for just such a chance as this."

Chapter Thirty Five

"I've sent them both to Crichton, sir, and we'd best follow soon, for reasons you're well aware of." Bothwell paused. "But first there's a specimen of man that I want you to see."

Patrick frowned, looking interested; without a word, he followed Bothwell down the hall and into the library. There were four men in the room.

"There's our culprit, sir." Bothwell pointed to the only man who wasn't one of his henchmen. Sym was buttoning his shirt, which was badly torn, with very nervous fingers; his coat lay on the floor beside him, and he had evidently been roughly divested of his boots, because his stockings were rumpled and pulled awry.

Bothwell hooked his thumbs in his belt and regarded his victim with a wicked smile, calculated to bring terror to his captive. "Have you been roughly treated, sir?" he mocked.

Graham said, "Your Lordship, we was gentle as lambs." He smiled broadly.

"I'm sure you were, Graham." Bothwell turned to Patrick. "Sir, I'd like you to look at this document which my men found on yonder filthy rogue." From the inner pocket of his coat he took a heavy white letter and handed it to Patrick.

The seal had already been broken by Bothwell, so Patrick unfolded the parchment, walked over to the light and held the document down so that the candlelight fell on it. He read it swiftly, folded it again, and handed it back to Bothwell.

"To what questions has he already responded, my lord?"

"His name is Sym; he is employed by Lord Morton, and he knows nothing of the correspondence he carried."

Sym had put his hands over his eyes, and he was standing, shivering. He didn't see the motion Bothwell made to Graham, so the first thing Sym knew his hands were seized and pulled away from his face, so that he had to look at Bothwell and Patrick—which was the last thing he wanted to do.

"I beg you, sirs," he faltered.

Bothwell said, "Strip him, Graham."

Sym cried out in terror; Graham let go his hands, whereupon Sym promptly clapped them to his face again. "I'll tell you all I know," he screamed through his fingers.

"Say 'your Lordship,'" growled Graham, seizing his hands again.

"Your Lordship," he quavered, and Bothwell turned aside to Patrick.

"*Voilà tout,*" he murmured, and Patrick winked and looked pleased. "*Tel maître, tel valet.* All right, Sym," he went on, "you were employed by Lord Morton. You are carrying a letter. Did you know that the letter was dangerous, Sym?"

"No, your Lordship."

"You weren't aware that the correspondence you carefully wore beneath your shirt was treasonable?"

"No, your Lordship."

"You're lying, Sym. Is it truly necessary for me to warn you again?" Bothwell made a motion toward Graham, but Sym interrupted hastily.

"I swear I didn't know it was treason, sir, I swear I didn't."

Bothwell and Patrick looked unbelieving, and finally Bothwell said, "To whom were you to deliver this message?" They both waited; this was the answer they really wanted. Would they hear the name they wished to hear?

"Maitland," Sym cried, desperately. "I swear it's the truth! Why don't you believe me?"

Patrick said solemnly, "We do, Sym." He had a wonderful smile on his face, and he said to Bothwell, "Then that little *billet-doux* was from Morton to Maitland."

Bothwell opened the letter again; he was smiling too, and he said with one eyebrow raised, "If we could only read it."

Patrick shrugged. "I can break that cipher, Francis, part of it, anyway. But the best part is that it obviously is Morton's handwriting. We'll have a devil of a time proving it was to go to Maitland, though, with only this rascal's word for it." He sighed, and was thoughtful. His words made Sym thoughtful too.

"They'll kill me," he burst out.

Bothwell looked surprised. "Somebody should." He was preoccupied, thinking about this letter, with its list of names that were all aliases for other famous names.

"But they'll kill me!"

Patrick explained, "He thinks when they know we've caught him, the safest thing to do with him is to slit his throat. I believe he's right, at that."

Graham asked, "Shall I slit it now?"

Sym recoiled in terror, and the rest of the men laughed; then Patrick said, "Tell me something, Sym. How long have you been in Lord Morton's employ?"

Sym wrenched his mind from the idea of his approaching demise. "Two years, sir."

"Two years." Patrick repeated it slowly. "Then perhaps you know something about the murder of an old hag named Campbell. Do you, Sym?"

Sym started to shake his head; but now, what difference did it make? "Aye, sir," he confessed, miserably.

"Did you murder her?" The tone was so insistent that Sym answered quickly, "No, sir. But I seen it done, I did."

Patrick frowned in such a manner that Sym's fears came rushing back. "I didn't do it, sir, and . . . he didn't mean to . . . He was trying to make her tell where the money was, and she just rocked back and forth and screamed, till he got mad, sir. He hit her . . . and she died."

Patrick said, "Just as I thought, if you'll remember, Francis. And, by the way, Sym, who is 'he?' "

"Lord Morton, sir," Sym paused, surprised. "I thought you knew, sir."

"We did." Bothwell lied with equanimity. "We wanted to hear you say it." He regarded Sym in silence for a minute. "Sym, do you know that the letter you carried contained a list of the successors to the crown? Sym, your life isn't worth five shillings, isn't worth a farthing. When Lord Morton knows you have been our prisoner—" He drew his hand across his throat and made a sucking noise, so terrifying to Sym that he grasped Graham for support.

Graham grunted. "Lay no hands on me, cuz," he said, stepping back.

"So, Sym, put your filthy feet inside those boots. I'll give you two pounds, and you get yourself over the Border, into England."

Sym stammered, "Thank you, my lord. Oh, your Lordship, thank you."

Bothwell said, "Don't thank me. I want to worry Morton." He yawned, watched the shaking Sym put on his footgear, and he tucked the letter back into his pocket.

"Now out the window with you!"

Sym obliged with alacrity, although he had hoped that Bothwell would offer him sanctuary. Graham closed the window and blew out the candles. They left the room.

"We don't have much time," Bothwell murmured to Patrick, as they mounted their horses.

"Aye."

Bothwell smiled.

"I fear, sir, that I'll ride the eight miles to Crichton, just to kiss my wife goodbye again. In that respect, you're more fortunate than I."

Patrick said nothing. He and Bothwell were riding abreast. Behind them came the reassuring hoofbeats of forty well-armed escorts. He was traveling toward Crichton, where Janet waited for him, but tonight Bothwell would leave; he was sure of it. They would ride eight more miles together and then it would be the end.

When they were four miles from Crichton, Bothwell said suddenly, "We shall reach Crichton just in time. Pursuit will surely come, sir."

"And quickly." Patrick leaned forward in the saddle. "Francis, what do you want me to do this time?"

Bothwell said abruptly, "I'd like you to take care of Anne." They galloped on in silence; Patrick wondered what he was thinking, but Bothwell did not speak again.

In the courtyard he flung himself off his horse, ran up the wide steps of the new wing he had built, and met Anne just as he rounded the gallery.

"Lord Bothwell is here?" she cried, and was out in the hall before anyone could answer her. There was no one in the hall, but it really would not have mattered. She put her arms around him; he was dirty, he smelled of the stables, and his rough beard scratched her cheek. He held her so tightly that the pistol in his belt hurt her flesh, and she wondered why she had been concerned with what she should say to him.

She expected him to kiss her; she expected him to lift her in his arms and carry her. She was surprised when he put her from him, and she realized he was looking over her head at someone. She knew it must be Patrick. The two men gazed at each other. Anne didn't know why Patrick was frowning so questioningly. "What's the matter?" she gasped.

Bothwell smiled ruefully. "You have only to look out toward the east."

Anne ran to the window at the end of the hall. It was the nearest window, and it faced the south, but she had no thought for directions now. The courtyard was lit by wavering torches; there were three horsemen who had evidently just galloped through the big gates, and while she watched, one flung himself off his horse, and the two others reined in sharply. One of them was Burley. He looked more intently serious than she had ever seen him. It sent fear through her. Impulsively she tried to open the window, but it stuck fast, and she whirled around, looking for the tall figure of her husband.

"Why don't they close the gates?" she cried, still banging

ineffectually at the window. "Why don't they close the gates?" Those big iron gates meant security for her; they shut out the world.

Bothwell was standing by her elbow; he looked down on the courtyard and the familiar scene it presented to his eyes, to his very senses. He too saw Burley, and he evidently recognized the two other men. "They're loyal, are they not, sir?" He spoke in a low voice to Patrick. Patrick was standing with bent head and drawn brows, his big hands hanging loosely at his sides.

"What is it, Francis?" Anne asked, her voice shaking.

"It's Jamie Stewart, thinking to lay hands on me." He didn't smile, but he had a faintly rueful expression on his face. They were ready, the orders had already gone out, and now . . . There were steps on the wide stairs, the heavy tread of men booted and running. Bothwell looked at Anne; she had grasped his arm, and to him she looked entrancingly lovely.

"I'll help you fight," she stammered.

At that he grinned, sending a look at Patrick that told her he was really amused and delighted with her response. "I'll take you to your room," he said. "D'ye think I want Andrew and young Burley unsettled for life by you in your dressing-gown?"

"Francis!" she cried. He was taking her arm, leading her along. "What does that matter now?" She was almost crying, and then she burst out again. "Why don't you tell them to close the gates?"

They were standing at the door of her room; at the balcony, the two approaching men and Gibson heard her, and they heard Bothwell say, "The gates are to remain open."

Then the door closed; they saw the flick of her satin skirts, and then nothing but the closed oaken door. He was going to try to explain briefly. "There will be no resistance at Crichton, lassie. No resistance. Patrick knows what to do. The King's men may enter; they may search. Do you understand me? There will be no resistance."

"But why?" She stared up at his face. "Why?" The word was a cry.

"Because it would be useless. Let Jamie bottle me up here, and he'll send to Edinburgh for cannon to blast every stone from these walls. Crichton's not built for siege, lassie; Crichton was built to live in. I built part of it, and I'll not stand by and watch it burn, watch it raked with cannon, knowing that you are in it, knowing that my only son is in it."

It was the most serious speech he had ever made to her; she stood frozen and immobile, watching his face. She took in the sharp angle of his jaw, the firm masculine mouth. Her eyes lingered on his heavy brows, on the thick springy hair, and then she lifted her hand and laid it gently on the side of his face, against the high cheekbones, and her fingers traced slowly over the slight hollow below the cheekbone. "I love you," she said, and she smiled. "Believe me, Francis, I love you. Remember that when you are gone, no matter where you are."

He drew her into his arms; he held her close against him, burying his face in her hair, kissing the curve of her throat. "I'll be back," he whispered. "Some day, sweetheart, some day. I may be long, but I'll come back."

She put her arms around his neck, cradling his head against her breast. Soon he would be gone; soon he would be riding away. He would be hunted, fugitive. She tried to keep back the tears. "Keep away from the wenches," she whispered, "and if you go to sea . . ." She stopped abruptly; she could not say any more.

"Keep away from the mermaids." He ended it for her. He tipped up her chin and said, "If Jamie Stewart could see you now, even he wouldn't have the heart to tear me away from your arms." He kissed her mouth, and then he straightened up, holding her away from him. "But don't let me catch you going out in that . . ." He waved his hand at her revealing gown. "Not even for the King, madam." He leaned down and kissed her again. "You smell of roses," he said—and that was the last word she heard from him. He closed the door behind him unhurriedly; she heard his retreating footsteps down the hall.

Patrick was waiting; he was standing at the top of the steps. Bothwell held out his hand, and Patrick put his in it. Their hands fell apart after a long second; they went down the shallow steps, their feet sounding loud in the stillness that pervaded the hushed and expectant castle. When they reached the bottom, they strode along to the huge doors. There was no one in the courtyard now but one man—and Valentine.

On the threshold of the castle Bothwell paused and said, "I'll see you when I can."

"I'll take care of everything." Patrick watched the tall figure stride away from him. Bothwell swung up into the saddle. Man and horse made a magnificent figure; it was etched on Patrick's mind.

The horse and man were strong and powerful, but there were no trappings this time. The saddle was old and scarred and Bothwell was wearing no armor. His jacket was of leather; it was old, too, and his boots were worn. He had no tasseled helmet but wore a plaid cap on the side of his head.

In the distance Patrick could hear the sound of horses, the blare of a trumpet, the jingling of harnesses. He could vision the trappings of the royal force, the floating banners, the gleam of musketeers. He stared for the last time at the picture in front of him—the man and the horse. Bothwell was waiting so that his enemies should know he had quit the castle. That was the plan and Patrick knew it. But now it was almost time. Bothwell lifted his hand from the pommel; he held the reins in the other. "You know," he said, "when my uncle left Crichton, with such pursuit as this, he didn't even have a saddle."

Patrick saw the familiar grin, he saw one big ungloved hand raised in farewell; then horse and man disappeared, slowly, out through the big iron gates that stood open so wide.

Chapter Thirty Six

James Stewart was riding with his men. Behind him echoed the sounds of armor, horses and the lumbering of cannon; ahead of him Crichton Castle gleamed like a jewel in the blackness.

In the courtyard the torches threw their light, and from almost every window, light glittered. James Stewart was riding fast; his prize was almost in his hands. Too long now had be been flouted by the Border lord, too long had his most impudent subject ridden abroad with impunity, recklessly thrusting aside the royal authority. Now it was to be ended; the castle was almost within his grasp.

James looked ahead eagerly. He could see plainly now, those gates which oddly enough stood open and suddenly he saw a horse and man ride out of them, slowly. Even at this distance, James recognized that figure.

But Bothwell was leaving nothing to chance. He spurred his horse suddenly, galloping uphill, away from the royal army, and just as suddenly reined in, making a picture against the sky. He fired the barrel of one pistol; then he shouted, "A Bothwell!"

The cry had a taunting ring as it echoed over the rolling hills. For a second, James was paralyzed by the insolence. He had stopped dead at the sight of the figure, and now he raised his own voice. "After him! After him!"

From the cavalcade many men responded, breaking ranks, obeying the royal order, pell mell in desperate haste, so that a number of the horses collided, unseating their riders. Amidst the whinnying of the mounts, and the shouts of the pursuers, Bothwell still stood on the hillside, waiting.

Looking down on the trim army which had come to trap him, he thought— This was his land, his castle. These rolling hills were his. What army had a right here, but his? Forfeiture meant nothing to the Border lord. What parliaments said or did to a scrap of paper made no difference to him. These lands were his. He wanted to defend them, he wanted to ride alone against that army, dashing down the hill to protect what was his own. A fierce rage swept over him. There was no fear, only anger, anger at his impotence, anger at having to flee and not to fight. On that hillside he felt an implacable hatred for his enemies, for they had driven him to this, driven him to flight.

He couldn't see that he had ever behaved wrongly. Four years ago, when he had spoken for his Queen's right to life, he had suffered imprisonment. One year ago, he had been trapped and flung into prison on the flimsiest of charges. He had escaped. What other course had been open to him? And now, what other course was available?

He sat immobile, watching the men who were galloping toward him. He put his pistol back in his belt; it was of no use at distances like these. Then he wheeled his horse sharply, and under the flying hoofs the dirt sprang up and was kicked aside. He galloped off into the night.

"After him!" James shouted again, and since his commands had already been obeyed, he fell into a steady cursing. There, on the bare hillside, as the ground sloped gently away to the lazy frozen Tyne, he swore, and he continued till after the figure of Bothwell had long disappeared.

James was frustrated, angry, and cold. You couldn't keep warm in Scotland in winter unless you rode at full gallop. He spurred his mount; those big gates were still open, and, with a number of his train, he rode right up to the doors.

They creaked slightly as they opened for him. James dismounted with the aid of two men, and ascended the shallow steps, looking around. This was the principal dwelling place of the Earls of Bothwell, but they held these lands, these houses, at the pleasure of the crown. James came forward slowly; he advanced into the hall, his plumed hat riding high on his head.

"Sir." The King's voice was metallic, and Patrick swept the cap off his curls. Patrick's face was set and tense; he didn't know what awaited him, and he dropped to one knee.

"Your Majesty." That was all he said. He could think of nothing else.

James said slowly, "It grieves your prince to find you here. You may stand, sir." His voice was weary.

Patrick rose to his feet. "The castle of Crichton is open, and honored to receive you, Sire."

"Honored?" James sneered openly.

"It is an honor to receive Your Majesty." Patrick said quietly. "It is always an honor. To me, though, it is regrettable that it is necessary for you to come on such an errand!"

That kind of intercession for Bothwell made James flush with anger. "You openly regret my actions?" The sentence burst out.

"Not that, Sir. But I regret all—that has gone before." He was silent, and then he said, forcefully, "Your Grace, do not ask me to desert him. Don't ask me, for I cannot!"

"Cannot? Those are strange words, sir, to use to your King." James wanted to sigh; he was angry, but he was suddenly regretful too. This man who stood before him, he had been trustworthy. Now James knew with clarity that he always would trust him, and yet between them stood the figure of the unruly renegade Border lord. It struck him then that this conversation was odd; the two of them might have been talking, as they had done so often before, in the anteroom at Holyrood, instead of in a vast empty hall where the wind whistled shrilly and the huge stairway went up into the shadows.

James glanced over his shoulder. The doors were still open, and his retinue had come in after him; they had formed a sort of wedge behind their monarch, spreading out in an open V. Patrick saw them too, but he saw them in a kind of daze. It was all over now. From the very beginning he had seen this coming, for the days of feudalism were over; gone was the time when a subject could flout the royal authority for any but a short length of time. James seemed to read his mind.

"I waited long to do this, sir."

Both men were silent again; both were thinking of the night outside, and the man who had fled into its darkness. James knew they would never catch Bothwell tonight.

James continued speaking. "I wish to see the Countess of Bothwell." He glanced over his shoulder again, seeing the men in armor, their plumed helmets tucked neatly under one arm, and there was suddenly more light, for torches had been brought in.

Patrick said slowly, "Is that a command, Sir?"

James's anger rushed back. "By God's son, it is a command," he roared. "And the countess may bring the keys to this dwelling."

Patrick bowed. He turned away, and he went upstairs slowly, his shadow growing longer as he ascended. In just a minute they heard his step again. James looked up expectantly, but he was alone. Patrick descended slowly; his eyes went over the hall beneath, with his King standing in the center, the courtiers, dressed for battle, and the soldiers, behind him, and over all, the flickering light that streamed unsteadily from the wind-blown torches. He'd wanted to spare her this, but it was useless. He remembered the old warning he'd given her, a year ago, and he had deliberately left her to face her King by herself. She alone could accomplish a miracle, and he would give her every chance to do it. He stepped off the last step and looked upwards. "Lady Bothwell is coming, Sire." Anne stood at the top of the stairway.

There was complete silence in the hall below. Anne looked down on a sea of upturned faces, and past them. Beyond the big doors, the courtyard was filled to overflowing with men and horses. Those faces below her—she could have recognized any of them if she had tried, for they belonged to men she had danced with, courtiers, noblemen. She saw none of them; she saw nothing but her King.

Only obedience moved her feet forward. In obedience to his

command she had picked up the nearest cloak; snatching it from a cupboard, settling its maroon velvet folds about her body, and she could not have chosen a better color for this stone hall. The lights glimmered softly on the rich velvet pile, running fingers of warmth over the sable fur that swept down the front of the cape and swirled around the full skirt. Anne had put one hand on the balustrade to steady herself, and in the other white hand she carried the heavy, huge keys that unlocked the massive gates and doors of Crichton Castle. Step after step she took, her slippers making no sound, but when she got to the bottom step, she stopped completely for just a second. In that second she remembered that she had covered her head; she raised one hand and pushed back the hood of her cape, letting it fall backward, letting her hand drop to her side again.

It was a gesture of submission. Now her face was released from the shadow of her cape, and the men watching her realized how lovely she was, how unconsciously alluring. She was a fit mate for her husband. The very sight of her made every man remember the tall powerful figure of the Border lord.

Anne descended the last step; she walked the few feet that separated her from James, and she knelt, her cape fanning out against the stones. Her blonde head was bent, her fingers were clasped over the heavy black iron keys, and Patrick, behind her, clenched his hands helplessly.

James looked down on her bent head. Then his eyes swept the hall briefly. He had lost his anger, he had lost it as she came down the steps toward him, but now it was indeed fitting that she should be so beautiful. It heightened his sense of power. With pleasure he studied the angle of her head, the rich honey-colored hair, the sweep of her black lashes; and he wanted to see her eyes. So he spoke.

"Madam, are those the keys to this dwelling?"

She did what he wanted; she raised her head, and looked up at him. "Aye, Your Majesty," she whispered.

He didn't let her rise. He said, "Give them to me," and he stretched out his gloved hand while she laid the keys into his fingers. James took them, scrutinized them. The hall was deathly silent. "Madam, you willfully married Francis Hepburn after he had been put to the horn, after he had been denounced outlaw. Since that time you have received him here, have tended to his wounds and hurts, gained by him in unlawful pursuits. Have you not?"

Her head was still raised to his. "Aye, Your Majesty." Her voice was low, but it carried in the stillness.

"So you have followed a course of unduty to the crown of this realm. Therefore the keys to this dwelling will remain with me, in my possession!" Anne said nothing, and James remembered the time he had kissed her. He said, "You may rise," and, surprisingly, he held out his hand.

Anne was too shaken to thank him. She rose, but James still had to look down at her. Hence the sense of power stayed with him, and he wanted to punish her. "Because you admit your complicity, because you would receive your husband again—" He paused, hoping she would contradict him, but she did not, and this open confession of her love annoyed James. "Because of that, you will be warded in Edinburgh Castle for as long as I deem it necessary."

Anne's face whitened. It was not the threat of imprisonment that frightened her; it was the implication that when Bothwell was safely caught, she would be freed. She stood stock-still, her eyes pleading with James. It couldn't be possible that a few minutes ago she had been held in her husband's arms, and now—she closed her eyes, trying to see his face, remembering her last words to him. "Your Majesty—" she held out her hands—"only one request I beg of you!"

James frowned, but he was pleased. "What is it?" he asked gruffly.

"My wee laddie; I cannot leave him, Sir. I beg you let me take my bairn and Lord Bothwell's daughter with me!"

Of all requests, James had not expected this. He stared, the soldiers with him stared, and none of them but would have exchanged places with James so that a man's generosity could be regally given. Patrick unclenched his hands, and he also thought of the political advantages this story would have.

Sympathy beat hard in the breast of every man who watched; James felt it, and it made his voice even sharper.

"Your request is granted, madam."

Everyone sighed. Anne murmured, "You are kind, Sir." And then she stood in front of him helplessly, for he hadn't dismissed her. She seemed to realize then that she had a large and attentive audience, and her violet eyes swept the entourage for the first time, before returning to James.

"You may ready yourself, madam; you may take personal servants." His words were an anticlimax to all that had gone before. Anne made her curtsy, Patrick took her arm, and together they mounted the steps. Down in the bare hall, James watched as their figures slowly went away from him.

Chapter Thirty Seven

ANNE left Crichton at eleven o'clock at night. Janet had helped her pack. There were just a few belongings; the rest could come later, including the featherbeds. Janet had wanted to go with her.

"No," said Patrick brusquely. "I'm going to take you to Borthwick."

Behind his back Anne shook her head at Janet, who stared; and Patrick frowned at both of them.

Anne went down the steps slowly; her own garrison filled the courtyard. She carried the baby, and little Janet clung fast to Marie's hand. Patrick put Anne in the coach.

"I shall see you tomorrow," he said only.

"Oh, Patrick," Anne said.

"Francis will be safe." He leaned down and kissed her. "Goodbye, lass."

He watched the coach turn; it clattered out of the courtyard and up the rutted road to the capital. It was accompanied by part of the garrison, and Patrick was more worried about the safety of the men than he was about Anne. He'd follow as soon as he could. He swung around to Janet.

"I had wanted to take you to London for your honeymoon," he said, and he sighed a little. "Instead it will have to be Borthwick for you, tonight, at least."

Janet said, "Patrick, do you like this dress?"

He drew his brows together. "No," he said, "and where's your cloak? You'll freeze."

"It's upstairs," she answered. "If we went to London, I could buy clothes, too."

He took her arm, drawing her into the library where the fire burned. "Stay here," he said. "I've orders to give, and I'll be back in some minutes. I've already talked to David Hepburn, but I want to see Bothwell's bailiff before we go."

She waited for him in front of the fire, curling up on one of the fireside benches. He was gone about thirty minutes and when he came back he stood in the center of the room, looking around as if for the last time.

"Well," he said finally, taking his eyes away from the old basket-hilted sword that hung over the mantle—the sword that had been taken from the hand of the second Earl as he lay mortally wounded on the battlefield at Flodden—"we must go now, Janet. There is nothing more to be done."

"No," said Janet stubbornly. "I'll not go to Borthwick."

"Why?" He came over beside her. "Why?"

"My head hurts," she said meekly.

"Does it?" he asked. "I thought it had stopped aching." He sat down on the bench wearily. "In the name of God, whether or not it hurts, there's nowhere else to go tonight."

"Where will Lord Bothwell go?"

Patrick looked into the fire. "Francis? Why he's probably asleep by now, in an inn, somewhere in the Borders. There are dozens which would shield him, Janet."

"But you said he had no money."

"He left all he had with me, for Anne. And he may be asleep by a fire, in a clearing in Ettrick forest. We've slept that way."

"He would want to be by himself?"

"He might."

"Patrick, he has not admitted defeat!"

"And do you think I have? But a man can fight a losing fight only so long. How does your head feel?"

"Better," she said.

He stood up. "Then we had best start for Borthwick."

Janet said slowly, "So this is what it will be like."

He frowned. "What are you talking about?"

"Being married. I'll not go to Borthwick," she ended, defiantly.

"Mistress, for God's sake, have you taken leave of your senses? D'ye want to start for Edinburgh now? Is that your heart's desire?"

She sat on the bench with her knees drawn up and her hands locked around them. He sat opposite her. "Patrick," she said softly, "I hardly knew him, but I hated to see him go, too. But he'll come back. I know he will."

Patrick didn't move. "You're wrong."

"I know I'm not," she said earnestly. "I know I'm not wrong."

He smiled a little, and then he thought of the letter they had intercepted tonight. Right now it reposed in one of the big worn boots that Bothwell was wearing. "Perhaps you are right," he conceded, finally.

She rose and came over to him, standing in front of him. "Patrick, now that I'm here, why do you act as though I were not?"

"I'm not accustomed to having females around. Sympathetic ones."

"Will I always have to remind you?"

He looked up at her. "I definitely do not like that dress."

"I knew you would not."

"You did? Is that why you made it?"

"No, sir. Anne told me. She told me a deal about you."

"I'll warrant she did." He grinned, and suddenly he stood up again and put his hands on her shoulders.

"Must we go now?" she asked.

"No," said Patrick. "Now that you've reminded me there is a female about, I'm not so likely to forget it."

Chapter Thirty Eight

THE Earl of Morton sat with his feet comfortably propped up on a stool in front of the low burning fire. His doublet was undone, the better to accommodate his ample supper, and the better to digest it. He drowsed contentedly, letting his head droop forward.

Outside the night was fine. There was spring in the air, and against the casement windows the branches of the apple trees tapped gently, making little brushing sounds that lulled Morton to sleep.

It was peaceful in the country; he was glad he had come. Although the last few months had been outwardly peaceful in the city, and Maitland was still absent from court, there was unrest, unquiet of late, simmering under the surface. Truly, if it weren't some of the reinstated Stewarts glowering at him in court, then it was Maitland's messages making him nervous, and James's jibes bringing the flush to his face. Morton wished he could control those flushes, either of anger or of outraged pride, but he'd never been able to stop the telltale blood.

The apple branches tapped at the window again, and he glanced over. He could see them outside. Then he looked back to the fire, and let his head droop lower on his chest. He began to snore a little.

One loud snort brought him up short. He sat up, startled, for somewhere in the darkened room a voice said, "Morton, you bear distinct resemblance to an untrussed fowl."

"Who said that?" Morton whispered the words, turning his head slowly, carefully searching the room with widened eyes.

"I'm right here, Morton. D'ye feel that? A wee bit of cold steel?"

"How did you get here? How did you get across the room?"

"On silent feet, Morton. I've learned to move silently." There was a chuckle. "I've been waiting for you for four weeks, Morton—almost a month. I knew you would come, sooner or later, and time makes not so much difference to me. I came in that window while you snored, and then I moved to this spot behind your chair. But do not scream, sir. Do not scream—or you'll shout your way into hell."

"What do you want?" Morton tried to sit forward, but the pressure of the weapon against his left shoulder didn't lessen.

"I want to talk with you. I'm not going to ask you for your word of honor—to be quiet while we talk. I'm going to warn you that any tricks—and you'll pay heavily, Morton. I'm not even going to lock the door. If anyone knocks, you may tell him not to disturb you. Now . . ." There was the scraping sound of a chair being dragged; it was pulled into Morton's line of vision, and the uninvited guest settled himself in it, just opposite Morton, right in front of the fire.

Morton stared. He stared at the scarred boots, the tarnished silver spurs, the leather coat and breeks; he stared at the gleaming dagger held in big, capable, blunt-nailed fingers; he stared at the face of his guest. "Bothwell," he said disjointedly, "what do you want to say to me?"

"A considerable." The Earl reached over and poured himself a glass of the wine that stood on the table. He sipped it appreciatively. "I don't often get anything as good as this, Morton. Rations are light lately, too." He smiled wryly, settling himself comfortably, giving Morton the awful impression that he was going to stay a long while.

"You are alone, my lord?"

Bothwell glanced up from the wine cup. He smiled again. "Looking for information, sir? If you want the truth, Morton, I'm well attended yet. Though there's no money." He watched Morton digest his words, which were quite untrue, for only Gibson and the faithful Graham had been permitted to follow him this winter in the Border hills and caves; only the three of them had, alone, eluded the law of the land.

"Is there anything else you'd like to ask me?"

Morton's eyes were limpid and dark with curiosity and fear. He kept staring at Bothwell as though he couldn't believe it was really he. All kinds of memories came flashing into his mind, all kinds of scenes. He remembered the first time he had ever seen the young earl; he remembered him at court, as a youngster, always striding rapidly, as though the walls of the room were much too close about him, and the room itself too small. He remembered the reports of his first duel; he remembered seeing him on the deck of a ship that James and he had inspected before it left port; he remembered him vividly the day he had told James that he deserved hanging if he'd let his mother die.

"How have you lived these months, Bothwell?" He sat forward in his chair. Scared as he was, what was this other kind of life like? What did it hold that was so fascinating?

"Morton, I've lived in caves, which abound in Liddesdale, as perhaps you've heard. I've lived in small inns. I've lived in some of my own houses, on the Border. I've lived in English estates. You know all that—why do you ask?"

"But . . . what have you done?"

Bothwell grinned. "Everything," he said succinctly. "And waited for you."

"I know," Morton said, almost as though he were in complete agreement with the Earl. "We all know. You should see the list of complaints from the Border, Bothwell. You should see them!"

The Border lord looked his usual guilty self. "Morton, if anyone should tell you that I led those raids, do not believe them, and," he continued, "you may tell them that I hold no

King's commission, and what my Borderers do is no concern of mine."

"You are deliberately letting them run wild, Bothwell. You are—and you know it."

"Do I?" He poured another cup of wine. "And although this is very pleasant, sir, we'll get to our business now." He paused again, laying the dagger across his knee, measuring the very short distance that separated him from Morton. He said slowly, "You needn't be afraid of me, Morton. You needn't be afraid at all, because I—I am in possession of a piece of paper which will hang you, sir. I scarce need to kill you myself."

Morton didn't speak, and Bothwell poured him a cup of wine, which he handed over. "A few months ago, I intercepted a letter, sir, which is in cipher, and which contains a list of the successions to the crown."

Morton's hand froze onto the cup. What he had been fearing these many months, then, was true! He stuttered, he tried to drink, and choked on his wine. "I'll explain," he muttered weakly.

Bothwell waved him aside. "Pray, do not explain. It matters little enough to me. You had best save your explanations for the court." He grinned wickedly.

Morton tossed off the wine, wishing it were strongest brandy. But his mind was beginning to function. Perhaps it would be possible to summon aid. All he needed was a few seconds—but first, he must discover more. He asked, "You have that piece of paper with you, Bothwell? Because if you do, I'll pay high! I'll pay you all I can get, I swear it before Almighty God!"

"Leave God out of it." Bothwell frowned, and Morton winced, because that frown had a devilish look. Quick fear ran through him; the Earl of Bothwell had been immeasurably hardened by these months of fugitive life. Morton was afraid, and he wanted to scream for help.

Bothwell leaned forward and slapped Morton across the face with the back of his hand. "You witless rabbit," he muttered, "keep your tongue quiet! Had you thought I wasn't watching you?" He relaxed back in his chair easily. "Now, don't play, Morton. Remember I'm no lord of the land; there's a price on my head, and I don't intend to pay it—not yet awhile."

The tone was so bitter that Morton said, "You'll die for this—for all you've done." Then he was silent; he wondered how he'd got the courage to say that.

"I may die—but I'll not die in chains! Remember that, Morton!" Bothwell put down the wine cup, crossed his legs, and held the gleaming dagger in one hand. "Now listen to me. I don't have that letter. Patrick Galbraith has it." He swung his boot carefully, wondering if the crackle of paper in it could be heard. It wasn't, and it made him smile, because Morton had been so unnerved by the statement that he had cowered back in his chair, almost gasping.

"Sir Patrick has it?"

"Aye," Bothwell lied, pleasantly. "So there is another matter I wish to speak to you about, and this previous disclosure should loosen your tongue. I want to know, Morton, about a stonemason named Campbell, who was murdered twenty-eight years ago. I want to know about his wife, who was murdered during Yuletide, one year ago. I want to know why you killed her. Now talk, Morton, quickly."

"The letter," Morton gasped.

"We deciphered it, Morton. Or rather, Patrick did. For some reason you made a list of the succession to the Scottish crown. If you didn't mean harm to James, why did you write that letter?"

"It was a mistake . . ."

"Don't blubber. Of course it was a mistake—a very grave one, for you. Now tell me about Mrs. Campbell. You killed her. Why?"

"I didn't kill her!"

"You lie. You killed her by a blow on the head, given in anger, because she wouldn't answer your questions. This time, if you don't answer mine, Sir Patrick will give that letter to

James. So talk, Morton, talk! I don't have much more time."

Morton said tremulously, "There is a mystery about a room in Stirling Castle. There is a mystery about what Campbell did there, that night, twenty-eight years ago. I thought she knew where the money was, and what happened that night. But she wouldn't tell me, Bothwell, she wouldn't tell me."

Bothwell had heard only one word. "Stirling?" He frowned thoughtfully, and he stretched his legs out again. "What room in Stirling?"

"A small room off the banquet hall—I think. I know nothing, don't you understand?"

The Border lord leaned forward. "Talk, Morton. Remember that piece of paper in Edinburgh!"

"D'ye think I've forgot?" Morton trembled with emotion. "How could I forget?" And he buried his face in his hands. "If I could only make you understand that I too know nothing. Except that room. Maitland gave that away one night. He's old enough to know something about twenty-eight years ago. I'm not, Bothwell."

Bothwell had been listening patiently. He looked at Morton long and steadily, and Morton thought he was going to say something pertinent, but instead, Bothwell said impassively, "Jesus, you sicken me." He got to his feet, stood for a moment, and added, "Come on, Morton."

"What?" Morton was so amazed that he forgot his terror.

"We're going, you and I. Get stirring; fasten your clothes and move yourself."

Morton hugged himself in a way that reminded Bothwell of Sym. But he did fasten his doublet. He gazed at Bothwell imploringly, and finally he asked, "Where are we going?"

The answer was short. "Stirling." Bothwell was reckoning the distance. "You can walk that far, Morton. 'Tisn't but twa miles. Lucky for you."

Actually, the two miles seemed very short to Morton. His feet seemed to eat up the distance to the bulking castle which they could see when they were still fully a mile from it, for Stirling topped a craggy rock, and its outlines in the moonlight were very plain. They could even see the rocky ramp down which the horsemen would come flying when the court was in residence in Stirling.

Often the turrets of the castle were shrouded in mist, but tonight the benevolent moon illumined all its ramparts. Sometimes trees concealed their view as they walked; sometimes a hill would intervene, but when that hill was topped, there was the castle again, ever nearer.

Morton began to hang back. He shot glances at the face of his companion, but Bothwell's expression told Morton nothing; only the Earl's steady pace told Morton that there was no use protesting.

"Bothwell, I'm not sure what room it is." Morton was trembling, with both the exertion of keeping up to Bothwell's long-legged stride, and his own pressing fears.

"Keep quiet." That was the only answer he got. Bothwell swung along, not knowing himself what he was going to do once the castle had been reached. At the bottom of the steep incline leading to its gates, he paused.

"Are we going right up to the entrance?" Morton could not forbear asking the question.

"Certainly. They'll think we're castle servants." Bothwell shrugged. That was the least of his worries. "Now look, Morton, I'm accustomed to housebreaking; you're not. So, if you don't want to get killed, see that ye do as I say. After all, there's little enough danger. There'll be no one here, save a few servants and some empty bedsteads." As he walked up the ramp boldly, he added, "Remember, do as I say."

Morton nodded silently. However unwilling a partner in crime he might be, he still wanted to escape from this alive. He trudged along at Bothwell's side, panting with effort at the steepness of the ascent.

At the top, Bothwell turned to the right, winding around the base of the walls, along a path quite clear in the moonlight. He didn't hurry; he knew better than to hurry. Around the corner there was less light. The shadows lay deep, and for the first time he stopped completely. There was a small door in the wall. He took out a bunch of keys and carefully fitted the first key in the lock. Nothing happened. He took another key, trying each one on the chain, and he had tried all but one, when the lock turned. Eagerly, he put his hand on the door to push it open, but when it didn't move, he swore softly, took out the key, and stood regarding the bolted door. He pushed back his cap a little, put the keys back, and drew from his pocket a length of coiled rope. He turned to Morton.

"Hand me that sword," he said.

Morton drew back fearfully. Bothwell grasped his arm, wrenching the sword from its sheath. Regardless of noise, he sent it flying over the rocks, while Morton whimpered protestingly. Bothwell said nothing. He bound Morton's hands neatly behind his back. "This insures your waiting for me," he explained pleasantly. The other end of the rope he fastened around his own wrist, and he was up and over the wall before Morton had time to realize why he had been bound to his captor.

Morton prayed silently. He hoped the door would never open, but there it was, gaping in the blackness, and he felt himself pulled into the void with any but gentle hands. He stumbled backwards, keeping his balance with an effort. His feet hurt already from climbing and walking in his thin-soled house shoes. "Oh," he gasped.

"I'll untie you," he heard Bothwell say. "I'm loath enough to be bound to you in any way whatsoever."

"How can you jest?" Morton looked around in terror.

"Jest? I was never more serious." Bothwell coiled the rope again neatly and put it back into his pocket. "This is fine rope, Morton. It will bear my weight. I've used it many times, sir." He grinned. "Now, shall I take your hand?"

"Aye," whispered Morton.

Bothwell looked down at him in real amazement. "You poor whoreson coward," he said, commiseratingly. Then he asked seriously, "Morton, what in the name of the devil are you afraid of?"

What was he afraid of? Morton looked at the great walls

ahead of them, and he heard the stealthy, rustling night sounds. He visioned the rooms lying in clammy darkness. Then he gave a sudden gasp, for Bothwell had pricked his arm with the point of his dagger.

"It's not a dream," muttered Bothwell. "I'll bleed the fear out of you. This way!" He led, and Morton followed, around the base of the castle, until they reached another door in the outside wall, which Bothwell carefully unlocked, leaving the door standing open just a bit, so that it wouldn't be easily observed. "Our outgate," he whispered. "You see, up there?" He pointed, and Morton knew those windows well enough. They were the windows of the great reception hall and gallery; the small panes gleamed in the moonlight.

"But how do we get in?"

"Easily," was the reply. He approached the nearest window. It was small, and he knocked out a pane with his elbow, a sharp, quick blow, and they could hear the glass tinkle to the floor inside. Bothwell put his hand through the frame; the window opened. "You first," he said, and he hoisted Morton rudely into the window. "There, you see." They stood together in Stirling Castle, the moonlight making patterns on the stone floor. "Don't step on the glass, lambie," he mocked; "you'll hurt your wee toes."

Morton stepped around the glass gingerly; he knew his way, too, here, and he knew that the door opposite led upstairs. He ascended those stairs behind Bothwell and he was amazed that the Earl moved so softly on those heavy boots. Morton himself stumbled over the top step, and lurched into the small room at the top.

It was completely bare. There was nothing in it, nothing but the same pattern of moonlight on the floor, and it was frighteningly silent, clammy and cold. Morton shivered as he stood and watched Bothwell cross the floor, open the door to the gallery. There the moonlight illumined the long room; the tables that could seat sixty persons were ghostly plain, the oaken floors shimmered, and the stone fireplaces were sunk in shadow. Bothwell closed the door again and looked around this small room. It was part of a suite; on one side of its fireplace was the door to the stairway, on the other a door leading to another of the rooms in the suite. There was only one window, and Bothwell went to it, opening it wide.

He leaned his elbow on the sill and regarded the room with puzzled eyes. He wished Patrick were there. He thought of him only briefly, though; how many weeks had it now been since he had seen him? And, oddly enough, he remembered with special clarity the first time he had talked with Patrick about his discovery of the cache of gold coins, and the murdered stonemason. Patrick had said, "You're going the wrong way. Stonemason leads to house, castle, walls. Start from there!"

Bothwell stared hard at the bare stone walls. "The floor is wooden," he remarked, aloud, and Morton jumped, for nothing had been said in the last few minutes.

Bothwell did not move, but his eyes roamed the room. The very act made him see that first kitchen in which he had stood, wondering where the walls concealed a treasure. In a second, he was on his knees before the fourth stone up, to the right of the fireplace.

He had brought a broad-bladed chisel, which he carried, but he had no hammer. Instead, he used the heavy hilt of his dagger. At the bottom of that fourth stone he started his steady pounding.

Morton came close, peering over his shoulder. "Get out of the light," he was told rudely, and then Bothwell worked on, interspersing his labors with remarks. "You will see now, Morton, the complements with which I ply my trade as an outlaw. When Sir Patrick gives that piece of paper to James Stewart, which he will do any time now, be sure to equip yourself with everything you have seen me use tonight. And don't forget the piece of rope, Morton. That is highly important."

He hammered on, loosened mortar powdering the floor. "In my back pocket is a torch, Morton, but it is wise to pick moonlight nights, as we do on the Border." He stood up, began to edge the chisel deeper into the corner of the uneven stone.

"If you can, carry a pistol, although it is regrettable that we haven't progressed to rapid-fire guns. However, there is a limit to what one man can carry easily. Hence, you see, my pistols are left behind, in my saddle holsters."

"Stop," said Morton, hoarsely.

"The prospect frightens you, does it? But two years ago you and Maitland labored to put me in this position. Aye, you worked hard at making King Jamie believe I intended to take his life, and you are still working at that, Morton. If Jamie weren't afraid of me, I'd have been able to talk to him before this, but I can't get near him, Morton, because of you."

"You forced Maitland out!"

"Aye, and much good it did me; much good it did me, to leave Jamie unmolested that day at Leith. I thought he'd know then I meant no harm to him. It is poetic justice that now you'll know what it means to have a charge of treason over your head, especially since you really deserve the charge, Morton." He chuckled, but his eyes were serious, intent on the stone that was loosened now. He bent nearer, crouching down.

"Bothwell, don't!"

"You want me to take bribes, Morton? How high will you pay?"

"I'll pay you every farthing I can lay my hands on!"

"Good," said Bothwell, getting to his feet. "Hand me your purse; I'll warrant you have it with you." He smiled with pleasure when the heavy leather purse was put in his hand. He weighed it and tucked it in his jacket. "Now I'll get to work again." He knelt down, and the little room was filled once more with the sound of steady hammering. "But, Morton, that was a bit of robbery, you know. I'd like also the jewels in your ears, and on your fingers, sir; so hand them over too. And I've no intention of interfering with the course of justice; you can't bribe me, Morton, especially since I'm a thief anyway."

"Bothwell!" Morton knelt down too. He was drawing the rings—he was wearing three—from his fleshy fingers. "Please, I'll give you more than these."

"I don't want more." Bothwell only glanced at the jewelry

held out to him. "This will be ample. I'm a man of simple wants, sir, but seeing you hang is something I'd pay very high for. Very high. I warned you, because I wanted information from you, and because I wanted you with me tonight. If anyone should come, you have only to tell them who you are. Then I'll be safe also, and if you do that, I'll give you two weeks before the letter goes to James." Bothwell stopped; he put the chisel under the edge of the stone. "Now!" he said, but first he put Morton's rings in his pocket. "Now!"

Morton forgot his fears. His eyes were glued to the big stone that was being inched from its place. It was moving—slowly—but moving. What could be behind it? A fortune in gold? What could there be, and how had Bothwell known the spot to pick? Morton whispered, "This was what Maitland didn't know about the room."

"This may not be its secret." Bothwell pushed out the words, for it took all his strength to move the stone. "It's stuck, fast, farther back," he muttered, heaving on the edge with all his force. Morton watched the muscles in his back and neck grow taut; he watched the big hands try for a grip on the rock.

"It's looser," Morton cried, excited and eager. "Here, I'll help." He seized the dagger, which had been laid on the floor, and, taking the hilt, tried to push the wide blade under the far edge.

"Don't break that," Bothwell said quickly. He stood up, bending over, getting his knee under the stone that was halfway out from the wall. He was breathing hard now, partly from his exertions and partly from the suspense. In a second, the secret, if there was a secret, would be revealed.

"It's out!" Morton gasped, with shortened breath. He was holding one edge of the stone, and carefully he helped Bothwell lay their burden on the floor. He almost crushed his fingers. He straightened up quickly. "What's in there?"

Bothwell had already stretched his arms into the cavity laid open. His fingers closed around the handle of an oblong box which he drew toward him, and when it came out, free, he carried it—for it was light—over to the square of floor where the moonlight lay. He didn't open it. He knelt beside it, and he didn't want to open it, for some reason. He didn't know why, but he didn't like to touch the box; there was something familiar about it. He stared at it. Only three feet long, it looked like—it looked like a miniature casket. And suddenly he remembered Patrick saying, "A crypt," and he could hear his own voice answering, "Why do you call it a crypt?" and Patrick had frowned and said, "Oh, I don't know."

"Is it a treasure, Bothwell?" Morton sank to his knees beside it.

"No," said Bothwell, slowly. "I don't know what it is, Morton. But it is too light to hold gold. It's too light to hold much of anything, Morton—except bones."

Morton blanched. His hands had reached out to lift the lid, which, oddly enough, wasn't fastened, and they stopped short; Morton's fingers just brushed against the dusty wood, and he drew them back hastily. The two of them stared at the little box.

"Let's put it back," Morton whispered.

"I'd like to," Bothwell said, "but I can't, Morton. I must see it." He lifted the lid, and it flew open, clattering back against the floor.

"A blanket!" Bothwell gritted his teeth. Now he was sure that he didn't want to disturb that blanket. The closely woven wool felt distasteful, even to his hard hands, and he saw the letter J embroidered in still gleaming silk. Then he lifted the edge of the wool.

That was all he needed, but when he had done that, ruthlessly he plucked the whole of the little blanket off its closely guarded, now defenseless, secret. At long last the Earl of Bothwell said, "No wonder that Campbell was murdered."

Morton crossed himself, and kneeling there in front of the little casket, he trembled and stared. Surely, he thought, he couldn't be here, in this room, with its hidden crypt, with its ghostly secrets!

"Twenty-seven years," said Bothwell slowly, "and I'd say it was a six-months-old babe." He replaced the blanket carefully, covering the small pitiful skeleton.

The lid was still open. Both men saw clearly that woven letter J, embroidered so carefully on the blanket, and Bothwell said, "D'ye realize what you've seen tonight, Morton?"

"Close it. Put it back." Morton stood, trembling.

"Men have died for knowing less than this." Bothwell took satisfaction in scaring Morton, but he did replace the lid; he picked up the box in his big hands, walking noiselessly back to the gaping wall. He felt like a ghoul; the tough Borderer murmured, "Heaven forgive me for disturbing a wee bairn's grave."

"Aye," said Morton piously, "but whose grave, Bothwell, whose?"

Bothwell withdrew his hands from the cavity. He lifted his shoulders as he said, "Perhaps an illegitimate, perhaps the heir to the throne. Perhaps the real heir. Who knows, Morton? We won't." He swung around suddenly, and his voice was louder. "But I know this. This child's body casts real doubt as to the heir to the Scottish throne, and what are we going to do with that knowledge, Morton? What can we do with it?"

Morton was going to say, "Forget it," but he didn't. His eyes grew crafty; he was thinking rapidly. "Some knowledge is worth money, Bothwell." A little smile creased his eyes.

Bothwell was looking down at the stone he had yet to replace, but he didn't need to glance at Morton to know his expression. "You tell this to James, Morton, and you'll not get money, unless you expect to spend it in hell. Here, help me with this stone."

"Aye, my lord."

Morton stooped obediently, working his plump fingers under the uneven edge of the stone. He heaved with all his strength, and for the first time tonight he felt a little better. Now he and Bothwell shared a secret, a terrible, dangerous secret; but at least they shared it, and perhaps Bothwell would know how to use it. Morton would not be afraid if the Border lord was his partner in crime. And perhaps this secret shared would be a basis for working out an agreement about that letter, the letter which lay in the hands of Sir Patrick Galbraith.

Morton heaved on the stone, raising his side of it, setting it carefully on the platform of rock from which it had come.

"I'll do the rest," murmured Bothwell, intent on his task. "You use your hands, and scrape up what you can of the crumbled mortar, then spread the rest with your feet."

Again Morton obeyed, without a word. There was no sound in the room outside of their light quick breathing and the dull scraping as Bothwell inched the stone into place. Morton was on his hands and knees, filling his hands and then his pockets with the whitish dust.

"Just so you don't leave any of it near the base of this stone." Bothwell glanced over his shoulder as Morton worked.

"I can't see very well," Morton complained. He stood up, and began to shuffle his feet, scattering the remainder of the telltale dust, leaning over every once in a while to blow at it lustily.

The sight of Morton's industry amused Bothwell. He was almost finished himself, and he started to say, "Good work," when he felt his whole body stiffen and he stood immobile, waiting for the sounds which would herald the danger that he had sensed.

Morton heard the second noise—outside the walls. His face turned white as the dust on his hands; he had been in the act of blowing and that changed to a sudden intake of breath. "What was that?" he gasped.

"Be quiet," Bothwell said tensely, working furiously, pushing the stone, his whole weight braced against the recalcitrant rock. He must finish replacing this stone, or tonight's work might well have been left undone. "Get to one side of the door to the stairs," he ordered. That was the safest place, for if they came up the stairs, they might run right by.

Morton was frozen to his place. He didn't move, and his horrified eyes fastened themselves on Bothwell imploringly. "Do something, Bothwell," he moaned. "We'll be caught here!"

Bothwell didn't answer. All his strength was needed to edge the stone back where it had come from. He braced himself for the final shove on the corners, listening now, for the sounds were nearer. Voices could be heard clearly, and the stamp of feet.

"Oh, God in Heaven," Morton moaned, hugging himself. "Hurry, Bothwell. What will we do?"

A hoarse cry from below seemed to fill the tiny room. Morton was at last galvanized into action. He rushed to the window and looked out; he could see nothing but the shadows of vague running shapes. "They're below us," he sobbed, whirling from the window, seeing Bothwell still working at his task. "I'm not staying here!" he cried, helplessly. He wanted aid; he wanted advice, but it was not forthcoming, for all of Bothwell's efforts were centered on that one stone. Morton tried to remember what Bothwell had said, and he did—he was to go behind the door. He stepped toward that vantage place, and then he heard the sounds of feet on the steps below. It was his undoing; he took to his heels and ran.

Bothwell heard the steps on the stairs too. They were coming quickly. Desperately, with every ounce of his powerful muscles, he gave one last shove at the stone, stopped to pick up his dagger, and he passed the door to the stairs just as it was flung open, just as it crashed back against the wall, pinning him there, hidden, safe, for the minute he needed.

Morton had gained the gallery. He rounded the first table; he had lost a shoe, but he was not aware of it. He ran past the long table, clear in the moonlight, and he was clear too, so clear that the four men who had come up the stairs from the room below, with its broken window, could see him plainly. One of them yelled, "There he is!" and another ran toward him at top speed, but the other two paused just past the doorway to the gallery, raising the long hagbuts that were already loaded.

The shots rang out in quick succession—deafening, ominously reverberating—and the two blinding flashes of gunfire lit the gallery with an unearthly glow. The light caught Morton's figure like a dark image turned to stone, and then he crumpled slowly. He tried to clutch the table as he went down, but his fingers lost their grip. He sank slowly to the floor.

The guns had spoken. A second later, Bothwell stepped over to the window. He heard the man who was kneeling over Morton say, "It's Lord Morton. He's dead!" And the Border lord climbed over the sill and jumped.

It was twenty feet to the ground. He hadn't had time to lower himself part of that distance. He had done nothing but jump, thankful that he had earlier left the window open. The breath was knocked out of him, his ankles felt like numbed blocks, and on his hands and knees he crawled toward the door he had so carefully unlocked.

As Bothwell closed the gate behind him, he was thinking that now he was the only person who knew that a child's body, wrapped in a blanket embroidered with the letter J, lay behind a wall in a room in Stirling Castle.

Chapter Thirty Nine

MARGARET VINSTAR climbed the steps of Borthwick Tower slowly. It was a long flight, steep and almost straight. She was dressed in a riding habit. She had changed her clothes hastily, after she had kissed Isobel goodnight and retired to her own room. She had chosen velvet, a deep green velvet, and even her tiny plumed hat was of the same material and the same color.

It had been almost two hours since she had left Isobel in the hall. Now she was close to the top of the long flight; she climbed the last steps, and she emerged into a tiny square room with rounded corners. The windows were on every side—narrow—but from them the whole of the surrounding countryside could be viewed.

She leaned her elbows on the window that looked toward the black bulk of Crichton Castle. She saw the river plainly, as it wound around the valley; the wooded spots between here and Crichton were like bunches of bushes clumped together.

It was one o'clock. Motionless she waited, never leaving her particular window, her hands clasped close together to keep them warm. The cold was bitter. Outside it should be even more bitter, for these thick stone walls did keep out the winter wind. Yet there was nothing to be seen on the frozen ground below. The river wound its way, and no shapes crossed the white patches of ground, or the dark bare earth where the snow had melted.

Margaret did not hear the clock downstairs strike two. She knew only that she had waited long, and still from the sleeping castle of Borthwick there had been no sounds, and there had been nothing to see from her high window.

At half after the hour, way below her, a dark figure crossed from a small wooded patch, out of her range of vision. The figure was masked; it moved swiftly, and yet with unhurried swiftness, and the postern door of Borthwick Castle was, curiously enough, unlocked. It was only two minutes more before the barred door to the tower yielded to his touch, and up above him Margaret heard the steps on the stone stairs.

She turned—not quickly, but very slowly. There was so little reality to this night that she seemed to be obeying other commands than those of her own nerves and senses. In a second he would reach the top, and she would know.

He did not need to remove the black half-mask. "You are alive," she said evenly.

"Rather dramatically so, madam." He tossed the mask to the floor, coming close to her side. He did not speak; he did not touch her, but went to the window, looking out himself. He was silent for a long time. "They are all dead," he said finally. "It was Jedburgh justice, madam, or Border justice, if you want it that way."

She did not move. "I saw nothing, Francis. Nothing."

"Hardly. This country is very familiar to me. I did not intend to be seen. But I admit I was flattered. You sent ten men to capture one lone man."

"Not capture. Kill." She turned her white face toward him, and her lips moved with the slightest trembling. "Francis, before we talk more—if you let me talk more—I beg you know this much. I love you."

He did not answer for a long time. "I had twenty men with me, Margaret. It was most simple to surround and dispense Jedburgh justice, and let the river have the bodies. The only bad part of it was that it was very cold, waiting."

"I know. I was cold, too."

Bothwell lifted his hand and turned her face to his. "You

are beautiful," he said. "You thought I would go to my death for that beauty."

"I would have died if you had," she said suddenly. "And now perhaps I'll die because you have lived. That was the most dreadful part of it, Francis. There was no choice."

"You move in glamor. I had loved you. I left my wife for you, one night at Hailes Castle."

"Francis, do you know the tale of the man who was blessed with the love of women? An old witch fell in love with him, and kept him chained to her until he sought death. Did you know that tale?"

"Margaret, listen.

> " 'The things that do attain
> the happy life be these, I find.
> The riches left, not got with pain,
> the fruitful ground, the quiet mind.
> Such sleeps as may beguile the night—' "

He paused before the last line—

> " 'Ne wish for death, ne fear his might.' "

"I do not want those," she said. "They are not for me. But I could not chain you, Francis, so I betrayed you to keep you from another woman."

"You betrayed Murray. You sent Logie to his death. You were the instrument of the murder of a girl you did not even know. A lass you sent to Logie, with a message that you could not come."

"Aye, it is true. But Francis, if I had not sent her, everyone would have suspected that it was I who lured him to the spot."

He nodded. "You thought we would assume that Logie had planned secretly to meet the lass. But she puzzled us, Margaret. For she was not bonnie."

"I know. Certainly it was better to send an ugly girl to the arms of Morpheus than deprive a bonnie one of life. Was that cruel, Francis? Patrick said he could not help me. I asked him once."

"There is no help for you now," he said. "Last night Morton died. Did you know that?"

Her answer was expressionless. "Aye. I told him once he was not clever enough to catch you, Francis. And neither was I."

"But I came to know you, Margaret. He did not. He saw only the beauty and the treachery; he looked at you with desire and fear."

He turned away and leaned his elbows on the sill. From this window James Hepburn had watched a hostile army draw close to the walls, and within them had been his wife, his Queen. Down the steep stairway he had run, hand in hand with Mary, to go out by himself, to seek help from his Borderers. But that had not been help enough.

Now he, Francis Hepburn, stood here. "All my life I've tried to keep faith."

She understood him. He had fought valiantly too, with all the weapons at his command, with all the strength of body and the cunning of mind. "You inherited the fire," she said. "Some men do."

"I'm going to leave Scotland," he said suddenly. "I must leave, and let Anne live there, at Crichton, where I want my son to grow to manhood. But before I go, I'm going to kill you, Margaret, so that Anne will be safe."

"So that Murray and Logie shall be avenged."

"Not for revenge, Margaret, believe me."

She took a step back from him; the moonlight came in the narrow window, but she did not retreat further. She knew there was no hope for pity. "Francis," she whispered. She was standing almost at the top of the stairway.

He raised one arm. The blow sent her backward, and she did not cry out. From the very top of the steps he watched her fall. Then he ran swiftly down to kneel at her side.

Her gray eyes were closed. Her little cap had fallen off, but her green velvet cloak had wrapped itself around her body. He slipped one hand under her head, and raised it, but her eyes did not open, and as he lifted her, he noticed a trickle of blood from one ear. Gently he laid her down, in the very position in which she had come to rest at the foot of the stone stairway.

She lived twelve hours longer. He spent the time watching at her bedside, but she never spoke, and when her eyes opened once, she did not know him. As she had requested of him, one night at Hailes, he took her body to Hermitage and buried her in the cemetery on the hill, just outside the tiny chapel. When the sun was in the west, the great stone walls of Hermitage laid their shadow across her grave.

Part Six

Chapter Forty

"It's eight o'clock, madam."

Janet glanced at the clock. "It lacks five minutes to the hour, Geordie." She picked up a ring and slipped it on her finger. "You may rest assured, however, that your master will be wakened on time. On the precise minute, in fact."

She went into her bedroom. Patrick was still sound asleep, and she sat down carefully on the side of the bed and smoothed back the tousled curls with one hand. "It's eight o'clock, sweetheart."

He yawned, turning over on his side to put his arm around her. "How do you feel this morning, Janet?"

"Well. Hungry. I want to have breakfast with you."

He yawned again. "Pleasure, madam." He stretched lazily, and Janet rose and went over to the window.

"It's a lovely day, Patrick. Warm. I'd like to walk up and see Anne."

"No." He sat up and regarded her intently. "That's too long a walk—to the castle—and all uphill. Take the coach." He was silent a minute and then he asked, "Were there any twins in your family?"

Janet turned from the window. "Aye."

"Where?" he asked seriously.

She smiled at him. "Here," she said, pointing to herself. "Lord, Patrick, I must be carrying twins. Or are there any elephants in your family?"

"Only two," he said, "so the strain is not strong. That is a becoming dress, madam."

"It has a matching cape. Marie helped. Will you be home tonight to dine with me?"

"Aye. I'll be in the city all day. And now I must hurry. I want to see James."

Astride his favorite brown gelding, he met James Stewart just as the King and his retinue were riding out for the day's hunt. It was about ten o'clock in the morning. Here in the Canongate the fields stretched green, the daffodils bloomed, the air was sweet with the scent of flowering fruit trees. James had dismounted for some reason, so that when Patrick rode up, the King was standing, a circle of courtiers around him. Patrick dismounted too, leaving his horse with a page, and, cap in hand, he walked over to James.

Patrick noted with approval that James was accompanied this morning by the Stewart contingent. They thronged around James. Maitland was far away, the day was fine, and for the first time in weeks, Patrick felt a glow of hope that was intensified by James's hearty greeting. James turned aside from the badly-dressed girl in front of him, to welcome Patrick.

"And I suppose you are on your way to hard work," James concluded, smiling. "Now you see, I am working too." He indicated the girl, who seemed to be the center of attraction.

"Who is the lass?" asked Patrick, curiously.

James took up that question. "Who are you?" he asked.

She shivered. "Jennie, Sire. The saddler's daughter."

"And do you have a saddle for His Majesty?" asked Patrick, raising one eyebrow, and running his hazel eyes over her figure.

James guffawed, and Atholl and the Duke of Lennox edged closer, to see what was happening.

Patrick said, "Well, speak up, lass. Has the cat your tongue? What do you want of His Highness?"

"I have a letter for him—for His Majesty," she said, holding out a piece of paper, moist with perspiration from her damp hands.

James looked amazed. He took the paper and began to read, but he had read no more than a line, before he began to curse heartily.

Jennie winced; she put her hands over her ears, and James read on. The letter was not long. James handed it to Patrick, and at the same time he said emphatically and disgustedly, "Christ's son!"

Jennie gasped. "You see, Sire, it is true!" Then she looked horrified by her own temerity, and braced herself for the rage of her sovereign.

Patrick had run his eyes over the paper. "What's true?"

"The letter!" Jennie cried. "It is wicked, this city, it is horrible, wicked, ungodly, lewd. Your mouths are foul." She pointed at Patrick.

"Christ's son!" roared James again, and again Jennie winced. "Your Majesty," she begged, "do not take the name of the Lord in vain!"

James was so angry he was speechless, and Patrick said, "Why, lass, His Majesty is not cursing. He is calling out the name of one of his men. None of us curses, lass." Patrick swung around and shouted, "Christsone! Where are you?"

James looked around, and when one of his men came forward hastily, he couldn't contain himself; he shook with laughter. Jennie's horrified face and Patrick's delighted expression drove him further.

"There really is someone by that name?" he gasped.

Patrick said soberly, "Here he is, Sire."

James said, "Just look at this letter. Did you ever see anything sillier?" He began to read it again, and then he turned and handed it to Atholl, while the Duke peered over his shoulder to read it.

"Oh, we do many other things at court too, lass," put in the Duke, fixing Jennie with wide eyes. "So you're the saddler's daughter?"

"I'd say she didn't know many gaits. Why should she?" Patrick grinned at James. "Let's see your ankles, Jennie."

Jennie's hands went to her skirts. She pressed them down

firmly, and she cried, remembering a phrase of the letter, "We of the people deplore the lewdness of the court and city; we—"

Patrick interrupted. "His Majesty has no wish to listen to lies, Jennie. You've been deluded, child." He looked at James, and James looked back helplessly; so Patrick whispered, "It might be well, Sire, to send her to the Queen. Her Majesty can take care of her."

James nodded. Jennie would carry a better tale if the Queen would see her.

James handed the letter back. "Take this to Her Majesty, Jennie."

"Christsone will take you," put in Patrick, and James roared with laughter, clutching Atholl. Jennie disappeared.

James had never felt better; he loved nothing more than to laugh. With affection he put his hand on Patrick's arm. "You've been absent from court, sir," he reminded. "It should give you pleasure to introduce your lady to court."

"It would, Sire." Patrick smiled ruefully. "I thank Your Majesty." He said nothing else, but James knew only too well what he was thinking. The image of Anne's face came into James's mind; how lovely, how fair she had been that night when she had knelt to him at Crichton.

"Where are you going now, sir? Why don't you join us?"

"I'm on my way to Edinburgh Castle, Sire." Patrick swung his cap between his fingers.

"With the rest of the gallants," James added. He glanced around at the men with him. "I am fortunate to have any of these with me!" He laughed a little. Anne held court in Edinburgh Castle every afternoon in rooms furnished elegantly and plentifully supplied with liquor and food and sandalwood fires, bought with the money of the man who stood in front of him. James thought of that money, he thought too of the wit and ease with which Patrick had handled the little fanatic Jennie, who objected to the morals of the court. He examined Patrick again. His clothes were so perfect that they never failed to make James wish he could look like that. "I am sic a scrub," he said, plaintively, "with only two pairs of silk stockings to my name."

Patrick said politely, "If I might have the honor of Your Majesty's presence at supper tomorrow, I'd be delighted to present my bride, Sire."

James knew that meant a present of half a dozen pairs of silk stockings. "Charmed, sir." He rubbed his cheek, and then he said, gruffly, "The Countess of Bothwell has outstayed her welcome at the castle. She may go home, sir, before she gets me in any more hot water. A King should know better than to fish in drumely waters." He tugged at his short beard and smiled. "The jade has every gallant at court coming to see her bairn's christening this afternoon!"

Patrick laughed. "Sire, I'm very happy about your decision. Let me convey my thanks, and those of my cousin."

James said, still remembering how lovely she had looked the last time he had seen her, "Tell your cousin I expect to hear her say her thanks to her prince." He turned away, making a mental note to tell the Queen that they were dining out the next night, and Patrick turned away too. He was in a hurry to tell Anne that she was free.

Anne had a suite of rooms in the castle. Patrick walked through the anteroom; he could hear her voice coming from her dressing room and she was saying, "I'll not see anyone, Marie. Tell them to go away!" There was the sound of a slight sob and then Marie's voice came, lower.

"*Chérie*, it might be His Grace. It might be Lord Atholl."

"I don't care!" Anne stamped her foot. "But see who it is."

"It's I." Patrick closed the door behind him just as Anne closed her mouth, for she had been about to break into a torrent of speech at the knave who would dare to walk in on her.

"You may stay while I finish dressing," she told him, over her shoulder. She had on a flowing dressing gown which opened down the front and showed her flouncing petticoats.

"So you're not in a very good humor, I see." He grinned, pointed to a page to pour him a drink, and relaxed into a chair, looking at her in the mirror.

She swung her slipper from the toe of her bare foot, alternately watching him, and watching Marie do her hair. Patrick had his drink, and he told the page to leave. Anne started to say, "How dare you?" but she decided against it. She said, sweetly, "Won't you have any water with your brandy, sir?"

"No, thank you." He sipped it slowly. "What's the matter this morning?"

Her hands were in her lap, and she was pleating and repleating a fold of her petticoat, crushing the satin beneath her fingers. "I'm so unhappy," she burst out.

"You were not yesterday."

She glared. "What has yesterday to do with it? Oh, Patrick, when am I going to get out of this poxey place?"

"Today," he answered equably. "I just saw James."

But she still pouted, and he was amazed that there was so little response to his news. Perhaps this would please her. "And I have a letter to you, from Francis." He reached in his coat and drew it out.

She jumped to her feet, whirling around, losing a slipper in her haste to reach him. "Give it me," she cried, taking the letter in her hands, looking longingly at the heavy writing. His hands had touched this paper too.

She didn't open it right away. "I wonder he has bothered to write me," she said at last, thrusting out her lower lip belligerently. "Sometimes I hate him so!"

Patrick watched her return to her stool with much swirling of petticoats. "Why don't you read it?" he suggested, lazily. "And stop having tantrums, they hardly amuse me. You act like an indignant virgin."

"Do not insult me!" She glared again, and he laughed, while Marie said calmly, "Please, be still a minute, your Ladyship."

Patrick said, "Who has been bringing you gossip about Francis?"

" 'Twasn't women," she snapped.

"Well, men, then. They all want your favor, Anne."

She smiled at him, thanking him for the compliment. "But do you know what he has been doing? Do you know that he was at Edenhall in England, for a fortnight party, and then he went to the horse races—do you know that? He was there for a week, and came back to Scotland just in time for the salmon fishing. He stayed at his favorite inn at Lanholme, and just last Thursday, mind, he was playing football. Why, he was seen plainly. Lowder saw him on the field there, along the River Esk! That horrible, murderous game!"

Patrick laughed with enjoyment, and some envy. He sighed, thinking of the opening of the salmon season, thinking about football. He looked around the stone walls that confined him, and sighed again.

"What did you expect him to be doing?" he asked. Then he sobered. "As a matter of fact, Annie, he has done some other things too." He thought of the letter he had received himself that morning, but that was not for her ears. "Today, Annie, I saw a list of the complaints and requests for redress from the Border. There has never been so much unrest on the Borders, never so many raids, never ones in which there was quite so much burning and looting. Two of the complaints list 'wives stolen,' along with the mares and kine."

Anne didn't care how many wives were stolen, but Patrick said sharply, "Wife stealing was a hanging offense when Francis was Keeper of Liddesdale."

That made her think. She glanced at him, questioningly, and he answered, "Now that he is not at Hermitage, the Border is wild. I suspect him of leading some of these raids himself; but Anne, if this keeps up, he'll lose Elizabeth's good will as well as James's. In Cumberland, Her Majesty's tenants there—Walter Caverly, gentleman, his house broken into and goods taken worth two hundred pounds, himself carried off prisoner to Scotland; in Gilsland, eighteen oxen and kine, twenty-four horses, household stuff, bedding and apparel—Annie, the list is the longest I've ever seen! The total amount of money stolen from England—only in monies, now—was two thousand and four hundred and fifty pounds, besides the ransom of forty-six prisoners!"

"You think he will lose Elizabeth's favor?" That was all that mattered to Anne.

"I don't know." He regarded the brandy in his glass and frowned.

Anne frowned too. She had been holding her letter, postponing the joy of opening it, but now she couldn't wait any longer. "Excuse me," she murmured. She skimmed through it, saw it was brief, as his letters usually were, and began to read it slowly, drinking in the familiar writing. "My dearest wife," Bothwell had begun, "I wish I had more news for you than I have. Everything is very quiet here"—Anne grimaced as she read that—"and, except for a brief trip north, I have been in Kelso since Friday. Roderick was here to meet me. The King's men tried to take him captive in Haddington last week, and he was rescued by the crowd at the market place! I'm allowing him to remain with me until Crichton is returned to you, and you need a bailiff. Heaven grant you will, some day, lass.

"I have been thinking well over our problems and I have reached one conclusion. It seems to me that the best thing for me to do is to go to France and take advantage of the hospitality of the French King. So I am seeing about some hounds and horses to take with me. I want to be careful about the choice, and tomorrow I'm going to Berwick concerning them.

"I would plan to be absent for a year. Crichton will be given back to you as soon as I leave; I'm sure of that, and perhaps time, the mother of truth, will solve our present difficulties. God keep you and the bairns well and safe."

There was nothing more, only the scrawled signature, and written at the bottom, "From the Moss Tower, Kelso, the twenty-fourth day of June."

"What does he say?" Patrick asked.

Anne put the letter to her face. "He's going away, Patrick, he's going away! And all he can think about is the hounds and horses he's picking to take with him! I'm shut up in this horrid, plaguey place, and he's enjoying himself!"

"You knew all this before you married him." Patrick stood up, yawned a little to show how uninterested he was, and went over to the door. "Now let me tell you something. I could have secured your release from this 'plaguey place' months ago, but Francis thought it best that you remain here, with the bairns, in comparative safety and in compliance with the King's orders.

Secondly, I have advised him to leave Scotland, even though, as you are well aware, there is a plot afoot to bring him back to court. I say you are well aware of it advisedly, for you have been dipping your fingers into a good bit of intrigue, you and Lennox and Atholl, together with Atholl's countess and the Lord Ochiltree."

"You kept me here? You know about—" She could hardly believe what she'd heard. She was only astonished now; anger would come later.

"Of course I know, and Francis knows. His orders to you are to keep strictly away from any plots, intrigues, or anything even smacking of underhanded involvements. But he will allow you your harmless flirtations."

Anne picked up a heavy brush and threw it at him, but he paid no attention to it, beyond waiting for the clatter to die down before he resumed. "I am going to Kelso in a few days. Do you have any message for him?"

"If I'm free, why can I not go to Kelso too, Patrick?" she asked, pleadingly.

"Because you cannot."

"I will anyway," she said, defiantly, and then she smiled. "He'd not send me home."

"Wouldn't he? No, I don't think he would, because he told me to tell you that he absolutely forbids your coming—and to make sure of your obedience, he has sent for David Hepburn. You'll have a hard time getting past his eye, lass, because your lord has ordered David to accompany you everywhere."

"Oh," she cried, unbelievingly, "how dared he?"

"He does not want you in the Borders, creeping into corners!"

He paused, then continued, seriously. "One more word. You have it within your power to win over James Stewart. For God's sake concentrate on that, and don't put your fingers into any political pie. Instead, concoct a perfume that will go to His Majesty's head." He adjusted the short cape that swung over one shoulder, and that was the last she saw of him.

He reached Kelso five days later and arrived at the Moss Tower in the late afternoon. It stood outside the town, near the

Abbey, the old Abbey, whose revenues Mary Stewart had bestowed on Francis Hepburn when he was but three years old, a sturdy laughing toddler who was not only her nephew, but the nephew of the man she loved. The Moss Tower was an old peel tower, its gray weathered stones rising ugly and green, and even the gnarled fruit trees in its garden were covered with moss. A low stone dyke enclosed the whole property.

Lord Bothwell was not at home. He was across the fields, behind the stables, and Patrick followed the pointing finger, tired as he was. He skirted the stables. He could see Bothwell plainly across the moor. Patrick spurred his weary mount; he would have come galloping right up to the small knot of men down the hill, but one of them started toward him, waving a hand, running. Patrick slowed his pace, frowning. He reined in some few feet from the Earl, and Bothwell turned and strode over to him.

Patrick dismounted, and together they stood there, smiling at each other, and neither said that it had been a long time, or that he was glad to see the other. Instead, Bothwell said, "Look at him, sir." He turned and pointed to the horse that two men held.

"So that's why I couldn't come dashing up." Patrick nodded, and looked with admiration at the tense animal that liked neither the men who held him, nor the saddle which had just been put on him.

"He's nervous enough already," said Bothwell. "He looks like his sire, doesn't he?"

Patrick transferred his gaze across the field to where Valentine was contentedly grazing. "He does that," he agreed, and his eyes were covetous as they rested on the young stallion. "You were right about the mare," he added. "Are you going to ride him?"

"Aye, man, and now." Bothwell smiled, and Patrick forgot that it had been months since they had seen each other; it might have been yesterday that he had left the Borders. This was so familiar—even the faint haze that hung over the spring afternoon and lay across the distant hills. He forgot his weariness;

indeed it had disappeared. His eyes shone. "You're wearing short spurs, Francis. Very short."

Bothwell said, "I don't want to dig too deep. These'll prick him badly enough. Just look at him, sir!"

Both men looked and approved, and Bothwell continued, "He doesn't like that saddle, does he? I'd better get in it before he breaks loose." He started away, and he called back, "I named him Corbie. He's blacker than a raven, and should be as fleet!" There was a man at each side of the horse's head, and Bothwell put one boot in the stirrup, and was in the saddle.

"Stand away!" The warning was given, the men jumped away, and for a moment Corbie stood motionless with surprise. Then he tossed his head up, way up, but it was jerked back again, hard, so that it hurt his mouth.

Bothwell was crouched in the saddle. He used neither whip nor spurs. He maintained his seat, which was difficult enough, and he used his hands hard, but not hard enough to cut Corbie's mouth. He let Corbie fight it out against those hard hands for quite a while, long enough for the horse to know that he couldn't unseat his rider.

Then he used the short spurs, pricking Corbie's flanks with sharp insistent thrusts. Corbie fled across the field. Faster and faster he went; surely a horse couldn't go faster than his flying hoofs were taking him, and yet there was always that insistent pricking, that devilish pain in his tender flanks. He raced on, clearing one hill, and then the next, finding the broad moor underneath his feet, and thundering across it. His mouth hurt, he was being pulled around, and he tried to shake off his burden. He came around as bidden, but there were the spurs again, and he felt strength and speed welling up in him again, and back across the moor his hoofs carried him, faster, faster.

The sweat was pouring off Bothwell's face. He was wearing only a shirt and breeches, and the shirt clung to his back and chest and armpits. The horse was failing a little now; he was slowing a bit. Bothwell let him have his head across the moor, but when they reached the hills again, he used the short spurs mercilessly, driving them in deep. Corbie didn't wince this time.

He took the sharp pain, came bounding up the crest of the hill, down again, past the men who were watching, and up he started to the brow of the hill. All the way up he went, till the men beneath were small dots. But Corbie's breath was failing, even though his pace had hardly slackened. In a last burst of effort he thundered to the very top, and for the first time he heard a low voice, harsh yet soft, and a firm hand was laid on his head just below his ear. Corbie came to a stop.

The reins were pulled gently. Obediently Corbie turned; he started down the hill slowly, to the men who waited outside the stable door. His head was high, his lips curled back from the white teeth, but he stood still while Bothwell jumped down beside him. "Good lad," he said proudly, "good Corbie," and he reached up one hand to the horse's neck, pulling gently at the black mane. "He's fit for a King, isn't he, sir?"

Patrick said slowly. "Aye, Francis. He is a king." He forgot he was going to congratulate Bothwell on his riding; he remembered suddenly that Bothwell was going away, and that Corbie would go with him, as a present to the King of France. Patrick said, "I'm going to take this saddle off you, Corbie." He reached for the buckles. Corbie trembled a bit and stood still again, while that other voice said, "I was with you when you were born, Corbie, and you were a braw foal, but I didn't realize then that you would be so magnificent."

The saddle was taken from Patrick's hands by one of the stablers. He and Bothwell stood there together, looking at Corbie. Bothwell knew what Patrick was thinking. He kicked at the dirt with one boot. Patrick wanted Corbie, and Bothwell said gruffly, "Well, let's go in, man, you must be weary enough." He tossed aside the whip he hadn't used, and turned on his heel.

The Moss Tower was lacking in comfort. Patrick sprawled across a bed laid in deerskins, because there were no chairs in Bothwell's room, and he was eating from the only table, hunking off pieces of meat with his own knife. At the foot of the bed, Bothwell sat hunched forward, his pewter tankard clasped in his hands. His boots lay on the floor and he seemed to be entirely concerned with the way he curled his toes in his stockings. "There's a horse meet at Carlisle tomorrow," he was saying, and then he suddenly drank off all his ale and blurted, "Patrick, I must go!"

Patrick said nothing. It was almost dark, and the wavering rushlight made the room shadowy. It was true enough, anyway. The Border lord couldn't stay much longer in Scotland. Even now it was a daily question of eluding the law, of moving from place to place, of being hunted, fugitive.

"After I left Stirling that night," Bothwell said, "and after I learned that Morton was really dead, I wrote you. You see, there is no evidence, probably, that involves Maitland. There is no evidence against him at all. Only you and I know that James may not be the real heir to the throne. You and I know there is the body of a child, wrapped in a blanket that bears James's initial. And I'm willing to go away for a while, and rest on those laurels. I'm going to write to James, telling him I still consider myself a loyal subject, telling him I'm willing to endure exile, if that is what he wants. And I'm going to commit Anne and my son to His Majesty's care. It seems it's the only thing I can do, now."

Patrick had stopped eating. "I think you're right, Francis. I've always thought it were best to leave Scotland, for a while. Later, you and I may find some way to use the information we both have, if voluntary exile doesn't work. But first, there is one more message I promised to deliver. There is a powerful faction at court which is working for your return. That faction includes the Queen."

Bothwell drew in his breath. Carelessly, he broke off a piece of cheese, crumbling it in his fingers. "Go on," he said.

"I was appointed to bring you the message. You see, Francis, there is fear that the King has decided to bring Maitland back to court. He needs a Secretary of State, and none of the Stewarts seems to qualify. As you can understand," Patrick put in dryly. "But they don't like the idea of Maitland. They think you're the only man who can stop it, and they're willing to sign a bond to that effect."

"Sign a bond?" Bothwell asked the question, but it wasn't a question. Bonds were common things in Scotland. You signed them for protection, so that your accomplices in any plot had their names down on paper. It was like hunting in packs; numbers made you safe. "They would sign a bond to the effect that they are all with me—if I promise to rid them of Maitland?" His voice was low.

"Aye, and they promise military help."

Bothwell tossed a piece of cheese into his mouth, and stared at the fingers of one hand, at the blackened nail of his middle finger which someone had stepped on the last time he had played football.

Patrick was tense, waiting for his answer, not knowing what the answer would be. He didn't approve, personally. "They would sign a bond," he repeated inanely. "What shall I tell them, Francis?"

Bothwell stood up. He walked over to the fire, turned, and hooked his thumbs in his belt. "Tell them I'll see them in hell," he said briefly. "Or, better, I'll tell them myself."

Chapter Forty One

The twenty-first of July, 1593, was a Sunday. It was a beautiful, sunny day, and in the blue sky only a few puffy white clouds rode high over the city. It was a day that invited play, and ordinarily the churches would have been half empty. But today the King was in the city, and attending the morning services.

The church of St. Giles was crowded. Although the papist trappings had been removed—for this was the church in which John Knox had preached his communion services, by the light of flaring torches, at four o'clock on a bitter winter morning—nothing could spoil the stone arches, the wonderful windows, and it was these James studied as the sermon went on over his head. He scratched at his chin, pulled at his short beard, and heard nothing of the words that poured from Mr. Bruce, the minister. James was thinking of Maitland, far away in the country, in temporary banishment, and James was thinking that he needed Maitland back—and then he thought of the hatreds which that would arouse. He stared in front of himself unseeingly. Maitland was old, the Lord knew he wouldn't live much longer anyway, and James reflected petulantly that it would save him a good deal of trouble if the Lord would take Maitland to His all-encompassing bosom. Still, James needed a secretary, and Maitland was an intellectual, whereas these Stewarts who crowded around James now, at this very instant, none of them listening to what was being said—and certainly if anybody should profit by a sermon it was one of them, who knew nothing but how to wield a sword, ride a horse, or bed a wench—certainly these Stewarts couldn't help him. None of them, except mayhap one, who was deep in his own Borders, eluding the law with his usual flamboyance.

James sighed. What was the minister saying? He did not care. He thought of his mother, who, they said, had been all quicksilver and gaiety, in the days before life had laid such shadows over her path. "I am a Stewart, too," he repeated, silently. For years he had clung to that phrase; when his birth had been questioned, when his manners, his looks, his poverty as a monarch were mocked at, he had hugged those words to himself. They were really the only things he had, those four words. They meant he would inherit the throne of England; they marked him of far higher birth than any bastard Queen of England. Back of James was the blood of the Guises, the Bruces, the royal Stewarts. They were his heritage, even as they were of the man most closely related to him, the outlawed Bothwell. Where was he now?

James wondered, and way to the south, the Earl was already up and ahorse, riding northward. That morning, while James was deciding to recall Maitland, the Border lord was thinking of his wife. That thought was driving him north, to the city of Edinburgh, and for still a few hours, there was nothing to show, outwardly, that the two events were to have their effect.

The sermon went on. It had an hour yet to run, as Mr. Bruce had figured it. He took a deep breath, and launched himself again, and the King still stared ahead. By this time, the Earl of Bothwell, accompanied by Patrick and an escort of forty men, was clattering over the wide roads north.

Anne was in church too. She was quite far back from her King; she couldn't even see him, surrounded as he was by his courtiers. She had waited for fully an hour now, and perhaps it would be just as long a time again that she would have to wait. Even though it was hot in these confining walls, she shivered.

She was dressed all in white, shiny satin. Her gloves, embroidered with seed pearls, were white satin, and her tiny change purse, too, that swung from one finger by a gold ring.

Anne tried to listen to what Mr. Bruce was saying, but even if she did listen, she couldn't understand him, for his speech was mixing politics with the Almighty, and Anne was very much confused. Quietly she opened her Bible. It fell open easily to a place where a small mirror was concealed, and Anne studied her curls, and her powder, and noted that her mouth was satisfactorily red. She studied her reflection until an errant gleam of sun caught the mirror, and she closed the book hastily, with a guilty look at the persons nearest her. They had noticed it, she thought ruefully, and she endeavored to look innocent. If they'd been listening, they wouldn't have noticed her! Some day, she must ask Bothwell to explain what these ministers meant. She could see him laugh at her, if she did ask, and he seemed so near that she closed her eyes and imagined how it would be if he could stand next to her in church, where all the people could see both of them. They'd stare at us far more than they do at James, she thought contentedly, relishing the idea.

Anne had placed her stool just to the left of one of the stone pillars. Over her head an arch of stone flared upward, and to her right, a large window let in the light. She tipped her head back a little, letting it rest against the stone. It was a hard head-rest, and accordingly she had decided to be more proper and bow her head, when the sudden stir of the congregation roused her. She kept herself from leaping to her feet. Instead, she composed her skirts, as a lady should, shook out her trailing cape, and stood aside from her stool, looking aloof and bored.

Her page scooped up the three-legged stool in one hand, and waited. Anne waited, and the people behind her perforce waited too. It wasn't until up ahead of her she saw James move, that she herself started forward belatedly, toward the center aisle. She must keep close to him; she didn't want to precede him by much.

The sunlight was brilliant outside. Anne thought briefly that the sun always looked wonderful shining on her hair. On the other hand, the thick mists always clung to her eyelashes, and that was a devastating effect too. Anne saw Lennox first, carrying his hat in one hand, and he was smiling broadly, evidently at something Lord Ochiltree had said to him. Anne's heart was beating fast, and her hands tightened prayerfully over her book. She made her way forward toward James.

The men around him seemed to melt away, but she hardly saw them. She was conscious of the warm sun, the noise in the street, and the many, many people, and then James himself, standing in front of her, looking surprised.

Anne didn't waste a second. Even though it seemed to her that half the occupants of Edinburgh were raptly gazing at her and James, she did what she had planned two days before. Without a word, she dropped to her knees in front of the completely astonished James. She bent her head over her book, and murmured, "Your Majesty," and then her head lifted, tilted so that the sun caught lights in her curls, and she put out her clasped hands.

"Your Majesty," she said pleadingly, hesitantly, her eyes holding his. She couldn't find words with which to continue.

James, never quick with his tongue, couldn't find words either. Heads craned, the crowd jostled closer, almost forgetting that their King was in their midst, and everyone was fascinated with this scene. All eyes were riveted on the kneeling figure in glistening white satin and the standing figure of her sovereign, his own velvets and silks rivaling the most magnificent of his courtiers.

"Sire," whispered Anne, "I wish to beg forgiveness from Your Majesty, and to hear your own voice grant it to me."

James cleared his throat; he glanced around, noticed how many spectators there were, and then looked down again at the face upturned to his. "Madame," he said, finding his tongue, "you may have my forgiveness." Then he looked slightly embarrassed.

"I prayed in church—all through the service—that I would hear Your Majesty say those words to me." She sighed so convincingly that even James had the momentary illusion that he believed she had so prayed. But his sense of humor was beginning to assert itself, and a smile twitched the corners of his mouth.

"I am the willing instrument of the Almighty," he said, low. "You may rise, madam."

Anne was undeterred by the slyness. She was playing a role, and she had already rehearsed her lines, her attitudes. She stood in front of James, still looking up at him as a countess should when she begs her King to forgive her. The wind caught at her cape, swinging it back, ruffling the skirt of her full gown. The sun glittered on the jewels and dress of the surrounding nobility, and in the breathless silence Anne said, "Your Majesty, I prayed you would not believe the lies that are told you about Lord Bothwell!"

Inside, her stomach quivered as she said the bold words, but her eyes were as melting as ever. James's face hardened, but Anne rushed on, heedless. "I swear," and she put her hand over her heart, "that Lord Bothwell never has, and never will, mean any harm to you, his King! I pray and beg you, Sire, believe one you have so generously forgiven! Grant forgiveness to him, too!"

"Do not spoil our friendship, madam!" James scowled threateningly.

"I speak the truth," she said, bravely. She had appropriated one of Bothwell's expressions, that she had seen him write. "Time is the mother of truth, and Sire, time will tell I speak truly! Oh, Your Grace, do not be angry with me!"

James bit his lip to hide his recurrent smile. His eyes crinkled, and then narrowed a bit. "You wee winsome witch," he murmured. "You'd blandish your prince, would you not?"

"*S'il vous plaît*," she whispered back, and for the first time she smiled, dropping her long lashes.

"My cousin," went on James, "was always an excellent judge of horseflesh and women." His mustache twitched and then his full mouth closed tightly. He watched her.

Anne kept her eyes down, demurely. "Sir, my wee bairn is honored to be your kin."

James smiled, both at the answer, which was so feminine a

retaliation, and at the practicality behind it. He made up his mind swiftly. Indeed he had always known he would do this. "Madam," he said firmly, "it has been bruited about that the lands of the earldom of Bothwell were to be redistributed. Those who say this are not privy to the truth, whether or not time is the mother of it." He grinned a little and added, "To you and your son, madam, Crichton will belong, so long as I am ruler of this realm!" Then James decided to be dramatic; he was a Stewart! "My royal word on't!"

Anne's eyes filled with tears. Generosity, like the picture of the Virgin and her Babe, moved Anne to emotional tears, and those tears did cling to her lashes, just as the Scottish mist did. "I thank Your Majesty," she said, trembling. "I hope I am worthy of Your Majesty's greatness." And she truly believed that her King was divinely appointed, even if he did slyly point out her charms. "I'll try to be more worthy of Your Majesty," she promised, remembering her own humble birth, suddenly forgetting her own efforts, her own long labors to attain her ends. She decided that James was responsible for all her honors. "Your Majesty, you have done me such honors! I shall pray for Your Majesty every night!"

James smiled. He felt exhilarated and happy. Why was it that he could always talk to Anne with such aplomb, when he so often stuttered and stammered with other people? She made him forget that he ever did stutter. She was curtsying to him now, and he watched her with pleasure. He knew he had acquitted himself well in this encounter, and all of his court and most of the city had witnessed it. He gave her his hand regally, feeling her soft lips against his hard knuckles.

"Madam," he said firmly, "I look to the pleasure of your company some evening soon." He hardly heard her thanks, he hardly heard her farewell, so intent was he on the curve of her mouth as she spoke, and the light of the sun on her hair, and the lovely, tantalizing whiff of her scent. He was brought back to earth by Lennox.

"What a wench," sighed the Duke, and he stared after her too . . .

The day wore on. It was so peaceful a Sunday. James read most of the afternoon. He wrote a long letter to Elizabeth, complaining about his allowance, which was overdue as usual, and he had a long nap that was momentarily interrupted by shouts from the tennis courts, where the ebullient Stewarts were gathered that afternoon. Later, James had supper, alone with Lennox.

At ten precisely, Lennox left His Majesty's chambers—but when he left the palace, he did not go in the direction of his own house, which lay at the rear of the royal palace; he didn't call for his horse. He made his way alone, unattended and unobserved, up the Canongate. He didn't intend to be unobserved; he was going to call on Patrick, and it made no difference to Lennox whether anyone saw him or not. He wasn't even sure that Patrick was back from the Borders yet. He was calling to find out.

He knocked on the door. The house was oddly dark, but Lennox knocked anyway, not caring how many servants he roused. But no lights came on, no steps sounded. Lennox started to turn away, when the door swung open quietly, softly, and a low, twangy voice said, "Come in, your Grace. Softly."

Lennox stiffened. He wasn't accustomed to orders, and he was about to snort and launch on a diatribe when the voice said, "It's Gibson, sir. The Lord is here."

Lennox knew instantly whom he meant. The Borderers often used that reverent word for Bothwell, as though he were the only or the greatest lord. He couldn't stop one word of disbelief. "Here?" he whispered, incredulously.

"Aye, sir." Gibson moved ahead of Lennox through the dark hallway, and ushered the Duke into the study.

The curtains were tightly drawn. There was light here, gleaming light from the wax candles. Lennox's mind took in first the luxuriousness of the house he walked through, and he was conscious of a pang of envy for Patrick's wealth. Then the door closed behind him, and the tall figure who seemed almost incased in leather, from his boots to his jacket, rose to his feet.

"How are you, man?" asked Bothwell, holding out his hand.

"A wee bit surprised," smiled the Duke, taking the big hand in his strong grip. "Just a wee bit," he added, his eyes leaving Bothwell for a minute, so that he could greet Patrick. "I had no notion that you were here, sir."

Patrick was standing. He had risen when Lennox entered, and now he said, waving Lennox to a chair, "Please sit, sir."

Lennox sat and Patrick relaxed into his own chair behind his table, but Bothwell walked over to the bare fireplace, leaning his elbow on the mantel.

There was an odd quiet in the room. Lennox felt as though he were an intruder, and that both these other men would rather he had never come. He felt that they had been deep in a conversation that concerned only the two of them. He was uneasy, uncomfortable, and he frowned, looking from one to the other.

Patrick's face was drawn. He looked weary, very weary, which was surprising. As for Bothwell—he was different tonight, too. So far, he had hardly smiled at Lennox; his face was set, the lines around his mouth were accentuated. Lennox endeavored to break the awkward silence.

"Are you not drinking?" he asked.

"No," said Patrick. Then he seemed to realize he was being very rude, and he smiled at Lennox, glancing from him to Bothwell, as if the Duke should understand that with Bothwell here in the house, it was hardly politic to call a servant for the wine or whatever Lennox wanted.

Lennox said quickly, "I didn't realize, sir," and then both men were startled out of their calm by an explosion from the Border lord.

Bothwell had been fingering the base of a silver candelabra on the mantle. He half-raised it, set it down again with a bang, and growled out, "Call all your servants. By Christ, I'll call them mysel'!" He strode to the door, flung it open with a resounding crash, and his voice bellowed through the hallway.

Patrick started to leap to his feet, Lennox was frozen in his chair, and Gibson's white face peered in the room.

"Tell somebody I want some whiskey!"

Gibson muttered, "Aye, my lord." When Bothwell turned,

Gibson looked imploringly at Patrick, and then he disappeared quickly. Bothwell banged the door shut.

"Are you afraid to be here with me, sirs?" Standing there by the door, arrogant and proud, he mocked them. "Are you afraid?"

Patrick jumped to his feet. He leaned over the table, his own anger boiling to the surface. "D'ye impute cowardice to me, sir—" He broke off as Gibson knocked on the door.

"Here's the whiskey," said Lennox, in tones of heartfelt relief.

Gibson entered the room. He was bearing a tray with a silver jug and glasses as light as blown bubbles. He poured three glasses, during which time he shot anxious glances at his master; then he left the room discreetly. He had hardly closed the door, before Bothwell opened it again. "You forgot the water," he said, loudly enough for his voice to echo through the whole house.

Patrick said, "Francis, you're a fool!" He had left his table, and he picked up a glass of whiskey and drank it all. "A fool," he repeated more calmly, and he grinned. "D'ye really want the water?"

"No," growled Bothwell, and then he too grinned, transferred his gaze to Lennox. "Will you drink, sir?" he inquired.

Patrick handed the Duke a filled glass. He said, "Don't relax yet, your Grace. I doubt if the Border lord is quite over his bad temper."

Bothwell said, "Your heavy Scot humor, sir," and he and Patrick eyed each other silently.

Lennox sipped the strong brew, wishing for water himself, or wishing he had wine, or that he dared ask for it. He sighed, and thought it might be well to change the subject before these two volatile tempers clashed again.

"Where are you going, Francis?" he asked.

The Earl's face darkened. "To Caithness," he snapped. "I'm trying to decide between piracy and the court of France."

Patrick set his glass down with a bang. "You'll hang yet!" he burst out.

Bothwell said equably, "Why should you care, sir? If I take

to the sea, you may have Corbie. That's what you want, isn't it?"

Lennox wrung his hands. "Do you have ships?"

"Aye," countered Bothwell briefly. "I can count on ships." But he hardly looked at Lennox. His eyes were still on Patrick.

Lennox said placatingly. "Your bonnie countess has won James Stewart, my lord. You should have seen her this morning, kneeling to him in the street!"

"She'll never do that again!" His mouth set, and then he said quite calmly, "I'm going away, Lennox. I don't know where, but I'm going. I'm through with this hole-and-corner business. I'm through with it!"

Lennox said slowly, "I had a crack with James tonight. While we supped he told me, just tonight—and I'm the only one who knows—that he had decided to recall Maitland."

Nothing was said, and Lennox thought of the plans they all had made to restore Bothwell to the royal favor. "Sir Patrick told you of our plans, did he not, my lord?"

There was silence again, and then Bothwell said sneeringly, "Fair promises and foul performances. Is that what you mean, Lennox?"

Lennox clenched his hands. "That was not courteous," he countered, quietly.

"Truth seldom is," Bothwell came back, quickly. "If I ever do anything, Lennox, it will be myself who does it—not half the court."

Lennox put in swiftly, "But they would support you, later. We would all support you."

Patrick came to attention. What was Lennox trying to do? "I'm afraid it would take more than your support, Lennox," he said, gravely.

Bothwell glanced at him, and from him to Lennox. "So Maitland will be recalled?" He was quiet; he was thinking grimly that with Maitland back, he himself might just as well not bother to voluntarily exile himself. "If it's true, I might as well take to piracy." He walked over and refilled his glass.

"Oh, it's true enough," said Lennox, cheerfully. "Much as we all hate Maitland, James is set on his return."

Bothwell regarded the Duke over the rim of his glass. "You thought I could stop it?"

"Aye, my lord. You are the only one who can. That is why we tried to enlist your support, and are willing to give all of ours. I, Atholl, Ochiltree, of course, the Master of Gray . . ." And he went on down a list ending up with the Lairds of Johnston, Burley, the Kers.

"Don't include my name," said Patrick grimly. This time it was he who was on the verge of losing his temper. Had all his warnings been in vain? Was Francis Hepburn to follow so closely in the footsteps of the fourth Earl of Bothwell?

Bothwell did not answer him. Their eyes clashed, and he said suddenly, "James told you tonight about Maitland?" He seemed to be trying to make himself realize it was the truth.

"Aye, my lord," said Lennox definitely, "tonight, this Sunday, the twenty-first of July, Jamie told me."

Bothwell said, "I know well enough I can count on the men you've named, Lennox." His dark eyes gleamed with excitement. It rushed through him, the old eagerness welling up, the old desire to give battle, and not to submit. The King was at Holyrood; clearly he could see it, just a half-mile away—the big palace, with its many adjoining buildings, stables, clustered close to it—with the houses of the nobility gathered around it, so near that they pushed at the royal palace. The one nearest was the town house of the Gowries.

Bothwell said, "Tell me, Lennox is it true that Lady Gowrie is in residence in the city?"

Lennox nodded. "She and the Lady Alice, and her two young sons."

"Ah," said Bothwell, with a world of satisfaction in his tone. Between the Gowrie mansion and the palace was a narrow dingy passage that led into the many huge kitchens of Holyrood.

Lennox couldn't contain himself. "We would all help," he blurted, eagerly. If Maitland got back into power, where would he, Lennox, be?

"I do not want help, sir." Bothwell hooked his thumbs in his belt. He was remembering. "In the first year, in the first months of my outlawry," he said, "I took the royal castle of Loughmaben. The King's garrison was bothering my Borderers. I entered the castle myself, first, secretly, disguised in woman's dress." He swung around to Patrick. "I'm going, sir. Will you have my horse brought?"

"Francis," said Patrick slowly, "oh, Francis, why?"

Lennox looked down at his shoes. Patrick came over to Bothwell, and the two stood there. Bothwell said slowly, "Let me think, then. I must think it all out—straight. Tell them to bring me my horse; I want no escort. I'll have Gibson stay here."

He started out into the hall, Lennox leaping up and starting after him. "What are you going to do, Bothwell?" He was panting with excitement.

"I don't know, sir, but if I do anything, I'll do it quickly, I'll do it soon. Tomorrow. Or Tuesday."

He went down the long hall and rode off abruptly, down the Canongate. He was observed "riding brazenly down the Canongate," so that many years later you might read a letter and see those words carefully preserved in the State papers on parchment yellow with age, with the sand still clinging to its roughness.

He was riding for Dunbar, the great ancient ruined fortress which had been associated with the Hepburns since Patrick Hepburn had defended it with the Lady Jane Beaufort, widow of James the First of Scotland; it was at Dunbar that James Hepburn had taken Mary, Queen of Scots; it was to the ruined Dunbar that Francis Hepburn was riding.

"Thou'rt safe if thou reach Dunbar, afore the gloamin's grey." The old poem ran through his mind. But it was already night; he was galloping through it and he knew that what he had told Patrick was untrue, and that Patrick knew it too. He had already decided.

He would not, could not leave now. He couldn't leave Anne, he could not leave his own son, to the mercy of a restored Maitland. It was not the time for the Border lord to throw in the gauntlet. It was not the time, even though Patrick thought it was, and this time, he would not involve Patrick, who would take care of Anne, if aught went wrong. And it well might with the perils that hedged the venture. Success was only one door of the dozens through which he might pass at the end of this excursion. But he would take the chance—in the hope that he might win through to a life with his lass and his bairn. Yes, he would take the chance, and he would take it soon.

He was riding for Dunbar, through the night, and the Borders lay near. While he rode, he reviewed in his mind the capture of the royal castle of Loughmaben, going over every step. There was only one thing that was different about that former coup. The castle of Loughmaben had not housed a King.

Chapter Forty Two

The night was very dark. There was no moon, and the glittering stars accentuated the blackness of the sky that arched over the city. It was very still.

Outside the city walls, in the country stillness, a figure suddenly detached itself from the shadows. A low whistle had pulled him from his sanctuary. He came forward, and toward him came two mounted figures. If there had been a watcher, he would have seen the two men dismount, and then all three of them disappear into the grove of trees from which the first had come.

There was not much time for words. Bothwell shook hands with Captain Ormuiston; he asked him briefly if all his orders had been carried out, and he received the Captain's assurances with only a short acknowledgment.

Gibson said little; he was watching Bothwell intently, affectionately.

"My horse," Bothwell said. "See that this old harness is removed before I need him tomorrow. Tonight I go on foot."

"And you a Borderer." Gibson smiled.

"The men," said Bothwell. "How is their temper?"

Ormuiston raised one eyebrow. "Splendid, my lord. Eager." He looked amused at his choice of words.

Bothwell nodded; there was need for no more talk, then. Now that he had done all that was possible to insure success, the rest was in the hands of the gods. "Goodbye, then," he said softly.

"Tell them to remember Loughmaben—and this time, too, I shall go ahead, to prepare the way."

"I'll tell them, my lord." Ormuiston took the reins of Bothwell's horse. "I'll tell them you have gone ahead, and God be with you."

Bothwell started away, and Gibson called, in a whisper, "Good luck, my lord."

The Earl waved his hand; he left the shadow of the trees and broke into an easy run. He covered the distance between the men he had left behind and the old wall in front of him in two minutes, and he landed on all fours, in the cemetery of Old Greyfriars Churchyard.

The church and the cemetery lay in inky blackness; the long oblong building was black, the branches of the trees were black; there was no sound. Bothwell picked himself up, brushed off his hands. He came toward the building slowly, edging around the ancient church on silent feet. The wet grass beneath his boots gave way to his weight, but when he left the churchyard behind, the grass had resiliently stood straight again, and no one could know that a man had walked through the cloistered grounds that night.

Bothwell emerged onto Candlemakers' Row. This curving street ended at the Grassmarket, but Bothwell turned the other way, slipping next into a dark alley, and following a devious and twisted path, past Thieves' Row, past the ruined Kirk O' Field, where murder had been done to a King of Scotland twenty-seven years ago. The going became easier; there was less chance of detection, for he was on the south back of the Canongate.

Fine houses sat back from the winding road. Suddenly he left the road, cutting through gardens; he crossed an orchard diagonally, making always toward the palace of Holyrood which lay at the bottom of the hill, the palace into whose grounds both streets finally ended, joining each other at the foot of the hill.

He left the orchard, passed another lighted house; then boldly, almost hugging one great mansion, he emerged onto the Canongate itself, arriving thus by trespasser's methods.

He walked jauntily down the Canongate; only three hundred

yards lay between him and his own house—he saw its lights, but there were no torchlight processions coming up the hill, no gallivanting nobility.

He turned into the grounds of his own house brazenly, but once on the walk, he slipped into the gardens and rounded the corner of the house.

Anne was giving a party. He could hear the laughter and music from the first floor gallery, and in the library were a few men who had deserted the gallery for a gambling game.

Bothwell leaned up against the old appletree. Right opposite him was the library, and he was looking straight at Patrick, as Patrick shook the dice box in one hand, his face intent. The dice rolled, Patrick smiled, and unconsciously Bothwell smiled back at him.

"Lucky throw," one of the men said, and Bothwell could hear plainly. "Why are you honoring us with your presence tonight, sir?"

Patrick still had the dice. "Janet wanted to come," he said, absently.

Lord Ochiltree said, "But you'll not dance, will you, sir?"

"By God, no," said Patrick and threw the dice.

Bothwell wanted to laugh; then his attention was taken by voices above him and he saw Anne. There was a man with her, and she was looking out the window. She said nothing, or if she did he could not hear her, and he stared upward, curiously, as if she were a stranger, a beautiful woman he might never see again but would remember the sight of with pleasure. Then she turned away; he could see just the back of her head, and as she was lost to his sight he realized she was wearing the sapphire earrings he had given her at Hermitage.

He leaned back against the tree comfortably; he had plenty of time. This was his house, yet he could not enter it, and the fact caused him no disquiet. He felt no envy for the men who sat so safely inside the paneled room. They gambled with bits of bone and money.

He was alone. Now nothing belonged to him but himself,

and there was not one coin in his pockets. He, a Borderer, had left even his closest companion, his horse, behind. He was free; he was alone, and there was no headier wine than for a man to go forth thus.

He hitched his belt and turned, cutting through the orchard between his house and Patrick's. Now only a quarter of a mile separated him from his destination.

The town house of the Gowries lay behind and adjacent to the royal palace. He knew his way well, for there had been nights when he had come this way before, and on the first floor of the mansion lights showed from the windows. The stones of a chimney, the ivy, made it an easy climb, and once up, he edged sideways slowly, looked in the window, and being satisfied with what he saw, knocked three times, lightly.

Alice Ruthven was alone in her room; she was ready for bed. When she heard the three knocks, she thought she hadn't heard aright. It couldn't be possible.

She approached the window slowly, staring at it. Surely she had imagined the sharp raps; yet if she had heard them, it could be only one man; no one else would know. She drew close to the tiny paned glass and she heard them again. The knocks were lighter than before, as if the man who knocked knew she was close to the window, and knew there was no need to rouse her. Her hand went to the catch; the window swung open. Her mind went back two years, to the first time she had waited for him, in May, a long time ago. Then he had leaned on the sill and smiled his delighted smile at her. He had hung there on the sill and he had said, "Come and kiss me, lass."

On this night two years and some months later, there he was again, his elbows on the sill and how he was supported she did not know. "Come and kiss me, lass," he said and, reaching up one hand, he doffed his cap gravely.

Alice said, with a catch in her voice, "Francis! Oh, Francis!" She put her hands around his neck and kissed him.

He swung in the window, closing it after him. Alice stared up at him; he was tanned, dark with the sun, and his eyebrows, dark as they were, were bleached on the tips. She could see it as she stood so close to him.

"Why did you say that, my lord?"

"You remembered too. And I used to feel so guilty when I'd come in that window." He smiled.

"You did not," she contradicted.

"I did, wench. But it was worth it."

She could not resist smiling back at his impudent grin, but she saw that he did feel guilty now, not because of her, but because of her mother, whom he had always liked. She saw too that as long as he had desired her, his guilt had remained conveniently in the background. He could not help his selfishness, she thought, or, if he could help it, she forgave him anyway. "Where have you been, Francis?" she asked. "All these long months, where have you been?"

"In the Borders." His voice was low; he was in danger here, even though she did not seem to realize it. He wanted to stay here no longer than necessary. He had been with her about five minutes; he began to wonder whether his plans had miscarried, or whether he was early. At that moment, to his relief, there was a soft rap on the door.

Alice's face blanched; she looked wildly around the room, as if she were wondering where she could hide him, when he himself walked forward boldly and opened the door. Alice saw her sister come into the room.

Alice's sister was the Countess of Atholl; she was a lady-in-waiting to the Queen, and why was she so unsurprised to see the Earl of Bothwell?

She slipped into the room, like a conspirator in a drama; she took Bothwell's hands, and held her face up for a kiss, which Bothwell promptly bestowed on her lips, as from one member of the Stewart clan to another member. "It's a pleasure to see you again, madam."

Lady Atholl wrung her hands a little. "I'm all atremble, Francis. I'll take to my bed after this. But Her Majesty is waiting."

Alice stared harder; she had been forgot by both of them, for

Bothwell was ready to move on. "You knew Francis was coming tonight?" she asked her sister.

"Be quiet, Alice," Lady Atholl admonished. "Certainly I knew Francis was coming."

"Aye, and it's time I was leaving." Francis put his big hand on Alice's shoulder. "I may see you in the morning, lass, and tell not even a wee bird you've seen me tonight."

Alice did not have time for another word; they had both gone when suddenly Lady Atholl put her head back in the door. "Do not quit your room before morning, Alice. Promise your word!"

She was so insistent that Alice said promptly, "I swear it."

In the corridor outside, Bothwell was following Lady Atholl, following close on her trail. "James has retired, my lord," she whispered. "The palace is asleep."

"Good," said Bothwell briefly. Now they could talk no more, for he was beginning the most dangerous part of his journey.

The Gowrie mansion was connected to Holyrood Palace by a passage open at all times. Lady Atholl led him down a curving back stairway; she moved ahead of him swiftly, and the candle she carried flickered with her hurried walk.

They had entered the passage now; they had left the Gowrie mansion behind. "Do not hasten." Bothwell's voice was intent. Nothing was so suspicious as furtive haste. He came abreast of her, taking her arm, bending over her solicitously. This pose would help conceal his height.

He felt the kitchen tiles beneath his feet. The palace kitchens were like caverns, stretching; fire still smoldered on one hearth, and a barefooted cook slept in a hard wooden chair just a few feet from him as he walked past. The kitchens smelled; there was the odor of wines, for the wine cellars were here, too, and then the corridor went by an old door that led to a small cemetery outside. He had left the palace that way quite a few times.

They emerged into the palace proper. Bothwell took the candle from Lady Atholl's hand, laying it on the floor, close to the walls. He tensed as he saw a figure ahead of him, and Lady Atholl shrank nervously against the wall.

Bothwell put his arm around her. "*Sois assurée,*" he whispered. The servant could not understand, he saw the attitude of the pair and he passed on.

The huge galleries were silent and empty; the kingly apartments were dark. Downstairs, the Captain of the Guard and his cronies were deep in a card game, and only once during the evening did the Captain take a turn through the halls. He took this sortie about five minutes after Bothwell had slipped into the Queen's apartments.

The Queen had known he was coming. A letter had reached her by the hands of Lady Atholl, this afternoon. She was alone; her women had been retired, and she waited for him by herself.

Lady Atholl had knocked but once, and he had come into the room. Lady Atholl's task was done; she had conveyed Bothwell into the palace and now she must seek her bed; she was under orders not to leave her room before morning.

The apartment in which Bothwell stood was spacious and lovely. Oriental carpets were underfoot; the hangings of the bed were cloth-of-gold. The Queen was standing in front of the fireplace whose overhanging mantle was taller than she was.

She was dressed in satin, in a large hooped gown, and pearls were lustrous in her hair. She looked at her visitor with her blue eyes; she watched him cross the room to her, and she looked down on his dark head as he knelt.

He took the hand she gave him, kissed it, and rose. He towered over her, she had to tip her head way back to see his face, and the element of recklessness, of danger, which he carried with him pressed her with its excitement.

"My lord," she murmured helplessly.

Bothwell glanced back at the door through which he had entered. Solid oak though it was, it was not much of a barrier between him and certain death. She had wanted to see him, and now he doubted whether she would be of any help to him. Bluntly, he spoke his thoughts aloud. "I should not have come, Your Grace."

She took her eyes from the gay cap that dangled from his fingers. This was quite a different man from the gay gallant she had missed so much. Although he was dressed the same, he was not the man who had so impudently visited her at Dalkeith. She had had her ladies then, and that had been a prank. Tonight was different, frighteningly so. Lord, should they find him here now!

"Would they kill you right here?" she gasped, her imagination lurid.

He said, "I do not kill so easily, Madam." He could not help smiling at the sight of her face. "They would scarce kill me here."

"They would not?"

He shook his head, still smiling. "Certainly not. They would wait at least till we were in the hall. Consider your good name." But his eyes had already picked a convenient window, and he continued, "Do I have your permission to lock this door?" He started toward the door to the hall.

"Aye, sir." The answer was breathless, and she was silent, watching him turn the heavy key.

He walked back to her; she had sunk down into a carved chair, her hands gripping the arms. Noiselessly he pulled over another chair. "You are frightened, and no wonder."

"I am not, my lord," she lied bravely.

He crossed his legs and rested his hands on his knees. "You wished to see me, Madam?"

"Aye," she said uncertainly. "Francis." She said his name as though she were assuring herself that she knew him well.

"Well, I am here."

She gave a coquettish laugh. "Aye, you are, my lord. Very much so. Francis, have your shoulders got wider? And your legs longer?"

"I think I stopped growing some time ago, Madam."

He was impatient and she saw it plainly. She said quickly, "His Majesty has decided to recall Maitland."

"I know."

"That is why I wanted to see you."

He looked straight at her. "I have a thousand men just south of the city. Camped for the night."

Her eyes were fastened on his dark ones. "Only a thousand?" she whispered.

He frowned. "They will be ample, Madam, should we succeed. If we do not succeed, there will be fewer killed, fewer Border wives to mourn their dead."

"If we should not succeed?" she repeated.

"We might fail," he said dryly. "And Maitland be the victor, then." As he said it, he forgot the presence of his Queen. "Christ's blood, what a joy to put a length of steel through him!"

She recoiled, but the violence of the words fascinated her. "But," she temporized, "Huntly killed Lord Murray."

"The hand that holds the dagger does not always commit the crime!"

She knew that he meant that James, her husband, had commissioned Huntly to find Murray. "His Majesty swore to me, swore to me, that he did not tell Huntly to do murder!"

He rose abruptly, pacing the room. She was sure he did not believe her, and she was too astonished to be offended. Never before had she been treated like this. He paced on, oblivious to her, and finally he turned to face her.

"I shall not kill Maitland, Madam. He's too old."

"Francis," she said. "You are different, and yet not different."

"I follow a basic pattern," he said lightly. "But it's a wee bit different, shall we say, than it used to be. Madam, I've come to the conclusion that having a wife and heir sobers a man. I've changed the cut of my jib."

"A pox on your jib, my lord. Tell me what you are going to do."

He looked past her to another oaken door. It was heavy, it was the door to the King's bedroom and it had a massive lock. He said intently, "You must trust me, Madam. Will you lock that door?"

She turned her head, following his eyes, seeing the door as though for the first time. She had already decided to lock the door, but suddenly that was less important than the man with her. She remembered a sentence he had recently uttered; she wanted to talk about him. "Change or no, you follow a basic pattern, my lord." She rose and began to walk toward the door.

At her words and her action, he stood too. "Aye, Madam," he said, his eyes intent on her. "A very basic pattern. I, like most men, am activated and maintained through love, hate, ambition, vanity, or even humbleness. I was born a peer of the realm; I've no desire to relinquish my rights, my lands. And because of my own pattern, Patrick tells me, I've lost them; tonight, in the same way, I intend to regain them."

Her hand was on the lock of the door. "Francis, what have you done these last months?"

"Practiced the art of outlawry. Or thievery, if you'd have it that way."

She smiled. "When may I open this, Francis?"

"When I tell you," he replied bluntly; but even as he spoke, he dropped to one knee, placing her hand on his head in a gesture of fidelity, and when he got to his feet he was smiling at her very respectfully. "Your Majesty, first I shall go through the door. My word, my oath, that no harm shall come to you and yours. You may lock it after I have gone." He kissed her hand, and very slowly opened the door, closing it behind him gently. He stood alone in James's bedroom.

The room was lighted. Dimly, but lighted, for a candle burned on the bedside table. Like a statue Bothwell stood in front of the door; the waiting was nerve-wracking, but he must wait, until he heard the lock turn. He froze his muscles into one entity; the shadowy room seemed to come closer to him, and he breathed so lightly that he could easily hear the breathing of his sleeping monarch and his page.

The page lay only a few feet from Bothwell. He slept youthfully, sprawled across the narrow trundle bed, one arm dangling over the side.

The candle flickered, throwing a golden glow over the bare night table. Bothwell was so near it he could see the lines of the book that still lay open, as James must have put it down before he went to sleep. He was so near he could read the lines; his eyes made them out slowly.

"So we'll go no more aroving—"

He did not need to read past the first few words; he knew what they said. James the Fifth, his grandfather, had written them, and Bothwell repeated the rest of the verse in his head.

"Aroving in the night.
We'll go no more aroving,
Let the moon shine e'er so bright."

They were all of a piece with his own life; they reminded him of the Border slogan, "We'll have moonlight again." But would there be? Death was all around him here. Let that page wake, and his cries would bring the whole palace down around their heads. Bothwell fixed him with narrowed eyes, waiting for the first movement that might herald disaster.

"We'll go no more aroving." The words had a lonely sound. How long had he stood here, waiting? Almost a full minute passed before he heard the faint scrape of the key. Then there was silence again.

He thought he could still hear the click of the key turned in the lock as he made his way across the danger-laden room. He heard James's breathing; the page stirred, settled again; and Bothwell passed the curtained bed, went by a window that was tight shut against the night air. Six more steps placed him before another door.

"God grant the hinges are oiled." His hand went to the catch, his fingers laid about it lightly, experimentally. The latch clicked, and he did not wait longer; his very presence might waken one of the sleeping men; even in slumber they might sense him. He must leave this room, regardless of noise.

The door swung open about a foot. He slipped through the opening, and without waiting he closed the door.

Chapter Forty Three

The anteroom of the King lay deep in darkness. Only the night light from the window embrasure picked up the room's furniture, blurring its outlines, leaving the chairs, the King's table, smudges against the deeper black of the curtained walls.

Those walls were arras-hung; the stiff brocade trailed to the floor, so that errant drafts could not scurry too gleefully under the royal feet. The curtains were so heavy that a man could lie behind them with ease.

The clock on the mantle was the only sound in the room. It ticked very lazily along, gave a wheeze, and then chimed five times, slowly, deliberately. Bothwell took that time to change his position lightly.

"Five o'clock." He did not say the words aloud, although there was less danger in being caught now, trapped like an animal against a stone wall. He was still careful, and he shifted his legs soundlessly, flexing his knees.

He had been lying on his side; he took up less space when he was propped on one elbow. Now he turned on his stomach, stretching out flat, and he permitted himself the luxury of a long sigh.

This was no place to sleep or rest. It was stuffy and dirty here; it smelled of dust. And the floor was harder than the pine-needled floor of the forest, where he could have a fire, and where he could see the stars above him at night.

He put his head down, and his heavy buckle pressed into his

stomach. He was uncomfortable. He had not been able to sleep. The castle—this room, its floors and walls—had pressed him in, and emphasized the fact that only his thoughts could roam the Border hills tonight.

A sudden noise made him stiffen, but brutally he forced himself to relax. On nights like this the bloody past of this royal dwelling must stir and warn those bold enough to interfere once more with the heavy sovereign authority. And if something went wrong, if there were betrayal and treachery, he would probably not live to see the face of the man or woman who even now might be pulling his horse into the outer courtyard, or mounting the silent stairway.

The clock struck the half hour and as the sound died away, he found everything else swept away by that one consideration —time. Morning was only minutes away. At this very moment his Borderers should be reaching the capital. They would be riding their swift, small Border horses. Their leather jacks would be their protection against sword thrusts. Some would wear rapiers, but most would stick to the light sharp-bladed axe slung in the saddles. There would be one company of hagbutters, their weapons loaded—men he had trained himself in guerilla warfare. And there were artillerymen, too, with their field guns mounted on sturdy carts. He himself had supervised their construction, from the first scrape of the saw to the hewn wheels that had iron rimming the tough Scottish oak.

The sun was up. Its first red streaks clawed at the sky, and he pushed back the curtains and stepped from behind them. In the empty room he stood very tall; he took out a handkerchief and dusted his shoulders, his boots. He crossed the room, making no effort to be silent. The waiting was over. The curtains at the window had not been drawn; he could look into the outer courts of Holyrood, and see the city going uphill away from him. The dawn was here; the gray houses were plainer against the gray and red sky and he stood motionless at the window for five minutes longer.

Then he opened the casement. The day was going to be warm, and the southeast wind fanned into the room, cool now at morning. He waited at the open window, his hand resting lightly on his sword hilt. He was relaxed, but he felt the tenseness rising in him, like a warm tide, that brought the blood beating in his temples. He was waiting, he was listening, for the first triumphant sounding of the Border war horns.

They seemed very loud to him when they first sounded. The trumpets' blare was like a clarion call to arms. The breeze caught the notes, wafted them through the open windows of the palace. His dark eyes glinted with the excitement, and he stood rigidly.

It was almost as if the palace had not heard the trumpets; it had only stirred in its sleep at their advent, so the sudden stentorian cries that rent the air burst in upon an unsuspecting, still sleeping, royalty and nobles. To Bothwell they were the sound of avenging angels; the voices were Lowland voices, and they shouted his name.

"A Bothwell!" At the sound he whirled from the window. While they captured the palace, he captured the King. Across the room his long stride carried him in ten steps; his hand was on the door, and he flung it open with such violence that it burst open and was crashed against the other wall. In front of Francis Hepburn was Jamie Stewart.

For one long second the two men stared at one another, and no word was spoken. Bothwell breathed lightly; he stood on the threshold of the room; he did not move and neither did James.

He had not seen James for two years, and he was a little surprised to find him just the same. James's mouth was open, and his tongue was still too big for his mouth. And James was not fully dressed, but was clutching at his robe.

Still James did not speak; his eyes fastened on Bothwell, as if he were reminding himself that Bothwell was just the same, too; he was just as big, and just as wide-shouldered. James watched one brown hand reach for its near sword hilt; he watched while the sword was drawn, and its glittering length of steel laid bare.

"My good bairn." Bothwell's voice was low, and its twangy

accent so familiar that James began to tremble. "You that have given out that I sought your life—behold, it is now in this hand!"

James opened his mouth to scream. What he had feared so long had come true, and through his mind went the innumerable times this scene had been reacted in his imaginings. "You traitor," he burst out. "You false traitor!" He whirled from Bothwell, reaching out his hand to the door so near him. He pulled at it frantically, and when he could not open the door, he knew why Bothwell had not pursued him, why the Earl was still standing easily, blocking the other entrance to the room. He had not run after James because he knew that the door to the Queen's chamber was locked.

Flight was not possible. He pulled his robe close around him. Then he turned.

"Traitors all!" He cried it not only at Bothwell, but at all those who had conspired against him, at the person who had locked this door. "You may strike, if you dare!"

Bothwell stood silent. James was fearful, but he had summoned his courage. They had not met for two years, and now they stood thus.

"I am no traitor," said Bothwell slowly.

James stiffened, and he heard Bothwell say again, "I am no traitor."

The quiet sentence filled the room. James stared at his kinsman; he did not know what was coming next.

"You," he began, trying to control his voice.

Bothwell took a step forward; he dropped to one knee. "Your Majesty," he said, "you may have my sword."

There was no one but James to see the sudden, dramatic gesture.

"I do not want your sword; I do not want it," James said, petulantly, in just the tone of voice that Bothwell had often heard him use when they were younger.

"I offer it to you," said Bothwell, patiently, as to a child, and James was prodded into coming closer.

Bothwell lifted the sword to his lips, then he raised his head and looked at James. "My sword belongs to Scotland, and so to you. You may take it and do with it what you will."

James looked down on his enemy's head. When his fingers closed around the shining hilt of the weapon, they touched his cousin's hand. Then Bothwell's hand came away, and he knelt at James's feet, helpless, unarmed.

"Francis," said James slowly.

"Aye, Sir?" Bothwell looked up.

"You may rise, Francis. You may have this back." Neatly James reversed the rapier, and Bothwell took it back, held it for a second, and sheathed it. He was searching for words.

"Hear me with patience, Sir, a moment. I had no other avenue than this."

"No?" James said nothing else.

"No," said Bothwell, frowning. "I swear to God you've done me wrong. You left me no other course than—"

"Violence?" James interrupted.

Bothwell was accustomed to arguing with James. It seemed very usual. "Not violence, Sir. The only way I could come to you was with ample guards."

James said dryly, "I lament your favorite form of doing, then." He regarded his cousin long, and then he said forcefully, "Francis, did Elizabeth have aught to do with this? By the allegiance you owe me, by the faith you bear me, by the favor you hope to find, do not conceal from me the traffic you have had with the Queen of England!"

Bothwell stared at James, who was still holding his robe tight, but looking more of a king now. He said bluntly, "Save in so far as Elizabeth yielded me the benefit of her country, for the preservation of my life and liberty, so narrowly sought by my adversaries, I've had no dealings with her."

"She had naught to do with this?" James scowled a bit. "You swear it?"

"I swear it, by all the gold in Spain, the silver in Scotland."

James said, "I trust my dear sister little, Francis."

Bothwell fingered his cap. "I think you could, Sir. I think it only wise to make an enduring friendship with her. She has her whims, but what woman hasn't, monarch or not?" He smiled.

"Aye, that's true," said James. For the first time, he smiled a little.

"After all, she is merely woman."

They stood in companionable silence for a minute. Then Bothwell said, "She is canny. But I'd be friends with her."

"Have you forgotten so soon my dear mother's death?"

Bothwell was surprised at the vehemence of James's question. "But I wanted to fight then, four years ago. If you, my liege, have forgiven it long since, why should I not forget it, so long after?"

His cousin's usual straightforwardness reassured James; he reminded himself again that Bothwell was just the same.

Bothwell continued, practically, "What has gone, is gone. You receive an allowance from her; you are her heir. For God's sake, Sir, let's be honest."

James grinned. "Do you think I deal in honesty?"

"With yourself, you should. You can fool no one, if you also fool yourself. That's no way to gamble. You must first know the worth of your own cards."

"Aye," said James. "Then from what you have just said, I am not a prisoner."

Bothwell wanted to smile, but he kept his face impassive. "I've come to crave your pardon, Sir, and only that."

James was silent. "My pardon?"

"Aye, Sir, your royal pardon, so that I may prove to you in deed what I have said today."

"You proceeded on great necessity, Francis." James smiled. For the second time, he smiled, almost impishly, but he felt a need to quibble more. "You are still under indictment for witchcraft, my lord. You are aware of that?"

Bothwell hesitated. Then he smiled back at James. "The devil's a sworn liar from the beginning, Sir. Would you take his word against mine? But I'm ready to stand my trial." He stopped. He knew he must be cautious, but it was so hard to be careful when all he wanted stood ready to take. "I shall stand trial, at the next Assizes, if that is Your Majesty's wish."

James nodded, as if he had been quite expecting that answer. "That will be the fourteenth of August, my lord. You will be summoned." He tilted his head to see Bothwell's face, and he too remembered that even as they talked here together, he, James, was not free. But neither was Bothwell. They were bound together, by nationality, by age, by blood. And he, the King, would have to make concessions. Bothwell was waiting for them, despite all the smoothness that overlaid his easy manner. He was waiting. He and his Borderers, who held the castle.

"I will deliver to you a royal pardon, Francis. It will be signed by the town bailies, and six preachers of the Kirk. I shall then sign it myself."

Bothwell thought of Anne. "Aye, Sir," he said. His eyes met James's. They were both breathing a little quickly, and again Bothwell waited. There was one thing more he wanted, and he knew that it was in James's mind too. Would the King say it himself, offer it, or would the Earl of Bothwell have to ask?

"Maitland," said James.

Again their eyes held, and James continued. This time it was he who thought of his wife. "Maitland shall be forbidden court." He waited now, and he was conscious of a momentary trepidation that this revenge would not be sufficient to suit the Border lord.

Bothwell said slowly, repeating almost what he had said to the Queen, "Maitland is old."

James knew what the words meant, and he looked relieved. His nobles were so in love with their feuding. "Then, Francis—" He broke off.

"All will be well, Sir." Bothwell smiled. He said lightly, because this would be important to James, "If Your Grace would place Lord Ochiltree in command of the palace guard, we might feel the easier." He bowed deferentially. "I mention it because I assume it would be your own thought."

James smiled wryly. "Aye," he said. "Ochiltree is a good man."

There were sounds in the next room. Both men could hear

footsteps, voices, and James looked uncertainly at Bothwell.

"That will be Sir Patrick," Bothwell said, and he could hardly wait to see him. "And his Grace, the Duke of Lennox, and others of our kin, Sir."

"Whoever they are, they may wait," said James royally. "They may wait a wee space."

He put his hand on Bothwell's arm, drawing him through the anteroom, where the Earl had waited long lonely hours last night, and led him to the window embrasure. They looked down on the outer courts of Holyrood.

The courts were full. The mob surged beneath them, the city bells that had summoned them rang out, and the King raised his hand in greeting, in such a way that it would be plain to all that he had his other hand on Bothwell's arm. Bothwell cast a sidelong glance at James, to see how he received the shouts of joy. The King was smiling, and Bothwell raised his own hand to wave it to the crowd. The cheers rose in a fresh crescendo.

When they had subsided a little, James spoke again, smiling slyly. "As you say, I much imagine Sir Patrick will be here, his Grace, the Duke of Lennox, and others of our kin. I shall inform them of your pardon, Francis. I shall inform them myself."

He raised his hand again, this time placing it upon Bothwell's shoulder. And now the voices of the crowd swelled to a thundering roar; the people waved to the tall figure of the Border lord. He had come back.

Chapter Forty Four

BOTHWELL went all the way down the steps of Holyrood Castle and out into the bright morning sunlight, with Patrick beside him, before either of them spoke.

Then Patrick said feelingly, "Let's go to your house and drink a toast." He stared at Bothwell long and hard.

"My head will not come off," Bothwell grinned and put his hand at his neck. He pointed back at the castle. "He's safe, the bairn, our Jamie Stewart. And I'm safe, too, for once."

Patrick waited until he was astride his horse to say more; he noted that Bothwell's bodyguard, which usually consisted of twenty men, had grown to fifty. Ahead of those men, they rode slowly out of the palace gates. "I see that you are aware you must still be careful."

"I am."

"But guards are not important." Patrick flung out his hand to indicate their escort. "Francis, you are certainly aware that you have committed high treason?"

Bothwell shrugged. "Your tone reminds me of the time we first met."

"I reminded you then of the danger of your power. That warning still holds, Francis."

"I know that, sir. I wanted to talk with you, too. I did not tell James that there is a crypt in a room in Stirling Castle."

After a minute Patrick said, "You were wise."

"I hold a card in reserve, besides a royal pardon."

"And it is too dangerous a card to play until all else is lost."

They were passing Patrick's house; they were almost at their destination. Impulsively he laid his hand on Bothwell's arm. "Mayhap I am too cautious. 'Tis but a counter-balance to your foolhardiness. Yet when all is said, no prudence would have won the day as you have. And it has been won. We are no longer outlaws, and we are well fortified against future threats."

Bothwell dismounted, nodding to left and right, greeting the gentlemen who had come to pay their homage to the man who had just accomplished the overthrow of Maitland, and who had elevated himself again to the royal favor. Bothwell stopped just short of the lintel. It seemed to him a long time since he had stood there.

Suddenly, he heard voices from the gallery, and he had started up the steps when a woman came down toward him. Janet met him on the wide landing, and swept him a curtsy.

Bothwell stared. "You are Janet," he said. "You look different, lass."

"I've lived with Patrick for six months," she said sweetly.

Bothwell smiled at Patrick. "My comments on that might be too lengthy or too revealing." He looked up, listening to the voices from above. "Where is Anne? I do not hear her."

"Anne?" said Janet. "Why, Anne has gone, my lord."

"Gone?" He looked so incredulous that Janet smiled. "How could she be gone?"

"Anne has gone to Crichton, my lord. She has not been to Crichton for six months. You know she was released less than three weeks ago, sir."

Bothwell turned. "Anne's at Crichton?" He had started down the steps, when Patrick caught at his arm.

"Francis! You cannot go now!"

Janet said, "Anne left me here, as your hostess."

"Aye, Francis. And you have much else to do before you can leave the city. Ochiltree is waiting for commands; Ormuiston wants to know how many troops, if any, should be left at the palace; Lennox awaits you upstairs."

"Holy Christ," said Bothwell; he hooked his thumbs in his belt and scowled.

Patrick laughed at him with real amusement. "Your marital affairs must wait," he jibed. "You will have to deal with your wench later."

He stopped and eyed Bothwell sharply. Then he too frowned, as Bothwell started down the steps away from him and Janet. "Francis," he said warningly.

Bothwell swung around, speaking to Janet. "If my wife left you here as my hostess, Patrick can take care of my duties." His boots made heavy sounds on the steps as he went away from them and he stopped for a moment at the bottom. "God knows I've been circumspect enough this morning."

Patrick looked incredulous. "You were circumspect? This morning?"

"After I cornered James, I was. I was most cautious and respectful."

"Francis," Patrick said again, helplessly. He ran down the steps.

Bothwell turned; he waved, and said, "Valentine's fresh." His tone was low. Patrick barely heard him, and before he could reply the Border lord and Gibson had galloped off down the Canongate.

Even through the city Gibson had trouble keeping up the pace Bothwell had set. At times, he came abreast of his master, and when he did, he shot anxious sidelong glances at his face. But when they left the city behind, Gibson lagged.

"I can't keep up with you," he shouted.

Bothwell did not answer. The sudden, swift anger he had felt when he learned that Anne was not waiting for him was not dispelled. He was beginning to believe he had done this for her alone; he had thought that, he had said it to the Queen last night. But as he rode, he wondered whether it was entirely true. God's wound, if it were, it was for the ungratefulest wench alive.

For this much was true. He had wanted to lay his victory at her feet, and she had not been there to receive it. He swore silently, and he started to slacken Valentine's gallop. He was a fool to go after her. Distinctly he remembered standing in the library in the Edinburgh house, and telling Anne that he had not followed a runaway wife; he had followed her because she was going into obvious danger.

He slowed the pace to a walk. Only a very few miles lay between him and Crichton now—and she would be there. But why should he follow? He thought of Patrick's last words, and his last call to him. He jerked at the reins. He should go back to Edinburgh. That was where he belonged. There was too much left behind him that was unfinished. He had done all this for her, but she had not even waited for him.

He had mounted a steep hill. Below him lay his own lands; they stretched away from him, on each side. To the east lay the sea and Hailes, to the south lay Crichton. In a few minutes he would see its towers.

Suddenly he grinned and brought his whip down sharply on Valentine's flanks. She was too near, his wife, his fair and wayward Annie. Too near and too exactly the way he would have her. The very reason he was riding toward her at once angrily and eagerly was that she was the right wench for him. And that was why he had risked his life last night. Soon he would see Crichton; soon he would see her again. They were both his to keep now.

He had gained the crest of the next hill, and now he and Valentine thundered down into the valley. Ahead lay the towers of Crichton Castle.